The Salvation of Henry Maxwell

by

Lee Lindauer

Copyright Notice
This is a work of fiction. Names, characters, places, and incidents are either the product of the author's imagination or are used fictitiously, and any resemblance to actual persons living or dead, business establishments, events, or locales, is entirely coincidental.

The Salvation of Henry Maxwell

COPYRIGHT © 2024 by Julius Leland Lindauer

All rights reserved. No part of this book may be used or reproduced in any manner whatsoever without written permission of the author or The Wild Rose Press, Inc. except in the case of brief quotations embodied in critical articles or reviews.
Contact Information: info@thewildrosepress.com

Cover Art by *The Wild Rose Press, Inc.*

The Wild Rose Press, Inc.
PO Box 708
Adams Basin, NY 14410-0708
Visit us at www.thewildrosepress.com

Publishing History
First Edition, 2024
Trade Paperback ISBN 978-1-5092-5705-8
Digital ISBN 978-1-5092-5706-5

Published in the United States of America

Dedication

With love and gratitude, I dedicate this novel to Teri, my remarkable wife for her unwavering support and inspiration in walking every step of the journey with me.

Prologue

Excerpt from the novel Lady Julia's Sarcophagus
Dunlap & Finch, Publishers
London, 1892

How often over the years have I dreamed of reaching my sweet darling Julia's afterworld? Yet I lacked the mental acuteness to facilitate such an everlasting reunion, never really understanding the unearthly skills necessary to penetrate the boundary between life and death. Just as I had resigned myself to the fact that I may never grasp the mechanism of the process, the answers came slowly in short bursts of psychic infusions. For the first time, I heard her calling my name.

And now, the only roadblock to deliverance is the tempest howling across the muck-soaked grass and among the mossy granite spires. I wipe the intermittent rain off my wind-blown face, not allowing the storm to hinder my passage. Behind me, the swaying trees obscure the deep-dead gloom of the manor. Ahead a shrouded moon hovers above the stately mausoleum at the end of my journey. I am within grasp. The moor beckons, the colour of salvation strips the darkness away...

Sir Alston Chatsworth shifts uncomfortably in bed, the dream melting into his wakeful world. Reaching over to the left side, he knows deep in his heart Lady Julia is not there. But her scent still permeates the old baroque-style poster bed, one that she had chosen for their wedding night. Was he expecting to cherish the comfort of her being? Soaked in sweat, he sits up, his eyes exploding in a cascading rivulet of blinks. Expecting complete silence, there is none, for the voice that escapes his dream now lives in his world.

The pounding in his chest furthers his awareness. The dreams, the nightly trances now have a voice calling out his name. He presses his palms over his ears, thinking the susurration will cease, but the softness of the whispering summon remains, a Siren's lure weaving within the undercurrents of the manor's stale air.

Again, he stares at her side, expecting a miracle of miracles. A crack of thunder breaks the distant drone, a thickening storm develops, sucking at the drafty hearths in every room and flogging tree branches against the narrow-arched windows, scratching and scraping like claws from the netherworld. Shadows permeate, roiling in and out as the scant light of a moon flickers, creased by the racing clouds. Not understanding the delicacy of the situation, he has to find the source of the voice.

Levering out of bed, he lights a candle and exits the bedroom. Dressed only in his nightshirt, he feels the chill of the night as more thunder booms. Tightening the drawstrings around his collar, he creeps ever so warily down the hallway, descending the grand stairway, spiraling his way to the Great Hall below, as dark and uninviting as it has been since Lady Julia's death. Lightning streaks through the narrow windows, flashing bits of melancholy off the dull furniture and dusty draperies, a gloomy and torturous room even when touched by the soft glint of a candle, or a rare late-afternoon sun gleaming through the windows. It had been a joyous and wondrous place at one time, now only a doleful vastness.

His ears twitch, the eerie voice repeating his name, a weak singsong. Gazing around, he imagines Julia's presence. The furnishing are the same, but her touch of decoration and happiness have long disappeared. The lone candle ripples shadows along the faded tapestries hanging lackluster from the high walls. "Julia, my Julia, have you come back?" he whispers. Panicked, he stumbles toward the back of the manor, following the voice in the air that now seems to force him outside.

Fleeing the manor, he staggers barefoot along the worn path that winds across the hill toward the moorlands. Traversing the slope of a mossy and brush-filled knoll, the muddy and rocky spurs of worn granite gouge his bare feet, cutting and slicing. They are bleeding, but he pushes on. The fierce winds pelt him with driven rain as he nears the top. He stops to catch his breath as he views the infinite breadth of peat and bog. Wiping the rain from his bleary eyes, he glimpses a pinpoint of light in the distance. Is it real, an illusion? Has insanity finally thrust him over the edge into the realm of paranoia and the world of ghosts and demons? Blinking, the faint light flitters through the woods.

The rain increases, battering the mud-encrusted path with a noise that overwhelms the voice, now a weak whisper. He moves swiftly circling down, his bloody feet sucking against the mud, the pain no longer entering his mind. The light still blinks on and off amongst a thicket of trees, finding refuge within the branches and autumn leaves. As he pushes farther up the hill, the night pulls at his weary soul as the woods thin and the neoclassical mausoleum in all its egregious grandeur rises from the barren peat below the pinnacle of High Haven. Julia envisioned this their final resting place, a stately and eternal home, elevated above the surrounding sea of moorlands where sunrises and sunsets would live forever.

He trudges across the moor, between the short folds and deep shadows of peat. At every high point, he stops to take his bearing, and ere morning his journey would be complete, the sea of peat and bogs behind him forever in his mortal past. The rain begins to lessen, but a spiraling mist driven by the breeze coming off the channel rolls upward ever so slowly, engulfing the face of the mausoleum.

The moon shows itself as he nears, bare, twisted trees surround the tomb, the mist flowing unhindered through the short wrought-iron fence and weedy patch. The stately, discoloured granite façade, a dreariness of depraved stone and weathered cracks etched with the name of Chatsworth, is now wrapped in a growth of invasive vines. He stops, frozen. For several minutes, he doesn't move, nor take his eyes off the door. The last time he'd been to High Haven was when his beloved was entombed. The anguish and loneliness of his existence ever since has tapped his emotions until nothing remains.

The mist thickens; the breeze diminishes. Suddenly, the mausoleum appears to shimmer, small feeble vibrations dance in the moonlight. He rushes through the gate, and the rasp of hinges sounds like the singsong he'd heard earlier. He does not fear anymore. *The door opens and the brilliance of a figure emerges...*

Chapter 1

June 10, 2013

Nerves on fire, a three-alarm blaze, or just a feverish state of mind. Nobody to hold her hand, no one to relieve her suspicions, no one to say it will be okay. Right now, Jessica couldn't tell if she was rushing full throttle to or away from the flames, but by the look of dejection on co-workers she passed in the hallway, it became clear—her time to burn at the stake approached.

She'd heard the rumors floating around the last few days, Medical to be downsized, Business and Tax Departments short-changed. Worst of all, Criminal Defense, white-collar and general practice, the whole nineteenth floor to be trimmed to a bare minimum. Even her old boss, soft-spoken Dan Flanigan, was too embarrassed to give her the word. Any paralegals left would be a win.

She'd been in Criminal for a little less than a year, two trials under her belt, all successful, but her future now appeared to be going up in smoke. Too many lawsuits and ethical complaints. Not by her, of course. The California State Bar had already disciplined three associates for unprofessional conduct. Disbarment the next step. Along with the public perception and unfortunate publicity, once proud Criminal begged for mercy. Rumors persisted Jergens Whitman &

Bonoventura had made the untimely and dreadful decision to downsize Criminal to a skeleton crew. Only active cases would go forward. So her immediate crisis, a mortgage she secured on a new one-bedroom condominium in the Mission District. Lucky to beat the competition, great location, near work, a bit more than she could afford, but who was keeping score? Next position, on the streets?

In a mindless stupor, she reached the end of the hallway where it made a sharp ninety-degree turn to the left. Cutting the corner, she came close to running into Pete Redden. Both stopped in mid stride, apologizing to one another for lack of awareness. Pete's face shaded pale with his eyes somber red, reading like chapters of despondency in a sad, tear-jerker novel.

Pete took a deep breath and wiped the sweat off his forehead. "Rumors are true. I'm gone."

Pete had a wife and two young kids. In her mind, he deserved to stay.

"Hell of a way to end a Friday."

"So sorry for you and Kaitlin, and the kids."

"We'll be fine. Don't worry about us. What about you?"

"On my way now. I'm positive I'll be pink slipped."

"Well, if you do, keep in touch, we'll hammer down a drink or two. A joy working with you."

"You, too." She nodded. "Take care."

He cracked an artificial smile and disappeared around the corner.

She continued down the hallway looking for Room 1744. Her pulse quickened as she saw the open door. Collecting her composure, she entered. Surprised, Marsha Hauser, a sixty-plus-year-old fixture of Family

Law sat gazing over a pile of files on the desk. She knew Marsha from last year's Christmas party and a couple of other office functions. Knowing everyone in JWB was impossible as it was one of the largest law firms in San Francisco with over three hundred attorneys--or so it was.

"Jessica, nice to see you." She motioned toward an uncomfortable-looking chair. *Electric*, she imagined, sliding into it. Marsha didn't hesitate. "How are you coping with all the turmoil?"

"End of the world, I guess."

"A damn bloodbath for sure. Few have been spared, junior, senior associates. Three partners decided to jump the sinking ship and retire. Administrative staff, paralegals. Almost everyone's taking a whipping."

"Marsha aren't you in Family Law? This is HR, isn't it?"

"Well, you can imagine HR being hit hard with all the furloughs, dismissals. I'm here to help them process this massacre." She leaned back and stared at Jessica. "So, any thoughts on your future?"

There, out in the open. No sense to say she'd been laid off, obvious when one's future is brought up. "I guess I'll be looking for work," she mustered.

Marsha smiled. "Now why would you do that?"

Had she heard correctly? "What do you mean? I need a job, have a condo, and high mortgage. I like to eat, too."

Marsha's smile widened. "I'm only asking because you haven't been fired."

She sat speechless. "I don't understand."

Marsha leaned back, smiling. "Oh, I owe you an apology. HR is not my forte. I obviously didn't make myself clear."

She took a deep breath. "You had me going. Like everyone else, I thought for sure I'd been sacked."

"You're one of the lucky ones, Jessica. There's added value in you. You've been retained."

Confusion muddled her mind. "Did I hear you say I'm not fired?"

"Criminal is where you'd like to be, but Criminal is on life support. Family Law is thriving, and we could use the help."

Family Law, one place she didn't feel the excitement—but a job's a job. "This is all so strange. Are you offering me a job in Family Law?"

"Well, it's one of our stronger divisions, and no ethic complaints I'm aware of."

"So, where's my added value in Family?"

"Let's talk about your background first." Marsha opened a file on her desk. "You graduated from UC Davis Law School three years ago, passed the bar, began working at JWB. Not only do you possess a law degree, but you first earned a master's in clinical psychology."

Jessica took a deep, agonizing breath, feeling the bottom drop out from under her. She pointed at the file. "I'm sure it explains why I left and went to law school."

"It does. I understand why you left the profession. I wasn't in your shoes, but I would've done the same thing. You were hired because of your potential as an attorney, not a psychologist. Even though you gave up psychology, you still have the background. I believe you're the right person for the job."

"I left psychology because—" She cleared her throat. "Right person for the job?"

"Let me explain the situation. We handle a fair

number of conservatorships. JWB has a celebrity client, Henry Maxwell. You're much younger than me. Does his name ring a bell?"

"The old movie star. I thought he'd be dead by now."

"The one and the same, still alive. He was as formidable in horror movies as Vincent Price et al. They were the kings of that genre back in the sixties. I remember going to Saturday matinees to get the heebie-jeebies scared out of me. Henry Maxwell movies, graveyards, creepy dungeons, grisly corpses, the whole ball of wax."

"And JWB is his legal guardian?"

Marsha nodded. "We've represented his interests for over forty-five years."

"So why the conservatorship?"

"Ever since the accident, we've become more involved in his finances and day-to-day affairs."

"Accident?"

"Three years ago, he came close to getting killed. A delivery truck hit his car. Ended up in a coma for over three months, bleeding in the brain. Gets around now with the aid of a cane. Has memory problems that still plague him to this day. Forgets what he's done—and hallucinations. Because of all of that, the courts appointed us conservator until they believe he's competent, if—and when that ever happens."

"And now?"

"A year ago, Henry's cognitive health and depression improved enough that the conservatorship was to be dissolved. Then, he regressed, went into a shell, and his condition became severe. Our responsibility is to keep his affairs in order. His mental deterioration is a concern, so we want to be in a position such that the state of California doesn't call all the shots."

Jessica didn't like the direction this conversation was headed. "You're staring at me, Marsha."

"I'm not asking you to perform a professional evaluation. With your background, being around him, and observing, you may be able to figure out what caused his decline and offer suggestions. Your resume qualifies you more than anyone else in the firm."

"How am I supposed to do that?" she demanded, raising her voice. "Call him up, get an appointment, put him on a couch and evaluate him, and then provide counseling." She began to shake. "You know how well that turned out. Read the file!"

"Let me psychoanalyze you for a moment. Three years with the firm. Your training in psychology on those two criminal cases you worked on was noticed. Dan Flanigan remarked on your ability in that regard."

Jessica shook her head at the compliment. "He's too kind."

"This isn't a pie-in-the-sky scheme. We've a court order to do one of two things. Observe him twenty-four-seven in his environment, or two, petition the courts to have him admitted for psychological evaluation for as long as it takes. We think that's unwarranted. This isn't an experiment. There are conservatorships all around the country implemented by courts the same way, and they've been successful. Henry lives alone in a huge house, or mansion I must admit. He needs help. We want you to move in with him for a few weeks. Find out what makes him tick."

"Are you kidding?" she exclaimed in a fit of

disbelief. "I can't just show up with my suitcase and ask where's my room."

"Easier than trying to locate a new job, don't you think? He's aware enough to understand that legalities have him boxed in, so to speak."

Jessica rolled her eyes in disbelief. "You're kidding, right?"

"If I was, we wouldn't be offering you the job. Think of this as a vacation. Good time to escape the Bay Area and get away from this dismal office for a while. He can't decline you or whoever as a guest, and he knows it. Very shrewd, but we have him over a barrel."

Chapter 2

The thought of pressing and grinding in the olive oil extraction building conjured up a few fantasies. *Isn't that what an olive press does—press and grind*? At least Cody Stevens thought so, his lips curling in anticipation. "Hurry, duck under here," he said, pulling up the rusted barbed wire.

"Are you sure?" Holly asked, stepping below the razor-sharp barbs in the fence, brushing back the brunette strands falling in her eyes. "What if someone catches us?"

"Who would do that? This place is haunted," he teased, letting out a blood-curdling cackle while shining the flashlight on his contorted face.

"Stop it," she said, slugging him on the arm.

He twisted away, laughing, deflecting her latest blow. "That's what I've been told. Nobody in their right mind would want to come here, at night no less." He gazed into Holly's eyes. They were less than thrilled. But she was a trooper. More than once, she had succumbed to his wishes. He pointed the flashlight beam along a worn path winding through a wooded area. A minute later, they came out in a clearing. They stopped, staring at the old stone building. Twilight made the façade look like a craggy farmhouse set amidst a dying forest, leafless branches casting ghastly, twisted shadows across the walls. She hedged, not wanting to go any farther.

"The dark makes it creepy."

"Trust me. This will be a memory for the ages." Grabbing her by the hand, he pulled her along. "Olives no more. Let's christen this fucker."

Pushing closer, he shined the light through the doorway. Dark and empty, free of debris, except for a few beer cans, an empty whiskey bottle, plastic water bottles and an assortment of cigarette butts. The gable roof had missing slats on its rotting timbers. A two-foot-wide trench dissected the concrete floor, where rock weights once hung providing the force to work the press. He sidestepped it and unfurled the blanket he carried.

Holly curled a lock of hair with her finger, smiling bashfully as she approached. *Getting into the game*, he thought, his prospects racing at a lustful pace. He removed his shoes and shirt and unbuckled his pants. They dropped like lead weights. He rushed up to her, wildly kissing her on the lips, stroking her hair. Pulling her halter top off over her head, he cupped her breasts and kissed them; her nipples igniting in the dim light. She tugged his underwear down below his ankles and stroked his penis. Hard as a rock. He fell on his back, drawing her down. Brushing a strand from her eyes, she closed over him, ready to do him justice when a putrid stench made her gag.

Rising, she said, "Do you smell that?"

He groaned, pissed he'd missed the oral ecstasy he was about to receive. He got up and grabbed the flashlight and sniffed around. Checking all corners of the building, he didn't see anything that would be a cause for the rank odor, hanging with a sickening sweetness. The light beam raked over a cellar door propped open against the far wall. Naked, he walked over and shined the light down an opening. The stairs disappeared into darkness, the stench wafting up from below. He pulled his hand over his mouth and nose, attempting to keep from losing it.

She came up beside him, pulling her halter back on. "What is it?"

"Something's rotting." He started down the stairs.

She latched onto his arm and yanked. "I'm scared. Let's leave!"

He turned toward her. "You stay here. I'll check it out. Likely a dead animal that got caught below. Sick and died, nothing more."

She protested.

He ignored her and stepped on the rickety, old wooden stairs. "I'll only take a minute."

As he neared the bottom, he felt a jolt. Holly crunched behind him, holding her nose. Curiosity got her, couldn't help herself. He raked the cellar with the flashlight. Several rats scurried out from under a pile of lumber. She screamed. Cody swallowed hard. *Just rats*, he kept telling himself.

Moving toward the center of the room, he saw a door opening in the wall next to the lumber. She came up on his heels, placing her hands on his shoulders, causing him to jump. Taking a deep breath, careful not to step on broken glass, he walked through the opening, shining the light around. The room was empty and twice as big as the one they'd left. In the middle a rickety, wooden table stood, leaning to one side. Cody assumed it was where bushels of olives would have been stored before grinding. He noticed a tubular mound of some kind, a blanket or sheet draped over a lump five or six feet long. The stench became unbearable.

"Please, Cody, let's leave!" she pleaded, finding it impossible not to lose it.

"Let me check one thing. Then, I promise, we'll get the hell out of here." He examined the sheet, faded white, stained with dark spots throughout. Cody's pulse raced out of control. Did he need to see what was underneath? An unknown force kept him from turning and running away. Reaching the end of the sheet he pulled it back. A rat scurried toward him and leaped off the table. She screamed.

"It's okay," he yelled, attempting to calm her down. "Nothing to fear." He looked back at the sheet, and there exposed, scuffed and tattered oxfords, the soles curled and punctured. He reached up and tugged the sheet up a little more. His worst fears. Two legs attached to the shoes, covered by a ragged pair of jeans.

A curtain of fear closed in; the chasm of curiosity ran deep. One voice in his head told him he had to know. A louder voice yelled, *Get the hell out of here, you moron. What the fuck are you doing down here?*

Relegating his decision-making to the toss of a coin, it came up heads. The first voice won. Without a thought, he grabbed the sheet and yanked it off.

His shattered nerves scraped the bottomless pit of his psyche. Face up on the table, supine to the world, lay a body, not just a body, but a man, a repulsive form, rigid, cheeks blistered, lips cracked. Holly screamed in fear. Cody stood transfixed, unable to move. It was not so much the sight of the dead man; in every visible orifice maggots oozed and slithered, out of the nose, ears, mouth, and empty eye sockets, hundreds if not thousands.

There, upon his chest as if in a funeral coffin, the

unfortunate soul held between his fingers, embracing so gently, his detached eyeballs, glinting under the spell of Cody's flashlight beam. Horrified, Cody pulled Holly into the other room. As they neared the stairs, a loud bang reverberated down the opening. "Christ," he screamed. "The damn door closed!" He rushed up the stairs and pushed against the door. Locked. "Open the door, you asshole, whoever you are! This is no joke!" He waited a second and heard something rustling, scrounging around above—and the heinous utterance of snickering.

And then silence, absolute silence. Shaken and panicked, he turned and shined the light on Holly. Her face said it all.

Chapter 3

Sergeant Detective Stanley Brown pulled the handkerchief away from his nose long enough to tell Deputy Crowley to make sure the coroner communicated the time of deaths to him as soon as possible. He glanced back at the three bodies, and for the life of him, this was the most repugnant murder scene he'd ever laid eyes upon in his twenty-seven years of investigations for the Los Angeles County Sheriff's Department.

"What's spinning in your mind right now? What's your take?"

The deputy wiped the sweat from his brow. "Two kids, body on the table. Close to the grisliest thing I've seen."

He wasn't satisfied. "That's not what I'm asking. What do you see here?"

"Yeah, I get it, two different murder events— Never in my wildest dreams."

"And?"

"The body with the maggots has been here a while, the kids, not so long. I'll make sure time of death of all the victims is a priority with the medical examiner."

"So, the old man murdered first, is that your take?"

"The murderer is one sadist SOB. Gets his jollies with creepy things. The boy and girl show up. Wrong place, wrong time."

Brown patted his mouth with his handkerchief.

"That's one possibility, but there's another. Yes, the old man, gruesome is too kind for the condition we found him in. The killer's a psycho, cut and dry, had no choice but to eliminate the teens from spoiling his little macabre playtime. He includes them in his murderous act, with a little flair. Second scenario, the old man used as a lure. The maggots are the flourish. This old place has always been a local teen hangout, you know teenagers and how they get into these types of things. Drinking beer, smoking weed, having sex, you know what I mean. If the old man's detestable murder was a lure, we have a serious problem on our hands."

"It could happen again, that's the scary thing," Crowley groaned.

"It could."

"You know, the creepy part is if the maggot body was staged, a put on, you know, like some of those fright movies we saw as kids. Whoever did this is one sick bastard. We need to find him fast."

Brown walked back to the table where personnel were wrapping up the man's body in a bag. Who, for the love of God, would have gouged out the poor fellow's eyes from his sockets and arranged them on his chest like olives waiting for a martini? Was the murderer leaving a trademark of his handicraft? And what about the stench, the rotting flesh, the maggots? How long had he been here? And the two kids. The boy found naked, testicles severed, throat slit. The girl, nipples slashed, throat slit. He sneezed into his handkerchief and watched as they carried the wrapped bodies up the stairs. Crowley walked over and said, "It's the young ones that get to me."

"Thinking of your own, Nate?"

He looked torn. "Who wouldn't? I have two

daughters. I can't imagine what it's going to be like to contact the parents when identification is done."

"I feel your pain. Unfortunately, that task of notifying the parents is on my agenda." He wiped the sweat from his forehead. "Maybe you crave a little bit of that old-time religion to remove this image from your memory banks. I sure as hell know I'm going to need it."

He gazed up at Brown, a good six inches taller. "Would they let a poor white boy like me in your church? I don't think I'm worth saving."

"Oh, I'll check with the pastor. I'll put in a good word for you. Then, the congregation will have no choice but to accept your pale ass with open arms."

The deputy smiled. A second later, his grim expression returned. "What about the boy and girl? They were just fooling around. Did they deserve such horrible deaths for that? What does God say about all this?"

He paused a moment, then said, "It's *Him* who made them human. And that's what they were doing, being human. I think *He* understands."

"I like the way you think."

Brown patted the deputy on the back and headed for the stairs. He waited a few minutes, left the old building and watched as they loaded the two teenagers into a waiting vehicle.

Walking the path where the two kids came from, he examined their car off the main Malibu Canyon road where a deputy had spotted it. The wallet and driver's license were found in the glove compartment. His name was Cody Stevens. The girl had yet to be identified. His brain was working overtime. What about the murderer? Where did he come from? Deputies were examining another old road leading from the other side of the building. Maybe they'd find some tracks to investigate.

Another thing his tired old body didn't need was another serial killer. Creepy serial killers were the worst. You never knew where the next victim would pop up, and under what circumstances. The Manson murders came to mind, but so far, this one had that beat by a mile. Charles was a saint compared to what he'd seen today. *God, this could be a hard slog. At least it's not Monday.*

Chapter 4

It is now a devil's shadow, blanketing this barren land of short grass and peat in windswept mists that flail across the vista of natural and Neolithic granite spires. And there, among the loftiest of the tors, High Haven points to the clouds like a piteous marker directing the wayward traveler. Onto Walton-On-Sea and the east cliffs, and the dreary sadness that is Chatsworth Manor.
—BB Barmore,
Lady Julia's Sarcophagus

Jessica's first view of Henry Maxwell's mansion was on the last curve up the canyon. Pulling off the road, she rolled her window down and stared up in utter panic. Situated high on the edge of a craggy precipice, she swore she'd been transported to the far side of the Carpathians. An intolerable fear swelled, sweat beading through her epidermis, her veins on fire. This was no ordinary movie star residence—this was a castle, complete with medieval towers and soaring turrets, draped in gloom and shadows in the late afternoon haze of the Santa Monica Mountains. Fuzzy fortress ramparts took control in the warrens of her trembling mind.

...and the flying monkeys, swooping down from the battlements, combing the canyon, searching...

Allowing her dizziness to subside, she sucked in a hollow breath, pulled her Subaru back on the asphalt and continued her journey, all the while believing Marsha had a vendetta against her. The road leveled off and she drove into a private drive with a wrought-iron gate and large stone pilasters topped with hideous-looking gargoyles. Entering a code on the box, she watched the gate creep open, then drove up the smooth circular drive, stopping off-center of the apex. This atrocity won in the out-of-place category, sticking out like a gangrene thumb. She sat for a moment, her mind rushing off into a thousand worlds of possibilities.

She'd hoped to arrive sooner, but a few miscellaneous items delayed her arrival. During the long drive from the San Francisco office, she had plenty of time to analyze her mission. No question Marsha had sentenced her to the job from hell. Sure, she'd worked a couple of years as a clinical psychologist. Solving human behavioral problems didn't fit her personality, so she took up law, and guess where that got her? Wasn't she an attorney, not a caretaker—and not a savior? Without ever meeting Henry Maxwell, she figured he likely needed professional psychiatric care and prescribed meds. At thirty-six years of age, would it be too late to find a third career?

She stared at the massive behemoth, the intricate stonework, the Gothic detail. Towers with battlements bookended the covered entry, crenellations along the roof added to the castle anatomy. A balcony floated high above the arched entrance, sinister-looking windows, like glazed cat eyes, gaped down from above. It didn't fit with the other mansions that graced the road up the canyon, modern and contemporary, owned by other celebrities or those of obscene wealth. A sense of despair and anxiety swept over her. This would be the perfect backdrop for one of Edgar Allan Poe's short stories.

A gathering of clouds drifted overhead, tempering the unusual oppressive heat to a modest level. She turned her attention to the gardens in front of the castle and scanned the expanse of the bleak landscape, grass brown and dying. In the center, a one-time majestic fountain stood in disregard, now dry, choked with windblown debris. The only green in the flower beds were weeds, a sickening impression that a caretaker was no longer employed.

She heard her cell phone ping. She grabbed it and answered in a panic. "This is Jessica."

"Hi, Tom Caswell. Sorry, I told you I'd introduce you. Unfortunately, I'm tied up in a huge traffic jam on the Santa Monica Freeway. Can't even get to the coast highway."

"Oh," she said, not liking the idea of being here without Caswell, whom she had spoken to a day earlier. "I'll wait until you arrive."

A deep sigh. "I'm afraid that might be a while. It could be a couple of hours, if not tomorrow."

She glanced at the castle, struggling with a sudden cold shiver. It was late afternoon, the sun scraping the western horizon.

"Tomorrow then. I can find a motel in Malibu for the night."

"Henry's expecting you today. It's best to meet that deadline."

Vulnerability swelled, leaving her in the wilderness to fend for herself with a person she hadn't met yet, one that began to unnerve her. "Oh, I can't—I mean—I don't feel comfortable not being introduced."

"I understand, I really do, but it won't be a problem.

I'd give Henry a call, although he never answers the phone."

Now, she knew she was over her head. Her brain fogged. "What if he doesn't answer the door?"

"He's waiting and knows he has to follow the rules and accept your presence."

"What, just open the door and saunter on in! You've got to be kidding." She gaped at the stone goliath. "This is crazy."

"Oh, don't worry. I do it all the time. I know what you're thinking. This house is enough to give anyone the creeps.

"No kidding?"

"Don't be intimidated when you go inside. He's expecting you, with or without me. You'll enter the Grand Foyer. He used to entertain there, throwing lavish parties for Hollywood's elites. He's a pussycat, caustic as hell at times, but once you get to know him, I'm positive he'll open up a bit. Don't bother knocking. He'd never answer and he let his last housekeeper go a couple of months ago. I suspect he's either in the den down the hallway on your right, or out on the back veranda. He spends a lot of time staring down the canyon, soaking up the sun, although it's about to disappear."

She shook her head, still in disbelief.

"Jessica, you still with me?"

"I haven't run away yet if that's what you mean?"

"You'll do fine. Just call out his name. I'll check on you later when I'm out of this fiasco."

The line went dead. A raw chill ran down her spine. Marsha never indicated the job might start this way. On her own, this was unthinkable. And it would be dark soon. Her eyes stared at the monstrosity. She started to shake, and she hadn't even knocked on the front door.

Sliding out of the seat, she walked across the drive, up the steps to the covered entry. For several minutes, her gaze a blank look. The elliptical wooden doors gawked back with malice. Instead of a doorbell, a black-iron door knocker hung on the massive double door. Closer examination revealed a dragon head with fiery eyes and a red tongue. Caswell told her to enter and call out Maxwell's name. She clutched the knocker, braving its icy response, and banged it against the door. Several seconds, nothing. She knocked again. Nothing. Sucking in a deep breath, she reached for the latch. It turned unhindered.

Opening the heavy door, she stared inside. Nothing but a pitch-black void. With her stomach stuck in her throat, she crossed the threshold. Her senses at once caught a drift of the perverse as a noxious scent of fear swept over her. The breadth and height of the room overwhelmed, dark and shadowy, pointed archways at every corner, shadows hiding lightless nooks and crevices. Massive, faded tapestries sagged from walls, a coat of arms beyond. She could barely make out the ceiling, too high to distinguish any pattern. The floor's gray tiles deepened her sense of foreboding. She had just stepped back into time, into an earlier era of cold stone and creepiness, far removed from the comfort of modern drywall and delightfully painted rooms.

Her heart thumped louder as she moved through the space. Grime grated under her feet. Likely hadn't been swept or mopped in some time. A couple of elongated windows above allowed what daylight remained. Other than a few side tables and elaborate antiques, emptiness and a lack of vibrancy completed the theme.

"Mr. Maxwell," her voice sputtered and cracked. She spoke again, louder. Only echoes returned off the walls.

The house gave her reason to fear. The darkness circled her, inching closer in diametric suffocation, the shadows pulsating with each bit of daylight that diminished. Her breathing became forced. Was she being watched? A set of stone stairs curved up a wall to the second floor, her eyes following to a landing that disappeared in blackness. She questioned the thought of climbing into the unfathomable and dying a terrifying death at the hands of something beyond the living.

She looked to her right, a Gothic archway above the entrance to a drab hallway. Caswell mentioned a den. She looked closer, swearing the shadows grew deeper, the darkness darkening. Sweat peppered her forehead as a cold breeze funneled her way. She remembered the veranda. Why not try that first? Would he not be outside and not wasting away in this gloom?

She trod across the Grand Foyer, trembling with each step. She moved under the coat of arms and into another room. Her hand swiped a series of cobwebs that penetrated the opening. Aware her stamina was being tested, she continued. She wiped a finger on one of the hallway tables. More dust and webs. Another confirmation that the housekeeper had been let go. Her thoughts deepened. Who would even want this job? More layers of grit crunched beneath her shoes.

An assortment of medieval weapons were displayed. Sneaking around this morbid place, what if he came upon her, forgetting she was coming? This man wasn't all there, from what she had been told. Wild scenarios began to invade her sane mind. Had she been a woman of lesser mental stability, she'd have let her emotions take control, fly through the front door and be halfway down the canyon by now. But she knew better. Her job wouldn't allow her to be that woman.

The dimness brightened. She stepped into the next room, with full-length windows and a double glass door. The ghoulish space changed into the unexpected, as if night had pivoted into day. She saw the back of the castle and an open patio. Structured with heavy timbers that spanned the length, the ceiling soared twenty or more feet high. What remained of daylight struck the floor through the windows giving a view of the back garden and woods beyond. Bits and pieces of furniture dotted the space. At least this room didn't have the oppressive medieval adornments like the previous ones.

She headed over to the glass doors, opened one, and stepped out onto the veranda, a terrazzo patio with a variety of outdoor furnishings. She filled her lungs with fresh air, relieved she'd extracted herself from the bowels of the nightmarish castle. She spied a swimming pool that stood in the center with a fire pit nearby. Leaves and algae covered the surface. It hadn't been cleaned or serviced in weeks, if not months. Neglected, just as the interior and front gardens had been.

She scanned the rest of the veranda. "Mr. Maxwell, are you out here?" she asked with a tepid voice. After no response, she examined every sunny corner, looking in deck chairs, and glancing across the gardens to the south and the woods beyond. Wilting and browning, same as the front. She shook her head in defeat. The last of the sun slanted below the distant hills to the west. Retreating through the double doors, she left the sanity of approaching twilight for the discomfort of imminent darkness. Back through the macabre weapons of death and into the Grand Foyer.

Swallowing hard, she again eyed the Gothic arch she saw earlier. She entered, wiping at a cobweb that swept into her vision. At the end, there were two doors. She opened the wooden door on her left. Still in shadow, she could make out shelves of books on every wall. There was an odor, a musty scent of old paper. Several newspapers littered the rectangular table. The ceiling was vaulted, not quite as high as that in the foyer, but the space felt just as cold—and menacing. She searched and didn't see any evidence of Maxwell hiding in the shadows, ready to spring. The sensation of pending doom still suffused her thoughts.

Exiting, she took a long, hard look at the other door. The den? Having no choice and realizing dusk was settling over the castle, she noticed the door ajar. She pushed it open, and like the library, a pair of lofty windows provided paltry light. She waited, allowing her light-starved eyes to adjust, making out a stone fireplace filling an entire wall to her right. The remaining walls appeared to be finished with wood paneling. Two chairs facing the fireplace offered a cozy scene, or so she tried to convince herself. At the far end, she glimpsed a wooden desk and a high-backed leather chair.

Repressing a shudder, she stepped into the room. As she neared the center of the den, she heard a bleating, sibilant noise, somewhere inside. Sucking in a breath, she approached, keeping her eyes on the chair. It was coal-black, yet she swore she saw something shimmer in it. She moved closer. Finally, the form of a body emerged. Repressing a nervous tremble, she stared at whom she assumed was Henry Maxwell, snoring.

His arms rested on his lap, hands turned up as if in acceptance of something—or nothing. Even in the dimness, she could see he was a miserable-looking lump of an old man with a long neck, unshaven pale face, aged and lined. His earlobes hung like roosting brown bats, his remaining hair raked-thin and the color of ash. She thought she could see a long scar near the top of his left ear disappear into his scalp. From the car accident, she assumed. A pair of bifocals rested on the end of his nose; an engraved cane lay on the desk.

She drew her shoulders together and whispered, "Mr. Maxwell."

No response.

A little louder. "Mr. Maxwell, can you hear me?"

A slight stir. One leg stretched out. His nose twitched, sniffed the air, then his eyes shot open, crisp, and fiery. They angled her direction in a nano-second with a vicious look of disdain.

"Who the hell are you?" Maxwell hissed, pushing his glasses up on his nose.

She swallowed hard. "Jessica Barrow, from Jergins Whitman & Bonoventura."

Maxwell straightened up in the chair, yawned, and licked his lips. "So, you've been sent to save me from myself. How charming."

"No, sir," she said, trying to keep from shaking. "I've been sent to find out how better we can serve you."

Maxwell grunted, leaned forward, and reached for his cane. Finding it, and with effort, he pushed himself up. He stood tall, imposing. His eyes blazed. The den swirled, swallowing her up, framing his stature until nothing else existed.

"JWB is a thorn in my side, considering all the bills

I've received over the years," he said, moving from behind the desk, and hovering over her, his mouth a rictus gape.

Feeling weak, she saw the resemblance to the old movie posters Marsha had shown her. There was a handsome tone to his wrinkled face, striking, screen worthy but with a terrifying appeal.

"We want to make sure everything is as it should be. After all, we value you as a client," she choked out.

"Oh, piss on it," he barked. "I'm a wreck of an old man. There's nothing to salvage here, so you're wasting your time."

She took a step backward, wanting nothing more than to smack Marsha for sending her here. "Tom Caswell was to be here—to introduce us."

"Tom, he's useless. Probably best he's not here. Now that you're here, don't think this is a princess's castle. This house is what is both good…and *bad*. The good dissolved years ago. Only *bad* since. Every corner, every nook, every cranny, every passageway, every room has its secrets. It takes a certain soul to live here, that is if you have one. And if you do," he leaned forward, peering at her with displeasure, "the stone walls suck you into their hideous past, and don't let go. I doubt you have what it takes to stay here." He leaned on his cane; his voice softened. "But it's your decision…I suppose."

She nodded unconsciously.

"Now let's get on the same page," he said, his tall frame straightening up. "Because of this silly California conservatorship law, I have no say in the matter but to put up with you, whether it's one week or a month. Let's hope it doesn't go that far. I'm more than capable of managing my own affairs, as you and your incompetent firm already know. So, here are my rules. If you have any questions—and I'm sure you will, you may ask, but don't expect answers. I like my privacy. Don't get in my space and I won't get in yours—and don't spy on me!"

He edged slowly toward the door.

"I will be staying here," Jessica squeaked. "You've been told, I assume."

Maxwell stopped, spun around. "How convenient. Don't anticipate room service. There are several bedrooms on the second floor. Take your pick. Stay off the third floor. Never, I warn you, never take those stairs up, or my private elevator off the motor court. That's my exclusive domain. You may wander anywhere else in this house of horrors if you so desire. I will not be responsible for your…safety. You are in charge of your own meals and groceries. I can handle my own needs. And don't expect me to entertain you."

He continued across the den and out the door, never looking back.

She clutched her hand over her chest and felt the dread of darkness immerse her soul.

Chapter 5

Close to midnight, Henry Maxwell found himself back in his leather recliner, contemplating the senseless timeline of his pitiful life. *You're conceived, you're birthed, you're nurtured, you learn, you err, you apologize, you err again, you love, you lose, you grieve, you continue to err, you despise, you blame, you hate, you grow old, you wither—you die. DEAD...AND...BURIED.* The norm for a good portion of the world's human population—a long box, six feet under, topped with the finest loam or the siltiest, clayey soil from any poor man's cornfield. He had better accommodations reserved. Though this latter stage was closing in, he was not quite ready. He ran his hand over an old revolver he once brandished in a movie.

And the newspaper, a two-day-old edition of the LA *Times*. He picked it up and glanced at the front-page headline: THREE BODIES DISCOVERED IN ABANDONED OLIVE OIL PROCESSING BUILDING IN MALIBU CANYON. He had read it and reread it and reread it again, and every time, he relived the scene. The descriptive newsprint said it all...two teenagers, a boy and a girl mutilated, found with a man's decomposing body... Surprised the building still existed. *Dark Stairs*, one of his early films, was alive and well. Not the highlight of his career, but the killing of the teenagers added a twist. Was he crazy? *Always have been*, he admitted, his lips curling with a sordid grin. He was crazy, crazier than crazy, and he knew it, but at this moment, it had no bearing on what, if anything, he'd already done.

His self-destructive thoughts struggled for a foothold when a slender arc of light pierced the windows above, adding little detail to the eeriness of the high indistinguishable ceiling. A boom of thunder followed. The squall outside, a Pacific sleeper, grew, stabs of lightning and rumbles now controlled the artistry of the nocturne. Next, the rain would come, and the saturation of the fire-raped hillsides would run with avalanches of mud. Welcome to lovely Southern California, home of the rich and famous…and the crazy. Things never change.

Two months after Lillian died, Maxwell sat in Dr. Ewe Kopf's office, searching for answers. Maybe he had some.

"I can prescribe something to help you sleep," Kopf offered, "but that would only be a temporary solution."

"Christ sakes, Ewe. You treated Lillian for depression all these years. She's gone now, my life is miserable. Most times I want to be gone, too. Is that so hard to understand?"

Kopf straightened up in his chair and scribbled on a yellow pad he held. He looked at Maxwell with apologies screaming from his eyes. "First of all, stop blaming yourself," he said. "If you must blame, blame me. I cared for her. Serious clinical depression, but not critical. We both understood her drug dependence. I admit failure. I couldn't reach her. Some patients respond, others don't. Lillian was in that group. If I could do this all over again, I'd try different methods,

I'm one hundred percent sure I would have gotten the same result. Therapy is not always successful; it's buried in the statistical sciences. Win some, lose some, a percentage problem. Your hope is to win more than you lose."

He didn't say anything. What was there t' say at this point?

"You're still here, Henry," Kopf continued. "The ball's in your court and we must both work toward a common goal. Life goes on, for me, for you, for the entire world. The question: Where do you go from here?"

He shrugged. "I don't know."

"Let's look at this from a different angle. Lillian aside for the moment, what's your biggest regret?"

"Trust me, I have several."

"Yes, we all do, but you must have one. What is it?"

"Dammit, Ewe. You know the answer. My career is a shamble. When she died, I quit. Global Pictures imploded. I drove them into bankruptcy. My last film wasn't released because I couldn't finish it. It would have been my best, my legacy. I'm a quitter, Ewe. I walked away. I couldn't act, even if it was the final thing I did on earth. For God's sake, I couldn't!"

Another boom exploded through the night. This kind of storm brought back celluloid memories of his past. Amazing what editors and sound engineers could do for a movie. Tonight, fear like never before swept over him. The massive house creaked and groaned with every blast of wind whistling against the windows. He straightened up shaking. Through the clamor of thunder, he swore he heard something coming from the other side of his castle domain. He palmed the gun. It had another purpose, but for some odd reason, the outside bluster misdirected his thoughts. He never liked guns. Nevertheless, he handled them as props during his glory days, but here he brandished it as an instrument of inevitability. *The tempest, my god, the storm!* The revolver twitched in his hand.

He stood up and walked into the hallway. The haunting streaks of light and shadows fluttered along the walls and ceilings. Moving through the bleakness, he tested the floor with his cane. Lights out. He assumed the woman hunkered upstairs in her room, crouched under the bed covers like all young women during stormy nights. So far, she'd been unobtrusive.

He took a few steps across the Grand Foyer. Again, that sound, a rattling. He moved under the coat of arms, past the medieval weapons and into the next room. An occasional lightning bolt tossed shadows. One of the doors to the veranda pivoted back and forth with each gust of wind. He sighed. Only the creaking from the hinges and the rattle from a loose pane of glass in the door. He shook his head in disgust. *If I wasn't in such a state of mind, I would have had a little maintenance done.*

His feeble eyes detected movement. He froze, squinting through the window. Outside on the other side, did he not see little pinpoints of light flickering on and off? Growing up in Ohio's Hocking Hills, fireflies were common. He kept staring. More points of light floated in and out, circling, rising, flirting. Busy sparks of light just as he remembered. But in California? There were no fireflies here, yet they flashed on and off, organizing, taking shape.

The rain blurred his view, the flashing light points swept out an outline, the whitest apparition, hypnotic, a long white gown, floating across the deck, down the stairs, into the garden. Cold sweat settled over him. His chest tightened. He'd worked with illusions in the movies, but this was real, a hundred levels above what those special effects people did in the sixties. He stood motionless. He gazed on in wonder. *My eyes—they wither, they lie! No, it is true—I see it!*

His life had been lived in the real and make-believe world. A few ghosts now and then shouldn't be a reason to be terrified. Clutching the revolver with strength he never realized, he moved out onto the veranda. Raindrops pelted his face, soaking through his robe. He neared the stairs and waited. Clouds were lifting, the squall starting to ease, a mist formed cloaking the surrounding woods. Maxwell drew his attention to the pathway extending across the garden into the trees. Something, unexplainable, tugged at his senses, his memory, pulling at him with effervescence.

As the drizzle subsided, he wiped the moisture from his face, now mostly sweat. His aged heart sped with an exhilaration he hadn't felt in years. A mental infusion of courage flooded his mind, the will to keep on pulled him. The gun in his hand slipped from his fingers and fell with a clang.

Forgetting the weapon, he gripped his cane, and stepped down onto the path, twisting across the garden and fading into a grouping of trees. For some odd reason, his worn knee didn't bother him as he followed a wide bend. He tried to remember the last time he had been beyond the woods, perhaps three or four years. His breathing increased at a rapid rate as he exited the trees and found himself in the statuary garden. Emotions intensified. This had been Lillian's favorite place. For a moment, he examined the Greek statues lining the agora, the Grecian plaza. A new moon haloing through the lifting clouds, brightened the white marble gods. He smiled, remembering the times he and Lillian would spend long evenings sitting on a bench near the statues. There would be laughter and intense conversations, a solving of the world's problems, and planning for their bright future. But that world, once so filled with immense happiness and pleasure, tragically vanished.

Shutting out his thoughts, an eerie shrill from the far end of the statues solidified his reality. Again…a fluttering glow…a white specter.

"Who are you?" Henry begged, as the wind picked up and the rain roared back.

Arthritic bad knee or not, he stumbled forward. Reaching the end of the statuary line, he stopped and brushed raindrops from his eyes. He saw a fading specter fluttering beyond the base of Zeus, a lone sentinel in its own right.

…and High Haven marks his journey, pointing the way to the end of time and the beginning of eternity.

He caught his breath when the apparition whirled. An otherworldly form for sure. As fast as it appeared, it faded into the trees.

Henry took two steps and staggered a bit farther, exhausted. His knees throbbed, and his heart raced toward atrophy. He had never ventured this far in years. The mist returned and so did his fear of the unknown. So close to ending his life tonight, yet there may be a reason to remain on this planet a little longer.

Chapter 6

Early the next morning, Jessica woke, disoriented, her nightgown drenched, sweat slick on her face. It took all her willpower to stay after brooming the cobwebs from the nightstand and the corners of the room. Thoughts of spiders or other crawly things walking over her kept her up most of the night. In case she needed a quick escape, she chose the closest room near the stairs.

Her reality became crystal clear—she'd hardly slept; eyes trained on the door waiting for the knob to turn. Here, a strange, unstable man roamed around a gargantuan, creepy old castle, keeping her from calling Marsha on several occasions to chew her out and offer her resignation, but every time she put the phone down.

After crawling from bed, she dressed. At seven-thirty, she opened her door and stepped out, the second floor as unkempt and filthy as below. She shuddered. Down the dreary hall, she saw a spray of light filtering up the massive stairwell from the Grand Foyer. With relief, she headed toward the stairs, having survived her first night. Surviving her first morning was yet to be seen.

What would their conversation be when and if she found him again? Where would she look first? Finding the kitchen, the scene stopped her cold. Spread out before her was the aftermath of a cyclone, piles of soiled dishes stacked like round towers, cups and glasses in disarray, some overturned, empty takeout boxes and an overflowing garbage can. A broken plate lay on the floor with remnants of chicken bones. And the stench, something putrid drifting across her nose coming from the sink. She spotted Maxwell in his robe, sitting in the breakfast room. He presented himself as disheveled as he did when she first met him. Gathering her courage, she walked over. "Good morning," fluttered from her mouth.

He peered up from the table, his whole face contorted, an assortment of wrinkles, sags, and puffiness. His left eye twitched, the accident scar dancing along his temple. He grumbled, took a sip from a mug. "Pot of coffee in the kitchen. Help yourself."

Reluctant to view the disgusting mess again, but determined to keep the conversation going, she retreated to the kitchen. After a futile search, she took one of the dirty cups from the counter, found a scrub brush with soap, cleaned and rinsed it. What about a little cream? Opening the refrigerator door, she gagged then closed it. If any was there, she'd leave it, it had a life of its own by now. Giving up, she returned to the morning sitting room with the nagging fear she would falter trying to converse with the old man. Taking a chair across from him, she sat down, hoping to survive the morning in his presence.

"Thanks for the coffee."

He didn't say anything, cupping his mug with both hands, staring at her with suspicion. "So how does Marsha Hauser convince someone as pretty as you to come to my rescue?" he asked.

She blushed. "No convincing. This is my job, you're a valued client."

"Oh, come now, sweetheart. You can do better than that. You, and all those other rat-assed attorneys at JWB, why you? What's your specialty the other leeches there couldn't handle?"

"I'm not partnered yet, so I do what I'm assigned."

Maxwell leaned in, his left eye still twitching. "My imagination, or do you have some unique skill? What's in your skillset that will save this worthless old bundle of bones you're looking at? Tell me, what makes you qualified?"

Jessica knew better than to tell him about her background in psychology. That would likely set him off. "I like to talk to people and learn about them. From what I understand, your life is remarkable."

He shook his head. "Total hogwash. Whatever happened in the past is gone; no more. Now, I'm an old man waiting out my remaining days. Shouldn't be difficult to comprehend."

"Why this imminent yearning for finality? You appear healthy for your age. Philanthropic I've been told. And you still have a lot to give. Why throw it all away now?"

"Cause I'm tired, dearie."

"Then let's talk about your profession. I mean, you were in the movies. Fascinating."

"Ancient history. Nothing to discuss."

"Nothing? You're before my time, but I did my research, and I'm honored to have the opportunity to discuss with someone from the movie business. Not every day one meets a celebrity."

Another grunt. "Have you ever seen any of my pictures?" His voice rose. "Or do you go to those huge budget blockbusters that dominate nowadays, or those baseless forced thrillers or tedious, teary-eyed dramas? Astronomical budgets, special effects, computer crap!

They don't give a damn about storytelling, just spending gobs of money. They've lost the art of making motion pictures. It's gone—all gone, destroyed by the almighty dollar." He paused. "Let me guess, you're a romance and touchy-feely kind of girl?"

"To answer your first question, no, I've never seen one of your movies. As to your second, in general, I rarely go to the movies. And if they're all about the allmighty dollar, I see you've gotten your share. As for your last question, I don't consider myself touchy-feely." Her eyes drifted around her surroundings.

"Touché, my sweet little princess." He gave her a sliver of a smile.

"I know I'm an inconvenience," she said. "Drop right in and upset your routine. I apologize, I really do, but I don't write the laws on conservatorships. Believe me, I want to be out of your life as quickly as possible."

"Do as you must, but like I told you yesterday, I'm not running a hotel here."

"I understand. That brings up another point. How does Tom Caswell fit into your life?"

Maxwell grumped. "He's an old acquaintance. Don't listen to a thing he says."

Jessica recognized a touch of animosity. "Why not?"

"Because he never amounted to a hill of beans. I could never figure out why he couldn't make anything out of his life. Even his sleazy father, who did work on my films, was an ass. The apple doesn't fall far from the tree. Now, move on."

She turned her head and looked back in the kitchen. "Okay if I had things tidied up a bit around here? I know you could use the help."

A slight hesitation. "Whatever makes you feel at home but leave me out of it, and don't go snooping, chasing after me."

"I wouldn't think of it."

"There's an extra key to this place in one of those hallway tables in the foyer. Alarm? Never had one. Always relied on the security gate out front. You have the code. You may need it if you're out carousing at night. I was young once, I remember. Don't expect me to open the door late at night. Now leave me in peace." He pointed at one of the windows. "The sun is coming through the clouds flooding my space. I wish to enjoy my coffee in privacy."

Jessica had been dismissed. She left, thankful he didn't rip her head off.

Chapter 7

At midnight, Maxwell shuffled from the path onto the smooth surface of the agora. He moved down the procession of statues, polished white-hot marble from the light of a dazzling crescent. Deathly quiet, save the tapping of his cane on the brick pavers. The last several days, the uncertainty controlled. Tonight, he would look for another appearance.

He stopped, taking a much-needed breath. To his right, a presence loomed on the murky fringes. *No, no, it's nothing*, he told himself, only the moon's rays bouncing off the old greenhouse. Still standing after all these years. A few glass panes survived unshattered. Earthquakes, mudslides, torrential rains, high winds, everything mother nature could hurl at it. He hobbled over, amazed at how it looked after years of neglect. A fitting tribute to Lillian, but without foresight, he let it sink into disrepair. He cursed himself for being so careless.

He found the door, somehow attached, half open. He tried to remember how often he ventured inside as she worked her magic with flowers. He took a step to enter but hesitated, considering how many times she entered through this opening. Thousands, perhaps? Sucking in a deep breath, he crossed the threshold into the empty space. Dried grass covered the dirt floor overtaking a row of wooden potting tables, rickety and deteriorating. In the murk, a few old broken clay pots stacked in a corner stood out, like centuries-old artifacts waiting to be discovered by an archeologist. Above, several panels of glass were missing.

He imagined decades earlier, when Lillian would work hours separating stock, raising flowers from seeds, and planning future landscape arrangements. He remembered the chalkboard at the end of one of the worktables. Which one, he couldn't remember, but that didn't matter. She kept meticulous notes, orders, and instructions. Like a fine-tuned Swiss watch, the gardens were impeccable, never shabby, always tidy. Purple and yellow daisies in winter and red roses in summer. Spring and fall were the best times of transition, in seasons and in people. She appeared happier in autumn.

Maxwell stared at the non-existent chalkboard. For a long time, he didn't stir, ruminating about the list of chores she would write down for the gardener. He marveled about the assorted chalk she would use, like the different shades and hues of flowers.

She died, her fingers gripping an orange piece. He never forgot the color, the investigative report, or how excited she had been for the dahlia project. Determining the perfect locations to plant were critical in Lillian's plan. She would fuss over each variety trying to achieve the best complement to pair with the statues. He recalled the chalkboard the police had photographed. The scribbled colors were vivid. Aphrodite, goddess of love, and beauty—bright red, to maximize desire and pleasure. Dionysus, god of wine and drunkenness, of parties and theater—pink pompon to emphasize a festive look. Hades, god of hell and the dead—burnt orange, a ball variety.

The Salvation of Henry Maxwell

On and on, Lillian decorated every statue with dahlias based on classification and color. Still engrained deep in his grieving mind, the last notation, a scribble travelling in a hectic line off the edge of the board. The Sheriff's investigation determined the culprit, a syringe on the table. Analyzed, it still held a small amount of atropine solution, a concentrate of deadly moonflower.

Maxwell thought long and hard about the report. Earlier this evening, he scrounged around and found it buried in an old shoebox. They stated overdose by intravenous injection of a mixed concoction of moonflower. Now why did he not question the findings at the time? She did cultivate a variety of moonflower for the showy flowers, the scientific name, datura wrightii, well aware of the danger when ingested in potent quantities. It indicated several cuttings were spread out over her worktable near the syringe. He could not buy the fact that she had injected the mixture. At the time, Maxwell disagreed, but no other explanation surfaced, too grief stricken to argue against the evidence, knowing her dependence on drugs. He felt a tightening in his chest. Sweat appeared on his forehead, glistening in the moonlight.

He admonished himself. Why didn't he object to the report? She held the title as the most conscientious person he'd ever met. Yes, controlled substances, amphetamines, anti-depressants, muscle relaxers, all harmful, but intravenous moonflower? He sensed a rage building. He never challenged the coroner's conclusions. His sudden movement surprised him as he swung his cane in protest, striking one of the pots, clay fragments flying every direction of what remained of the pot.

Strange only now did he believe Lillian's death no

accident. The two-inch chalk she clutched in her fist became suspect. Toxicologists suggested the atropine in her system would have caused intense discomfort along with confusion and hallucinations. She vomited outside the door after tripping over a bag of insecticide, the pain becoming excruciating. The bag was covered with vomit. Why had he not questioned this? Lillian did not allow toxins in her garden, only organic insecticides. After that, she stumbled, falling at least two more times before reaching the agora. There, she vomited a second time, seizures beginning to take control. Why didn't she move toward the house and dial emergency? Instead, she went the other direction. The report emphasized delirium was a contributing factor. Halfway down the agora, she vomited a third time. He visualized the horrific scene, not unlike some of his movies.

Regaining her feet, she lurched along, eyes likely swinging back and forth between the statues, no doubt hallucinating. Apollo must have stared blindly at her, strumming his lyre. No doubt she heard his music, a dark and resonating eeriness, like a distant cry for help. And Artemis, stringing her bow and pointing the arrow at her. Down at the end, she would have recognized the massive Zeus. waving his scepter. Certainly, she heard his verbal banter, as he passed judgment on her while the gods lent their ears.

She never made it as far as Zeus. Situated between Eros and Aphrodite, she collapsed, the chalk still gripped in her hand. Why had she carried it this far? And why here? Maxwell walked down the agora and stopped at the spot where she was found.

He glanced to his right and stared at Aphrodite. What thoughts went through her mind as she peered up at the goddess? And when she died, did she want to scribble something on the pavers? The report mentioned the chalk but didn't give a reason she had brought it from the greenhouse. Medical experts theorized, because of the pain, her hand muscles had constricted, unable to drop it. *Hogwash!* Her outstretched arm pointed toward the statues.

Why for God's sake did he remember all this so well, now? His love was Lillian, but her passion was Greek mythology. Many evenings along the agora she would be animated, discussing the gods. Oh, how he now wished he understood her devotion to the mythical.

Chapter 8

Maxwell leaned on the counter across from Lannie Goodrich, chief health officer for the district office of the Los Angeles Department of Environmental Health on Wilshire Blvd. Middle-aged, clean shaven, with black curly hair and wearing glasses, he flipped through a notebook, plastic-lined pages of different poisonous plant varieties.

"Is this something you're cultivating in your garden?" Goodrich asked, somewhat curious as to why an older gentleman with a worn-looking fedora would be asking about the particulars of moonflower.

"I understand it's dangerous," Maxwell said, eyeing Goodrich with a full-face grin.

"Yes, it can be, but it's not against the law to grow them, if that's your question."

"I've given it some thought, but since I'm getting on in years, I didn't want to be responsible if someone got sick from this plant."

Goodrich turned the notebook around. "Here's a picture of one variety of moonflower. Other names are nightshade and datura."

"How poisonous?"

"Can be deadly. It wouldn't be in here if it wasn't. Every part of the plant is toxic, the seeds, leaves, roots, stems. If you are planning to cultivate it, just take extra precaution and wear gloves, and don't let your dog chew on them, could be lethal."

He stepped back and leaned on his cane, both hands on the handle. "Let's go with a little fiction here," he said, smiling. "If I was to poison someone with moonflower, how'd I go about doing it?"

Goodrich straightened up and eyed the old man. "You can't be serious, now, are you, Mr.—"

He extended his hand across the counter. "Henry Maxwell."

Goodrich took his hand and laughed. "You had me going there for a bit." He kept his eyes on the old man, thinking something was here he couldn't put his finger on.

"Listen, Lannie," Maxwell said in a subdued voice. "I used to be in the flicks back in the day, and I'm talking when you probably were still in diapers. I've been asked to do another one. Even at my age, my fans can't get enough of me. Very gratifying, but I've had my time in front of the camera. I surmise I'm just an easy pushover. The screenwriter is having trouble designing a perfect murder. I suggested moonflower, so that's why I'm here. Screenwriter's a nephew; thought I'd help him out a bit."

Goodrich took his eyeglasses off and wiped them with a tissue and replaced them. He glanced at Maxwell. "Son of a gun, you kinda look like who you say you are. A little older since the movies I saw when younger, reruns on television. Well, I'll be, I know this office is in Beverly Hills, but to this day, I've never seen a movie star come through those doors. Only once or twice we'd get a call from some celebrity whose kid overdosed on this or that, Ecstasy at the top of the list. My, my, isn't this something?"

"I appreciate you having a remembrance of those

movies back then."

"I do remember watching a few of them. Can't recall you ever using poison, but you had other methods. Some were downright creepy, like suffocation in a coffin, things like that."

"Oh, yes, of course, *Devil's Details*. I enjoyed that one. Tell you what, I believe all the means of demise for one person or another have been tried in the movies. I'm sure moonflower poisoning has been used as well, but I'm still intrigued. Could you lend me your expertise? This being a poison control center, I imagine you have a wealth of information that might be helpful."

"To answer your question, I'd suggest the seeds be ground up, leaves shredded and boiled in water, make a tea so to speak."

"Use in a syringe?"

"Yeah, that may work."

"Interesting. So if my screenwriter nephew asks me what's the ingredient that's poisonous, what do I tell him."

"Just a second." Goodrich walked back into another room and returned carrying a massive technical manual. He placed it down, checked the index and turned to a page. "Says here the predominant toxins are atropine and scopolamine. These are toxic to the human body. They're also used in surgery and for other medical uses, even to manage other poisonings."

Maxwell raised an eyebrow. "Really, a poison that can be used as an antidote for other poisonings. That's interesting."

He nodded. "I guess that's not that uncommon. If you think about it, anti-venom is made from snake venom. We've seen a few rattlesnake cases come

The Salvation of Henry Maxwell

through here over the years."

He swirled this information in his mind. Thinking back forty-plus years ago was a major, daunting task, when attempting to remember things that were in the report on Lillian's cause of death. And why now had he started to put what facts he had together?

"Is there something else I can help you with, Mr. Maxwell?"

"You said other poisons this atropine can treat. What would some of those be?"

Goodrich slid his finger down the page, reading. "Mushroom poisonings, organophosphate insecticides, things like Malathion, Diazinon."

"Does it say how atropine would handle that?"

"Intravenous. Acts as a block of the chemical messenger in the insecticide. A little bit more science than I'm familiar with."

A smile erupted across Maxwell's face. "You've been more than helpful." He tipped his hat and on the way out said, "See you in the movies."

Chapter 9

That afternoon, Jessica sat on one of the veranda deck chairs, pleased she'd found a cleaning service who would be by tomorrow to undertake, in what her mind would be a massive task. A housekeeper was also on her agenda, although not right away. That might be too much for Henry to absorb all at once. Earlier in the day, she hired a reputable gardening company who was more than happy to have a new contract. If she could get the estate cleaned up and back to respectability, maybe he'd open up, and she could kiss this assignment goodbye. For certain, the zillionaires living up the canyon wouldn't be complaining so loud about the looney actor from the sixties letting his property decline into a trash heap, depressing their property values.

She heard footsteps on the veranda. Thinking it was Maxwell, she turned, and to her surprise, a tall, fiftyish, well-structured man approached, wearing khaki shorts and a long-sleeved shirt with rolled-up cuffs.

"Jessica, Tom Caswell," he said. "Sorry I missed you yesterday."

They shook hands. "I took your advice, met Mr. Maxwell, and did survive the night."

"You'll continue to survive. The sunny backside helps alleviate the ghoulish nature of the house."

"Castle," she shuddered.

Caswell nodded. "Castle, indeed." He looked

The Salvation of Henry Maxwell

around. "I didn't check the den for Henry."

"I haven't seen him since this morning. We had a cup of coffee together. Not much conversation, although he is allowing me to have this place tidied up."

Tom pulled up a chair and sat down. "You move fast. That's good news."

"So far, If he's helpless, he hides it well."

"Some days are like that. He has mood shifts. Never can tell what Henry will show up."

"How long have you known Mr. Maxwell?"

"Forever, it seems. My dad worked as a special effects director on most of his films. I was just a kid. When I wasn't in school, he would take me down to the set, and sometimes Lillian would be there."

"Maxwell's wife?"

"Yes. She kind of took me under her wing in those days. My mother died when I was four." He sighed. "Lillian was as close to a mother as I've ever had. After she passed, things got strained, but I never gave up on Henry."

The click of a walking stick on the terrazzo perked Jessica's ears. She turned her head to see Maxwell lumbering over, stopping in front of Caswell.

"Well, well, what have we here," he said, leaning on his cane. "My uninvited guest and my… dear…old…friend. Both plotting against me, I'm sure."

"Now, Henry, you know that's not true," Caswell said.

"Oh, come now, Tom," he said, smirking. "You know I'm kidding. I love you like a son. I might add, more than Roy ever did."

She swore smoke came out of Caswell's ears.

"No need to bring him up," Caswell said. "We've

hashed all that stuff out years ago."

"Who's Roy?" she asked, not wanting to be left out of the conversation.

Caswell kept a keen eye on Maxwell. "He's my father. I haven't seen him in years."

"Yes, poor old Roy got bent out of shape when Lillian took an interest in Tom. He couldn't handle being pushed aside, but he more than deserved it. Isn't that right, Tom?"

Tom stood, irritated. "That's your recollection."

"There's more to the story, isn't there?" Maxwell gave him a rough look, then glanced at Jessica. "You two keep plotting now, I've things to do." He hobbled across the veranda and back into the house.

She didn't respond, not understanding the exchange.

"That's been my life with Henry. I try my best to be of help, knowing what he's been through. To one of the biggest names in Hollywood in the sixties to who he is today. Hard to understand. Quite sad, really. It's not a jovial relationship, but he hasn't told me to hit the road. Not yet anyway. We'll talk later, just wanted to finally check-in." He left, leaving Jessica with more unanswered questions.

That night, she lay silently, eyes unblinking, thinking. Grief was one of the hardest responses to the loss of a loved one, emotionally, but physically as well. She remembered well from her undergraduate classes at UC Davis, the five stages of grief—denial, anger, bargaining, depression, and acceptance, in that order. From what she read; Maxwell had reached the acceptance stage years before the accident. Afterwards, he backtracked to the fourth stage, depression. The question dug at her. Why? And what about this tension between Henry and Tom? She slid out of bed and checked the time. 11:15.

A hot shower would be welcome, but a quick stroll outside to catch a breath of fresh air would be more relaxing. At this hour of the night, Maxwell must be asleep. He told her he stayed on the third floor. Her foray onto the veranda should not arouse him from sleep.

Retrieving a headlamp she had with her, she stepped out into the hallway. Dark and dingy, like before. Taking her time, she walked down the curved stairway, the beam showing the way, casting wayward shadows along the walls, shadows that sprang and disintegrated. She shuddered, wondering where she got the guts to move through the dark in this creepy, manmade cavern. As imagined, the rest of the house remained pitch dark, the way Henry liked it for some odd reason. Maxwell kept to his room but turning on lights might go against his wishes. Why risk it.

She wound her way to the front door. Again, the idea of being an intruder shot through her mind. Her inner voice reminded her this was the home of an actor who played malevolent characters. He mastered them well because *he understands what evil is*. Would she really be able to sit through one of Maxwell's films? Her scaredy-cat brain convinced her she was living one now. Shaking her head, wanting nothing more than to unscramble her presence of mind, she found the door latch. Locked. She felt a little relief.

Working her way back to the other side of the cold, cavernous space through the large stone-clad rooms, she passed through the Great Hall to the door to the veranda. She noticed the loose pane of glass and made a mental note to have it fixed. Stepping out onto the terrazzo deck, she turned her flashlight off. She flopped in a chair away from the pool in shadows, as the glow from the LA basin provided a slight radiance. Her presence here would be hidden. She looked across the lawn down the canyon at the distant lights of Malibu. Broken clouds streamed by, lifting off the Pacific and adding elevated humidity. After a hurried day, breathing in the moisture-laden air brought satisfaction to a job well done. Getting Maxwell to accept her help in arranging housekeeping and gardeners remained a small victory; now if she could challenge him to open a little bit more. If the death of his wife some decades before was the problem, what was the solution?

A metallic click roused her attention. She straightened up in the chair as the shuffle of feet drew closer. An outside light came on and Maxwell came out of shadow on the far side, his cane probing his way towards the garden. She slunk back, not wanting to make a sound. He reached the stairs and negotiated his way down. Shining a flashlight, he picked along the path that curled toward the woods, guiding himself without any trouble. Jessica started to get up but thought otherwise. This would not be a suitable time to show herself. Treading on thin ice seemed to be her trademark. Just wait and see what happens.

And wait she did. At 12:35, she saw a pinpoint of light flaring out of the woods. Maxwell was returning, his flashlight raking ahead. She stayed back in the chair, waiting as he trudged through the garden. Several times he stopped to catch his breath. After another minute or two, he neared the stairs and plodded up. He reached the veranda, paused, huffing and wheezing. Satisfied, he walked back to the door and disappeared. The light turned off. She waited another fifteen minutes, then eased out of the chair in the darkness, wondering what had drawn Maxwell into the woods this time of night.

Chapter 10

The house on Diego Street was one of several forties-style Spanish ranchers, all similar in appearance with rough-textured stucco and red-clay tile roofs. Yasuo Tashiro, Yaz to his friends and close acquaintances, lived here alone. At one time a film editor who worked for a few studios in Hollywood, he was seen as somewhat of a celebrity in the neighborhood. When prompted about working in the motion picture industry, he would offer what he could, chitchatting about the films he had the opportunity to edit, low budget, along with a couple of better-financed movies. Having retired over a decade ago, he now lived south of where he grew up near the Feather River.

He kept a vegetable garden in his back yard with a few tangerine trees. The rows of radishes, carrots and zucchini brought satisfaction. He had learned tilling of soil from his parents, who learned from their parents, and if he had a family himself, he would be handing down the joys of gardening to them.

He bent down and turned the knob on one of the irrigation bibs. Enough watering today. He glanced to the west and caught the last glimpse of the sun disappearing over the horizon. Pausing, he thought of the call he had received a while back from a Professor Grovene of UCLA. The professor's expertise was B-movies. Had he sent the professor a list of the film inventory in his private collection? He tried to remember. And it came to him. He sent it a day or two ago. Rolling his eyes, he cursed himself for having such a geezer mind.

He headed back to the house. Reaching the door, he pushed in, and proceeded to the refrigerator. Time to rustle up something simple for dinner. "Losing my mind again," he whispered. "What about a bottle of wine?" He walked out into the hallway and opened the door to the basement. Turning on a light switch, he moved down the stairs and into a partially finished space that held a workbench, tools, and an old sofa against one of the walls. At the far end, he walked over to the door to the vault. He proceeded down another half-set of stairs.

Bomb shelter then, the sixties long gone, but now a perfect place for wine storage and reels of celluloid. Yaz, former film editor, was an expert on preservation. After he bought the house, he added additional ventilation and a supplemental air-handling unit, keeping the space at fifty degrees Fahrenheit and thirty-five percent relative humidity. Although the temperature was a little high for storing film, reds and whites from the vine were thankful for the chilling.

He pulled out a local Cabernet Sauvignon from one of the wine racks. A fitting tribute to a perfect day. Cradling the bottle, he walked past shelves of 35 mm canisters, original celluloid, now considered collector items. At last count, he thought he had at least sixty different titles. His eyes caught the taped title on a canister, *The Remnant*, released in 1961, part of a double feature, a rage at the time. For a budget of $110,000, it barely broke even.

He admired the remaining collection with satisfaction, then turned to leave. He stopped in his tracks. A man stood next to the storage racks, examining a bottle of wine. Unshaven, with a shaggy mane of tousled red hair, the stranger wore a scuffed-up black-and-gray varsity jacket with no name or insignia. A long cloth satchel hung over one shoulder. Yaz sucked in a disturbed breath.

The man stared at him; his eyes flickered like spinning tops. "Merlot, 2009. Not bad I suppose. Good year, do you think?"

Stunned, Yaz asked, "Who are you?"

The stranger replaced the Merlot. "I buy films," he said. He walked along the storage shelves, rolling his eyes over the canisters, examining the titles.

"Those—those are not for sale! Now, who are you to come into my house uninvited?"

"Hey, no need to be nervous. "I'm a collector, like you." He continued to examine the film canisters, moving a little closer. He kept his interest on the shelves as he reached into the satchel, retrieved a long-barrel pistol, pointed it at Yaz and pulled the trigger.

Yaz didn't have time to react. First, a blunt pop sounded, and a red-feathered dart pierced his chest, a slight prick. He seized the dart at the same time he dropped the Cabernet Sauvignon. The bottle shattered and splattered wine across the floor. Pulling the needle out, he glanced back at the stranger in shock. Dizziness overtook his senses. He buckled onto his knees and fell over. Struggling for a solid breath, his muscles atrophied and sweat pooled on his forehead as he drifted into a deep sleep.

Chapter 11

David Grovene sat in disbelief reading the online story in the *Sacramento Bee* after a colleague alerted him. Yasuo Tashiro, the celluloid film collector, was dead. He reached out to him a while back, taking a while to track him down. He was one of the few still living who was an expert on B-movies as he edited many of them in the sixties. He was eager to have his collection of films examined by an academic, someone in a better position to assure their preservation. Two days ago, David received Tashiro's written inventory.

According to the newspaper, Tashiro may have suffered a medical issue in the storage vault. A quick call directed him to the Sacramento Police Department and a Detective Matt Hardrick. David gave him his credentials and explained why he'd called.

"I planned to meet Mr. Tashiro the day after tomorrow in Sacramento. I found out about his death in the morning paper."

"Why the interest in him?" Hardrick asked. "Did you know him?"

"No, never met, although we've talked by phone a couple of times. He sent me a written inventory of his films. I'm researching the history of old celluloids. He kindly invited me to look over his private collection."

A slight pause followed. "We're still investigating."

"Medical issue?"

"He sent you a list of his films?"

"Yes, I have them."

"You say you're a professor at UCLA, would you still like the opportunity to examine them?"

"I won't say no. Examining his collection would further my research."

Hardrick's voice became accommodating. "We may need your expertise. How soon could you come to Sacramento?"

Something else going on here. "My schedule is rather empty now. I could get there tomorrow."

"The sooner the better."

"Sounds serious."

A short pause. "Mr. Tashiro died under unusual circumstances."

The next day, David flew to Sacramento and rented a car. He arrived at Tashiro's house a little after 3:00 p.m. Yellow ribbon surrounded the property. He walked up to the front door, and a young police officer came out and asked for his name. Satisfied, he escorted him inside and down to the basement. Another man waited outside the entry to the vault in a white dress shirt with rolled-up sleeves, green tie and pleated trousers. He stuck out his hand. "Mr. Grovene, thanks for coming, I'm Matt Hardrick."

"Pleasure."

"Follow me." He retreated down the stairs. David followed.

"Old bomb shelter. The Cold War, everyone afraid of getting nuked by the Soviets."

"Before my time."

Hardrick grinned. "Mine too." Upon entering the room, David felt a chill from the high humidity. A rack of wines set against one wall and a couple of self-standing shelves filled with canisters took up the interior space. Like a cave, Tashiro tackled two problems with one solution.

"I'd tell you not to touch anything, but we've already gone over everything with a fine-tooth comb, dusted for prints, the whole ball of wax. Over here are the films."

David stood in the aisle and admired the storage racks, like bookshelves in a library. But instead of books, flat metal canisters were stacked to the top with identification labels. The sight delighted him, transporting him back to his teen years, waiting for the magic of cinema on a Saturday afternoon. The matinee, a place to escape to, where dreams and futures were imagined. And when the strip of film broke, the tormented impatience that followed, with him and his friends waiting for the projectionist to splice the pieces back together so the adventure could continue. No doubt about his obsession, the world of celluloid—the faint odor of vinegar always brought out the excitement. His nose twitched with joy as he took in another deep inhalation. Tashiro's vault was a testament to the power of long-lost cinema.

He estimated at least sixty or seventy different spools of film took up space. At the far end, the burgundy-colored concrete floor stood out. And then, the black marking of what appeared to be an outline of a body.

Hardrick caught his gaze. "That's where we found him. He dropped a bottle of wine, a Cabernet from Woodward Canyon, Washington State." He grumbled. "Guess California wines weren't to his liking."

David let the scene soak in. "You said his death was suspicious. Why?"

"Autopsy showed a needle mark on his chest. Likely a dart shot from a wildlife tranquilizer gun containing the drug Etorphine. I doubt Tashiro would have allowed someone to stick a needle in his chest without a fight. No evidence of that. The coroner almost overlooked checking for elevated levels of the chemical makeup in his bloodstream until he saw the needle mark."

"Any theories?"

Hardrick shook his head. "We haven't figured out a motive. We checked around the house. Nothing appears to be out of place that we can tell. He has an older sister in Santa Cruz. After calming down, she didn't think he had anything of value hidden in his house, nor did he have any enemies. We'd appreciate it if you would go through what you see here and determine if the films add up to the list he supplied you. Maybe he had a million dollars buried in one of the cans." He cracked a smile.

"I'll be glad to." David reached into his briefcase and pulled out his list of films. "This may take time. I need to verify the list. Might even want to view parts of them on the film editor over there." He pointed to a bizarre-looking piece of equipment with empty spools attached to the top of a box with wires and cables. He walked over and examined it closer, an older model of a Steenbeck flatbed editor like the one they had back at the UCLA film lab.

"Doable, do you think?"

David scanned the racks of canisters. "Into tomorrow, I suspect."

"We appreciate your expertise and rapid response. I'll check back later. Officer Peyton will remain upstairs.

If you find anything, give me a call." He turned and left.

David proceeded to go through the canisters, a menagerie of B-movies, one at a time. The strong odor of old film permeated his nostrils with each can he opened. The longer the reels stayed in the cans, the stronger the vinegar trace. Most didn't receive the critical review that would have propelled them up the ladder of motion picture success, but here they were, successful or not, a portion of cinematic history.

His found himself on cloud nine when he located the 1963 classic, *Once Upon a Nightmare*. He recalled it being part of a Halloween program years ago on television. And another film, *Devil's Trance*. Never understood why it didn't do well at the box office. This happened quite often with small studios when distribution was hard to get.

With each canister, he took the film out and ran the couple hundred or so frames through the editor. So far, things checked out, nothing missing. Reaching the end of one of the shelves, he picked up the last one, *Lady Julia's Sarcophagus*, another unknown. He marked it off Tashiro's list. The date on the can read 1968.

He looked closer at the reel. It appeared to be older than a film shot in the sixties. Slipping it out of the canister, he took a whiff, his nose twitched. He unraveled a few frames and sure enough, written on the spool edge, the word "nitrate"—and black-and-white to boot. Discontinued in 1952, acetate-based films replaced the vintage nitrate which had to be handled and preserved in proper facilities. Low temperature, and humidity, something more sophisticated than Tashiro's bomb shelter.

David wound the reel on the editing machine.

Looking through the viewfinder, he rolled through several frames. Pulling back, he rubbed his weary eyes. The deteriorated quality made viewing difficult. Nitrate films broke down if improperly stored. At least the title read an original copy of *Crypt of the Damned*, released in 1951.

Not surprising, there were hundreds of B-movies from the fifties and sixties. Most of them were nothing more now than a long-lost hazy video that had been downloaded to YouTube. Had the real *Lady Julia's Sarcophagus* been replaced with this older film, *Crypt of the Damned*? A clever deception, hiding another film in a mismarked canister.

He called Hardrick and let him know what he found. Either Tashiro knew about the misplaced films, or he didn't. Finishing the call, David sat back and contemplated his discovery.

From a snooping perspective, what about *Crypt of the Damned*? And did *Lady Julia's Sarcophagus* really exist?

Chapter 12

On his first day back from Sacramento, David Grovene had a revelation. Why would someone exchange the unknown *Lady Julia's Sarcophagus* for a film by the name *Crypt of the Damned*? Did Tashiro make a mistake, or did he intentionally mislead? If that was the case, *Lady Julia's Sarcophagus* may have been a dummy, and never existed. Even a complete search of the National Film Registry database in the Library of Congress did not mention such a film.

The real intrigue: where did this rare, original celluloid copy of *Crypt of the Damned* come from? A garage sale, bought on eBay, or did Tashiro purchase at a film outlet store? What about one of the film festivals like Cinecon or Cinevent, places where classic movies changed hands? Then again, another option. Stolen films always found a way to follow the money, like in the world of pilfered Rembrandts and Picassos. Therefore, it wasn't unusual for the passionate cinephile to seek out old classic films in their original format, those kept in climate-controlled vaults and under pristine condition.

Now David thought like a police investigator. He should call Matt Hardrick to see if their investigation considered where the switched film originated. He stopped short of picking up the phone when another revelation hit him. Who would be an expert on rare B-movies other than Dart Darling, cinephile extraordinaire?

Late afternoon the next day, David took Hwy 210 to I-15 and two hours later arrived in Victorville on the edge of the Mojave Desert. As sundown approached, he found the gravel lane on the east side of town, headed to the southeast until he came into view of the ramshackle adobe structure tucked away from civilization. He parked in front of the house surrounded by a couple of junked up dune buggies, one missing an engine, an old rusting '63 Jeep, a few dead appliances and other throwaway scrap metal. Dart's property looked like something out of a Mad Max movie. Only the silhouette of Joshua trees and cholla cactus in the twilight kept things in perspective that he was in the desert and not a salvage yard. He took his time exiting his car in the waning light, picking his way carefully, watching for rattlesnakes. Dart hacked the head off one last time he visited, an image now forever seared in his brain.

"Well, my, my, looky who's here," an old Gabby Hayes lookalike exclaimed, standing in the doorway. A whiskered face with narrow eyes, slicked-back wiry hair, he wore jeans, faded leather vest with a red plaid shirt. Even in the hell of summer, never shorts, explaining being a Nebraska farm boy, jeans were the norm.

"You knew I was coming. I called, didn't I?" David said.

"Surely you did; you did surely," Dart said, weaving about. "Come on in out of the heat. Still 'bout 103."

He followed him inside, the same mismatched furniture, clutter, and odor of wet rags. He hoped he'd swept out any rattlesnakes lurking under the furniture.

"Let's go downstairs, cooler. I reckon that's your reason you're here."

"You got me pegged," David said with a grin.

Dart pulled a throw rug away, exposing a trap door. He opened it and stepped down on the first rung of a ladder. A few seconds later, the opening lit up. David climbed down into a cool and dry concrete cellar. More than once he perused Dart's collection of classic 35 mm movies, several still on perishable nitrate film. He lived in a ramshackle place, but his storage vault was light-years ahead of most collectors in the hobby of film preservation. He spent years digitizing them, but the essence of his collection were the celluloid originals. He passed between shelves holding hundreds of canisters, catalogued according to genre and release date. He inhaled, letting the acidity invigorate him, knowing there was something singular about being surrounded by reels preserving stories from the past. This was a hidden sanctuary, a lost library of Alexandria, a library of audio and visual history, the quintessence of time recorded frame by frame. Although the digital age enhanced the preservation and protection of long-ago cinematic works, to collectors and hard-driven cinephiles, original films were as seductive as a mesmerizing ride on a time machine.

"You look awestruck every time you come down here, another cinephile bent on a nitrate fix," Dart said, acknowledging the excitement on David's face.

"Like a kid in the candy store. I can't help myself. Give Thomas Edison credit." He pawed through a shelf of Western classics, amazed at the collection. How he acquired them never came up.

"And I'm one of Edison's disciples," Dart said, "and here is entertainment for this evening." He pulled out a canister.

"What's the movie?"

"From a collector in Irvine. *Fury at Furnace Creek.*"

"A western?"

"Victor Mature and Coleen Gray. What a sweetheart she was. Released in 1948." He tucked the canister under his arm and headed for the ladder. David followed to the back of the house where Dart stepped outside, opened a door into a small attached shed and entered, threading the film on an old 35 mm film projector. Looking out among the rocks, David could make out the house-size, flat-faced boulder thirty yards away painted white. Like the drive-in movies, he mused. Every time he came to pry information, he was obligated to join in the evening's entertainment.

Stepping back inside the house and out of the heat, Dart poured a couple of shots of Jim Beam and they both took a seat facing the picture window. With a remote control, he started the projector, and a beam of light collided with the rock. Sound blared from inside speakers. For the next hour and a half, Victor Mature and Coleen Gray worked their magic below the starry sky of the Mojave Desert. How many times had he seen an old movie under the stars in Dart's presence? Too many to remember. He was like a kid again at the Saturday matinee, sipping his ice-cold Coca-Cola and chomping on a Milky Way candy bar.

After Dart rewound the spool, he took a sip of a second shot of whiskey. David declined the offering. "Tell me, Professor, you're here for more than the philosophy of celluloid, I bet."

"Looking for a film, *Lady Julia's Sarcophagus.* Ring a bell?"

"Can't say it does."

The Salvation of Henry Maxwell

"Here's another one. What about one called *Crypt of the Damned*?"

"Is the Pope Catholic?

"Suppose so, what about *Crypt of the Damned*?"

Dart gave him a long and prying stare, and a grin appeared. "Well now, you sly dog, you. I have underestimated your ability."

David raised a brow. "How so?"

"Come on, Professor. Now *yer* into finagling unknown films, classics or not, movin' in on my territory. That film never amounted to much. Only one copy I'm aware of, in horrible shape. Ain't worth a damn on the market, although I'd keep it in my collection. How'd you get it?"

"Let's just say I've seen a copy, nitrate based, not in the best condition. Who owns the other copy?"

Dart drained his whiskey. "Someone who loves to stay out of the limelight. He kind of works on his own...if you catch my drift. I've seen his stockpile, and *Crypt of the Damned* is there, along with a few other worthless strips of celluloid. You say there's another copy? Where at?"

"In Sacramento."

"Who's the owner?"

"In a canister labelled *Lady Julia's Sarcophagus*. It's in a sizable collection, although not as extensive as yours.

"Well, whose collection?"

"A man named Yasuo Tashiro. Ever hear of him?"

Dart shook his head. "Nope. I need to get with him and compare notes."

"Won't work. Mr. Tashiro's dead."

"Dead?"

"In the newspaper. Called the police since I was to meet Tashiro. Made the trip to Sacramento. They think the death is suspicious."

"Like homicide?"

David nodded. "I believe that film hadn't been in Tashiro's possession more than a few days."

Dart paced around the room. "Murder, damn, something right out of the movies. And nitrate based. Some collectors shy away from them because of the storage requirements. Not me, I like a good nitrate fix." He crinkled his nose with a grin." Better than a drag of weed, I say."

"Something about both films has a hold of me. How do we contact this someone who owns the other copy of *Crypt of the Damned*?

"Not easy."

"What's his name and how do I find him?"

Dart rubbed his chin. "Eddie Wilkerson. Hard to track him down. Listen, I'm as interested as you are. Why don't we both go. I know where he lives. If anyone knows a thing or two 'bout those two films you mentioned, Eddie's the one. He doesn't own a phone, likes to keep his whereabouts rather vague. "Tomorrow work for you?"

David nodded. "Tomorrow will work."

Chapter 13

It wasn't the desire to continue his research on B-movies as much as it was a craving. After visiting with Dart Darling the night before, David's memories of Saturday matinees resurfaced. The world of celluloid returned, the obsession, the countless hours as a teenager he'd borrow a 16 mm projector from the high school film department and immerse himself with Roy Rogers, Vincent Price, Abbot and Costello. It was a masterful drug, this old sphere of motion pictures, this relic from the past bridging the gap from vaudeville to digital. To see this visual medium die would be nothing short of criminal.

After agonizing for the last forty minutes trying to find a parking spot, he walked several blocks down Hollywood Boulevard following the Walk of Fame. Hundreds, if not thousands, of five-pointed celebrity stars embedded in the sidewalks. Fighting off the throngs of tourists, he reached his destination. More visitors milled around outside, snapping pictures, selfies, and overcrowding an already crowded place. Soon enough, he found Dart sitting in the entrance courtyard of the historical Grauman's Egyptian Theater. Today he wore the same shabby vest and worn jeans, his arms crossed. He appeared to be snoozing, like an extra from some forgotten western movie enjoying a much-needed nap.

"No sleeping on the job," David said.

Dart jerked his head up. "Sleeping! I'm contemplating everything and anything in the universe, and you shouldn't sneak up on a fella like that," he grumbled.

He shook his head in awe. "How'd you park so close? I walked half a mile, and I paid an arm and leg at one of those concrete garages."

"Well, I apologize, Professor. I should have told you my secret. I parked two miles away, took the bus. This is Hollywood. Ain't no parking here."

He glanced around at the theater. "I haven't been here in a while. Why'd you want to meet here?"

"You know the Cinecon film festival, coming up in a couple of months. Eddie sets up shop with sellers from across the country during the event."

"Why would he be here now?"

Dart stood and stretched. "Probably won't be, but you never know. Sometimes you can spot his old Cadillac driving by. Those in the business to buy or sell will flag him down, kinda like a druggie finding a pusher man." His rosy cheeks glowed. "Celluloid trading happens all year long. This is the epicenter for collectors."

"As in the underground?"

He moved within a few inches of David. "You never ask where a particular reel comes from. They won't tell. Part of the culture. These collector types will do anything to wrap their hands on a classic."

"So where to?"

"I talked to one of my buddies who hawks Hollywood trinkets. He shares the street with Eddie. Said he hadn't seen him in over a week. Thinks he's lying low, up in the canyon."

"Where's that?"

"Off the 405. I've been there once, the old Atwater Movie Ranch. Tons of movies filmed back in the sixties and seventies. Closed in eighty-six after they shot the last film, a revisionist western. New owners turned it into a wildlife park, zebras and giraffes and such. Folded a few years back. Eddie has a cabin up a small canyon, used to work for the park. Your car is the closest."

An hour later, they followed the 405 to an exit on N. Sepulveda Boulevard, then took a left fork until they came to a gate with a padlock. A sign declared private property.

"We walk from here?" David asked.

"Only a quarter mile or so." Dart added, "Time to stretch these legs."

Hopping the fence, they hiked up the dirt road which wound between some unusual sandstone formations. A small creek flowed through the scrub oak and chaparral. After another couple hundred yards the woodlands thickened, intertwined with hoodoos. The canyon narrowed, and the road petered out. Parked in a slight turnaround near a grouping of house-sized boulders, an old 1968 baby-blue Cadillac El Dorado stood out like a sore thumb.

"Eddie's celluloid pimp mobile. He's in town when you spot that monster on the street. His pride and joy."

David checked his watch, 2:20 in the afternoon and the heat rising. He walked over and glanced inside. "The windows are open."

Dart rushed over. "Nothing inside, that's good."

David eyed dust on the car seat, thinking the window had been open a while. He spotted a trail. After a couple of hundred feet, they found a rustic paint-peeled clapboard-sided cabin with a small porch overlooking the creek.

Dart ran up to the door and knocked. After a few seconds he yelled, "Eddie, you around?"

After seeing the murder scene in Sacramento, and the search for a film possibly tying Tashiro and Eddie together, there was ample reason to be uncomfortable. David walked to the back side of the cabin and spotted a set of cellar stairs.

"The front door is unlocked. Eddie isn't here."

"Could this be where he stores his films?" He motioned towards the stairs.

Dart stepped down the concrete steps, pushed the door open, fumbled for a light switch. "Strange, it's unlocked. Nothing here but Eddie's treasures. Must have at least a hundred canisters. A gold mine and nobody's watching the store."

"That can't be normal."

"Give me a few minutes to check the titles." Dart flipped through the canisters. "Well, well," he said, coming back up. He held a film canister, shoved it toward David. The title read *Crypt of the Damned*."

"You found the copy?" he asked.

Dart opened it. "Empty."

"You don't suppose—"

"The reel you found in Sacramento might at one time have called this can home."

"No time to postulate." David said. "Let's fan out."

They continued up the canyon, the heat beating down. The babbling of the creek didn't distract from David's discomfort. He admonished himself for leaving a bottle of water in the car, but knew better than to cup his hands into the creek for a drink, for fear of getting some water-borne disease. Not far from the cabin, he spotted a small, lean-to surrounded by a wood corral. A place for horses in the past. Maybe for some of the movies shot here, Westerns likely. His eyes traced around the corral, stopping at an open gate.

His thirst abated when something on the ground caught his attention. He bent down for a closer examination. Sure enough, huge paw prints. A shiver ran down his backside.

Dart showed up. "You look like you've seen a ghost."

"What's your take?"

Dart stooped down, squinted. "Mountain lion, if not mistaken."

"That's my guess. Just read they have started a comeback in the Simi Hills. Kind of unbelievable, since this area is bordered by two major highways, the 405 being one of them."

Dart cast his eyes around as if on lookout. "Could be watchin' us as we speak."

David followed the path the prints took, taking him to the backside of the lean-to and winding back into the chaparral. Deciding not to bushwhack his way to follow, he turned to leave. He caught the stench of something dead. Beyond, he saw a boulder and a raven on top preening its wings. Despite the fear of moving farther into the scrub, he pushed on, curious as to the odor. What he found stopped him cold. "Oh, shit!" he screamed.

Dart came running. Not far from David, the grisly remains of a body splayed out with cat-like paw prints all around. He made out the features of what once had been a human, a cage of bones and ripped clothing. The skull contorted, held on by traces of stringy skin. A detached arm rested near the corpse, the hand still recognizable but black and leathery.

"Goddammit, Eddie, you poor bastard," he groaned.

"Are you sure?"

He turned away. "Still has his mop of red hair."

Poor Eddie, for sure, David thought, trying to shake the tragedy spread out in front of him. The pertinent question remained. Was Eddie involved in Tashiro's death? He looked at Dart. "I think we'd better alert the authorities. Don't touch anything."

Dart stared at the ground, shoulders drooping. For once, David spotted a lone tear drifting down his friend's cheek.

Chapter 14

The haunted moon blurs, shrouded by drifting clouds impersonating hapless shapes and eyeless beasts from the far side of hell. This is a blissful sign. Comforting, welcoming phantoms tuck the night under the bed covers and signify the end of another miserable day of existence.
—BB Barmore,
Lady Julia's Sarcophagus

Henry Maxwell stared out into the blackness hiding the expanse of green grass, newly planted flower beds and manicured trees and shrubs. At a quarter to midnight, his weary eyes were unable to see the transformation, yet his nose indicated the loveliness stretching out in front, the aromatic scent of evening primrose and California Mock Orange floating in the air. All this a glory because of the young woman who appeared on his doorstep, uninvited, forced into his heartbroken life by a willfully ignorant judge. He took a deep breath and exhaled with satisfaction. Ever since the ghostly apparition, nothing else mattered.

He stepped off the veranda onto the path toward the woods, like so many nights before. He stopped and gazed into the sky. A hazy half-moon rose above the hills to the east adding definition to the path. With a sense of urgency, he crept into the woods, his cane guiding him through the shadows.

Emerging from the trees, the moonlight basked the procession of gods with a white radiance, a brilliance washing over the marble like liquid salt. Romance blossomed when he and Lillian would stroll together here under the torrid pull of the moon.

He tried to ignore his aches and pains. He moved on, reminiscing the exquisite times they made love here in a wicked, steamy fashion on a stand of grass along the colonnade. Naked, entangled, the scents, the sweat, the lust. Nothing like motion pictures back in the days of sixties puritanism in American film. Blood and violence acceptable, but a little human pleasure taboo. During their lovemaking, all the glorious gods of Greece would look down upon them with envy. *Zeus, known for his inhibitions*, Lillian would say. *Jealousy*, Maxwell would insist. These sojourns became a nightly ritual when he wasn't in demand at the studios, those rare moments between films.

She loved Greece. He remembered at least four or five trips to the land of the Olympians. Her happiness kept him rolling out film after film. Global Pictures earned obscene amounts of money because of him. He never denied it made him wealthy as well, and a celebrity. The competition to produce the genre of Gothic horror movies was at an all-time high. Why not be part of the phenomenon?

Reaching the end of the agora, Maxwell imagined Lillian by his side, hand in hand. The moon, now higher, sent rays of light poking around the statues, creating spooky lines falling across the walkway.

Pinpoints of white light swirling like a galaxy emerged to his right. Fireflies again, pulsating. Looking into the darkness of night, he saw the backside of an opalescent figure flittering like a butterfly.

Maxwell's breathing went into overdrive. He feared it wouldn't survive the excitement. This is the night...*yes, oh gods of Olympus, yes!* Shaking off the idea he might have cardiac arrest, he hobbled toward the mysterious flickering.

At the edge of the precipice, Lillian had installed an observation deck which provided a magnificent view of the boundless Pacific. He rediscovered the old path, overgrown and shabby, cutting into the face of a small ravine wet with a seep, snaking downward. Maxwell experienced a surge of youthful vigor the closer he came to the deck, working around the brush.

Once at the bottom, he sucked in the warm draft of air rising from below. Maneuvering clear of the few oak shrubs, not more than fifteen feet away the glowing apparition swayed. A woman, he swore, gazing out at the sparkling lights of Malibu backlighting her hair. Gasping for air, he searched his inner soul for the remnants of any courage he possessed. He limped over. As he neared, she turned her head and smiled. He struggled with his consciousness, his mind registering a vision long forgotten.

He does not shudder, stumble, or cry. Every past thought and dream since Lillian's death coalesces into one. His eyes rivet on her with a thousand emotions. Her flawless face and bright eyes beam with an eternal fervor, the way she was before she died. Her hair, an illusion of golden half-braids draped down to her shoulders, tied back with a jeweled-flower tiara. Dressed in the whitest, the brightest of Grecian robes, he rubs his eyes in disbelief. A hallucination, it would soon fade away. He waits for his vision to clear.

But there is no change. Lillian raises her hand and motions Maxwell to follow. As he complies, his cane slips from his hand, banging against the bench, rattling. He senses a transformation. His aches evaporate. He puts pressure on his left knee. The arthritis that he had dealt with for the last twenty years disappears. His fingers are no longer misshapen and weakened. He runs a hand across his face, the wrinkles smooth, bumps and hollows minimized, the flabs of skin hanging from his chin gone. He rakes his hair, a fullness long lost. He reaches toward Lillian; an unimagined happiness overwhelms him as she takes his outreached hand.

"My love," he says with tears in his eyes. Every instinct wants to pull her close and embrace her. His lips tremble. "You—you've come back."

Her smile deepens, her face young and pure, just as he remembered. He gains strength, knowing there was a purpose in finding her.

Together, hand in hand, they walk back to the agora.

Now, his clothes are tight fitting, his trousers too short. He searches for his cane, but he had dropped it. No need for that. Without questioning, he follows Lillian up the path along the ravine and back to the statuary colonnades.

Entering the agora, they move among the statues. Surrounded by the gods, they embrace, clinging to each other. He gazes into her eyes, her face as alluring as ever. "Do you remember our first visit to Greece? I just finished a film and we had a few weeks. The joy in your eyes. It was the first time we'd been overseas. Your happiness was all I needed to exist."

She pulls him next to Aphrodite, admiring it.

The Salvation of Henry Maxwell

"She was one of the most beautiful, the goddess of love and beauty," he says, gazing at the statue that mirrors Lillian. "Your radiance outshines Aphrodite." He stares into her eyes. "That is why I chose you. The best and wisest thing I ever did." God, how he wants to keep her close and shower endless kisses on every inch of her being. But would this make his dream fade? Would his dear Lillian evaporate into emptiness? He dare not take the chance.

As they walk side by side taking in the spectacular evening view, the twinkling lights of Malibu in the distance and the glow off the Pacific dazzle.

"It's like the Aegean Sea," Maxwell says. "Remember the bus ride from Athens to Cape Sounion to see the Temple of Poseidon? We heard the gods singing in the background."

She stares out at the ocean. Her goddess silhouette haloes from the city radiance coming off the waters. And in that instance, he listens for the love songs that she would sing.

The tightening in his throat lessens. She ushers back memories that he suppressed for years. He finds it hard to believe all this is real. Good or bad, but in his recollection, there were never any cruel recollections, all filled with happiness, except...

...he can't contain himself as he starts to cry. A dream, this must be a dream! The gentle touch of Lillian's hands caressing his arm ease any remaining pain. She smiles and puts her head on his shoulder.

He reaches around and slides his hand across her abdomen as tears streak down his cheek. Oh, how they had been robbed. He wants so much to kiss her, and bury her agony in an eternity of softness.

She pulls him along, stopping between Aphrodite and Eros. She turns back to Henry, still holding his hand. His world overflows with unanswered questions. She is sending him a signal, but what? If only she would reveal what happened that day. If only...

She keeps her emerald eyes pinned to his. They speak to him, telling him to plan.

He wipes a tear and nods. "I promise, I will..."

She lets go of his hand, and drifts away from the colonnade and disappears, her whitest of white robes fading into darkness.

Maxwell tried to compose himself. He blotted away another teardrop and inhaled a deep breath, as though the wind had been knocked from him. Taking a step, he felt throbbing return to his knees, and his clothes were fitting again. He knew it was a dream; he was no longer the young man he once was. Realizing he didn't have his cane, he started to move around, kicking something. His cane rattled and rolled across the pavers. Did he not drop it by the bench?

But how, I never...

He stooped down and picked it up, and returned to the house.

Chapter 15

Jessica left the castle at 9:00 a.m. sharp, descending the canyon to the Pacific Coast Highway. She connected to Interstate 10 and exited at La Cienega Boulevard. An hour later she pulled into the visitor's parking lot for Parkwood Towers in Los Angeles. Researching Henry's files, she found the name of Dr. Ewe Kopf, a psychiatrist who'd been treating Maxwell's wife, Lillian, until her death in 1968. Now in his early eighties, he agreed to meet with her at his condominium after she explained the situation.

Staring at the high-rise, she questioned if she made the right decision. This meeting brought her closer to the profession she left. Whether the idea would help, she hadn't a clue. After another minute of scrutiny, she slid out of the seat, entered the building and found his unit.

"May I offer you something to drink?" Kopf asked, pointing to a couple of chairs on the deck. "Coffee, soda, water?" He had steady blue eyes, a cue-ball head with shaved sides, and wore tan chinos and a red crewneck sweater. He appraised his visitor with an air of curiosity.

"Water would be fine," Jessica said.

Watching Kopf leave, she sat down in the cushioned wicker chair on the deck, admiring the gray-green Santa Monica Mountains to the north as she allowed the sun to wash across her cheeks.

"So, you're the attorney in charge of Henry's

affairs?" he asked, returning and handing her a bottle of Aquafina.

"My firm is overseeing Mr. Maxwell's conservatorship."

"Not more than a month ago, Henry dropped in on me out of the blue. We see each other now and then, but not often enough."

"What about his depression during these times?" she said taking a sip.

"I've tried to keep tabs on him, although I don't practice any more. After the accident, he did appear to aggravate his despondency, something he struggled with after Lillian passed. I wish I had a magic bullet to help him cope. Her death caused him immense emotional pain. He suffered a severe case of PGD, or—"

"Prolonged Grief Disorder."

Kopf looked at Jessica, surprised. "You know of PGD?"

"I just remember a psychology course I took in college," she said, not wanting to tell him about her first career. "Went into law instead." She smiled.

"I can't blame you."

"Mr. Maxwell's depression is why I asked to meet you."

"He's hard to fix. I think he will always be out of sorts until his dying days." He pushed himself up. "Please, follow me. Let me show you something.

He escorted Jessica back inside to his study, lined with volumes of books shelved along one wall. A desk took up space in the middle of the room, cluttered and overflowing with papers and periodicals including *The American Journal of Psychiatry*. She caught the date on one, November 2006. Old journals in an older man's office.

Kopf walked over to a file cabinet next to the bookshelf and searched through one of the drawers. He removed a yellow envelope, pulled out several photographs and handed them to Jessica.

"Those are photos of Henry and Lillian, and others, of course, taken at different times. Photos at studio parties, premieres, Hollywood functions. I attended a few of those. When Lillian passed away, her death was a major blow, not only for him personally, but professionally. He quit acting, without losing a beat." He pointed to a woman in one of the photographs. "Lillian."

She studied Lillian's photograph—beautiful, tall, graceful, with short, ash-blond hair, dressed in an elegant teal cocktail dress. The image portrayed a woman the center of attention, holding the others in the scene together. "Heartbreaking."

Kopf nodded. "A lovely woman, one of my patients. I remember the day she died. Shocked us all, Henry the most, of course. Never saw it coming, otherwise I would have done something different." He sank into the chair at the desk.

"Different? What?"

"I treated Lillian for persistent depression, working every angle I could think of to release her from that sad, mental grasp. It's an evil affliction."

"Why the depression?"

"A simple diagnosis. Their relationship was amazing. To everyone looking in from the outside, they lived and loved for each other. Unfortunately, another love affair got in the way."

Jessica's eyes widened.

"Not in the traditional sense. Work was his

mistress." He stood, examining Jessica. "You're too young, but back in the sixties, Henry was one of the biggest stars of those early Gothic horror movies. They were the rage at the time. He was a workaholic, two, sometimes three films a year. Always on set, rarely at home, away from that haunted mansion up the canyon. Lillian, alone most of the time by herself in that stone monstrosity. I believe staying there all that time would be a reason to depress any sane person. When he did come home, he treated her like a queen. Together, you couldn't help but notice the love they had for one another."

"What about friends or a social support group since Mr. Maxwell was gone a great deal of the time?"

"She had some. Not enough, perhaps."

"What about Henry, does he have any regular friends?"

"Tom Caswell stops by quite often. No one else comes to mind."

"What about Tom's father, Roy?"

Kopf's face turned pale. "He's another problem right out of the past."

"How so?"

"I shouldn't tell you this, doctor-patient confidentiality."

She found a chair, sat and kept her eyes on Kopf. "The conservatorship may need that information."

He shrugged. "Long time ago."

She nodded.

"Tom's mother died when he was four, I believe. Lillian mothered him, took him under her wing because his father never gave the kid the time of day. The boy started to accept her as the mother he lost, and it progressed to him developing pleasurable yearnings for her." He gazed up at Jessica in a guilty sort of way.

She rolled her eyes, imagining where this was headed.

"Truth is, my diagnosis was pure Freudian, an Oedipus type of complex. At the same time, Tom shunned Roy. Lillian wasn't his real mother, but he used her as a substitute. Henry told me at one point Roy stormed their home and threatened her, telling her to stay away from his son, or else."

"And Henry, wedged in the middle."

He nodded. "Too much like the movies. Again, I should have done something."

"Where is Roy, or is he still alive?"

"No idea."

"I understand she died from a drug overdose."

"Yes, moonflower she had in her garden. Gardening kept her sane, her passion when Henry was at work, but nobody knew she grew that wretched plant."

"And it killed her?"

He remained motionless, his eyes glistening. "It's my fault. I'm convinced I overmedicated her with anti-depressants. Those drugs led to me prescribing things like valium to help with her anxiety."

"What happened?"

He swallowed hard. "She was dependent on the drugs that I had been prescribing. Addicted. Until I realized what was occurring. I cut the prescriptions down, but the moonflower became a substitute. She overdosed. I'm to blame for her death as much as anyone."

Jessica watched Kopf struggle with the past.

He shrugged, allowing his melancholy eyes to

wander the room.

She felt sorry for the man. "What about you, wife, kids?"

"I had a wife. She died twenty-three years ago. Bladder cancer. No kids. We all experience our tragedies. Don't compare my loss to Henry's. I had time to prepare for Margaret's passing."

"You met Mr. Maxwell recently. Were you able to give him any hope?"

"We talked about his struggles. He said he was hallucinating. Very understandable with a patient who cannot shake their grief. I tried to emphasize to him that he needed to wrap his mind around the present. I encouraged him to think of the moments that made him happy. People still respect him. He needs to hear from them. Believe me, he still has friends if he'd only reach out to them." He stared at Jessica. "Would it be possible to invite them over for a get-together, something that would allow him to experience those enjoyable times from his past?"

Jessica nodded in agreement. "Loneliness can be a dagger. That's an interesting thought."

Kopf smiled. "You'd make a terrific psychiatrist."

"I'd bungle it for sure. Finding out the causes of Lillian's death explains a lot, but not enough to get Henry Maxwell back on track."

Chapter 16

Jessica watched with satisfaction as the pool man finished skimming out eucalyptus leaves that had blown in the night before. Compared to the last few days, no green algae, no brackish, fetid water. Equipment cleaned, serviced, walls scrubbed, chemical balance adjusted.

"Thanks again." She waved as the service man hurried away. As she turned to leave, Maxwell shuffled out to the veranda, a newspaper clutched under his left armpit, cane in hand. Instead of heading toward his umbrella and favorite chair, he walked her direction. Ever since her forced arrival, he went out of his way to dodge conversation.

"Morning Mr. Maxwell. The day is wonderful."

"Don't Maxwell me," he grumbled. "If you must, Henry will suffice." His eyes fell on the pool, the blue sheen of the water reflecting like a mirror.

"Do you swim, Henry?"

"Not in years, since…" His voice tailed off.

"You may enjoy it again."

"Lillian would spend time on the veranda when not working in her garden. Swimming, laying in the sun. The future…our future… She dreamed a lot."

Memories, pleasant and tragic, they all unite, birthed from the same source, intertwined. She realized how impossible it would be to separate them and relive only the joyous ones. "Do you want to talk about Lillian?"

"She's dead!"

She decided to chance it. "What can you tell me about her, Henry?" She gazed out over the gardens, and how they were transforming back into a lush sensation of beauty. "I imagine she had a major influence on all this at one time."

He fidgeted, dropped the newspaper. Jessica picked it up and handed it back. "Thank you." He nodded. "Her passion, all this color surrounding this decrepit pile of stone." His eyes narrowed as they swung her direction. "Friends would all 'ooh and aah' over her creations. The garden kept her sanity. When we were together, we spent more time in the gardens than inside."

"You don't need to convince me of that."

His gruff demeanor remained, throat tightened, eyes misting. "Arrangements were her specialty, beyond what most spectators could comprehend."

"I would have loved to have seen them."

He started to leave, then surveyed the rest of the veranda, looking back at the pool. "I must admit, you should oversee a restoration company, you know, they come in to fix disasters. This hunk of real estate hasn't looked this good in years."

"Thanks, I appreciate the compliment."

He nodded, glancing from the pool to an umbrella and his deck chair on the opposite end. "I'll be reading the paper and napping. Have a nice day, Ms. Barrow," he said, hobbling toward his chair, his cane clacking on the terrazzo.

"Enjoy your nap," she said, knowing he didn't hear. *The first time he'd instigated a conversation*, she thought. And what did he say about "being in charge of a restoration company"? Now the assignment didn't feel so overbearing. Progress may be slow, elusive, only in baby steps. Maybe she was sent here to be the mental restoration he needed? Marsha knew what she was doing. Now it was up to her to fulfill the mission.

Chapter 17

The sun dips beneath the hedge rows and the moon hangs low like a rising ghost. And the long road from SOMEWHERE continues onto a place called NOWHERE. Yet the men appear from every point, soot in their hair, toil beneath their fingernails, and dryness upon their lips. The beggars beg and Sir Alston Chatsworth draws rein and knocks the dust off his gray frock. To heal his restless soul, he will enter the working man's lair and bring about a donnybrook—and The Black Gull, with sawdust on the floor and the stench of ale in the air, has no fine china.
—BB Barmore,
Lady Julia's Sarcophagus

Olsen's Tavern was a rustic, blue clapboard hangout with an enormous frothy-looking surfer wave painted on the side. Built in the sixties on a high knoll, it commanded a superb view of the eastern end of Malibu and its string of celebrity-dotted beaches. Why the present owner kept possession of this local dive for over thirty years and why he never gave in to any offers to sell such a valued piece of real estate didn't make sense.

Maxwell pulled his Bentley into the gravel lot, parked among two bikes—both Harleys—an old Porsche 911, a red Dodge Challenger, and a faded white F-150 in need of a paint job. Wearing a brown fedora, gray tweed sport coat, and navy slacks, he exited, sniffing the salty mist rising off the Pacific. A slight chill stirred the air. Would his celebrity status from years past garnish attention? He didn't give a rat's ass. Just an ordinary eighty-five-year-old out to raise a little hell.

He stepped inside, leaned on his cane, and took a moment for his eyes to adjust. The dimly lit room had surfing posters plastered on all the walls and a smattering of autographed photos of local mid-level movie stars. There were few patrons this late on a Monday night, two men at the bar, a man and woman appearing too young to drink were in the rear playing a game of pool on the only billiard table sandwiched between flashing neon beer signs. A lone man sat in a far corner, talking on his phone. They all gave him the onceover. Two couples sitting nearby, dressed in bike leathers, whispered amongst themselves, glancing his direction, amused at the barely-able-to-walk geriatric.

He brushed off their stares and shuffled over to the bar. He took his time sliding onto the stool, removed his fedora, and hung his cane on the edge. The bartender, a thirtyish muscle-hunk of a man with shaved head and a half-sleeve Māori-style tattoo, pushed a napkin under Maxwell's nose. Maxwell's gaze slipped to the two men at the opposite end, checked their nosiness. Without a second thought, he said, "Glass of your best scotch, no ice."

The bartender appraised him, then grabbed a bottle of Glenfiddich single malt and poured two fingers. Maxwell stared at the bottle for a moment, questioning, *This is their finest*, then wrapped his hand around the glass, took a sip. He eyed the bartender, and said in a surly voice, "So this is the top of the line?"

The bartender rolled his eyes, not prepared for a question from someone who should be home in bed by now. He paused, then smiled. "Either an insult, or a well-researched joke." He leaned over the bar resting on both arms. "What's the punchline, gramps?"

Maxwell grinned. "No offense. Things are different from what I remember years ago." He hesitated, removed his eyeglasses, wiped them with the napkin and slid them back on. "Way before your time. Age seems to have caught up with this place."

The bartender nodded. "Caught up with the owner as well. He hasn't changed a thing. The tavern has history, locals don't mind. They keep coming back. We're not ritzy Malibu, or Hollywood, never have been."

"Not Hollywood. I like that, a dive that brings back memories of the olden days." He sucked in a breath. "Quaint, too."

The bartender drew another beer for one of the men at the other end. "Suppose you could say that. No need to change what's been working."

Maxwell turned around on his stool, staring at the other patrons. "Not a lot of folks here tonight. Tell me, how does this place stay in business?" he said in a booming voice to no one in particular.

"Dammit, some of us happen to like coming here, for peace and quiet," yelled the nearest man. Drab-faced, gray-bearded, with a sharp jawline, he appeared to be twenty years younger than Maxwell, and seemed irritated by the boisterous way the elderly man at the bar blabbered. "We like getting away from those egomaniacs and celebrity wannabes down in town." He eyed Maxwell with suspicion, as if he were one of those. "Like

Johnnie here says," pointing to the bartender, "this sure as hell ain't Hollywood."

"Amen to that," said one of the biker women.

A broad smile creased Maxwell's lips as he tossed the remaining scotch down. He motioned to the bartender. "I'll have another." He turned to face the gray-bearded man taking a swig of beer. "If I may ask, dear sir, what is your beef with Tinseltown?"

The man placed his mug down hard on the bar. "I am sick and tired of those celebrity types, rich, self-centered, driving fancy cars that say, 'I'm famous, you're not.' A bunch of assholes always pushing goddamn liberal causes." He threw his arm up, pointing to his right. "Look at all them that used to carouse down on Colony Beach, acting as if they owned the goddamn sand. Those days are gone, but nothing changed. Now just another fucked-up gated community. Those scumbags, they screw things up. Shit for brains I call them."

"So, dear sir, is that a well-researched fact about those folks?"

"Who needs research? Read the fucking papers, right there under your nose."

Maxwell's determined nature was becoming unearthed. "So, in your short-sighted worldview, everyone associated with Hollywood, or should I be specific, the movie industry, they're all assholes. Is that correct?"

The man nodded and said, "Now you're listening, and there ain't nothing short-sighted about it!"

Maxwell slid off his stool and moved closer to the man and sat back down, one stool separating them. He placed his cane on the bar. "Come on, dear sir, you can at least name one of those parasites that have concern for the planet?"

The man's eyes were full of rage. "Don't 'dear sir' me, fucker!"

He kept up the pressure, his voice becoming stronger, more confident the more he spoke. "How about that young actor DiCaprio, you know, the Titanic?"

"What about the asshole?"

"He puts his money to work. His foundation works for environmental causes, wildlife and habitat protection, climate change."

"He's a liberal commie. Don't give me crap 'bout climate change. What a fuckin' hoax!"

"What about George Clooney being involved in Darfur, helping to bring to light the genocide over there? You don't think that deserves a little credit?"

"Oh fuck 'em all. Darkie Africa, not my concern."

"And Willie Nelson, maybe not straight Hollywood, but a celebrity. What about the millions he's raised for Farm Aid?"

The gray-bearded man's temper reached a boiling point. He jumped off the stool and thrust his body into Maxwell's. "Why don't you get your old-man-ass up off that seat and vamoose the hell out of here before I escort you myself, you motherfucking loudmouth!"

The bartender came over and thrust his arms between the two. "Come on, Vern, let it go." Veins popping along his forehead, Vern backed away and sat down.

"Yes, Vern, let it go," Maxwell said. "You're all in a tizzy. You forgot about Audie Murphy. Remember him? The cowboy star of the fifties. One of the most decorated soldiers in World War II. A Hero, and

The Salvation of Henry Maxwell

Hollywood, all together. Two H's. He doesn't seem like an asshole to me." He kept his cool, his voice carried authority. His wrinkled and age-spotted face menaced the dingy-lit bar. Hard to believe he had the tenacity to start such an argument.

Vern's face turned red. He swiveled on his stool and stared into Maxwell's sneering eyes. "Shut the fuck up!"

His tone went up a half octave. "My, what a temper you have, Vern. You need therapy."

"All right, enough of this," the bartender said. He took Maxwell's glass away and looked him in the eye. "Sir, I'm going to have to ask you to leave."

Maxwell reached for his cane and slammed it down hard. The crack of the oaken walking stick on the copper-topped bar rattled throughout the tavern, shaking the bottles of spirits on the shelves. "My money's as good as Vern's," he shouted. Beneath his coat, he pulled out a small gun and laid it on the bar.

All eyes froze. One of the women began to cry.

The bartender rushed over. "Hey, that's not allowed in here." Reaching for it, Maxwell drew back the cane, striking the bartender's hand with surprising force. He fell back into the row of liquor. A bottle of Seagram's Dry Gin hit the floor and shattered. "God damn, you broke my hand," he screamed.

Maxwell leered deep into the bartender's eyes, inflicting a deadly stare. "I suggest for the time being, Johnnie, you stay comfortable behind the bar. I'll be glad to pay for the broken booze. Your hand, you're on your own."

The bartender didn't move, rubbing his swollen hand.

He returned his gaze to Vern and pushed the gun

closer. "Vern, be attentive. This is a Colt 41 caliber rimfire derringer, manufactured in 1879. It's a classic, antique weapon, great for self-defense. If my mind serves me well, I do believe I brandished it in *Once Upon a Nightmare*, with blanks, of course. Do you remember that one? One of my finest performances if I do say so myself. But this time, it's loaded with the real thing. I want you to listen to me and listen carefully."

Streams of sweat began to pour off Vern. He slunk back in his chair, unsure of what to do. He stared at the gun and back at Maxwell. Fear exploded from his eyes.

"Vern, I want you to pick up this weapon, this valuable antique, and I want you to cock the hammer, place the barrel against your head…and blow your goddamn brains out."

"What!" cried Vern. "You psycho or somethin'?"

"No, dear sir, I'm a gentleman working to rid the world of scum like you. Now pick it up and do it!" he taunted. He pushed the gun closer with his cane.

At that moment, the bartender sprang forward and swept his good hand across the bar, flinging the gun out of reach and away from Maxwell. One of the bikers picked it up off the floor and pointed it at Maxwell. "I got him covered."

Maxwell didn't appear surprised. His grin widened. He put his hat on, moved off the stool, making eye contact with each patron. They all stared back, wondering about this old man, coming here on a slow and quiet Monday night raising holy hell. He spotted an empty table, sat down, and with his cane, raked the condiments off, causing them to scatter across the room. The salt shaker ended under the pool table and the bottle of ketchup smashed into the bar, dripping contents onto the vinyl floor. The smell of sweet tomatoes mixed with the scent of spilled beer quickly spread.

"Oh, sorry about that," he said, laughing. He took his hat off and pretended to be reshaping it. "I think I've just made a mess." Everyone in the bar sat speechless, their mellow evening, without warning, had gone south. He glanced back at the bartender, who now had a phone to his ear.

Calling the cops. He let out a smile. *What took him so long?*

Chapter 18

Jessica sat in Marsha Hauser's office at JWB massaging her eyes. After the early morning flight to San Francisco, she rubbed her eyes after staring at her laptop for the last forty minutes reading a six-month-old *American Journal of Psychology* article authored by a former psych professor. Another, less critical reason she gave up clinical psychology as a career—the mind, always regressing. The reality of fixing those minds near impossible. Did she think law would be a better choice? Lawyers existed because of human weaknesses and transgressions. *They need therapy, too*, she mused.

Looking up upon hearing the shuffle of feet outside the door, Marsha entered in a tizzy carrying a Starbucks coffee cup in one hand and a leather portfolio in the other. She rushed over to her desk, tossed them down. "Sorry, got caught in traffic. Just like me to ask you to fly up on the early flight and I'm late for my own meeting."

Jessica closed her laptop. "No worries. Gave me time to figure out why Maxwell acts the way he does."

"Your theory?" Marsha asked, taking a seat.

"I just finished reading an article by a former psychology professor of mine."

"Learn anything?"

"Some."

"What about all this?" Marsha reached into the

portfolio and pulled out a newspaper clipping. "It made all the papers. Not sure why the interest, Maxwell's been forgotten for years."

"The bad news, a full half a day to arrange bail. The good news, the gun was empty. He's been charged with criminal mischief and disorderly conduct. Leaving the sheriff station, I couldn't believe all the cameras and reporters waiting outside, a zoo, and all the calls I got from newspapers, and magazines—*New York Times*, Associated Press, *People, Entertainment Weekly, The New Yorker. National Enquirer* had a story ready to go, all about the resurrection of the sinister actor from the old sixties horror movies. *Spilled ketchup now, spilled blood next?* The headline was already worked out."

Marsha waved the newspaper article. "*San Francisco Chronicle*. His arrest got around." She shook her head in disbelief. "How'd this get out so fast?"

"You tell me."

"Well, I'm somewhat in shock, but then, why are we surprised?"

"Inevitable, I guess."

"But not normal for eighty-five-year-olds to go bar hopping." She took a sip of coffee. "Cold. What did you learn from your former professor?"

"He seemed to agree with me. It boils down to irrational psychological behavior. He authored this paper, which deals with the elderly. In a nutshell, this type of conduct is not all that uncommon."

"But for seniors?"

"Why not? On the other hand, those that make irrational decisions might be psychotic."

Marsha didn't smile. "I don't like hearing that word. The judge should be informed."

Jessica leaned in. "I don't think Maxwell's psychotic, or I dare say, dangerous. His mind is capable of rational thought. I haven't detected anything that would make me conclude he's off his rocker."

"Why do you say that?"

"When I first arrived, entering the house scared me to death. My god, he lives in a damn castle, dreary, spooky, creepy. Tom Caswell told me he bought it because it reminded him of his films. He entertained a lot in his acting days. He had huge parties. He loved recreating scenes from his movies and scaring the pants off his guests by having them play games that brought out the horrors and mysteries of the castle. From what I understand, his friends would never turn down an invitation. Now, he doesn't entertain anymore. After a while, I got used to moving around the house, exploring different areas, but he never bothers me. When we're together, which is rare, he starts to talk. There's pain in his eyes, a huge sense of loneliness. The loss of his wife is still with him. Psychologists' term is loss aversion, where it is difficult to break the cycle of guilt of losing a loved one. His wife's death still haunts him, worse now after the accident."

"Something's going on in his head. I'll check again with the judge to see if we have to commit him for evaluation. I won't promise anything."

"Don't do it, please."

"I don't want you in danger." Marsha leaned on her desk and clasped her hands. "And I want to apologize again."

"For what?"

"For assigning you this task. I put your psychological background as the first criteria for this job.

That was wrong. I didn't consider your personal life."

"What's to consider. I'm not tied down."

Marsha took a deep breath, then exhaled. "I've taken advantage of the situation. I'm working you from every direction, pushing you without regard to the circumstances. I let my selfish interests take over, and to have you reengage with your psychological training, something you had reason to leave. At this point, I think it's best to relieve you of this task."

Jessica shook her head. "I appreciate your concern, but not now. He's bottled up a ton of emotion. Being a psychologist gave me the opportunity to gain experience in anxieties. For the first time in my life, I'm able to stop pitying myself. I never imagined I'd mentally survive one night in Henry's old castle, but so far, each night gets a little easier. I'm forced to adapt. This is turning out to be therapy for me."

Marsha smiled with relief.

"I must see a resolution to this. I'm making progress, believe me. To be removed now would be a mistake. I don't think he's cried in years, and I think he's close. Crying helps soothe the soul."

Marsha sat back down. "They call that the bliss hormone, right?"

She nodded. "He needs to go through that phase. By the way, didn't I tell you I had a meeting with one of Henry's old acquaintances, a psychiatrist who had treated his wife before she died? He suggested Henry should reconnect with old friends. We could throw a party at the house, a real social event."

"You serious?"

"I am. We need to check with his former publicist. Invitations could be sent out to friends and associates, if still alive."

Marsha nodded. "Interesting."

"It can't hurt. I know I can reach him. I really do."

Chapter 19

The next morning, Henry Maxwell gunned the engine on his 2011 Bentley and tore out of the open motor court in a fury. Jessica sucked in a deep breath, watching him disappear through the gate barely missing the gargoyle on his right. Rolling her eyes, she exhaled. She had no authority to stop him. After all, he wasn't a prisoner in his own home. He didn't share his destination or how long he'd be gone.

She went to the kitchen in hopes of having a cup of tea. Things were starting to take a turn for the better. The house had been cleaned, endless garbage removed, floors swept, mopped, and waxed, the furniture dusted, rugs vacuumed, shampooed, bathrooms and kitchen disinfected and spotless. With a little more luck, she hoped to hire a fulltime housekeeper. Maxwell grumbled, but didn't say no.

For the past week, her attention focused on his mental well-being. Little conversation ensued, only when something needed to be done. He ignored her issues and went his way. She went hers, determined to bring the house and grounds back to their glory.

Now the landscape had a new life. She looked out the breakfast room window, watching the new groundkeepers replant flowers. Maxwell didn't complain much after she took control, and she swore she detected a slight change in his disposition. Now would be a suitable time to check out the gardener's work, and in the process, do a little snooping. Without a second thought, she hurried out to the veranda and marveled at the renaissance. Soon, it would be back to the beauty it once displayed. She walked toward the west side of the house and moved down a set of stairs to a small, private patio. A perfect place for taking in the scene. Her eyes roamed to the distant Pacific, Maxwell possessing one of the most remarkable views she'd ever seen. A concrete wall separated her from the edge of the precipice. The house, or in her mind, castle, perched on a sheer escarpment of sandstone that ran the length of the property before fading into the brush and trees far below. She peered over the wall. A small path came from nowhere and wound into the shrubs and oaks clinging to the face of the cliff as if defying gravity. Vertigo kicked in, forcing her back. Fear of heights, one phobia she was never able to shake.

Back up the stairs, she glanced at the wooded area beyond. Curious, she wondered what drew Maxwell out around midnight? Stepping into the garden, she walked toward the woods, waving to one of the gardeners. She entered a mix of chaparral, interspersed with an assortment of subtropical and Mediterranean plantings. The well-marked trail was overgrown with native grasses and weeds. It traversed the side of the ridge, sloping down a few feet and winding through the overgrowth. After a sharp turn, it levelled off and came out into the open. She stared. A long plaza lay before her with a colonnade of statues lining both sides, as if she'd discovered a long-lost ruin.

Continuing along the pattern of paving bricks, she examined the effigies, all intricately sculptured mythological Greek gods. She could only guess the fortune that it took to carve such grand figures out of what appeared to be high-quality white marble. What drove Maxwell to have this facsimile of ancient Greece constructed? She picked her way, trying to decipher who each statue represented. Apollo, Athena, Hades, some with wings, some clothed, some naked, others wielding swords or musical instruments. All were seven or eight feet tall, stained from the weather, but pristine otherwise. At the far end stood Zeus, larger and taller than the rest.

Halfway down, she spotted a building to her right, hidden by hedges and trees. As she neared, she recognized a worn-out greenhouse. The door was off its hinges, half open. It hadn't been used in years. Moving inside, she nearly tripped over something dark gray, darting out past her. The blur of a tiger-tail disappeared out the door.

"Oh!"

A figure blocked her exit.

"Sorry, didn't mean to frighten you," Tom Caswell remarked.

Jessica felt relieved. "You just startled me. A stray cat almost did me in."

"Feral cats along the rim. I asked the gardener where you or Henry might be. He pointed this direction."

"Mr. Maxwell is gone. He didn't say where."

"He does that quite often. How are things with him, any better?"

"I do see minor improvement. With him away, I wanted to explore. He tends to come here at night."

"Yes, I'm aware."

"You do?"

He sighed. "He's searching for Lillian."

"Interesting."

"He still believes he can be in touch with her spirit."

"Is she part of the hallucinations he's experiencing?"

"I suppose so. And here, why not? This was Lillian's passion, these carvings and the agora. She brought me here as a boy. Taught me about the Olympians. So enthralled, I read *The Iliad* and *The Odyssey* at least three times."

Walking back to the statuary garden, she said, "This is quite impressive. His wife did all this?"

"She had a fascination with Greece. This was the place where she spent most of her time when Henry worked in the films. Three terraces follow this promontory dissecting the canyons, each one dropping a little lower than the previous one. The gardens are on the first terrace, these two colonnades of statues line the agora, a public space in Greek. I call it the avenue of gods. Out on the point is a third terrace. Too difficult to get to, surrounded by steep cliffs."

"Tom, it's none of my business, but I had a talk with Dr. Kopf."

It took a second for Caswell to react. "How'd you find out about him?"

"From our files."

"What'd he tell you?"

"He treated Lillian. I must ask. Please don't take it personally. Is it true your father once threatened her?"

He cleared his throat. "I don't know much about that."

"Do you know his whereabouts?"

No hesitation. "Why would you want to look him up?"

"I'm trying to shed a little light on Henry's background. Your father may remember something that can help me reach him a little deeper."

"Doubtful. I wouldn't have a clue where he is."

She nodded, pursuing this further might not be the best plan of action.

After a moment, Caswell faced her head on. "As a word of advice, I wouldn't let him catch us here. This is Lillian's sanctuary.

"Then let's get back."

"No sense getting him riled up if he returns."

"Henry told me her gardening killed her."

He waved his hand around, staring at the sculptures. "She did die here."

She thought back to the cause of death, a drug overdose. She saw sadness in Caswell's eyes. Together, they walked back to the house in silence.

Chapter 20

High above the east cliffs amidst the ruins of Sixby Abbey, Sir Alston Chatsworth came to contemplate his miserable past and make peace with his broken soul.
—BB Barmore,
Lady Julia's Sarcophagus

A time to clear his head, or muck it up. A crapshoot at best.

The last few days had brought a bombardment of disruptive, head-scratching decisions, all part of some bold plan. But for what purpose? The answer to that question became obvious. It all started in the garden. The addition of the young woman lawyer may have become a detriment, or an incentive—or the catalyst. Time would tell.

He blamed himself for not seeing Jessica before making his unannounced escape from the house. Since she bailed him out after his arrest at Olsen's Tavern, he'd grown accustomed to having a quick word with her once or twice during the day. The icy glares he gave her were, in most regards, unwarranted. She didn't deserve such rudeness, but getting her out of his life still floundered in his indecisive mind. If he would act sane, then all this conservatorship rubbish might end.

He shuffled along the worn path, snaking through the oaks, working his way down a short hill into a small, dry gully. It meandered, overgrown with weeds, the sun hot and direct. Dragonflies flittered about as he moved through the high grasses lining both sides of the path. Ants crisscrossed and grasshoppers chirped as he took his time to climb up the other side.

It had been several months since he'd taken this walk, always at times to let his mind flush away the dreariness of the castle and to pretend to get away from reality. He never met anyone on these walks as it was private property with a sign that indicated trespassers would be prosecuted. Shot on sight would have been more descriptive. *Save us all a little bit of time and frustration.* A chain link fence surrounded the several acres of land and a padlock kept people from entering through the gate. Thankfully, for him, he possessed a key.

With his arthritic legs and bad knee screaming in pain, he climbed a short rise, and on the horizon, the Pacific came in view. He stood for a couple of minutes leaning on his cane, catching his breath and waiting for the throbbing to subside. To his right, he gazed at the old mission, or what remained of San Miguel de Nuevo España, the only existing California Mission never given the proper attention and preservation it deserved. It was smaller in stature that the other missions, an estranged part of California's history of Spanish missions established in the eighteenth and early nineteenth centuries by the Franciscan order of the Catholic Church. The property, complete with an intimate courtyard, bell tower and tile roofs, ended up in private hands after the Spanish influence waned. As the years passed, it deteriorated further, the bell long ago stolen, the tiles on the roof cracked or missing, stone masonry falling in disrepair. Weeds covered the courtyards, always a place to ignore considering rattlesnakes sometimes slithered around in the hot sun.

Now in a ruinous state, not much had been done to preserve or restore it to its original condition. The California Historical Society had visions for restoration, but the present owner all but gave them the finger. Eccentric and rich, he didn't care for any type of government intervention. He only concerned himself with the value of the property. To hell with history, the acreage had development potential written all over it, condominiums and tennis courts. But for now, it was a forgotten piece of real estate.

Even now, the thought of preservation was the furthest thing from Maxwell's mind. Like the other night, when he realized he had a reason to be on this earth a little longer, the nagging voice in the back of his head kept reminding him of his newfound vision. He studied the structure and the blue-gray Pacific in the distance. His thinking clicked back and forth between fact and fiction.

...the shell of the old abbey, a ruinous collection of Gothic stone walls not unlike the remains of a roofless Greek temple, now overgrown with wild heather and straggling vines, stands as a lonely sentinel...

He neared the weathered arched double doors and saw the chain and padlock securing the latches. Again, he retrieved another key from his pocket, and opened it. A few seconds later, he wrestled the latch and pushed the door in. He didn't secure the keys by accident. In 1966 he starred in *The Sins of San Rafael*, which was filmed in and around the mission. At that time, the old structure and surroundings were well-maintained. He played a

Franciscan priest, more evil than godly. The prior owner of the property agreed Maxwell could visit any time as he took an interest in the mission and its history. As far as Maxwell could figure, the present owner didn't know he still retained a key. So be it, shame on him. Stepping inside, Maxwell's gaze bounced throughout the sanctuary, lit by four upper-story windows.

The sudden flapping of pigeons brought his attention to the furthest window, now shattered. Pigeon crap spread upon the ledges and on the floor. The broken window must have happened since his last visit a while back. He came here to meditate, to clear his mind. Not being a man of faith, when he sat in the pews he did get a vague grasp of the addiction of religion. But every time he visited he never understood the desire to believe. His needs took a different direction. Once inside the church, he couldn't stop from replaying in his head the morbid scenes from the movie, and to ask himself, Why? Why in the hell did he agree to do such a film? He did Gothic horror, not sensationalistic blood-splatter. To be a murderous, sadistic, evil priest one moment, and then a respected, loving, and virtuous person off set the next was nothing short of miraculous. As one of Hollywood's strongest critics once said, *if Henry Maxwell didn't have a personality disorder, then by gum, he's an actor's actor, and a damn fine one.*

He walked over to one of the few remaining pews, sat down, gazing up at the dark stained heavy roof timbers. Roosting pigeons flittered from beam to beam. Chalky white blobs drooped from the beams, and feathers drifted down in the sooty-looking air. Fitting, he thought, that it should come to this. Forgetting the pigeons, he swirled around in his mind the climactic scene from *The Sins of San Rafael*. To this day, he still couldn't believe the producers convinced the owner to allow such repugnance to be filmed inside the holy space instead of a mockup set at the studio. But this mission long ago gave up its faith-based roots. Mass hadn't been performed here in over a hundred and fifty years.

Would God forgive? Maybe God really didn't give a damn.

Maxwell didn't give a damn. After Lillian's death, he lost all belief. Other forces were at work, some insidious, some lacking in empathy, others of the weak variety, unwilling to be registered as a sign of mental instability.

He glanced around the sanctuary, the stark interior, whitewashed plaster walls, the occasional groupings of bright-colored tiles and the predella steps to the ornate tabernacle, broken and discolored. The wall below the shattered window was stained from rainwater leaking through. A slight puddle could be seen on the floor.

He studied the roof beam at the front of the altar. He would never be able to remove that one piece of heavy timber from his transgressions. How could he? That one scene always tore him apart because of its horrific nature, yet he replayed it time and time again in his worthless mind. He would never forget Father Agustin Isidrio de Duero. The narrative of the act stretched across his thoughts.

Camera's roll
Clapper Board, Scene 1
Take 1
Gloria Patri, et filio, et spiritui sancto. That bit of Latin would forever be entrenched in the inner workings of his grief-crusted memory. He continued to recite his

lines as if the camera still rolled.

We walk this earth as one with God. We look at evil as one studies the eyes of the sinner. This woman is damned because she has not accepted the glorious nature of the one God, and his beloved Son. By the grace of the Almighty and the good laws of the Spanish Empire, we have arrived to help these poor wretched souls from suffering eternal damnation.

Maxwell felt his eyes burn bright as the lines continued to roll through his mind.

This is the punishment for those who do not accept the splendor of the one true God.

Sweat dripped from every pore as he concluded the dialogue.

Following the traditions of Juan Fernándes de Lara, the Grand Inquisitor from Valencia, I will discharge this sentence. It pains me that this young woman must carry the burden of this edict into the depths of hell. One might think that this is a high price to pay for disobeying the Bible. This is God's just law. Therefore, we execute this auto-da-fé in a most humane manner and not by public burning. In nomine Patris, et Filii, et Spiritus Sancti.

Henry Maxwell lowered his gaze. His neck ached from staring at the wood beam. Rubbing his red and watery eyes, his thoughts were melting and unsure. He kept them pinned to the floor. Having revisited this scene over and over in his mind at least a thousand times, he again contemplated why he agreed to do such a gruesome bit of acting. But for whatever reason, he knew he had done a superb job of portraying Father Agustin Isidrio de Duero. It was as if he had completed the movie only yesterday.

Why did he ever think that coming back here would

be a place for reflection? It always ended this way. Yet, it made sense. He would continue to plan his immediate future and eternal demise and leave his next step to fate.

He pushed himself up and walked out of the church.

Chapter 21

"I don't think police work is my calling," David said over the phone.

"Didn't hurt to ask." Hardrick responded. "You realize you've made more headway on Yashiro's killing than anyone else in the department? We need your brains."

"At one time I considered investigative reporting before I went academia."

"You'd still make one hell of a detective. For your information, a Ventura County pathologist determined Eddie suffered a heart attack and the mountain lion finished him off. And another thing, they found a tranquilizer gun and several darts in Eddie's cabin."

He remembered Dart telling him Eddie used to work for the owners of the wildlife park. "Sounds incriminating?"

"We're waiting for forensics to get back. They should be able to determine if the tranquilizer gun is the same. We're thinking he meant to tranquilize Tashiro and the dosage was too strong?"

David thought long and hard. "This is getting crazier by the minute."

"I couldn't agree more. For your edification, the authorities didn't find a reel by the name of *Lady Julia's Sarcophagus* at the cabin."

Now, more than ever, he convinced himself *Crypt of*

the Damned was a decoy. Then where the hell was *Lady Julia's Sarcophagus*?

He thanked Hardrick for the information, stood from his desk and walked over to a file cabinet. Reaching in, he pulled out a folder. Everything he uncovered about those films, akin to the B-side of a 45-rpm record, became more complicated. B-movies played the flip side of a double matinee. Now two celluloid motion pictures centered his research—one stolen, ending up in a murdered man's collection?

What started as an innocent project metamorphosized into a murder investigation. How in the hell did this happen, and what was so important about these old movies costing two people their lives? He needed to readjust his thinking. A flurry of thoughts came streaming by, sparking a memory. Most of Yashiro's work was with Global Pictures. Why not start there? If he went back to his original hypothesis, *Lady Julia's Sarcophagus* might be the key.

Opening the folder he retrieved from the cabinet, he reviewed his notes on Global, flipping through the pages, unable to find a complete listing of the films the studio produced. Locating people who worked there was going to be a huge undertaking. They would be advanced in years if alive at all. Tashiro, one of the last, now dead. Examining his notes, he found the name Emma Sandstrom written on a scrap of paper, the wife of one of Global's controlling partners. After many phone calls, he tracked her down, a resident in an assisted living center near Santa Monica.

Two hours later, he checked in at the front desk, and asked to speak with Emma Sandstrom. "Always in the sunroom this time of day," the young receptionist said.

The Salvation of Henry Maxwell

"Follow me."

She led him into a brightly lit room with enough potted plants to give it a jungle feel. A stately looking nonagenarian with light-rimmed glasses, a face etched with wrinkles and white hair pulled back sat next to the window. Hearing him, she looked up from reading. He could see she had all her faculties. This brought a sigh of relief. The receptionist introduced him, then left.

"Well, sit down, young man," Emma said, placing her book aside.

"Thanks for seeing me," David said, introducing himself and the reason for his visit. Pulling over a well-padded wicker chair, he said, "I apologize for dropping in cold like this."

"Oh, nonsense. Not that I have a busy schedule." Her eyes twinkled. "Nice to see a new face around here. Everyone is so old." She snickered.

He returned her smile. "So, if I may, what can you tell me about Global Pictures?"

"So many years ago, I'm afraid."

"I researched a little about your husband. I understand he died about two months before Global went bankrupt?"

"Plane crash. Both Marshall and Oscar didn't survive. And that was the end."

"Why was that?"

"They were the studio brains." She thought a moment, and then added, "I blame one man more than the accident."

"Who's that?" he asked.

"Henry Maxwell!" she said matter-of-factly. "I've tried to forget about him, but that bothersome fellow from his fan club is always pestering me." She poked at her eye, as if trying to dislodge something.

"Who would that be?"

"Name escapes me. Let me see, Jewish, like Oscar, I think. Yes, let's see—Arlen—Arlen Silvers, I believe. Always picking my old brain, won't leave me alone."

David nodded. He had done his research. Maxwell kept Global above water. Small, independent studios in the days of low-budget Hollywood had to have a cash cow to survive, a mega star whose popularity would make up for all the other flops the studio produced. They knew this, and they banked on it. Maxwell's brand outpaced all the others for most of the sixties.

"It's no secret. Henry Maxwell and Global Pictures paired well together back in the day."

"Yes, that's true."

"What happened?"

Emma rubbed her other eye. "They had financial problems. To be honest, Marshall tended to go out on a limb. Several projects never worked. They came close to finishing the last film Global did. They believed its release would bring them back into the black. He had high hopes. They died with him."

"Why?"

"Bad timing. Henry's wife overdosed, they said. Drugs. He quit before the final scene was shot. The studio found themselves in a bind, on the verge of collapsing. That's when Marshall and Oscar flew to New York to talk to some investors to carry them through." She sighed and shrank back into her chair. "They never made it."

He listened, wrestling with a vague notion. "What was the name of the film?"

"Wish I'd forgotten it long ago. *Lady Julia's*

Sarcophagus."

He froze. Why did he think he knew the answer before he asked the question? "You say Global never released it, all because Maxwell's wife died?"

Emma lifted her gaze and met David's stare. "Marshall pleaded with Henry to come to his senses. Only one more scene to shoot. The editors had all the credits rolled on the picture. just waiting for a five-minute finish and 'The End.' I never quit living after my husband's accident. Henry, though, ruined a studio, and so many lives."

David said nothing for a moment. He contemplated the hate Emma carried against Maxwell. Her hostility rose so quickly to the surface, as if her blame had slumbered for years. He sensed a relief in her weary eyes. Maxwell, one time the savior for Global, and then its destroyer.

"What was the film about?"

"A Gothic love story." She shook her head. "If you want me to recite the plot, don't ask. Too long ago."

"How successful would *Lady Julia's Sarcophagus* have been if it had been finished?"

She didn't hesitate. "Marshall said it would have been the greatest picture made by Global Pictures."

Chapter 22

Detective Sergeant Stanley Brown contemplated his career. Fifty-four years old, he served in investigations for fifteen of his twenty-six years with the department, and if he didn't spend another eight years investigating the worst that humanity offered, he wouldn't have enough financial resources to satisfy the bloodsuckers in his life. One ex-wife and three children, one who couldn't punch his way out of a paper bag, another boy who couldn't hold onto a job, and his youngest, a girl who hadn't figured out how to graduate from college. Add to that two mortgages and a Great Dane eating him out of house and home. If he managed that many years of stress, his mortgages would be satisfied, alimony out the window, the Great Dane in dog heaven and his pension would kick in. Although living that long himself would be a toss-up.

He picked up the photos of the murder scene in Malibu Canyon, paused, wondering why he would want to examine them again. Grisly, hideous, not enough words in the dictionary to describe the heinous affair and what they're up against. He glanced up from his desk as he heard the familiar voice of Deputy Crowley in conversation in the hallway. After they finished, the deputy came over tossing a manila envelope down.

"The man with the gouged eyes has been identified as one Dale Pocock, a homeless man from the inner city," Crowley said. "Method of death still undetermined due to the condition of the corpse. Time of death of the two other victims are in the forensics report. I'm sure you're biting at the bit."

Brown opened the envelope and took out the two-page report. Skimming through, he glanced up at the deputy. "So, this Pollock fellow was killed two days before the teenagers."

"That's Pocock."

"Okay, Pocock." He tossed the report down, and with the strained voice of someone who had seen enough of the rotten world's underside asked, "Why?"

"Seems to be a setup. I think we have a demented individual that kills for pleasure and uses his killings to attract more victims."

"Not even Jeffrey Dahmer fit that description."

"Neither does Jack the Ripper, even though both exhibited the same grisly methods. Saws, knives, body parts."

"Keep it to yourself, Crowley. The day's dragging, just to piss me off, not even noon."

"Yeah, I know. Hard to process what we saw. Don't seem right."

Brown smoothed back his thick, black mustache and sank deeper into his chair. "What about the maggots?"

Crowley cocked his head. "What about them?"

"Maggots are larvae."

"Okay, larvae turn into flies if I remember my junior high science."

"Go on," Brown insisted.

"Rotting body, maggots appear, isn't that mother nature?"

"Come on, think. Do your research. Those were full-blown maggots."

"Decaying corpse, flies lay eggs, maggots develop."

"Not that fast. Mature maggots, close to changing into flies. That can't happen in two days."

"What're you getting at?

"Fishing."

Crowley shook his head. "Fishing?"

"Maggots can be used for fishing bait. Damn effective. I've even used them a time or two. Here's what I think. I think the maggots were planted by our killer to set the scene."

"No kidding?"

"Think about it. The psycho we're looking for is a sadistic son of a bitch. He wanted the visual to be the most hideous we could ever imagine. He kills the poor Pollock fellow—"

"Pocock," Crowley corrected again.

"Okay, he murders this Pocock, takes him to the old stone building, gouges out his eyes, salts all his orifices—ears, nose, mouth, asshole, eye sockets—with maggots to make it mimic a real horror scene."

Crowley's face wrinkled and paled.

"You okay?"

"Yeah, yeah, fine, I think." He wiped his forehead. "But why?"

"To use Pocock as bait. That old building was used as a hangout for young people, a place to party. That was this bastard's goal, to draw in other victims to telegraph to the world how demented and sadistic he is."

"Where to now?"

"Check out every bait shop in the vicinity that sells maggots. A lot of these places raise them. Disgusting business, but like I said, fish go crazy to take a bite.

Someone must have sold a bunch of the slimy creatures, more than you would use to go fishing. Chances are, they'll remember who bought a large quantity of maggots."

"You're something, Stanley," Crowley said. "Really something. I'll get right onto it."

Chapter 23

Jessica finished putting groceries away in the kitchen when her cell phone rang. She didn't recognize the number. Hesitating, she answered, "Hello."

"Is this Jessica Barrow?" a voice inquired.

"Yes, what can I do for you?"

"Hi, my name's David Grovene. I'm on the faculty at UCLA, Department of Film, Television and Media Studies. I got your name from Marsha Hauser."

"Oh."

"Ms. Hauser suggested you and I get together. She explained your firm's association with Henry Maxwell. I'm involved in something concerning him. Is it possible to meet?"

Jessica paused a moment. "Where would you like to meet?"

"I could come to you."

"Thinking it might not be a good idea," she said. "I don't think I should be inviting guests here at this time. Would your office work?"

"Wonderful, this afternoon?"

This sounds intriguing. "Sure, that could work."

"I'll text my address and directions," David said.

After agreeing to a time, she hung up and called Marsha, who filled her in. She wanted to meet this professor, thinking he could help her with her relationship with Maxwell. She checked her watch. It would take a while, assuming the traffic wasn't a total nightmare, which was wishful thinking. She snuck a peek and noticed Maxwell sitting in a lounger next to the pool. Reading a newspaper, he appeared content.

She rushed upstairs to freshen up.

At 2:25, she pulled into a visitor parking spot on the UCLA campus. Ten minutes later, she found his building and office. The door was open. As she was ready to knock, a man, longish dark hair with a touch of gray looked up from his desk with a playful grin, his long-sleeved white shirt wrinkled and the collar fighting his chin for space. "Jessica, I presume. You made great time, come in." He offered a hand.

"Hi, Jessica Barrow."

"Please call me David. Thrilled we're able to meet so quickly."

"I talked to Marsha. She filled me in, something about police investigating a couple of old films." She gazed at the professor, thinking he didn't convey the air of a stuffy university type.

David spent the next five minutes describing how he got involved in the investigation and why a film by the name *Lady Julia's Sarcophagus* might be the key. Jessica opened her mouth to say something but held back, knowing quite well attempting to interpret Henry Maxwell's inner mind had become even more complex with two dead men somehow part of the equation.

"One of his movies?"

"Never released, from my understanding. Appears to be the epicenter of everything."

"Why wasn't it released?"

"His wife died suddenly. Stopped him cold. Despondent, he refused to complete the picture."

"His grief has been all-consuming since his wife's death decades earlier. How does this investigation involve you?"

"I'm a film theorist. I study old celluloid films from an academic perspective, not from a critique viewpoint. Part of my interest is in preservation and history."

"Are you thinking Mr. Maxwell can tell us why those two folks were murdered?"

David shook his head. "Not sure, but before he is asked, we need more information."

"Did Marsha tell you about my position in JWB's role as conservatorship?

"Only you were the right person for the job."

Jessica felt relieved, whether she mentioned her psychology background or not, did it really matter? "This *Lady Julia's Sarcophagus*, creepy as it sounds, reminds me of this humongous castle I'm having the honor of calling my temporary residence. It's the most massive and bizarre place on earth."

"I'd love to see it." He went on to detail how the death of Maxwell's wife brought the demise of Global Pictures and an end to his acting career.

"That's doesn't surprise me. He doesn't talk much. Made a little progress, but I'm still convinced he'll open up."

"There has to be a lot going on in his mind. Heck, he was one of the biggest stars in the Gothic horror genre back then."

Jessica bit her lip. "What's the movie about? If we had knowledge of the plot, it might help us understand how to approach Mr. Maxwell."

"He might be the only person left who remembers the movie's details. Most of those involved are deceased.

There may be others still alive, but without credits rolling, we're in the dark."

Jessica tilted her head, trying to make sense. "You mentioned Gothic. That takes me right back to what I experienced the last several days living in his monstrosity. I swear something macabre drifts out of the stone walls. It gets into your blood, a frightening existence. There's a chill in the air when I'm in that sinister place, and to think I am charged with staying there. I don't know how any sane person can live alone there like he does."

David leaned across his desk with a smile. "How about a tour? What's the chances you'll invite me?"

"No problem with me. I'd have to ask Mr. Maxwell first."

"I promise to behave. Tell him we're old friends. Tell him I'm doing a study on the B-movie era. That may pique his interest. Ask if he would be willing to be interviewed."

Jessica thought a moment, then nodded. "I know he won't grant interviews to the normal press, but for a professor working on something at one time dear to his heart, he might agree, bring some pride back, enough for him to begin to live again. We had a talk one day about movies in general. He might be ready to say more. I'll see what I can do. I'll give you a call tomorrow."

David couldn't contain his excitement. A smile covered his face.

Chapter 24

...and in the confines of the barren vaults and crypts, time and time again, a visitor will find himself lost within the vexing and twisting labyrinths and lose his sanity to an oblique form of stark horror.
—BB Barmore,
Lady Julia's Sarcophagus

Early the next afternoon, David Grovene eased his beat-up Honda hatchback into the circular driveway. If he hadn't gotten the opportunity to interview Henry Maxwell, he and Toby, his four-year-old overactive yellow lab, would be racing down the beach, smelling the salt air and kicking up the sand. But that could wait. No way would he miss this chance.

Sliding out of his seat, he stood looking over the roof of his car at the massive stone behemoth framed by the bookend battlements. Jessica Barrow didn't kid when she said he lived in a castle. If it were midnight, the moon flickering behind a procession of clouds, and a werewolf howling in the distance, he could fall into the spirit of things. No werewolves, but at least he would meet one of the kings of horror.

A shot of excitement coursed down to his toes as he shut the door and hurried up to the entry. He admired the dragon knocker. Pulse racing, he banged it hard. Several seconds later, the door opened.

"You're punctual," Jessica said, smiling.

"Wouldn't miss meeting *the* Henry Maxwell if my life depended on it," he said.

"Come in. I want your reaction."

David stepped inside and took in the massive foyer, amazed at the grandeur and architectural gloom it presented. For a moment, his mind left Jessica. His memory travelled back to the opening scenes of past horror movies he'd scrutinized and studied. He swore he recognized the large room in a few of the old Maxwell films. The cold stone walls pulsated a sense of evil, a definite chill in the air. Not exactly a loving and welcoming space. Yet he savored every minute of his surroundings and was anxious to ask the horror star himself why he lived in such a dreary, immense residence, mimicking scenes from his movies.

Jessica enjoyed watching his reaction. "Was I spot on?"

"You described it to a T."

"You should have seen it before it was cleaned. No more cobwebs as far as I can tell."

"Still looks creepy and ghoulish."

She nodded. "When I mentioned to him your academic interest in B-movies, he perked up. I think he wants to share his experiences. Follow me. He's in the den."

David trailed her across the lofty foyer, past the circular stairway and under one of the arches. He was no longer in the twentieth century. Years of studying the literature and films of the Gothic era paid off. He never felt more at home.

Near the end of the hallway, she pushed open a wooden door and they entered. Instead of stone, the walls were wood paneled. Along one wall, a fire flickered in an ornate fireplace. He couldn't believe his eyes. June, and eighty degrees outside. Yet a touch of cool air circulated.

"Don't be shy," a voice ripped from a corner of the room.

David looked closer, a figure sitting in a high-backed chair. He walked over. Maxwell's form sharpened; shadows scattered. The old horror star didn't rise.

"Pleased to meet you, Mr. Maxwell. I'm David Grovene," he said, offering an extended hand.

"I know who the hell you are. Take a seat. You too, Jessica."

Caught off guard, he drew his hand back and fell in a nearby chair.

"Tell me, Mr. Professor," his voice brusque, like dragging chains. "How am I to enlighten you today?"

"Do you mind if I record this?" he said, starting to overheat from the fireplace.

"If you must." Maxwell's voice moderated.

David wiped his forehead, took out a digital recorder and placed it on an end table. "Thanks for allowing me to visit, and thank you, Jessica, for setting this up." He gave her a smile. He gazed back at Maxwell. "My field of interest and research is in the Gothic period of film, and of film preservation. Let me start by asking about the B-movie era of the sixties. You made a name for yourself starring in, at my count, over thirty-two such films."

"Thirty-three. No big deal, it was an early time of my life. That's what I did."

"A very productive period. The Gothic horror genre found an audience, and you were a part of its success."

He grumbled. "So they say."

David cleared his throat. "I do believe, if not mistaken, some of the B-movies took on an A quality. They weren't always relegated to the double matinee formula."

"Since we're on the alphabet, how about C and C?" Maxwell asked.

"C and C?"

"Oh, come, Professor, A- and B-movies, now let's expand the alphabet. C and C, Cinemascope, and color, especially color. Blood is red, never black and white. Years later, the slasher genre overdid it. God help us when that happened. My pictures, if I say so, contained a certain romanticism, most of them, that is." He stroked his chin.

"There's romanticism attributed to Gothic literature for sure. It's a style that incorporates an emphasis on imagination, architecture, fears and desires. Your films delivered that aspect. *The Pillars of Hell*, one of my favorites. *Devil's Details*, another film that stretches elements of Walpole's *Castle of Otranto*. Your house here, for example, a castle by definition, has those architectural components of the genre—the stonework, pointed arches, medieval decoration. And back to the topic of blood. Red makes a great spectacle. People can relate to it on the screen as something terrifying, someone dying in a horrific manner."

"Very good, Mr. Grovene. You do wear your professor hat quite well. Thank you for acknowledging some of my pictures. Haunted houses and dreary castles all equate to what Gothic horror stood for—back then." Maxwell leaned back in his chair. "But a film or a novel is populated with people. They are the driving forces, and their psychology is critical to the genre." He glanced over to Jessica, the fire flickering off her irises. "Jessica, don't you agree?"

Startled, she sucked in a hasty breath. "Yes, I would think so."

"Why would you live in a house copying the backdrops of some of your films?" David asked.

"It was used in six. Why should I distinguish between reality and fantasy? I was comfortable on the set, I'm comfortable here."

"I swore I'd been here before, coming in the front door. Brings back the movies I've seen. On another subject, what can you tell me about your work with Global Pictures?"

Maxwell didn't answer. He rose, picked up his cane, and sauntered like a sloth over to the fireplace, pushed a button next to the mantel. The flame disappeared. "Don't tell your friends it's gas. I wouldn't want to break their everloving hearts thinking I wasn't authentic enough." He limped over to the door. "Please, I'll be right back. It will only be a minute or two." He left, the sound of shuffling feet and cane chinking on the floor muted as he went down the hallway.

David glanced over at Jessica. "One mention of Global, and he disappears. What do you think?"

"He doesn't want to discuss it, but I think he's opened up quite a bit."

"I sense he's messing with us. The fireplace—in June? He had it on for effect, to observe our reaction."

"Or maybe to help him cope with us. The eerie settings in his movies must have given him contentment, so he incorporated them in this mansion. This house is a living entity, his security blanket. It almost breathes on its own."

"That sounds psychological."

She smiled. "I'll fill you in later."

David tilted his head. "Did you hear something?"

"No, what?"

He stood, turning to the far wall. "What's that?"

Jessica jumped up and stared. "Is that a door that just popped open?"

He moved over. "Damn right. A door, hidden in the wood paneling." He eyed the door and the opening. "Secret passages were always an integral realm of Gothic." Inching closer, he clasped the edge of the narrow door, pulling it fully open. He stuck his head in, a set of stairs greeted him, stone treads winding down and disappearing into darkness.

"I just remembered something Tom Caswell told me," Jessica said. "He's a friend of Mr. Maxwell's. He used to have parties and games here. Subterranean passages are integral to this place." She pointed at the door. "That must be part of his fun."

A grin came over David's face. "He's testing us. He wants us to take these stairs. For him to tell us more, we have to appease him."

"You're not thinking of going down there, are you?"

"We have to pass the test." He took several steps into shadow. "Are you coming?"

****

Jessica rolled her eyes in disbelief. To enter was against her better judgment. But would she miss something, something interesting? Combating the fears she'd felt since arriving at the castle, she convinced herself this was doable. "I'm stronger now," she murmured. Pulling her lead feet off the floor, she crept over to the opening and stepped over the threshold. A warm draft swept up, aged and stale. After the first step, she coaxed herself downward, one step at a time. She reached the bottom in a subterranean room with stone walls and a high barrel roof. Light came from several flickering torches. David stood next to a standing set of iron armor, a medieval-looking trunk nearby. On the opposite wall, a wooden table with candles and a box of matches. Cobwebs were everywhere, draped over the two archways that led into what appeared to be darkened corridors. Her senses heightened, she asked, "More cobwebs? I can't take it."

He pulled one off the torch. and examined it. "Real as can be." He examined the wall, the stone laid end to end in a meticulous soldier coursing. "Never seen this type of masonry anywhere in Southern California. It doesn't look native. And the stonework, more European, as if this place is a few hundred years old, which doesn't make sense."

"Flickering torches. They can't be real."

"They're exact replicas from the medieval days, artificial, only electric."

The door from the den slammed shut.

"Well, well," David commented.

"This isn't good." A shaken Jessica responded, her voice straining. She rushed back up the stairs and pushed the door. It wouldn't budge. 'Now what?" she said, hollering down the stairwell.

"We have two choices. Those arched doorways. Right or left? This is part of his game."

"Game! I didn't sign up for a game!" she shrieked, huffing heavily. "You have a lot of faith in our safety, knowing him fifteen minutes."

"Gut instinct. Pretty obvious he's eccentric."

"And mentally unstable. Oh, god, I'll kill Marsha if I ever get out of here alive."

"Let's try this left corridor." He picked up two candleholders on the table and lighted the candles, handing one to Jessica.

She moaned deeply, then followed David into the passageway, angling downward, the air close to choking, the space a claustrophobic loneliness of sightless, abyssal confinement. Ghastly and daring, retching twists and turns of stone, the archetypal and ancient facsimile of a new world catacomb. Reaching a ninety-degree corner, she squeezed closer to David.

"Listen, I understand your concern." he said. "This is a test, I'm convinced."

"Testing, for what? Our sanity?" Her voice wavered.

"What I've learned from studying the Gothic literature and film genre, people read novels to get scared; they go to the movies to experience the terror. The only saving grace—they know once they close the book or walk out of the theater, they've survived when some of the characters didn't. Watching a movie you're still a spectator. Maxwell wants our reaction. He's challenging our resolve. Perhaps it's taking him back to better days when he entertained here."

Resigned, Jessica nodded. At this point, she had no other choice.

Turning the corner, they passed an intersecting corridor. A few feet farther, they came to a large wooden door with an arched top. David tried the massive latch and pushed the door open. A dark passageway greeted them. "You stay here."

"What? Where are you going? Let's go back, pound

on the door. Maxwell must be back in the den. I don't think we're meant to be down here."

"Just give me a second or two." He stepped inside. Before Jessica could protest, the door swung shut with a thud.

She rushed over and reached for the latch. "It won't open," she screamed.

David tried the same. The door didn't budge. "Listen, I'll find another way out of here."

"And leave me all alone!" The candle continued to flicker, fraying her nerves. "Please stay lit," she pleaded.

"Only a minute," he said. "Hang on, must be a pattern to Maxwell's thinking."

Now separated. Was this part of Maxwell's plan? The corridor she found herself in was dark and narrow. A miasma of decomposing loam hung in the air. "David, you still there?"

No response came from the other side of the door.

****

David crept along the passageway, his twinkling candle bouncing light off the stone walls. A stench of mildew twitched his nose, growing stronger. He turned another corner to his right and ended up at an iron-grille door. He shoved hard. It opened with a screech of the hinges.

His candle stopped flickering. Stale air greeted him on entry. He walked into the room through a large archway. There, a consortium of rotting wood articles—tables, chairs, an old armoire, a three-legged stool missing a leg. Along the edges of one wall—old wooden planks, some dusty beams, inset with a rickety plank half-door, hanging by one rusty hinge. Cobwebs everywhere.

Jessica, he remembered. How stupid, not trying to force open the door and stay with her. *What the hell was I thinking?* At that precise moment, the iron-grille door closed with a clang. He wheeled, coming close to dropping the candle. He rushed over and pushed at the door. Locked tight. Cursing, he realized he might be the dumbest SOB that ever walked the face of the earth, and now his appreciation and understanding of Maxwell began to turn.

He panned around, shining the candle in every corner, every indent, every niche. He shook his head in disgust. He was beginning to believe the man was mad. His mind now ran in circles, fear becoming reality. Game or not, where did he go wrong? Where was the secret lever to rid himself of captivity?

Yes, a lever, the old Gothic horror movies always had something that opened secret doors or freed prisoners. If Maxwell was truly testing them—where the hell was the lever? He paced, racking his brain—Maxwell's screen life—the terror—the escape. This charade had to be a repeat of his party games. His guests had to find a way out. He panned the candle around, scanned the walls. His eyes fell on a non-lit torch sticking out of the far wall on a stone holder. Hoping against hope, he rushed over and pulled down on the holder, he'd seen this before somewhere. Likely rusted, it rotated, giving him hope—and then with a snap, a clink of iron screeched. He glanced over, and the door swung open. He quickly dashed back into the corridor.

****

Jessica kept pounding on the door. Her fears skyrocketed. "David, talk to me! What's happening?" Her cries for help served no purpose other than to raise her hysterics. She couldn't think straight. Thick stone walls snuffed out her rattled pleas. Turning in circles, she wanted to scream again…and again, but her voice didn't respond. Her throat pulsated, sweat covered her body head to toe, the corridor steamy hot, yet she began to shiver. She tasted fear rising up, clogging her breathing. Swiveling her head back and forth, the walls moved in ready to crush her to oblivion, while a tingling prickle of doom crawled up her arms like a thousand spiders.

Her candle blinked. Panicked, her mind was now close to sheer delirium. Whirling around in a stupor, she clawed her way back through the convoluted passageway, back to the first room she and David started in. Why not wait here until someone opened up the door to the den? That would be the sensible thing to do. Pure foolishness to even think otherwise.

She examined the door on her right, and subconsciously entered the corridor. A dark labyrinth of intersecting passageways greeted her—low, narrow, springing off each direction. This maze struck her with a claustrophobic terror similar to the door she and David first entered and became separated. Everywhere the same dread, pulling her toward some seething mass of inevitability. Her throat, irritated from the confined, stale air, triggered her breathing to accelerate, almost to the point of hyperventilating.

She turned a corner, shadows weaving along the passageway. She stopped suddenly, frozen—and there in a small chamber, flashes bounced and danced—and along the far wall, a hangman's noose and its shadow swinging back and forth. The air remained calm, nothing to cause the pendulous motion. And yet, it swung…on and on…and on…

A solemn silhouette grew out of the stone, and the image seared her memory of a twelve-year-old boy—*Noah! His pleas were a challenge and a farewell. And in his eyes, loneliness cried out, the helpless trappings of targeted tormenting, the humiliation washing over him like an ocean wave of vicious acid. Stupid, ugly, fat, weird, all words meant to terrorize and inflict pain continued to resonate in his ears, saturating his mind with thoughts offering only one way out. She tried to counterbalance the teasing and abuse through counselling. Yet she failed, couldn't reach deep enough to convince him it wasn't his fault. But to no avail. Yes, she failed, and the nylon twine and garage rafters haunted her to this day.*

She fell back against the wall trembling, barely able to hold the candle. She let out a scream. Turning, she rushed back down the passageway, her mind on fire. Around another ninety-degree corner, she stopped at a set of steps going up.

No thoughts of where she was, she trod up the risers ending at another short corridor with a wooden door blocking her way. Suppressing images of Noah from her mind, she theorized she might be on the way back up to the main floor. She swore she hadn't climbed up the same distance as she did to go down.

A dreaded silence smothered her. Terror took over, pure, unmitigated terror. Why did she not stay in the den, not take the bait, stay away from the hysteria of an over-reactive mind? She should have expected this turning into a nightmare. She wanted to cry, but instead she tried the latch. The door opened. More stairs, no way! They went down, a never-ending trap of craziness—down, down, deep down—panic at every step. The candle began to flicker again and beyond the downward risers, she swore she heard something.

Suddenly the flame snuffed out. Pure darkness to accompany her hysteria, pitch black, nothing, no light. Would she ever regain her sight again? If there was light, would it ever reengage her optic nerves, and allow the sweet blessing of sight to renew? The dread of blindness now traumatized her thinking. She moved down the stairs, keeping her balance by hugging the wall on her right. After a couple of minutes, she imagined a far-off groaning of metal scraping. Tossing her fear aside, she hurried along another narrow passageway, feeling her way toward the sound.

And then a miracle. Her optic nerve still worked. A pinpoint of light came her way, dancing off the walls. She yelled, "David, that you?" Her heart rate was racing faster than her words.

"Jessica!" The response boomed her way.

The flicker of light grew stronger in the darkness. She rushed up and grabbed his arm. "Oh, am I glad to see you!"

"I should have my head examined for getting separated. Like a Halloween fright night. Are you okay?"

She nodded, out of breath.

"I'll admit, I was beginning to question my better judgment."

"What happened? How'd we finally meet?"

"This subterranean world is a series of passageways that jig and jag."

"Do you feel a breeze?" She pointed at another intersecting corridor.

David noticed her hair tossing. "I do."

"If it is what I think it is, we might find our way out."

"Feels like it's coming from there," he said, pointing. They turned and walked slowly, David protecting his candle flame so both could see. The draft was strengthening. Turning right at the intersection, they followed the tight passageway as the floor rose, ending at a set of stairs going up.

Climbing up, they came into a small room with a door at the end. Light could be seen between the bottom of the door and the threshold. David tried the knob and it opened. Full sunshine greeted them. They exhaled in unison and stepped out into the motor court. Allowing their eyes to adjust, they took a back exit to the east side of the castle and climbed another stair onto the veranda near the pool.

****

Maxwell sat in his favorite deck chair, clasping a cold glass of lemonade. A smile came across his face as he noticed Jessica and the professor fellow struggling up the last steps.

When she saw him, she rushed over and locked eyes. "How dare you pull a stunt like that!" she said in a strained and animated voice. Arms lashing about, she came close to hitting him.

"You survived, isn't that what counts?" Maxwell said, snickering. "You're a winner."

"You're a sick, sick man!"

"Then I take it you'll be leaving soon. Have you had enough keeping tabs on me?"

She kept a fiery stare pinned on him. "You're not that lucky. I'm here for the duration, so get used to it!"

Before he could respond, she turned on a dime and rushed back into the mansion.

He watched her disappear as David approached.

"So, what's your take?"

"You're good, maybe too good."

Maxwell pointed to another deck chair. "Sit down. "You deserve a whole lot of credit for extricating yourself out of that mess below. Not many people could do it in the old days."

"A ton of cobwebs down there."

"Alas, I haven't been there in years. More realistic now, don't you think?"

David pulled the chair over and sat down.

Maxwell poured a glass of lemonade and handed it over. "When Jessica settles down, she'll return. I don't think she likes being left in the dark. I admire that," he said with a sense of pride. He took a sip and lounged back. In a rather pleased voice, he said, "In a way, she's a lot like me." He placed the glass on the table and straightened in his chair. "Now, in the meantime, let me tell you about Global Pictures."

Chapter 25

The next day at the West Los Angeles Regional library, Maxwell opened a source on Greek mythology. Not any book, the one and only Edith Hamilton's *Mythology: Timeless Tales of Gods and Heroes*. He swore he had a copy in his own library. Likely, Lillian would have read it cover to cover a thousand times over. After looking for it close to an hour, no Edith was found.

Flipping through the index, his throat tightened as he found references to Aphrodite, Lillian's favorite, the one she saw in herself. He remembered her pointing in the general direction of the goddess of love and beauty in the garden when her body was found.

But why Aphrodite? Maxwell scanned all the references, searching for a reason she might have pointed at the statue. Did she spring from the foam of the sea as later poems denoted? He read on: Aphros, Greek for foam. Other characteristics fell out of the book. Not always strong, sometimes soft and weak, as in *The Iliad*. "Aphrodite, speak to me!"

Lowering the book, he noticed a young girl on the opposite end of the table, twelve or thirteen, with several books spread out. She stared at him.

"What's the problem?" he spat. "Never seen an old man read?"

Ignoring his gruffness, she said, "You're reading a classic."

"A little beyond your age to comprehend, I imagine," he said rather boldly. Out of the corner of his eye, he glimpsed another patron frowning. "So, what of it?" he repeated, almost whispering.

"I've read it tons of times," she said, not concerned with his rough demeanor. "What part are you looking at?"

"Skimming through it. Now if you don't mind, I'll—"

"Aphrodite is one of my favorites," she insisted.

"What'd you say?"

"What can I tell you about her?"

"Curious, that's all."

"She's the goddess of love."

"I know," he said, trying to keep his voice down.

"She wasn't always good, sometimes nasty."

"Listen, Miss—"

"My name's Sam."

He shook his head. "Sam, a boy's name."

"Samantha isn't, but I like Sam better." She grimaced. "My parents gave me an old-fashioned name."

"To each his or her own. What makes you think you can tell me something I don't know about Aphrodite?"

"She is one of the Twelve Great Olympians?"

Lillian had explained the divine Olympians to him once or twice. Feeling quite ignorant, he decided to let the girl talk. Maybe she would reveal something of value. Standing up, he moved next to her at the end of the table.

"Name's Henry. There's nothing new you can tell me, so prove me wrong."

"The Twelve lived in Olympia, a tall mountain. Aphrodite was Zeus' daughter."

The Salvation of Henry Maxwell

"I read different, something about her springing from the foam in the sea."

Sam gave him a slight grin. "Do you want the details?"

He raised an eyebrow. "Naturally."

"The seafoam was caused by Uranus's genitals being tossed into the sea?"

He almost croaked, hearing such a thing from this young girl. "Is that what you're learning in school?" he asked. "Not ladylike."

"Of course, my teachers wouldn't teach me everything. No, I read it here in these books. But in *The Iliad*, she's the daughter of Zeus and Dione. I like that version best."

"I would think so. And you've read *The Iliad*? Impossible."

She grinned.

He crooked his neck to stare straight at her. "Why would a girl your age have such knowledge about Greek Mythology? There are things in it that may not be so pleasant, or should I say, R-rated, beyond what a young person should be studying. You mentioned one of those."

"In school, pretty simple boring stuff, but in the library, it's different. Details, important facts, exciting stories."

"I could get in trouble talking to you about what the gods did and didn't do. Let's keep this clean. What else about Aphrodite?"

"Everything?"

He nodded. "Try me.

"Okay, here goes. She married Hephaestus."

He thought long and hard. "Who? I can't place him, he's not one of the statues in the garden."

"What garden?"

"Oh, just a bunch of marble gods. Nothing special."

"I'd like to see them."

"When you're a little older."

"Why?"

"Well—"

"I'm old enough. A naked god wouldn't freak me out."

Here we go again. "What about Hephaestus?"

"She was unfaithful to him. She had many lovers."

He realized he should get away and give up on his research before being accused of being a pedophile.

Sam continued, "Aphrodite's children, Iacchus, Phobos, Deimos, Eros, Anteros, Himeros, Pothos, and many more." She gave him a know-it-all smile. "Hephaestus was not their father."

Maxwell's head swam. Then he recalled the name Eros, remembering it was the statue next to Aphrodite. "Did you say Eros?"

"He was an Erotes."

He began to sweat. He'd heard that word before, years earlier. Lillian taught him a bit about young and handsome naked males with wings. Damn, if Eros and Erotic didn't stem from Erotes. And why did his ears perk up with Eros? Was she indicating him instead of Aphrodite?

"Are you okay, Henry?" Sam said, noticing his feverish expression. "If you want, I can explain all about the Erotes. Eros was—"

He frantically cut her off. "No—no need! I do believe, young lady, that you have answered all my questions, and for that, I am grateful."

Chapter 26

Stanley Brown was a strong man, worked out at least three times a week, bench pressed two hundred pounds, a respectable amount for his body type and mass. Along with free weights, an elliptical or a cardio rowing machine, he never skipped a sweat-inducing workout, his distraction after a demanding nerve-wracking day. But physical brawn had nothing to do with strength. Strength of character, the ability to know where you'd been and where you were headed, but most importantly, how you got there. Born and raised in the predominately black Watts neighborhood of Los Angeles, he never forgot his roots. He recalled in detail living in a crammed four-room apartment on East 106th Street. His father labored, working job to job, anything he could find. He died of a heart attack in 1965, the same year the infamous riots left thirty-four people dead, mostly blacks. Ten-year-old Stanley remembered it well, wanting to participate with the rioters, throwing bricks and bottles at the police because, at that tender age, he felt the discrimination and inequality of life. His mother snatched him by the ear and dragged him back home before he ended up a statistic.

To this day, he was grateful to her for her determination and courage in keeping him and his two brothers from straying, teaching them the rewards of honesty, hard work, and trust in the good Lord.

Character-building she called it, remaining a force in his life until her death three years ago. Courage and strength pushed him to where he was now. He knew strength came in different forms, and he tested the limits of his in scores of senseless human-induced situations with the Los Angeles County Sheriff's Department. He thought it couldn't get much worse. He reached his breaking point, a beginning atrophy not of his muscles but of his mental resilience.

Today he thought God had forsaken him and every other living, honest, moral person. Times like this tested one's faith. Macabre crime scenes had not made him immune, and the madness discovered at the old olive oil building made him question the theory of God's grace.

The visual front and center turned him to stone. Camera flashes and self-imposed silence from the investigators and forensic teams had dulled his senses. The young woman hung upside down by one leg, naked, from a high roof beam, her throat slit, the floor of the old Mission San Miguel de Nuevo España splattered in a dark crimson. He closed his eyes and took a deep breath. How do you process such images? Is there a secretion from an unknown gland that dulls the mind, makes the inhumane tolerable? Maybe something like endorphins, a magic peptide hormone that kicks in to rid the mind of pain. If not, what then? He opened his eyes, stared at the floor, trying to keep them from the pools of blood and the footprints that had tracked across. He swore every drop from the young woman drained from her body. He looked up and exhaled sharply as the horrific scene again flooded his vision. He turned as Deputy Crowley walked over in a trance.

He took another deep breath hoping to anesthetize

his mind. "Is the investigative team done with their work?"

The bags under Crowley's eyes were puffed up, like having a needle inserted and tons of silicone pumped in. He didn't look at all well. With a deep sigh, he said, "Yes, they've got what they need."

Brown's temper flared at the deputy in a fit of anger that caused every investigator and forensic technician to stop what they were doing. "Then get the poor woman down from there, now! Get my fucking drift?" He walked out of the sanctuary and vomited. When had he last cursed? He couldn't remember, but after what he'd seen, it may not be the last time.

Chapter 27

"How horribly insensitive of you!" Sir Benton said. "You have sent shivers down the spines of your friends and tested the boundaries of de rigueur. If any close acquaintances remain, and I doubt they will, including myself, you have only yourself to blame for your arrogance and foul words that carelessly flutter from your ungodly mouth. Good day, sir, and good riddance!"
—BB Barmore,
Lady Julia's Sarcophagus

Jessica stood at the edge of the pool studying several of Henry Maxwell's longtime friends and cinematic acquaintances. A string quartet played Bach in the background. The savory aroma of catered ribs, brisket, and smoked salmon from the opposite end of the veranda drifted across the gathering. When she asked Maxwell if he would be agreeable to having a few of his colleagues over, at first he shrugged it off, then later agreed it might be fun. "Folks I haven't seen in years, wonderful. Some alive—some dead. Maybe both will show up," he said, pleased with his joke.

When the invitees arrived, they signed a guest sheet and were escorted through the dreary castle to the veranda, strung with colorful lights. There, they were offered drinks and hors d'oeuvres. Maxwell made his entrance and seemed to enjoy socializing. From all appearances, his enthusiasm was sincere, seeing old friends and sharing old times.

Jessica watched with satisfaction, grateful Maxwell's publicist tracked down as many people as she could from his movie and philanthropic days. Some guests brought their significant others. At last count they numbered fifty-seven. Not too bad. Looking at the guest list, several old and new directors, three former cinematographers, an associate producer, one costume designer in her nineties and her grandson escort, a couple of screenplay writers, a retired newspaper columnist, his foundation executor, and a few actors, none that rang a bell.

Another person she wanted to invite was Roy Caswell. He must have some recollection on the relationship between Lillian and Tom that caused such drama back then. His whereabouts was never found.

David Grovene walked over. "What do you think?"

"So far, so good. He's mingling like we hoped."

"He does have a spark in his eyes."

"You're the expert on his movies. Do you recall any of these people from your research on his old films?"

"Yeah, I recognize a couple of them. Donald Appleton, a former director." He pointed to a short, overweight man with black-framed glasses. "That's his wife standing next to him. I think he directed Henry in *Chasm of Blood*, not one of Maxwell's greatest endeavors. And the bald fellow over in the corner surrounded by other guests. He's Frank Benedict, a character actor from the sixties. Starred in two or three of his movies."

She grinned at David. "You should introduce yourself. You're the movie expert. They may enjoy hearing about film preservation."

He sighed. "Not my party. How about a glass of wine?"

"Red would be great."

"Got it." He shuffled off in the direction of the bar.

"Jessica, this is wonderful," Tom Caswell said, coming up from behind. "I can see life in Henry."

"We can only hope it continues this way. By the way, I wanted to track down your father. I didn't want to exclude anyone."

He didn't look surprised. "He wouldn't have shown if he knew I was here."

She needed answers. "Why is there a such a rift between you and him?"

He scanned the crowd, uncomfortable. "I appreciate you for all you're doing here, but that part of my life is private."

Jessica raised a brow, thinking she'd touched a nerve. "Sorry, I won't ask again." David approached, carrying two glasses of wine.

"Tom Caswell, this is David Grovene," she said, accepting one of the glasses.

"I recognize your name."

"I'm on the faculty at UCLA, Film, Television and Media studies."

"I recall a few of your articles on film preservation in some of the entertainment magazines. You're an expert in that field."

"Very kind of you. I try to put preservation at the forefront. Old Hollywood is long gone, but we must take care of what treasures remain."

"I couldn't agree more."

Jessica sighted Dr. Ewe Kopf strutting across the

veranda. "If you two will excuse me, someone I need to see."

"Of course," Caswell said.

She feathered her way through the crowd and approached the former psychiatrist, thinking all the while about Tom's conflict with his father.

"I'm so happy you could make it," she said.

"Oh, Ms. Barrow," Kopf said. "Pleased to see you again."

"I want to thank you."

"For what?" he said, confused.

She waved around. "For being the catalyst for this successful gathering. You suggested having Henry's friends over. So far, your advice might be the tonic that has brought him back to life."

"Allowing the mind to relive better times helps overshadow the bad."

"Can I get you something?"

"No, thanks. I can't stay long. I don't drive well after dark."

"Well, I can't thank you enough for the suggestion."

"After talking to Henry, I think he's quite under control tonight, although I wouldn't want him to drink too much. He's on his second scotch."

She smiled. "I'll keep an eye on him. From all appearances, it means a lot to him."

Another man caught Kopf from behind and they began to chat. She started to work her way back toward David when a squat, frizzy-haired man with a pasty complexion and bulging eyes stopped her in her tracks. She tried not to stare.

"Jessica Barrow," he said in a nasal voice. "My name's Arlen Silvers. I'm president of Henry's fan club."

"A Henry Maxwell fan club. I didn't know one existed," she said, trying to ignore his toothy grin.

"Oh, yes, the club has been going strong. I was a big fan as a boy. I took over as president in 1986. Nowadays, with the internet, we've grown leaps and bounds, even though Henry quit acting a long time ago."

"Wow, Mr. Silvers. I can't imagine a fan club would exist after Henry's been out of the limelight all these years. And there are fans?"

"Tons of them, my dear. Some of the older ones have been with him since the beginning, but there's newer fans, grandkids and all. At least five thousand at my last count."

"Impressive. So—what drives folks to be a fan of someone who hasn't acted in decades?"

Silvers grabbed a champagne from a passing tray. "The movies. Henry's work is in a class by itself. Oh sure, there was Hammer Studio and Vincent, but Henry was king in my mind, where realism made the film, and of course, *blood*…lots of it."

She sensed the conversation moving away from her comfort level, wanting nothing more than to find a way to ditch him without being obvious. "Blood, yes," she said, startled as the word fell out. She felt uncomfortable talking to the squat man. His voice came across frightening, his ogre eyeballs intimidating.

"His films were the balm for the country back then. Kennedy, Cuban missile crisis, voting rights, Vietnam, you name it, the sixties, what a decade it was. The movies were strong medicine for a weak society."

She needed to change the subject. "Fascinating. Do you stay connected with Henry?"

"Oh, indeed. He hasn't been forgotten and he's gaining fans daily."

"That's wonderful."

Silvers took a sip of champagne. "I don't want to prod, but I understand you are an attorney working as conservator for Mr. Maxwell. I applaud you."

"Well, thanks. I believe we're making progress."

"The films, Ms. Barrow. They're the key."

She heard voices raised. She glanced over, Maxwell roaring, arms flaying. Her chance to escape. "If you'll excuse me, Mr. Silvers, I better check on Henry. Part of my job now as conservator."

"Don't let me keep you from your duties." He bowed.

Taking advantage of her opportunity, she rushed over to where Maxwell was berating Donald Appleton.

"The lean budget, barely enough to finish," Appleton groaned. "I'm quite convinced if we had more resources, *Chasm of Blood* would've broken records."

"Resources, hell!" Maxwell bellowed, becoming belligerent and waving his hand, spilling his scotch. "Global provided the same funding for that film as others, yet—and I do emphasize 'yet'—those other films did twice the business."

Appleton's face grew ruby red. "Then that's a point of disagreement."

He shook his head. "Oh, no, it's not. The movie fell flat, and if I must be so bold, your directorship lacked ingenuity. Marina Farley, the young actress who played Mary. You couldn't keep her character alive. I thought she had the talent, but you failed to light a fuse under her feet to get it out. Yes, I blame the director—and Donald, sorry to say, that's you!" He placed a finger tight against

Appleton's chest and pushed to drive his point home.

"Debbie, we're leaving. Our host doesn't have any manners."

"Oh, Debbie, Debbie," Maxwell said as if nothing had happened. "I apologize for ignoring you, after all these years. Must be tough living with this man. His retirement hasn't helped his disposition."

She glanced at Maxwell with disgust and pulled away. Appleton took her by the elbow and turned to leave.

"By the way, Debbie. You used to have the best set of knockers in Hollywood, but looking at you now, it appears your tits are drooping like a bloodhound's ears."

A chorus of gasps erupted from those nearby.

Both Appletons rushed through the crowd straight for the door.

"Oh, and thanks for coming," he laughed hysterically.

She couldn't believe what she just witnessed. David came over after hearing the commotion. "Did I just hear—"

"You did." "Do me a favor and give Mr. Appleton and his wife our deepest apologies. Lie to them, tell them Henry takes medications that sometimes affect his personality."

He nodded and went to find the couple.

She stared at Maxwell. All conversation ceased. Pulling next to Henry, she announced loudly to the crowd, "I think it's time we all sat down and enjoyed some mouthwatering barbeque."

"Brilliant idea," he beamed, back to his normal jovial form. "Everyone, please meet my new roommate, Jessica Barrow. Sweet young thing, attorney extraordinaire."

Embarrassed, with all eyes on her, she tried to assure the guests. "I don't think Mr. Maxwell meant any disrespect to Mr. Appleton and his wife."

"The hell I didn't," he responded. "That dick and his dime-store wife deserved it."

"Really, Henry," Doss Millikan, a former screenwriter said. "They didn't ask for that shellacking. You were part of that film just as much as Donald."

"Doss. I'm surprised you came tonight. Didn't know you had any friends."

Another murmur came from the crowd. Some began to leave.

Jessica witnessed the world crumbling around her.

"Oh, come now, folks," he said. "The night's still young. I'm sure I can pop a few more insults." He raised his glass in a toast. "How about it? Anyone else game?"

"You've lost my respect," a man from the diminishing crowd said.

"Well, now, Lars. If you have a problem with me, write it up on a sheet of paper and stick it up your fat, sorrowful ass!"

Jessica reached over and took Maxwell's glass. She couldn't believe what had happened. Something that started out so encouraging had turned into a disaster in the span of a few minutes. Most of the guests were now gone, having moved quickly off the veranda. She looked for Tom Caswell and Dr. Kopf. They were no longer present. Out of the corner of her eye, she caught Arlen Silvers slinking away.

David came running. "What the hell is going on?" he asked.

She was close to tears. "I've been so wrong about

him. He's a loose cannon, unfixable."

A voice boomed across the terrace loud and clear.

"Play some more Bach, will you," Maxwell shouted to the quartet.

The four young musicians, all women, transfixed with shock, began to play with no audience left. The looks on their faces were as sad as their music. Maxwell approached the caterer and picked up a plate. "How about some brisket with a kick of salmon? No sense letting this fancy feast go to waste."

Jessica buried her face in her hands, wanting to crawl into a hole.

Chapter 28

The next morning, Jessica stormed downstairs and found Maxwell in the breakfast nook, hands clasped around a cup of coffee. Time to let him have it with both barrels. "You do have a way with words, don't you?" she said, crowding in front of him, bitterness escaping her lips.

Maxwell's face peeked up. "Not sure what got into me. Must have been one scotch too many."

"Same excuse you gave for the tavern fiasco. I'm not buying any of that anymore. I thought it would be beneficial for you to reacquaint yourself with old friends and colleagues. Instead you have a flair for blowing things up beyond repair. If you continue along this road, I can't but wonder where this will end. Have you given that any thought?"

"It's not important."

"Not important? You're on the brink of a mental breakdown in the eyes of the court. Do you understand? They won't go easy."

He paused, not responding.

She shook her head in disgust. "How does a grown, mature man's mind work, can you tell me that?"

"Oh, don't give me that. I'm sure your father made bad decisions when you were growing up."

She struggled with an emptiness in her gut. "My father died when I was quite young. I don't think I had adequate time to know him."

Maxwell stared at his coffee cup, hands fidgeting. "Didn't mean to pry. Sorry."

"Pulling up my stakes here is a possibility. Then, you'd be on your own, and at the mercy of a merciless court. That's what you've been wanting all along. You may get your wish, and what future you have left will not be my concern."

He shrugged.

"I've been talking to Dr. Kopf."

He raised an eyebrow. "Last night, did you have him dissect me?"

"No, I just got off the phone with him before I came down. I told him what happened, and yes, he did some dissecting. Too bad it wasn't a full-fledged mental takedown."

Maxwell's smirk dissolved. "He's a washed-up shrink."

"That's your opinion. He did agree with you on one thing. A drink too many on top of battling depression may have given you the 'what the hell' effect. In other words, one insult leads to another, and another, and another because they feed your ego, make you the top of the world. Is that the case?"

"Who cares? Good to allow those bastards from the early days in on the facts. They screwed up a lot of things."

"And you're so perfect? Really? You've become out of control, defensive. Tom Caswell agrees."

"They're both fruitcakes, foolish sonsabitches, both of them."

She felt a sudden shift in his attitude. No sense stretching him any further. She stepped back. "When and

if you decide to grow up, you let me know. Otherwise…"
She turned and walked out of the room.

Maxwell took another sip of coffee.

Later that night, Jessica sat on the veranda in shadow, contemplating the stupendous mess Maxwell had caused. What was he up to with such habits? All her psychological training had run into roadblocks. Dr. Kopf may have come the closest to understanding his bizarre behavior. Not that any theory at this point made any sense.

Although it wasn't a nightly ritual, it happened two or three times a week. Sitting in a chair hidden in shadows, she watched as the foyer door swung open, an outside light illuminated, and Maxwell emerged, flashlight in hand. He strolled across the veranda, tapping his cane on the hard surface. She checked the time. 11:47. Within a couple of minutes, he stepped down into the garden and crossed the expanse of grass and flower beds, disappearing into the trees on the far side.

With promises made to him, she would never interfere with his affairs or spy on him. But after his defiance and ill-mannered, embarrassing performance last night, she had reason to go back on her word. She straightened up, rose from the chair, took a few steps, then hesitated. As much as she prided herself on keeping her word, this evening she wouldn't restrain herself. He'd lost all favors that were granted, with his antics.

She skipped down the steps and walked across the gardens and entered the grove of trees. Exiting on the other side, the sparse cloud cover reflected the eerie glow of the statues from the urban light bounce in the Los Angeles Basin. What she didn't expect—the rolling fog that started to engulf the bases of the statues. She could see it rise from the canyon and float up over the edge onto the agora. A chill ran down her spine. And why not? She was spying on the old king of horror and now found herself in his domain. What's next, a misty graveyard, bats flapping, blood-curdling screams? Attempting to relax, she knew coastal fogs in California were quite common in the drier summer months.

Or did she?

The fog kept rolling in, not rising too high. The tops of the statues were all visible. Not seeing any sign of Maxwell, she walked along the line of mythical gods, keeping her wits. Halfway down, she advanced stealthily past the old greenhouse, avoiding it as there may be more feral cats that would shriek if she were to disturb them, thus alerting him to her presence.

She froze, thinking she heard a voice drifting in the night air. Spotting a gap in the trees, she walked toward the precipice, the fog staying with her. The voice came and went, rising in volume with each step. The trees and shrubs thinned, and then the lights of Malibu stretched along the coast. Straight ahead, she spied an observation deck and Maxwell sitting on a bench. It appeared he was talking to someone.

She adjusted her stance, staying immobile. After a couple of minutes, she shifted and stepped on a twig. A loud snap. Whirling in a panic, she rushed back through the gap.

****

Maxwell's throat tensed into oblivion at the sound. He spun around and zeroed in on the path. Anger overtook the joy he was experiencing with his beloved.

Someone had followed.

He felt violated.

Jessica!

His clothes no longer felt tight and the arthritis in his legs returned. He turned back to face Lillian. She was no longer there.

And then the tears flowed, rivulets of sorrow, forever washing away the haunting rhapsody of his miserable soul.

Chapter 29

David Grovene arrived in Victorville a little after dusk. Less than two minutes later, Dart Darling ushered him into a chair in front of the big picture window. He waited for his desert friend to finish threading the film in the outside projector. "I'd offer you a Mr. Beam," Dart said, returning, "but I think we better both have our wits during this screening."

"No bourbon? This must be serious. You never really told me what this is about, but I'm sure I'll be enlightened," David said.

"Hang onto your hat. This is one helluva a ride."

He raised a brow.

"After seeing what happened to poor Eddie the other day and what you're 'bout to see, I feel as if my brain has been stomped on, like in one of those wild-ass Kung Fu movies." He sat down and picked up the remote. "This first Maxwell film is one named *Dark Stairs*. I will only show one scene, not too long, only a minute or two. I am sure you'll recall it since you're a buddy with one of Hollywood's former elites." He winked at David, pushed a button and the massive white rock burst into a shining beacon, and action ensued. After a couple of minutes, he turned the projector off.

"Remember that one?"

"Yeah, I was a kid when I first saw it. Mutilated decaying body, beyond pure Gothic horror, not typical

Maxwell."

"From Gothic to slasher genre in one clean swoop. Give me a minute." Dart went outside, changed reels, returned. *"The Sins of San Rafael* is a little more graphic."

He sat and watched. He took a deep breath. "How could I forget? I almost lost my admiration for Henry Maxwell then. Can't figure out what drove him to stray from his normal, literary Gothic horror genre. Most sadistic scene I'd ever seen him in, way too much slasher."

Dart rewound the reels. "Two scenes, two films. Terrifying, sickening, not the good old Henry."

"You're trying to tell me something. I'm still in the dark."

He fumbled for a word, then said, "Hell, I need a drink. Care for one?"

David declined. "Still got to drive home tonight."

He pulled a bottle off the shelf and poured a shot. "Here's to Jim," he said, polishing it off in one gulp. He walked over to a table and picked up a couple of articles clipped out of the newspapers. "Take a look at these."

David took his time reading them one by one. "Unbelievable! I remember them now. When I first saw stories, I just thought of another Manson-inspired killer, someone doing butchery. This is fucking unreal. Excuse my French."

"Damn, you know foreign languages as well. One well-rounded professor you are." Dart cracked a smile. "Not until I read about the last gruesome murder yesterday, the one at the old mission, did I put two and two together."

David stood, pacing in a circle. After a while, he

said, "Rotting corpse, two slashed bodies in the first scene and the hanging woman in the other with a slit throat. Do we have a copycat killer, mimicking those movie scenes?"

"We could, but let's stop a second. Compare the real murders with the movie ones. Can you see a connection?"

He thought a moment, then rolled his eyes. "What am I missing?"

Dart twisted his head. "Location, Professor, location, location. The slayings were committed at the same locales as the slaying scenes in Maxwell's movies."

He shook his head trying to shake the images, not wanting to believe what he'd seen and heard. "You've got to be kidding me?"

"Nope, I ain't. Identical to a T."

"For what purpose? Is the killer enthralled with Maxwell and gets his jolly's off by mimicking parts of the movies at the same locales where the scenes were…"

"Or?"

"Or what?"

Dart again twisted his head. "You said Maxwell was depressed. He flipped. Is he the killer?"

David remained silent for a moment. "No, I don't think—" He stopped mid-sentence. "He's an old man. Why now—how?"

Dart didn't say anything.

"I mean, yeah, he's a little off. Jessica and I had a strange Twilight Zone moment the first time I met him, but I can't imagine…"

"What? Finish your damn thought, Professor."

He slumped back into his chair. "We're assuming a

lot here. These could be murders from two different perpetrators. We don't know for sure it's the same person. Pass me a drink."

Dart poured two more bourbons. 'Hey, weirder things happen. Only a few years ago, a man killed several people in their own homes by wearing a hockey mask, mimicking Freddie Krueger in the film *A Nightmare on Elm Street*."

David felt a hollow unease in his gut. *And Jessica is living in that sinister old castle.* He shook the thought from his head. He stood up suddenly. "I got to go."

"You worried about the girl?"

"Wouldn't you, after what you've just told me?"

Dart nodded. "I won't keep you any further, Professor. One thing, though, there's a third film titled *The Chains*."

David's eyes grew wide as his mind slid into a mental fissure, his stomach churned and sweat slicked the back of his neck. "Oh, man!"

"All three films have been called *The Trilogy*."

"Are you thinking what I'm thinking?"

"Not to be the harbinger of bad news—but could that one —be next in line?"

"That's not comforting."

Dart rubbed his arms and grimaced. "Man, I'm sweating Jim right now."

"Do you have that film?"

He nodded.

"I might have missed that one as a kid. Don't tell me about it. I don't want to know right now."

"By the way, I have more information that might be helpful."

"What's that?" David said, searching for his car

keys.

A smile came across Dart's face. "The movie you're looking for, *Lady Julia's Sarcophagus*. I did some investigating. I never located a copy, but I learned something interesting."

David's hollow feeling diminished. "I've been thinking about that."

"I checked with another one of Eddie's contacts, a fellow out of New Jersey. I asked him if he'd ever heard of the film. He told me something he shouldn't have."

"Don't keep me in suspense. I'm getting used to your bombshells."

"Guy in New Jersey got an email a while back from Arlen Silvers."

David thought a moment. "Yeah, he runs Maxwell's fan club. I saw him at the party from the far side of the moon the other night."

"You need to tell me more about that. Sounds like an affair to end affairs."

"I'll do that when you have more bourbon to get rid of. I never got a chance to talk to him. Jessica did."

"You should have," Dart said, smiling. "Silvers put out a feeler about a Maxwell film that was never released, looking for a buyer. First estimates, it could be worth tens of thousands."

"And the film?"

"*Lady Julia's Sarcophagus*."

"Are you sure?"

"New Jersey sent me the e-mail correspondence he had with Silvers, who said he had in his possession a copy of an unknown unreleased Maxwell film, *Lady Julia's Sarcophagus*. Unless there's another strip of celluloid, and I doubt there is, that should be evidence enough."

"Dart, my old friend, what would I do without you?"

"Just keep me in mind when you become famous hanging out with those Hollywood types."

Chapter 30

Early the next morning, David called Detective Brown, who he learned was in charge of the investigations for the gruesome murders at the abandoned building in Malibu Canyon and the Mission San Miguel de Nuevo España.

"What are you trying to tell me, Mr. Grovene?" Brown asked after learning of David's credentials.

"I'm not implicating Henry Maxwell as a suspect. Those homicides I read about in the papers were committed at the exact same locale as those in the films. There appears to be a copycat killer mimicking the killings from these sixties movies."

A long silence, then, "No kidding?"

"One hundred percent."

"It would be helpful if you could come to the station and give us a full accounting."

"I have something to do this afternoon. Would this morning work?"

"The sooner, the better,"

David hung up and wondered if he was doing the right thing.

After meeting with Brown and offering what he knew about the two Maxwell films, David knocked on the door of the tan brick house which blended in with the sea of thousands of lookalikes in this modest West Los Angeles neighborhood. The small weedy front lawn of

Bermuda grass needed tender loving care as did the fronds from a date palm, hanging wilted and broken over the roof eave at the corner of the house.

Why hadn't he thought of this before? After the party from hell at Henry Maxwell's castle, he wished he'd spoken to Arlen Silvers after Dart said he may have the only copy of *Lady Julia's Sarcophagus*. Did the fan club president have anything to do with Yaz's murder? A trail of death seemed to relate to this rare Maxwell film. Maybe he should have contacted Detective Hardrick about the e-mail. Right now, he would try and get a feel for this individual.

After another knock, the door opened. Silvers himself, recognizable from the other night. David ignored the frown.

"Mr. Grovene," he said in his languid voice. "Won't you come in."

He stepped inside. "Thanks for seeing me. Sorry we didn't have a chance to chat the other night."

"Quite the night. I assume Henry has come back down to earth after exploding all those insults. So unlike him. They need to adjust his meds."

"Not sure why it went downhill."

"You're curious about the fan club. Very understandable. Let me show you around my pride and joy."

He followed Silvers through a small foyer, across a dull and colorless living room and down a set of stairs leading to the basement. The walls of the stairwell were lined with blood-red velvet wallpaper. At the bottom, Silvers flicked a switch. In the low-ambient light, they walked along a dark-blue corridor with life-size cutout images of Henry Maxwell as different characters from his movies, all illuminated by up lighting. Entering a larger room, plastered with old movie posters, each created for a Maxwell film. Standard 27 inches by 41 inches, framed and protected with non-glare glass. He moved down one wall, taking in the vintage artwork. First one, *Once Upon a Nightmare* costarring Byron Gibson and Tiffany Cobb. Next, the classic *Ancient Eyes*, with the sinister orbs of an otherworldly pharaoh holding a knife across the throat of a beautiful but terrified modern-day woman. Below the image, Color by Technicolor in fine print as if to make a point that gruesome scenes in color would convey to the senses more realism than black and white. He recalled that film being an answer to *The Mummy* with Boris Karloff, shot decades earlier. On and on, each poster brought back memories. He'd seen most of them.

"There's not a single poster from Henry's films that I don't have displayed here."

"I see that."

He followed Silvers into another room. Surprised, he found himself in a small theater. Plush recliners faced a movie screen covering the back wall, a projection booth next to the door. David couldn't help but glance at the vintage popcorn machine in the corner.

"I have a 35 mm projector. On occasion, I will show the artistry that Henry Maxwell has left us. To those that have an interest."

"Of course."

They entered another room, reminiscent of a museum. Original props, some on tables, others hanging from the walls, filled the space. Silvers pointed to a mass of surgical-looking tools. "From *The Mortician*, a scalpel and this beauty." He picked up a thick needle-like tool.

"This is called a trocar, inserted into the organs to relieve gas buildup. You do remember it being an important prop in the film?"

"The dead man it was used on wasn't dead."

Silvers' lips twisted into a creepy smile. "Yes, quite lovely." He moved on pointing out other props, a nemes, or pharaoh headdress, from *Ancient Eyes* and a full-size coffin from *The Pillars of Hell* propped up in a corner. Items of death became clear in David's mind. Seeing these on the big screen—and now, in the flesh, brought forth a whole new meaning—and on a different level. Exiting the room, they returned to the display of posters.

"I'm putting together an evening with Henry Maxwell as the star in a venue that would coincide with Cinecon next year. That's assuming he would be willing to be the guest of honor. Proceeds to go to charity, of course. "I've seen this done with Vincent Price. Don't know why we can't do one with Henry."

"I hope it's successful."

"Time will tell."

David saw an open door to his left. He looked in, a desk, a computer and some file cabinets.

"That's where I do the business for the fan club," Silvers said.

He nodded, staring at another assortment of posters on the right side of the door. The first showed a series of stairs descending into an aphotic abyss, *Dark Stairs*. He checked the next one, *The Sins of San Rafael*. A third film, *The Chains* completed the trio. He took a step back. For the oddest moment, he felt unnerved. These were the three films Dart had called *The Trilogy*. The two scenes he showed came from the first two movies. A sudden tremor resonated from his shoulders to his knees. He swore Silvers' breathing warmed the back of his neck. Shaking off an indication of unease, he spun to face the squat man. Their eyes met.

"Something wrong?" Silvers asked, testing David. "Those are some of Henry's greatest works."

"No—no, nothing. Just trying to recall them." He turned back to the posters, attempting to steady his drifting thoughts. Three films, glorifying the slasher genre that became popular in the seventies and eighties, a direct departure from the Gothic horror that defined Henry Maxwell's career. He studied the squat man. "A definite change from his more notable work, don't you think?"

Silvers looked offended. "Why do you say that? They possess the essence of evil, making Dracula look like an altar boy. Evil has no boundaries when time is involved. It continues, woven in the DNA of these fantastic characters."

"They were out of character. They're not what made Maxwell. It's his Gothic roles that got him recognized."

Silvers became animated. "So what! Isn't it the scare-factor that's important? Pure, unadulterated evil!"

David nodded, taking a step back. "In my opinion, that's not what movie goers remember about Maxwell."

With a cold, deliberate smirk, Silvers continued. "The blood splatter here is much more potent."

"I appreciate your passion for all of Maxwell's works, but there's one film that never got released. *Lady Julia's Sarcophagus*. What do you know of it?"

Silvers' facial expression turned to stone. His body language indicated the end of the interview. "Nothing, sorry." He hustled for the stairs.

David pressed him. "You're president of the fan

club. Maxwell himself must have mentioned this one to you and you know his history better than anyone. You know about every movie he starred in."

He became agitated. "I said I never heard of it."

And then a wild thought thundered into his brain. "I've information a man in Sacramento may have ties to the film. I guess that's my next stop."

Silvers' face grew pale.

David walked past Silvers and started up the stairs heading for the front door. *He's rattled*. He turned and extended his hand. "I really appreciated seeing your meticulous collection. Good to see Maxwell's fan club alive and well."

Silvers ignored his hand.

David thanked him again and left. Walking toward his car thinking, *what is it with this one movie that keeps me involved in police business?* Yes, he should talk to Hardrick…later.

Chapter 31

Sergeant Detective Stanley Brown sat at one side of the table, Detective Tony D'Angelo to his left, Henry Maxwell across from them, a blank look on his face as if in a daze. D'Angelo, ready to plow ahead, known as the Grand Interrogator of the Lost Hills Substation, reputed to be able to coerce a confession at least eighty percent of the time. Smooth-shaven, bulky, five-foot-seven at best, no evidence of emotion in his sapless expression. Today he wore out-of-style pleated Dockers, a wrinkled white shirt with rolled-up cuffs, and a loose red tie. Maybe his lack of fashion helped keep suspects off guard. One glance at him and the unsuspecting would think he'd be a walk in the park. Brown shook his head, waiting for the fireworks. He felt sorry for Henry Maxwell, still in a gray robe over satin pajamas. On closer examination, he didn't appear engaged. D'Angelo loved playing good cop, bad cop. And it wasn't hard to figure out which one he excelled at.

"Now, Mr. Maxwell," D'Angelo began, "this session is being recorded, video and audio, just in case this goes to court. Do you understand?"

He nodded.

"Do we also understand, you do not wish to remain silent and have counsel present?" Brown asked.

He raised his head. "I've been arrested, so what of it?"

The Salvation of Henry Maxwell

"Let the record indicate you've declined both offers." D'Angelo checked his watch. "It's 2:34 in the morning. I'm sure we'd all like to complete this as soon as possible, so let's not dally. Okay with you, Mr. Maxwell?"

He didn't respond, rubbing the bags beneath his eyes.

"Do you understand why you're here, Mr. Maxwell?" Brown asked.

"You tell me," he grumbled.

D'Angelo shook his head. "No, that's not how this works. You tell us, Mr. Movie Star. You tell us about these two films you starred in back in the sixties." He glanced at a yellow legal pad on the table. "*Dark Stairs* released in 1964. Remember? And, um, let's see, *The Sins of San Rafael*, released in 1965. Another creepy film?"

"Must have been before you were born, Tony. What are you, fiftyish?"

D'Angelo stared at Maxwell; his eyes magnified by the thick lenses on his glasses. "Forty-six, if you think that's important. Now, do you believe in reconnecting, Mr. Maxwell?"

Maxwell cocked his head at Brown.

"Just answer the questions, Mr. Maxwell," Brown said.

"Do you like reminiscing about old times, about old memories that take you back?" D'Angelo continued. "Do you imagine yourself reliving those times of film, fame, and the red-carpet premieres? It must have been quite a high. And all the mental stress you're experiencing, the depression that dogs you. Looking back over your recent arrest, I see you seem to have turned in a magnificent performance at a local hangout. Scared the living shit out of the patrons. What the hell would an eighty-five-year-old man be doing late at night out and about?"

"Is there a law against getting a drink, Tony?"

D'Angelo leaned forward, picked up the yellow note pad and prodded Maxwell's arm with it. "Really, Mr. Movie Star. Too much to drink, and at your age to go barroom carousing. According to the bartender, you had one scotch, never took a sip of the second one. Low tolerance for alcohol? I doubt that. You're old Hollywood, boozers all of you, back in the day."

"Cut to the chase, Tony," Maxwell demanded. "You're beginning to wear on me."

"The old olive press building, north end of Malibu Canyon. Three dead and mutilated bodies. Why'd you do it, Mr. Maxwell?"

He gave D'Angelo a troubled, surprised look.

"A tit for tat, didn't miss a thing in *Dark Stairs*, although this time the bodies weren't actors. The first body, a lure, maggots pure genius, just like in the movie."

He took a deep breath, wheezed when he exhaled.

"Where'd you procure the maggots? You sure used a lot of them, hundreds of the slimy little bastards."

"I don't have a clue what you're talking about."

"You don't, do you? Then explain how the four cardboard bait cans from Clem's Bait Shop in Santa Monica ended up in a storage room outside your motor court. We've checked around, Mr. Movie Star. Do you fish?"

"No," he said.

"We visited Clem's," Brown added. "Maggots as

bait aren't popular this time of year. But they did remember selling the cans three days before we discovered the murders in the extraction building."

He didn't respond.

"Stress is a powerful elixir," D'Angelo said. "It can make you do things you wouldn't think to do. We've learned a little bit about things you've seen, hallucinations you've had. Has that been the case?"

Maxwell's lower lip quivered. "What the hell would I know? I've lived too long to care anymore."

"Have you ever been back to the old Mission San Miguel de Nuevo España? Damn, I hope my Spanish is correct." He looked back at the notepad.

"I don't remember."

"Oh, please, Mr. Movie Star. Don't insult my intelligence. We have confirmation you've been there a few times in the past, the most recent a couple of days ago according to neighbors in the area, so don't tell me you don't fucking remember."

He blurted, "Yes, I've been there. I go to clear my head. The owners have allowed me access."

"Clear your head! Two days ago, several hours before the murder, you were there. Later, you visited to replay that sadistic movie. Would you like to confirm that, so we can get this over?"

He stayed silent, his hands fidgeting, his head drooping.

"How'd you find the young girl? Did you stalk her after she got off work serving drinks at the Chumash Resort Casino in Santa Ynez? Sweet Jesus, that's a two-hour drive up 101! Of course, she had to be Chumash, didn't she? Just like in the film. Let's get our details exact. That makes the reconnect so much more dramatic."

"I—I don't…"

"Don't remember?" D'Angelo shook his head. "I'm sure it'll come to you. I don't always remember the drives I've done, sometimes so boring you want to forget them. Pretty, wasn't she? A gorgeous young Indian maiden just like in *The Sins of San Rafael*. You know, I had to relook at that scene two or three times. My understanding is you were an accomplished actor. This killing was a duplicate of the one on film. You're authentic in the movies, authentic in real life. But I'm surprised you could cut the throat of such a beauty in a house of worship, of all places, and drool as her blood paints the floor bright red in front of the altar. Exciting, isn't it?"

"I—I don't…?"

"You don't know, yeah, I've heard that before. You're a sicko, man. You know it, I know it. Why don't you save us some time and tell us why you recreated those scenes? Trust me, it'll make it a lot easier down the road."

"I…said…I…don't…remember…anymore. And if I did, I don't give a damn!"

D'Angelo looked over at Brown and extended a hand. "Stanley, if I may."

Brown reached down under the table and pulled up a transparent Ziplock bag containing two shoes. "These are size ten, a Royale, low-top brown leather sneakers. Top of the line. Mr. Maxwell, are these yours?"

He stared at the shoes. "I have lots of shoes."

"They were taken from your closet," D'Angelo said. "An expensive shoe from my understanding, not your standard sneaker. We had a warrant. He turned the bag around so Maxwell could see the sole. "I won't take them out. Take a look. See the tread, the stairstep design." He placed a photograph next to the shoe. "That's a photo of a footprint in blood. the imprint, same type, stairsteps. Now these shoes were cleaned after you found out you stepped into the blood. But don't worry. We have technicians that can find the tiniest remnants of blood that likely remains. In fact, they are so good they can find dirt that you picked up off the floor of the olive extraction building too. Most up-to-date technology. You weren't watching your steps after you slit the woman's throat, walking willy-nilly across the blood-splattered floor." He shook his head. "Careless, very careless."

****

The room melted into a haze and Maxwell went into a dream—a dream so full of joy and happiness—a dream with Lillian, vivid with sensual smiles and radiating tingles, frolicking beneath the moon, playing hide-and-seek among the statues. He sensed her tenderness, her gentle touch that would greet him after a trying day. But it was on set, his films that kept overriding this sweetest of dreams. Films offered security and a wonderful life for Lillian and himself. This man Tony, this sleazy dago, insinuating things about his work, bad things. Maxwell began to sweat.

The old olive building, how can I forget? The bloated body in the cellar, grotesquely rotting, eyeballs resting on his maggot-squirming chest. The director had planned well. Herbert Bass, yes I remember his name. He pulled a coup with the grotesque corpse. I wanted real eyeballs, gleaming and shiny, dripping with vitreous, maybe from some real corpse. No, Herbie called for glass ones, like marbles. His only mistake, in my opinion. Come to think of it, Herbie died several years ago. A fantastic director, eyeballs or not. I must say that scene outclassed Vincent Price's Morella. *Oh, we had such positive competition, Vincent and me, all in good fun.*

And the two innocent intruders showing up unexpectedly. What a wonderful addition in the script. Two young people...a full life ahead for both. Their presence added so much to the scene. If only Herbie had given me better direction with such simple butchery. Still, it wasn't bad.

And what else did that dago Tony mention, a young woman hanging by her feet, blood dripping on the floor like a koshered lamb? Was I not there a while back, the old mission? The high roof beam where the rope hung, how did I ever get it up there without help?

He shook his head, touched his chest. *No pain yet.* Tears materialized.

But no matter. This was a Saturday matinee for kids. The audience craved more; they always did. And she was naked, of course. Screw those PG ratings. The teenagers loved it. Why not, I was magnificent. The second take is always the best. Practice makes perfect.

Maxwell sighed, relegated himself from his dreams and wiped his mouth. He looked up from the floor. "So, Tony, what is it you want from me?"

D'Angelo stood up and slammed the notepad back down on the table. "Why the hell did you do those sadistic pieces of surgery? And the young woman. For God's sake, man! Do you like to reconnect at the expense of living, breathing human flesh? Is that how your warped old mind now gets its jollies?"

Maxwell grabbed the notepad, tossing it back at

D'Angelo, hitting him in the head. His old eyes blazed a tempest. "Why not? Like in the movies, I like to kill! I killed them all. Any other questions?"

Chapter 32

Jessica dug into the oversized fruit bowl, shoving a spoonful of kiwi and strawberries into her mouth, savoring the explosion of flavor just as much as she savored spending a night away from Henry's ghoulish castle. She patted her lips with her napkin and looked across the table at her old college roommate who stared at her.

"It's obvious you needed a break," Heather said, amazed at her appetite.

"Thanks for letting me dump last night. And I still haven't told you all the stories. Too exhausting. It's as if he's an unruly teenager constantly getting into trouble, testing the limits of his parents. And in this scenario, I'm the parent."

"Ground him." Heather laughed.

"If it was only that easy." Jessica played with her spoon, stirring the bowl. "I haven't been able to isolate why he would pull all these shenanigans. He's not dumb, sharp as a tack."

"Well, you said so yourself. He wants you gone."

Jessica nodded. "True, and why I've stayed this long is beyond me. I mean, living in that dark, creepy, stone monster."

Heather took a sip of coffee. "How much longer do you think it'll take?"

"Not sure at this point. I've already been there close

to three weeks. I keep a report of how he's doing on a daily basis. The judge will make the decision. We either continue, or with luck, end the conservatorship."

"My advice, get away from there as best you can, assuming it doesn't interfere with your observations."

"The only saving grace is David."

"Wait a minute. Weren't you as mad at him as you were at Henry Maxwell after the experiences in the secret passageways?"

"At first, but truthfully, he's been very supportive, especially at the catastrophic party for Henry. I don't think I'd have the willpower to keep on if I didn't have him looking out for me."

"Then for your sake, I'm glad he's there. What else about him?"

"Recently, he's opened up."

"Go on."

"Married once."

"Once?"

"Right out of college. He worked in journalism, investigative reporting. She went to law school, where he supported her endeavor. After graduating, she decided they didn't have a lot in common. Bailed, went to Seattle."

"Nasty. Sounds like a leech."

"He wasn't surprised, knowing they weren't the best match. He didn't despair. Figured it was time for a change. Enrolled at UCLA, received his PhD and has been there ever since, last eight years on faculty."

"How'd he end up in your life?"

"Inquired about one of Henry's films."

"A new boyfriend?"

Jessica grinned. "You know me better."

"Way to go, girl!"

Jessica rolled her eyes as her phone pinged. She excused herself after learning it was a Detective Brown from the LA Sheriff's office. During their ten-minute conversation, she learned Henry was in custody, arrested on four counts of first-degree murder. Unbelievable! Would she ever get him and his affairs under control? She felt her blood pressure explode. Brown continued, explaining Maxwell first refused to have counsel present, but after the initial interrogation and a couple of hours to think about it in his jail cell, he gave Jessica's number as his attorney.

He filled her in on all the lurid details connected to his arrest and e-mailed her the pertinent reports filed in the case. She called Marsha to let her know the circumstances. Marsha suggested she assume the role of preliminary counsel as things would move quickly the first few days. Jessica objected, but she was overruled, reminding her of her previous job in Criminal. *Use your experience*, Marsha told her.

Saying goodbye to Heather after explaining her new dilemma, they agreed to meet again in the not-too-distant future. She didn't look forward to what lay ahead. Arriving back at the castle, she gathered her briefcase and made a change of clothes. She took stock of the details provided by Brown, put a great deal of thought to the timeline, did a quick review on bloodwork forensics, and ninety minutes later, raced down the canyon.

She pulled into the sheriff's station in Lost Hills. A deputy escorted her to a small room in the back. Two men stood, introduced themselves as Detectives Brown and D'Angelo.

"Please, have a seat," Brown instructed.

"Thank you," she said, sitting across the table.

"Thanks for coming, Ms. Barrow. I believe I filled you in on all the important details this morning, including the shoe prints, so we won't rehash them unless you have some questions. We've already interrogated Mr. Maxwell. However, earlier this morning, he asked to have counsel present, as he says he has thought long and hard about what he has submitted."

"We have his statement on record," D'Angelo added. "He has been given all legal rights afforded a suspect."

"May I see it?" She looked at Brown. "From what you're telling me, he admitted guilt to the four counts of homicide you described."

D'Angelo pushed several sheets of paper over. "Look at the last page of his initial interrogation."

Jessica recoiled at the thought Maxwell had committed murder. Pulling up the sheet she read: *Why not! Like in the movies, I like to kill! I killed them. Any other questions?* Jessica took a slow breath as she reread the sentences for the second time. "Oh, brother," slipped from her dry lips. She skimmed the other pages, the similarities of the killings to two of Maxwell's old movies, several forensic photographs. She laid them out on the table. "Well, that kind of sums it up."

A smile came over D'Angelo's face.

She leaned forward. A thought entered her mind. "Have you gentlemen come to any conclusion as to how an eighty-five-year-old man could have accomplished these sinister murders all by himself?"

"We'll get to that, I'm sure," D'Angelo said. "An accomplice is certainly not out of the question."

"If my client admitted to the crimes, did you ask him

why he would do such a thing?"

Brown gave Jessica an eye-popping gaze. He adjusted himself in his chair, his bulk wrapped in a white polo shirt, his armpits stained from perspiration. His eyes were tired. The long night of arrest and interrogation must have taken a toll. Interestingly, D'Angelo appeared wide awake, ready to have an answer for anything Jessica hurled his direction. There was an unforced silence between the two men.

Finally, D'Angelo broke the ice. "Our first investigation was to extract a confession. We were successful. With all due diligence, we have more questions for Mr. Maxwell."

Jessica looked at the detective. "That's good. I would not expect any less from the Los Angeles Sheriff's Department. And don't get me wrong. We all want justice, but I'm also charged with getting the best for my client."

"And we wouldn't expect any less," he said with a smile.

"Fair enough," Jessica said. "Now, for the record, JWB has full authority over Mr. Maxwell's well-being, as conservator as delivered by court order."

"We understand," Brown said.

"JWB handles his financial and daily affairs. He has for several years been suffering from severe depression. Sometimes, he says or does things totally out of character."

"Like murder," D'Angelo broke in with a smirk.

Jessica didn't flinch. "That's a possibility, although I don't believe murder is in his best interest. What I'm saying is, he has been known to cause controversy."

"Why would he do that?" Brown asked.

"Mr. Maxwell has been under duress, affecting his decision-making ability. You mentioned in his interrogation his encounter at the tavern. In your opinion, would that be normal for a man of his age?"

"Maybe not for any age," Brown suggested. "We're aware of his mental state."

"If I read your interrogation report correctly, you had a warrant and arrested him after midnight and interrogated a couple of hours later. That's a lot to happen in such a short time. Because of his mental condition, was it necessary to coerce a confession so fast, and at such a late hour?"

"Procedure, Ms. Barrow," D'Angelo answered. "That's our job."

Jessica took a deep, lung-filling breath. "We in the public appreciate what you do," she said. "And coming from the legal side of protecting the citizenry, we want our law enforcement partners to do it in a manner that gets to the truth. Because of the time at which Mr. Maxwell was interrogated, and considering his duress, I am positive a court of law would not like to find the confession acquired by taking advantage of his diminished mental capacity. Do you agree a fair and partial judge would throw out the questioning if it were proven the subject's judgment at time of interrogation was diminished?"

D'Angelo straightened up in his chair and raised an eyebrow. "Are you suggesting—"

"Yes, I suppose I am."

Brown jumped in. "There was no intent to take advantage of his condition." His eyes connected with D'Angelo's. "We also have the shoe prints. We want the truth as well. The evidence appears to be all here."

She looked at D'Angelo. "You had other questions? How about now? As Mr. Maxwell's counsel, I would like to have him present."

"Now?" D'Angelo didn't look happy.

Jessica nodded with a smile.

"Listen, that might not be wise at this time," D'Angelo said, sitting up straight.

Brown looked at D'Angelo with a frown, then back at Jessica. "I will have him brought up." He rose and left the room. D'Angelo folded his arms and sank back in his chair.

Ten minutes later, Henry Maxwell entered, disheveled and blurry-eyed, wearing an orange jump suit. Brown escorted him to Jessica's right. Maxwell leaned his cane against the table and slipped into the chair. He looked at Jessica with not so much as a hello. Jessica saw anxiety in Maxwell's eyes, something she hadn't noticed before.

"How're you coping?" she asked.

He grunted. "These clowns drug me here in the dead of night. How do you suppose I'm doing?"

She gave him a brief smile, seeing his gruffness hadn't changed. She drifted her gaze back to the detectives. "Let's talk about the warrant. You searched his house and found some maggot bait cans in the motor court. If I understand, you are tying those into the grisly murders at the old extraction building."

"That's correct," Brown said.

"What's the possibility those cans were planted by someone other than Mr. Maxwell?"

"No reason to think that at this time," Brown said.

"For now, then, let's talk about the shoes. How long before forensics confirms the blood on the shoes is from the victim?"

"Within forty-eight hours."

"Could they too have been planted?" she asked.

"His shoes. How do you suppose the blood got there? The prints are proof enough." He pointed to a photograph on the table. "Mr. Maxwell's right shoe and the prints match. That has been confirmed."

"I commend your forensics unit." She looked at Maxwell. "Henry, do you wear those shoes often?"

"If those are mine, I do wear them often. They are comfortable, as I have a high arch, painful at times."

"Do you wear them in public—in other words, would other people have seen them?"

"I imagine so."

"When's the last time you saw them?"

"I don't remember."

She turned her attention back to the detectives. "Again, I am suggesting those shoe prints at the scene might have been planted."

"Oh, please," D'Angelo blurted. "Let's stick to facts here, not theories."

"That's a great suggestion. Let's stick to the facts. Facts lead to the truth. I'm not arguing those aren't his shoes. It would be possible to steal them, prints placed in the blood, and the shoes replaced."

"Not likely." D'Angelo leaned back and folded his arms dismissively.

She continued, "Having read the crime report by Detective Brown, the young woman's body at the mission was discovered yesterday at 10:55 and the crime scene investigated at 12:30. Forensics concluded their on-site work at 2:57 and lab work was completed at 6:25 that evening. They determined the victim was killed at

12:05 am. Coroner indicated death was by hemorrhaging. So the time of death was June 27 in the morning. Examining blood coagulation, drying rate, body temperature cooling rates, stiffening and other postmortem parameters such as putrefaction, they estimated time of death. Did I understand this correctly?"

Brown nodded.

Maxwell rolled his eyes as a sign of boredom.

"So, the victim was killed a little after midnight on June 27. Did anyone ask Mr. Maxwell where he was at that time? In other words, did you gentlemen ask him if he had an alibi at the time of murder?"

Brown shook his head. "No, the evidence points directly to him. And he admitted to the killing."

Jessica gazed over at Maxwell. "Henry, do you remember where you were at midnight, or there abouts, on the night of June 26th and the morning of June 27th?"

He stayed silent, looking intently at Jessica. After a moment he answered. "Usually I walk in my garden, around midnight. It's routine. The most peaceful time of day and night."

"What about that night?" Brown asked. "Same routine?"

"I—I don't remember dates, just most nights."

D'Angelo shook his head. "Nothing new here. Move on."

"Maybe Henry can't recall the date exactly," Jessica ventured, "but I can."

All eyes fell on the woman attorney, except Maxwell's. He seemed to understand where this was headed.

"Ms. Barrow, what could you offer Mr. Maxwell?" Brown asked.

"As you are aware, I have been staying at his house the past few weeks as a requirement of the conservatorship JWB has been entrusted with. I would like to submit into your report that I can vouch for his presence in his garden at the time of the alleged murder of the young woman."

D'Angelo broke into a huge grin. "Really, your word on that. You think the courts will take your word for it without more definitive proof." He looked over at Brown. "Stanley, am I correct?"

"I'd like to hear more from Ms. Barrow," Brown said with a hint of curiosity.

"I would offer the shoes were taken from Henry's closet, prints planted, and returned. Same with the maggot cans. Henry's house is not secure."

D'Angelo shrugged. "Again, highly unlikely."

Jessica gazed into Maxwell's eyes. "I'd like to apologize for spying, Henry, and I know that was your only request. I have watched your comings and goings in the garden. I specifically remember that night. It was the night after your, shall I admit, unforgettable party. Do you remember now?"

Maxwell thought a moment, then nodded.

She gazed back at the detectives. "Now is the time to investigate those shoes a little more."

"Prints don't lie," D'Angelo snidely remarked.

"Henry, why do you use a cane?"

"My left knee is shot, from the accident, and arthritis. Christ, I'm an old man! How else you expect me to get around?"

"Because you have a problem on your left side, is it my understanding you use the cane on your right side, in other words, you hold it with your right hand? Canes are used opposite side of the limb being supported. Is that correct?"

Maxwell nodded.

She pointed back at one of the photographs on the table. "Where are the cane marks in the blood? His right shoe left blood prints." Her gaze bounced between D'Angelo and Brown. "I don't see any circular imprints caused by a cane used by the right hand. Oh, and by the way. Henry's cane is next to him. Why don't you check for blood residue on the tip?"

There was silence in the room.

Maxwell sat quietly in his seat, a slight grin tiptoeing across his face.

Chapter 33

A fiery orange disappears over the edge of the endless sea, a slow, lazy dissolution into the brine. Lady Julia leans back into the golden sling she built around his heart, a rising sun in the crux of his arms. And in that moment of ageless love, the east cliffs of Walton-On-Sea will never be the same.
—BB Barmore,
Lady Julia's Sarcophagus

It was 2:15 in the afternoon, dark in Maxwell's library. Jessica sat in shadow, her cheeks in the palms of her hands, elbows propped on the table.

David sat across from her, hands clasped resting on his abdomen. After hearing about her visit with law enforcement, he could tell she'd been under strain. He suggested an alternate reality.

"What if the young woman's murder happened in daylight?"

She gave him a look of exasperation. "Then I wouldn't be much use as an alibi."

He shook his head. "Yeah, stupid question. I apologize."

A long silence followed. Leaning back, she mused, "Still, no clues on who the real killer—or killers—are. Those two films have become a plague hanging over Henry."

"I met Arlen Silvers yesterday. He loves those movies, close to worships them."

"Why'd you want to see him?"

"For my benefit. My research. He's a strange person. I got quite the heebie-jeebies visiting with him."

"I thought the same when I met him at the party. Couldn't wait to lose him."

David shook his head in frustration. "Sorry, can't believe I still have the energy to continue thinking about my needs and wants with all this murder stuff going on."

"Has to be your nature. Do what you must to keep sane."

"I should put all this on hold. You're the one with the headaches."

She smiled. "I'm glad you noticed."

"Dart and I almost convinced ourselves Maxwell could have been involved, except for his age—"

"Dart?"

"Friend of mine. A great resource on B-movies. He made the connection between the murders and those two films. Similar sadistic scenes, real and make-believe, same locations. And I have a confession to make. Information is critical for law enforcement. I did contact Detective Brown and gave him a statement of facts on the films."

Jessica smiled. "Of course you had to share that with the detective. No apologies necessary. I'm glad you did."

"Thanks."

"Speaking of movies, are you still trying to find—"

"*Lady Julia's Sarcophagus*. I think Arlen Silver knows something. Maybe I should ask Henry for his perspective."

"I don't think he's ready to expose more of his

history—not now. Wait until this blows over, which we hope will be soon."

"Good point."

Jessica's cell phone pinged. She picked it up off the table and answered. After a *Yes* and *I'll be there*, she clicked it off. Looking relieved, she stood. "They've released him on a personal recognizance bond. He's still a suspect, but because of his age and a few details about the shoe prints, they decided they couldn't hold him. They want me to pick him up. I need to bring him some clothes, he only has his pajamas and robe."

David rose. "Need some help?"

She shook her head. "No...no, I'll handle it. I don't think two of us together will help his attitude." She pocketed her phone. "I'll give you a call afterwards."

He pulled her over and gave her a hug. "Be careful."

She nodded with a smile and walked out of the library.

On the drive to the station, Jessica called Tom Caswell to let him know she'd gotten Maxwell out of jail and was on her way to pick him up. He sounded thrilled, thanking her, reiterating he knew Henry couldn't be involved in the killings. Twenty-five minutes later, she picked Henry up at the Lost Hills station. No reporters hounding him. Hard to believe the word hadn't become public like his first arrest. On the way driving back to the castle, no words were exchanged. She waited for him to scold her for spying. The sentence, "How soon can you leave?" would surely come up.

He glared at her with bitter eyes. "I should send you packing for spying on me."

She didn't flinch. "I understand."

"Take 101 up to Point Dume. I want to show you

something."

"Wouldn't it be wise to get some rest? You've had a hard day and night."

"That's for later. Do as I say."

"All right. Give me directions."

Thirty-five minutes later, Jessica pulled off the road at a sign indicating Point Dume State Beach. Several other cars filled the lot. Overlooking the beaches below, the promontory jutted out over steep cliffs. She shook her head in awe, surprised she'd never been here before, a California native and all. For some odd reason, she felt a sense of peace.

Exiting the car, Maxwell trudged along a dirt path sloping downhill. Gulls soared overhead, riding an endless updraft. The unmistaken smell of seaweed and salt drifted up from below where a few people could be seen walking on the beach. She took in a deep breath of the aroma, feeling a renewed connection to her California roots. Shifting her thoughts back to Henry, she hoped he wouldn't trip and fall. He took his time negotiating the rim of the point, leveling out on a lookout. Catalina Island could be seen off in the hazy distance to the south and Santa Cruz to the west. He steadied himself, gazing at the blueness of the Pacific. She came up beside him. Her eyes narrowed in his direction thinking there were deep memories inside his head working free.

After a moment of silence, his voice cracked as he spoke. "Lillian and I used to come here quite often. It didn't matter the time of day or night. I swore Point Dume was made just for the two of us."

"I can see why. It's breathtaking."

His eyes swept the seascape. "We would reminisce

about our times in Greece along the Aegean. She had a great appreciation for classical architecture. She studied it in detail—the proportions, the orders, Ionic, Doric, Corinthian—the very grace of the ancient temples. Right before we married, I bought that behemoth in all its Gothic splendor. I thought she'd like it. She never did, considered the style grotesque. *Pointed arches, really*, she would complain. *All I see is deformity.*" Maxwell shook his head. "Then, her escape, she added the statuary garden and made it her domain. She wanted balance. As time moved on, I learned to appreciate the beauty she created, opposite the coldness of the stark castle."

Jessica swore a slight smile broke on his face.

"Right here, where we stand, always deserted. Never anyone. Not sure why." He smiled. "Maybe others sensed this space belonged to only us love birds." His eyes rolled skyward and took in a deep breath of the salty air, his thoughts drifting elsewhere. Returning his attention, he stared rather pensively straight ahead. Moisture filled his eyes.

She remained silent. He had brought her here for a reason; maybe as a chauffeur, maybe for something else. A rogue wave crashed into the rocks below and chatty seagulls continued to circle the point, catching the updraft. But why here? Did he want her conversation? "I would have loved to have met Lillian."

"Everyone swooned over her. I—" He wiped an eye. "Time doesn't make the pain melt. It only prolongs it."

"Henry," she said, knowing she had never called him Henry before. "I can't imagine the grief of her passing, all these years, but if I can help in any way, I…" She didn't continue.

Maxwell tilted his head. "Good intentions, I

understand. I'm an old man who is prone to plenty of stupidity. I'm not sure why I confessed to the murders in the first place. After a time in orange jail clothing, I realized I wasn't meant for jail. Thank you for spying."

She blushed. "Not my intent. Something kept drawing me to follow. "I'll never do it again."

"Don't ever say 'never.' I'm a firm believer the word 'never' will hinder good things from happening. I'm a prime example of not following my own advice. I quit that word years ago, never should have given up so easily. I think I'm in the mood to reclaim it." He seemed to want to smile again, but instead let his face return to the gloom. He stared down at the ground, tapping his cane once or twice on the hardpack.

Jessica looked up at Maxwell. His moistened eyes said it all. Memories held intense emotions. At the same time, she wiped a tear. No words could convey her heartfelt sympathy.

"I guess you'd better take me home. I'm tired." He started back up the trail.

How ironic this man, at times a rough and tumble character with an unpredictable nature, a man torn by emotion, and a man who could show his grief with ease.

Maybe he was human after all.

Chapter 34

It took Maxwell two hours rummaging through several cardboard boxes he kept in one of the storage rooms off the motor court. How the hell he remembered they were there was beyond his capacity to grasp. Fishing through stacks of photographs Lillian had stored away, he came across what he hoped would be the key to his search, an old polaroid depicting two young men. Dressed in white pants and blue short-sleeve shirts, each held a ribbon with a round silver metal attached, standing in front of what appeared to be a large white wall. On the back of the photo was scribbled the names: Francisco Cuervo, Javier Urruty, 1967.

Francisco had been their gardener, and the one he desperately wanted to track down. After Lillian's death, he disappeared, never to be seen again. That seemed strange at the time, stranger now. The polaroid provided a clue, a sense of hope. To his surprise he recalled Javier as being one of Francisco's friends, and as Maxwell's memory sharpened, he remembered Javier helping Francisco in the garden on occasion. Both men were young, hard workers. Racking his "old man" brain, he remembered they played a Basque form of handball. Javier was Basque. If he could locate him, maybe he could find Francisco.

****

Jessica bent over her laptop in the library, finishing

her weekly report to Marsha. Hearing a shuffling and clicking, she looked up. Maxwell entered, something he'd rarely done when she was working.

"Henry, good to see you. Everything okay today?"

He hobbled over. "I appreciate you driving me to Point Dume yesterday. It meant a lot."

She smiled. "My pleasure. Be glad to do it anytime."

"That would be nice. I want to ask another favor."

A sense of progress swept over her. *A step forward, he's opening up.* "Anything. What can I do for you?"

"I've been looking at old photos that Lillian had packed away, and one got me curious." He dropped the polaroid on the table.

"Who are the two young men?"

"One on the left is Francisco, our gardener when Lillian was alive. The other fellow his friend, Javier."

Jessica flipped it over, saw the names and date. "What's the sport, soccer?

"Not with white pants. It got me thinking. I remember Lillian telling me they played a Basque form of handball. I did a little checking. It's called pelota."

"Pelota. I've heard of that. I can see their hands, all taped up. Makes sense."

"This photo has stimulated my memory. Do you think I could find out where the photo was taken? In the background is a high wall. If that was the handball court, where is it?"

"Is there a reason to find this place?"

He shrugged. "Something to keep me occupied, I suppose.

She smiled. "I guess we start with the Basque community in the area. If this is handball, I can't imagine there would be a lot of places to play, especially back then. Let me do a little investigating."

****

Maxwell hadn't driven this much in at least a couple of years. Now, after negotiating several fast and furious highways, he found himself at his destination. Jessica ably found a location in East Los Angeles called Maravilla, the oldest Basque handball court in the area, still in operation. Another reason his respect for Jessica continued to grow.

Anxious, he parked. Across the street stood a high, tapered brick wall. Stepping out of the Bentley, he waited for traffic to clear, then trod across the street to a breezeway separating the court from a neighborhood grocery store. A few tables and chairs filled the space in what appeared to be a sitting area, where patrons could lunch on deli offerings from the store. He spotted a single man, chomping on a sandwich at one of the tables. Thin, graying hair, and a thick mustache. He wore a white polo shirt, gray twill pants, and sneakers. Maxwell figured he was ten to fifteen years younger.

Walking over, he removed his fedora and said, "Excuse me, do you live in this neighborhood?"

The man looked up, wiped his mouth with a napkin. "Long enough," he said with a deep Mexican accent. "Been here my whole life, no place to go."

Maxwell felt he hit the lottery. "My name's Henry, may I intrude for a couple of minutes?"

The man gazed at the Bentley across the street. "My friend, you are no *pachuco*, although your hat may work, and that's no Chevy Impala lowrider. Not from East LA." Then with a hint of curiosity and a smile he said, "Take a chair, Henry."

Maxwell raised an eyebrow, plopped down, and

placed the fedora and cane on a nearby seat. "And you are—"

"Juan. Try the *jamón* sandwich. Creamy goat cheese, *muy sabroso*."

"Juan, nice to meet you. I might give it a try, but for now, this is the first time I've been in East LA in many years. If I may, I have a question or two: is the handball court still in use?"

"*Si*, yes. Closed for a few years, new owners."

"And they play a Basque form of handball I understand?"

"Pelota. I played a little as a young man." He showed Maxwell his fingers, all like sausages. "That, *mi amigo*, is what the hard ball do to you." He laughed. "I am Basque. Family came here three generations ago, herded sheep in Kern County."

Maxwell studied the man's hands. "Very interesting. Very painful?"

"Why you ask?" he said, taking a bite of sandwich.

"Long story, but I am trying to find the whereabouts of a young man who played here back in the sixties."

"No longer young man, many years ago. What is his name?"

"Javier Urruty, not sure that's how you pronounce the last name."

A smile swept across Juan's face. "Urruty, *si*, everyone know Urruty. Javier, I remember. Very good player."

A streak of good fortune washed over Maxwell, like hitting the gold vein. "That's great. Is he still around?"

Juan's eyes drooped. "No, no. *Esta muerto*."

Maxwell's excitement deflated like air escaping a balloon as he understood a little Spanish. "How did he die?"

Juan noticed the disappointment on his face. "Why you ask?"

"I was hoping he could tell me the whereabouts of one of his friends."

"What is friend's name?"

"Francisco Cuervo. They played as a team in this handball."

Juan finished off his sandwich, took a drink from a bottle of Coca-Cola, and leaned back. "Maybe his sister can remember."

"Javier has a sister?"

"*Si*, Amaya, still in neighborhood."

Maxwell exhaled. *The journey continues*. "Where does she live?"

"You are in luck, Henry. Down the street over there, two blocks maybe, a pink house on the left."

Ten minutes later, Maxwell found the pink-colored ranch-style house with a small grassed yard surrounded by a white picket fence. If he'd known any better, he had passed this house two blocks before he arrived at the handball court. Parking in front, he peeled himself off the seat and walked up to the fence surrounding a colorful flower garden. He noticed a stooped-over woman on her knees spading through a strip of dirt surrounding the front of the house.

Opening the gate, he moseyed over and said, "Excuse me, are you Amaya Urruty?"

The woman straightened up on her knees and gazed at the stranger. "May I help you?"

"I was told down the street you are the sister of Javier Urruty?"

She pushed herself up the rest of the way. "Yes, my

brother, ya know," she said, with a staccato cadence. "Died."

"Sorry to hear."

She gave him a onceover, her brown eyes flooding over Maxwell in a flurry of uncertainty, as if asking why a nice old man would suddenly show up at her small casa in East LA.

"You know Javier?"

"No, Amaya, I never met him. He did have a friend, Francisco Cuervo, that I did know."

Amaya pulled off her gloves. "The sun is hot, come inside. We can talk." She dropped the gloves and walked up to the porch, opened the door. Maxwell followed. "Please, sit," she said, directing him to a sofa in her sparse living room with a gold-crested crucifix prominent on the wall. He sat, removed his hat. She sat opposite in a rocker. "What you want to know about Francisco?"

"He and Javier were handball partners I understand?"

Her tone of voice shifted. "They were friends and partners in pelota, that is all."

Maxwell sensed she was thinking what had been on his mind. "No, please, I am not implying anything else."

She nodded. "I did not approve of their friendship, thinking it would not look good for Javier. I am old; some things never change. I have my faith, ya know."

"I understand. Times do change. My only concern with finding Javier is that he may have had information on where I could find Francisco, nothing else."

"I haven't seen Francisco since Javier died, car accident."

"Sorry for your loss, Amaya, I really am."

"It is none of my concern as to why you look for Francisco, but there is a club down on Santa Monica Boulevard where he had a relationship with one of the workers. I don't remember the name of the club but the man's last name is Stone. Forgive me, *oh, Dios*."

Chapter 35

That evening, Maxwell hobbled up to the entrance, a copper-clad double door with two smoked-glass portholes. Club S.O.M.F., the name proclaimed, in fiery red and yellow on the neon sign. Confident, he opened the right-side door and entered a wide, garish, crème-colored hallway with a faux Louis XIV marble-top console along one wall and a lavishly decorated armchair along the other. Emanating deep within the dive, the techno dance beat rattled his teeth. After catching his breath, he continued down the corridor, the music intensifying.

A man wearing a pair of skin-tight spandex shorts and a white sleeveless undershirt brushed against Maxwell as he raced by. The man stopped on a dime. A distinctive fragrance of cologne filled the air. He lingered a few seconds, gave Maxwell a once-over, then said, "If this was Wednesday, we'd do an O.M.L.F."

"Stunned, Maxwell didn't have anything to say.

The man giggled, rushing out the door.

Gathering his bearings, Maxwell staggered on until he came to an intimate space, elaborately decorated with French provincial furniture. A curved marble reception desk like one found in a fancy hotel occupied the room. A sour-faced man with black hair and a trimmed goatee wearing a tight satin T-shirt sized him up.

"What can I do for you," he asked, with a tinge of

curiosity.

"What's an O.M.L.F.?" Maxwell asked.

The man mocked. "OLD MAN LET'S FUCK! Is that what you came for?"

Maxwell composed himself. "I'm looking for Gilbert Stone."

A slight hesitation. "No one here by that name." He leaned over, whispering, "Sir, this isn't the senior center. Are you sure you have the right place?"

Maxwell propped on the counter. "I understand the business model of this establishment, so, here's the deal. I've been busy all day tracking down this Mr. Stone and this is the one place that keeps popping up every time his name is mentioned. I'm told he works here."

"Sorry, don't know him."

Maxwell checked the admission price of one hundred dollars for non-members, posted on the wall. He pulled out a hundred, and tossed it on the counter. "I will pay for admittance and check it out myself."

The man picked up the bill, and stuffed it back in Maxwell's breast pocket with a smoothing pat. "Sorry, sir, don't think this place is your style. You wouldn't be comfortable romping inside. For your own safety, that is. Trust me, you don't belong here."

Maxwell's temper rose. He stared at the man straight in the eye. "I've been around the block a few times, I'm not naïve. I understand Stone works here, so I suggest you bring him to me." Maxwell reached into his pocket, took out another couple of hundreds, wadded them up with the third and with a flourish and caustic smile, stuffed them under the neckline of the man's shirt.

The man pulled them out, examined them and crammed them in his pocket.

"Lizzy will take you back. Stay with her."

Lizzy walked around the counter, a short figure with a buzz cut, ear and nose rings, covered with a mass of tattoos. Maxwell couldn't discern if male or female. "Follow me, Mr.—" she said with a rather male voice.

"You can call me Henry."

"Henry it is. This way," she said, keeping an eye on her guest, knowing he moved at a snail's pace.

"Tell me, Lizzy, Gilbert Stone does work here, doesn't he?"

She turned her head, smiled. "He does. You must understand Boz back there. He doesn't like strangers, those that don't fit the profile, know what I mean? No offense, but you don't fit the profile."

"Hardly." He sighed.

"No need to apologize. Hey, I'm trans, if that means anything. You find all types here, gays, a splattering of switch-hitters, lots of pans, lezzies of course. Don't act surprised at what you might see in the club."

"Yes, a club, understood."

They exited the corridor into a dance area. Flashing lights and boisterous beat music blared. A seventies-style reflective disco ball spun overhead. Men, he thought, were dancing, barely dressed. Several flat screen televisions were spaced around the room, showing what appeared to be gay porn. Along the perimeter, an assortment of tables were occupied. In the dim light, kissing and stroking took place. A few women dotted the place, lesbians he assumed. Anxiety began to affect him. Patrons stared his direction. Lizzy guided him across the dance floor past a go-go platform. A hairy-chested man with a thin pencil mustache danced, wearing only a see-through G-string. Beyond that, bartenders were busily filling drinks.

She took Maxwell by the arm. "Here, watch your step until we get out of the disco."

He didn't protest. Lizzy seemed to be a nice girl (or guy), not that it mattered. He appreciated the help.

They entered another hallway with several doors along the way. One door was open. Maxwell stopped, glancing inside. Wall sconces defined the scene. Mattresses on the floor, filled with men having their way. Body odor and sex permeated the space. In the corner a sling was hung from the ceiling, where two others were busy with each other. He couldn't tell what, but at this point, didn't want details.

Lizzy came up beside him. "This is the playroom, for those inclined. Not for you, Henry."

"Unlikely." He turned and stepped back into the hallway. "Everything is a go here."

"Everything and anything, busting a nut or two, you know what I mean?" She gave him a grin. "Keep with me, we're almost there."

"By the way, what does S.O.M.F. stand for? Has to be an acronym of some type."

She looked him in the eye. "SOME OTHER MOTHER FUCKER. Does that work?"

"I suppose so."

"If you're into this place, you could call it SIT ON MY FACE. Take your pick."

He was beginning to feel as if he'd gotten too much information. The world had changed. Down another corridor they went, past a booth with a man sitting inside. Lizzy walked up and said, "He's on the house."

The man nodded. "Go ahead."

"Follow me, Henry."

Around a corner they came out in a long room with several doors side by side. Men in various levels of dress, some naked, others with their pants pulled down. Near the door, a table contained bins of condoms and lubricants. Next to each door was a circular hole waist high. An assortment of body parts stuck out of holes. Now, he'd seen too much. He rolled his eyes, trying not to stare. He caught Lizzy looking at him.

"This is the S.O.M.F. Glory Hole. A club, remember?"

He nodded. Never in his wildest dreams would he have imagined how the world had changed. Were sex clubs really this open? Lizzy walked over to the third door and waited until one of the customers had completed his job with wild satisfaction. She knocked on the door. "Someone here for you." A minute later, the door sprang open.

"Go on inside," she said, motioning. "He's all yours. I'll wait. When you're done then, I'll escort you back."

He entered. The cubicle was cramped, no more than four feet by six feet with a narrow bench next to the hole. Gilbert Stone stood in the back of the space wiping his crotch down with a towel. He finished and wrapped the towel around his waist. He was tall, muscular, with a large swirling tattoo in rainbow colors etched on his chest depicting the American Flag. He had a few days' growth of beard and a shaved head.

He looked at Maxwell. "Do I know you?" he said, squinting.

"No, you don't…and I'm not here for any kind of…service."

Stone rubbed his jaw. "No kidding."

Maxwell eyed the bench. "May I?"

The Salvation of Henry Maxwell

Stone nodded, stepped back a bit and propped one foot on the end.

He sat down and leaned on his cane. "I'm here because you can help me find a friend of yours."

"Who would that be?"

"Francisco Cuervo."

Stone's face hardened. "Cisco? Why you looking for him?"

"Years ago, he was my gardener."

Stone straightened up, pointing a finger at Maxwell. A grin emerged on his face. "You're not that old movie star, are you?"

"I suppose so."

"A movie star coming to find me in this shithole. Man, I'm flattered."

"I need your help. I'm hoping you can lead me to Francisco."

Stone dropped his smile. "Why do you want to find him?"

Maxwell took his hat off and placed it on his lap. "Let's say, for old times' sake. I don't recollect having much interaction with him back in those days. I had reasons to think he was, you know, gay, but I never broached the subject. None of my business."

Stone raised an eyebrow. "Do homos frighten you? Maxwell, isn't it?"

"No—no, they don't. I'm an old man, doing my best to cope with a different world. My apologies."

Stone shook his head. "Quite all right."

"My old-man mouth sometimes gets the best of me."

"I understand your dilemma, coming to a place like this. How'd you get my name?"

"From one of Francisco's old friends. His sister gave

me your name."

Stone didn't flinch. "Has to be Javier."

"Yes, Javier Urruty, not sure about the pronunciation."

"Poor bastard. Passed away a while back. Both he and Francisco were good friends, if you get my drift. Yes, Javier, the Pyrenees Pansy, we'd tease."

"You knew them both?"

Stone nodded, stretched and pulled on a pair of Levi's. "Javier not much. Too straight, but Francisco...until—" He shook his head.

"What do you mean?"

"Health issues."

"I don't understand."

"Surprised the hell out of me. Francisco had HIV. That ended our time together."

Maxwell thought better about sitting on a bench in a place like this. He pushed himself up and plopped his hat on his head. "Sorry to hear. How's he doing?"

Stone's face turned distressed. "Not good. Last I heard, he was in hospice care. His HIV veered off into full blown AIDS."

Maxwell felt the air come out like he'd been punched in the gut. Hospice, what else could go wrong?

Chapter 36

The next afternoon, the sun spread a hazy veil across the flatlands of Orange County. Maxwell pulled his Bentley into the parking lot of Lasting Wishes, a residential end-of-life facility in the city of Cypress. He managed to get the address where Francisco was in hospice. Turning off the engine, he shook the edginess that multiplied on the drive. He couldn't remember the last time he'd driven this far from home. A few years at best. My God, he ruminated, how did he keep from getting run over by the zillion cars streaking by on the freeway? The last two days seemed as if he had driven a million miles on his fact-finding trips.

Stepping out of the Bentley, he walked up to the facility, which resembled a long ranch-style farmhouse with wrap-around porch. Maxwell entered a comfortably sized reception area decorated like a country hospitality room. Lots of pig and goose décor, fat-armed chairs and rustic end tables with crocheted doilies like oversized snowflakes beneath several ceramic figurines, a red barn, a tractor and a farmer with pitchfork. An assortment of magazines were spread out over a coffee table. A middle-aged brunette-haired woman behind the counter asked, "May I help you?"

He hobbled over. "I've come to visit a former friend of mine. Told he's here. His name is Francisco Cuervo."

"Yes, Mr. Cuervo is here. When did you last see

him?"

Maxwell lied. "Not more than two years ago."

"I must warn you; he's weak and is in generalized wasting. He cannot lift his arms more than a few inches. You might not recognize him, and because of a series of surgeries, he's had throat cancer. His vocal cords were removed."

He frowned.

"He can communicate by nodding."

"I understand. It's just, like, you know—I want to see him—before, you know."

"Very well." She pushed a button on the intercom and inquired, "Mary, please escort a gentleman to see Mr. Cuervo."

A minute later, a woman wearing a white nurse uniform appeared from down a long hallway. She had a pleasant smile, as this was a place where smiles would do the best good.

She handed him a mask. "Put this over your mouth and nose. It's not for your protection, but for Francisco's."

Taking the mask, he slipped the straps behind his ears.

Mary led the way back down the hallway to a room on their right. "Let me check him first," she said. She entered. A few seconds later she returned. "He's awake. You may go on in."

Nodding, Maxwell thanked her. Next to a wall, a fragile man lay in a hospital bed. He knew even under good circumstances he wouldn't have recognized him. He walked over. This was beyond any of his expectations. Covered with a sheet below his chest, his torso was withered and emaciated to the point his rib cage was exposed, almost skeletal-looking. His brown face was cracked like a sunbaked mud flat, his hair thin and wiry. A stand was positioned behind the bed with a venous IV inserted and taped to the crook of his arm. His eyes strayed to Maxwell, never leaving.

For the briefest of minutes, both men stared at each other. Maxwell said, "Francisco, do you remember me?" He pulled the mask down.

At first, Francisco didn't stir. His eyes rolled around as if thinking out loud, his fingers curled.

Maxwell found a nearby chair, towed it over and sat down. "It's been a lot of years."

A slow nod.

He looked at what remained of a healthy, vibrant hard-working, nineteen-year-old gardener. But that was decades ago. Maxwell came for answers. He wanted nothing more, but that didn't mean rushing him to communicate. Somehow, that young girl, Sam at the library, flicked a switch in his head. The statue of Eros held the key, and whether his former gardener was aware of it or not, the facts had to be discussed. He had no doubt Lillian left him a clue. The man was on his deathbed, and to go to the grave without acknowledging the truth would be a travesty. Maxwell hoped Francisco would want to clear his conscience.

"After Lillian's death, you said you couldn't continue since she died. You said you adored her, would do anything for her. Is that true?"

Francisco lowered his eyes, nodded yes.

Maxwell pulled his chair closer. A constriction tightened his chest. "When they found her, she was with the statues. Did you know that?"

Again, another positive nod.

"She was on the ground, pointing to one of the statues, dying." He came close to breaking into tears, crushed by what he just said.

Francisco straightened his fingers, then curled them again, and tried to lift his arms. Pain flushed from his eyes.

"Do you know which statue?"

Francisco's fingers continued to curl and unfurl.

"She taught you about the gods. She died near one named Eros. Why, Francisco?" He could feel his emotions tearing him apart.

Francisco's withered face tightened, wanting to force the words out, but it was futile. Frustrated, he blinked, sucking hard for another breath.

"Did you and Lillian ever discuss Eros?"

Francisco kept his eyes on Maxwell, nodding.

Would he be able to end those thousands of nights of grief and loneliness? He leaned close, within inches. He remembered Lillian discussing Eros and Francisco in the same vein. "Do you think she was trying to tell me something by dying at the feet of Eros?"

He hesitated, then closed his eyes for a moment, reopened them. They were wet with tears. He blinked once or twice.

Maxwell took a breath and continued, "Did she indicate you by pointing at the statue of Eros?"

There was no hesitation this time. He nodded.

He was so close, yet so far. Eros, one of the Erotes, sometimes associated with same-sex desire, a patron of homosexual love.

"The police report said she died from a drug overdose. Is that correct?" The question escaped his lips.

Francisco shook his head side to side.

In this solitude between two men miles apart, Maxwell felt he was on the cusp of truth. The frustration of not hearing Francisco's voice weighed on him. He gave him a long, hard stare. "How did she die, Francisco?"

He turned his hand and with a trembling finger, pointed at himself.

It was as if Maxwell's vital organs were squeezed through the eye of a needle. He could only grasp at Lillian's time of need, excruciating pain, her insides on fire, a difficult time breathing, stumbling along the agora knowing she was dying, but having the fortitude to leave a message.

"She was poisoned, wasn't she?" Maxwell strained to keep the agony from tightening his throat.

Francisco nodded.

"Did the contents of the syringe kill her?

Francisco's breathing became erratic. His eyes rolled upward, shaking his head back and forth.

He remembered the report and the bag of insecticide found outside the door. "Was she poisoned with insecticide?

He nodded quickly, then relaxed as if in relief.

"Why?"

There was no response, only the drooping of his eyelids.

"Who put you up to it, Francisco?"

He wanted to speak, lips quivering. Maxwell could only imagine he wanted to say who ordered him to do it.

"You must help me. All these years have been a toll on everyone, including you. Please, did she know this person well?"

Nodding, his eyes filled with tears. Exhaustion

overtook his frailty.

"Did I know him as well?"

Another nod.

Maxwell's mind was twisted in a paroxysm of pain like he had witnessed the tragic and horrible death of his beloved Lillian. And in the sterile environment of the hospice room, sweat glistened on the withered man's moribund face, the face of the man who had cruelly taken Lillian's life.

Francisco stared back; his teary eyes hinted at a deep request. He wanted to talk if only he could.

Forgiveness? No, he wasn't asking for that.

Compassion? Way too late for that.

Mercy? No *mercy*.

Justice? He was begging for *justice*! In a fit of agonizing suffering, Francisco curled his left hand and pointed to the IV port in the crook of his arm. His chest puffed up. His eyes strayed, his breathing wild and volatile, pleading to have the sentence carried out.

In one, smooth, irrational motion filled with mounting rage, Maxwell reached over the rails of the bed and pulled the needle out of Francisco's arm and let it dangle, drops of fluid dripping on the floor.

For a minute, he gazed at his former gardener with no pity. The pallor on his face was now transforming into a living corpse. His former gardener stared back and with what energy he had left, mouthed a thank you. With that he took a deep breath, eyes rolled to the ceiling, and in the solace of the room, relief etched upon his face.

With his hand clasped over the crown of his cane, Maxwell walked out the door, and never looked back.

Chapter 37

Maxwell shuffled along the Venice Beach boardwalk on a bright and sunny "good to be alive" afternoon, realizing he was out of place alongside the zillion tourists, throngs of skateboarders, rollerbladers, young men flexing their shirtless muscles and women in skimpy bikinis flaunting their attributes, zipping in a *see me, I'm special* manner.

His head still reeled from his visit at the hospice. Why Francisco? Whoever had put his gardener up to the task had a familiarity with the statuary garden. He searched his memory banks. A host of friends had visited the promenade of statues when Lillian held functions among the gods. A few garden parties, teas, a couple of weddings—that is all he could remember. But who would have wanted her dead?

At his age, he wondered how he could keep going, after decades of shunning the masses. He recognized the fact that he needed to get away from that horrendous pile of ancient stones he had called home for so many years of his life. Venice wasn't a prime location to spend time if the prerequisite was just to get out of the house. Fantasy land. The real world buried itself somewhere between here and there. He'd already seen a Malibu tavern, a gay sex club, and an end-of-life facility. Maybe Venice was California on steroids.

Come to think of it, why should he be out of place?

Jugglers, fortune-tellers, musicians, break-dancers, and street magicians filled the walkways. Performers, all of them. Why not a decrepit old movie star with a cane, wearing an overused fedora? He smiled. He hadn't been recognized in years, why would he be now? And if they did, he wouldn't give a rat's ass.

After several minutes, he hobbled off the boardwalk. To his right, a small park with a path circled between palm trees and cool grassy areas. He passed food and drink vendors and found a bench with a lone man holding a bag of popcorn, staring at the expanse of sand and rolling waves beyond. His shiny cue-ball head reflected the filtering sun coming through the palms.

Maxwell approached. "So, this your hangout, Ewe?'

Kopf looked up and took a deep breath of relief. "Henry. Take a seat, please. I am so glad you came."

He sat down. He gave Kopf an appreciative look. "Lots of young people's skin down here, Ewe."

"It makes an old man like me feel younger. Stretches the eye muscles, keeps them from becoming lethargic. Hell, nothing works anymore." He offered Maxwell some popcorn.

"No, thanks, sticks between my molars. I haven't been here in a hundred years."

"The activity soothes my nerves." Ewe retracted the bag and took a handful.

"I never was one for public places even when Lillian lived. She liked them. I bit my tongue."

"Of course, you do what you're told. I wanted to check up on you. After the party at the house the other night. I came close to calling you, then you called."

"I was something, wasn't I?"

"I left before the fireworks, but I have ears. And the

young woman, Jessica? How'd she handle your performance?"

"Better than I thought."

"She must like you, Henry."

He shook his head in a grateful sort of way. "She's strong."

"That's a fine compliment, coming from you. I'm thrilled to hear you say that."

"You're the shrink, Ewe. You have all the answers." Maxwell twisted on the bench. "It never ends. I'm trying my hardest to cope, like you keep telling me. Ancient history keeps raising its ugly head."

"That wouldn't include Tom Caswell, would it?"

"Why'd you raise his name?"

"Because he's at the center of everything that happened with Lillian. You've harbored that incident for years."

He nodded. "Tom treating her like more than a mother. At the same time, Roy never gave the kid the time of day."

"And Roy going off the deep end."

"She told me about it. She didn't know what to do. She never realized Tom saw her in a different light. I sort of felt sorry for the kid myself. But he was different, never had many friends." Maxwell shook his head. "I never caught on how bad it had become."

"He could never sustain a relationship."

"Where'd you hear that?"

Kopf tossed popcorn kernels to a group of pesky pigeons. "You told me that a few years back."

Maxwell watched the pigeons fight over the treat, then turned a quizzical eye back to Kopf. "Tom blamed me for Lillian's death. Thinking about it, I might have to agree."

"Nonsense! I treated Lillian. You attended to her needs best as a husband could. Don't blame yourself. We've discussed this endlessly, so move on."

"Did she ever confide in you about Tom?"

He nodded. "Of course, she did. We talked about him and Roy."

"The cheap bastard. Horrible father. Not until later, after she was gone, did he come out of the closet. Hard to believe he fathered that Godforsaken child of his.

Kopf leaned forward and crushed the empty popcorn bag.

Maxwell's emotions began to swell. *Why didn't I make the connection sooner?*

"Any idea where he is now?"

Maxwell shook his head.

Kopf slouched in his seat. "Out of the closet?"

He nodded, eyes staring into space, having drifted off into another world. The noise of children playing and adults talking and laughing along the promenade had all but disappeared. Only the high-pitched cooing of seagulls meshed with his thoughts, far, far away.

After a minute, Kopf reached over and touched Maxwell's knee. "Henry, you okay?"

He jumped, as if suddenly awakened. "Fine. Just thinking about Tom's worthless father."

"You know, the apple doesn't fall far from the tree."

"Then, maybe I should look him up."

"Henry, please just move on, enjoy your remaining days. Both you and I need to relax, feed the pigeons, and look at the pretty girls. Might help us live longer."

"You're the shrink, Ewe. I'll keep that in mind.

Chapter 38

It only took one day for Maxwell to track down Roy Caswell. Calling a few of the special effects companies in the LA basin made him easy to find, still working at a company in Pasadena.

Maxwell entered the front door of Digital Frames, and after introducing himself to the woman receptionist, he was escorted to Roy's office, a glass enclosed cubicle overlooking a massive design studio with complex computer equipment. Several people were focused over monitors and other bizarre-looking pieces of electronic and digital hardware. A large table in the middle of the high-ceiling room supported a model of some futuristic city with towering space-age buildings. An employee worked around all sides, photographing in a panoramic arc.

"Please, have a seat, Mr. Maxwell," she said. "I'll track Roy down."

He lumbered over to a chair next to the wall, giving him a view of the studio through the full-height glass partition. After a few minutes, a man, thin, balding, with a thick gray beard, appeared. He guessed Roy was mid-seventies by now.

"Henry," he said. "It's been a long time." He moved behind his desk.

"A lot of water under the bridge. Must be at least forty years. I can't believe you're still at it."

Roy nodded. "What else do I have?" He sat down. "You look well. The years haven't beat you up too bad."

"I'm still kicking. Other things have slowed me down."

"Can't imagine." He leaned back and stared at Maxwell. "You here to talk about Tom? He kept in touch with you, I understand."

"We could start there."

"He was a rotten kid. I was a rotten father. Never should have been a father. Go figure."

"Your estrangement was no secret."

"Like I said. I was a rotten father. Hard for me to rationalize paternal instincts. I tried to reconnect years later. He wouldn't take my calls or have anything to do with me. I don't fucking blame him. I do believe he has a screw loose. Not my genes. Mine are bad but not insane. Got it from his mother's side."

Maxwell turned his gaze to the studio.

Roy shifted in his seat. "As a young boy, his mother died. I couldn't keep him from drooling over Lillian. He wanted me out of the picture as much as I wished him gone."

"Why?"

"I wanted to kill him—or Lillian, one or the other—to put a stop to it."

Maxwell took a deep breath. "So, Roy, did you have my wife killed?"

He squinted. "I thought it was drugs."

"I think different."

Roy frowned. "Why do you think so?"

"I have my reasons."

"If I did, I wouldn't tell you," he snidely remarked. "Oh, how I wished her gone, no question. I didn't have a clue on how to control Tom. You're aware he loved her more than as a child looking for a mother."

"I've known that."

"Why didn't you tell her to slow down her motherly overtures?"

He shrank a little. "Guilty as charged. I should have."

"With her out of the picture, I hoped to have a chance to reconnect with him. Be the father I was never meant to be. And then—poof, she's gone. My problem solved." He fixed his eyes on Maxwell. "Tom's mental problems only got worse. As a weakling, I bailed. Most horrible fathers do the same thing."

He felt the urge to leap across the desk and strangle the bastard, knowing full well he was too old to do such a deed. After all these years, why would Roy admit to the murder he did or didn't do? His throat as tight as a vise, Maxwell returned his gaze to the studio, thinking he wanted to drop the conversation about Tom and Lillian. "Visual effects have changed over the years."

"At my age, I still have something to add. The old days, matte painting, miniature models, trick photography. You remember. We still do mockups once in a while to help our digital artists. Now it's all CGI."

"Computer something?"

"Computer generated imagery, 3-D digital modeling, compositing. A whole new world. We still use blue and green screens and mechanical effects, but computer software is king."

"You kept up well, Roy."

"I've been fortunate to still be in the business. In the last fifteen years, we've been nominated five times, won two Academy Awards."

"Congratulations." *You piece of crap.*

Roy gazed back at Maxwell with a smile. "You've lived long enough, time's irrelevant. As I said, I was a rotten father, and a rotten friend—and I despised Lillian. Hard for me to admit. I'm sorry for your loss."

Maxwell stared down at the floor, head bobbing. "I guess I never expected sympathy from you." He palmed his cane and pushed himself up out of the chair. "I won't rest until I get the truth."

"Find peace, Henry. I have," he said with a dismissive smile. He pointed across the design studio. "Misdirection, it's like magic. It fools people into screwing with the senses. Sometimes, what you're looking for is right under your nose."

"Thanks for the advice. I'll keep that in mind," Maxwell said as he walked out the door, hoping to hold his tears until he got away from the building.

Chapter 39

Lord Dedrick cowers on the edge of the precipice, knowing there are only two ways to settle his fate. One goes down, the other, north—and north is never a positive option. "And why now be one's own judge?" he offers in a desperate shriek that only the monsters of his mind hear. And they are listening, far below the fiery depths of reason on the breaking waves of the eastern cliffs.
—BB Barmore,
Lady Julia's Sarcophagus

The next day, Maxwell drove his Bentley into the warehouse district on the edge of Culver City, found an empty spot along Warner Drive. He took his time exiting, checking to make sure he brought everything he needed. As he stood outside the car, a splattering of raindrops greeted him. Looking to the northwest, a large cloud formed over the Santa Monica Mountains, hinting at a better than fifty percent chance for a good soaking. Reaching into the back seat, he pulled out an umbrella, just in case.

He hobbled up onto the sidewalk and walked down a delivery lane surrounded by a mismatch of warehouses. After a few minutes, he stopped and gazed at the concrete block structure straight ahead, painted white with a low-slung barrel roof. Built during World War II,

Global Pictures bought it afterwards. The building had a purpose, the perfect space for movie making, the purity of film far removed from the digital world of today, as the asshole Roy Caswell explained. Owned by Terra Firma Pictures, the warehouse served as an overflow sound stage near their primary lot.

He approached the entrance, pulled out a key from his pocket and unlocked the door. Just like the Spanish mission, the owners gave him access, as he served as a living ambassador to the long-lost memory of Global Pictures. Opening the door, he silenced the alarm. Fumbling around, he turned the light switch on. The cavernous space lit bright.

He negotiated his way through the maze of varied sets, stages, and sound partitions. At the far corner of the building, he paused, studying the scene, a replica of a Great Hall, like a dreary old English manor. An ornate, gray stone fireplace centered in the mockup with huge, framed paintings above depicting fifteenth-century nobility, all trimmed in gold-leaf frames. Several trophy heads of various English stags and a boar adorned the wall between the art. At one end, a curved staircase with wood-engraved railings soared up to a nonexistent second floor.

Even to this day, he was amazed at how realistic the backdrop portrayed a living, breathing panorama composed of artistic carpentry, paint, plastic, and papier-mâché. Built as an interchangeable scene, it was used in many Global films, altered to fit the age of the setting and story. At one time, it served as a hotel lobby, a public library, and now, an English manor's Great Hall. For decades, this corner of the building remained the same, a reminder of the last Global project.

He limped over to an electric panel at the side and flicked a couple more switches. Now the Great Hall came alive. A few wall torches blinked on. A flicker of faux fire rose from the fireplace, the impression of wood burning without the smoke. He shuffled over to a long mahogany table with several chairs and made himself comfortable, taking a seat at one end. He hung his cane on the edge and laid his umbrella down.

He questioned why Terra Firma preserved this sound stage, and this set in its original state. "Historical preservation" is all they would say. It didn't hurt that the CEO was a Gothic horror buff. Maxwell sat solemn for a moment, feeling a slight choke in his throat, gazing at the undisturbed setting of the second-to-last scene of *Lady Julia's Sarcophagus*. A tear stole down his cheek as he pondered the scene that was never shot, never to see the light of day.

He retrieved his cell phone from his pocket and placed it on the table. Jessica convinced him he needed it, and helped him pick out the latest model, teaching him how to use the different functions. He'd never owned a portable phone, let alone a smart one, until now. At first, he really didn't think it was necessary at his age, but after learning some of the things it could do, he withheld further judgment.

He laid a photograph face down next to the phone. As he waited, he reminisced about the thrill he experienced working on *Lady Julia's Sarcophagus*. He played Sir Alston Chatsworth, a man of means, who in some respects resembled him in real life—or was it the other way around?

A far door opened, taking him out of his reverie. His name echoed through the cavernous space.

"Come to the other end, to the old set," Maxwell yelled back.

The sound of shoes slapping on the concrete floor grew stronger. Around the corner of an isolated wall partition, a figure appeared, wearing a black raincoat. Seeing Henry, he continued over, marveling at the pseudo Great Hall.

"A few drops of rain out there," Kopf said, approaching the long table. His eyes took in the set. "I'd swear I traveled back in time, somewhere other than Culver City."

"Have a seat, Ewe. Welcome to Chatsworth Hall in the moors of Devon." He pointed to the chair at the opposite end of the table. "We can both pretend to be the barons of this kingdom by the sea."

Kopf pulled the chair out, sat, and chuckled. "Kingdom by the sea. Amusing. I've read Poe's *Annabelle Lee*. "I'm not here for dinner, I don't suppose?"

"No dinner. We have no kitchen, no servants. This place is a relic of the past. I apologize if I never invited you for any of my shoots here, Ewe. I get nervous when good friends are watching."

"Oh, not you, Henry. You never get nervous. You're a natural in front of a camera or a room full of friends…or enemies."

"I appreciate your support."

"Now tell me. You sounded upset when you phoned me. I thought we'd come to some sort of conclusion when we met in Venice. You appeared to be more upbeat then. Why the downside?"

Maxwell let out a subdued sigh. "I'm an old man, Ewe. At this age, nothing's going to change. Lillian's been gone for decades. And so should I."

"If I had a magic wand, I'd wave it here and now. But I don't. I only have advice. We both have only a few remaining years. We must use them wisely."

"A long life never guarantees happiness. Sometimes our wisdom is our downfall. Too many memories may lead to madness. Wouldn't it be great to let every little bit of recollection die out just like our woeful bodies decay? Take Lillian's garden, for instance. All those marble statues. You couldn't be around her without her sharing legends associated with each mythical god or goddess. In fact, Lillian paired people in her life with a statue that replicated that person."

"Interesting. Why bring that up?"

"That's my point, Ewe. Old information never dies. It comes back to haunt your inner being. For example, she saw herself as Aphrodite, goddess of love and beauty."

"She was a beautiful woman."

Maxwell smiled. "She compared me to Zeus. Can you imagine?"

"Of course, king of the gods. She adored you."

"Oh, and by the way. You were Apollo. How about that? God of music and healing. Medicine. There you go, Doctor Kopf, your namesake."

"No, I don't remember being Apollo."

"None of this matters now, Ewe. It's all trivia information that should have faded years ago. All ancient history, just like the gods themselves." His eyes brightened. "But there are some interesting connections."

Kopf's sharpened eyes stared at him. "Where's all this headed, Henry?"

"Walking through the statuary garden the other day, something occurred to me unexpectedly. This is where I must digress. Some memories can still have value after so many years."

"And what would they be?"

Maxwell leaned back, taking his time, analyzing how he would say it. "Ewe, what would you say if I told you Lillian's death wasn't accidental?"

Kopf blinked. "Henry, it does you no good to relive what happened decades ago. For your well-being, your health, your sanity, and as a friend and someone who understands the mind, for God's sake, let it go!"

He smoothed a wrinkle on his forehead.

Near silence. The crack of rolling thunder exploded from outside, shaking the old building. The wall torches flickered with each boom. Kopf's face turned pale. "Where in hell did you come up with that theory? Nineteen sixty-eight, a long time ago, and now you say it wasn't an accident. That goes against the coroner's report, the sheriff's report, everybody else's goddamn report."

"Hard to believe, but I tracked down the man who did it. He admitted as much, that he killed Lillian." He studied Kopf, watching his eye movements.

After what seemed like an eternity, Kopf asked, "At your age, why play detective, attempting to manufacture a theory? Is that it? What's gotten into you?"

"Francisco Cuervo was Lillian's gardener. You remember him, don't you, Ewe?"

A long pause. Kopf's face tightened. "No, I can't place him."

"Oh, come, Ewe. Francisco couldn't have slipped your mind. Lillian paired him with Eros, and now I understand. You visited her several times at the house during her therapy. Are you telling me you never met him?"

"No, can't recall ever meeting this Cueva, Cuervo, whatever. I believe I would remember if I did."

"Think, think, Ewe. Among other gardening chores, Francisco helped her work floral decorations in the statuary garden. She used to have afternoon wine socials among all those statues to benefit the Malibu Garden Club." He stared at Kopf. "Francisco killed Lillian, Ewe."

"How did you conclude this? You're not hallucinating, are you, Henry?"

"Right now, I can only say this whole affair is an ongoing Greek tragedy. Ironic, don't you think?" Maxwell kept his eyes trained on the psychiatrist, watching him become restless. He picked up the photograph and spun it across the table.

"Take a look, Ewe. That's a photo of you, Lillian, and the little man, Francisco. Taken at one of Lillian's garden affairs. If my mind serves me, you took part as one of the judges selecting the most dynamic, colorful, full-bodied arrangement that complimented each god. Dionysus won. Sorry it wasn't Apollo, but there you are, with Lillian and Francisco."

Kopf glanced at the photograph. His jaw tightened.

Maxwell's voice became stronger. "Now, Ewe, I assume the photo has triggered your memories. Remember Francisco now?"

Another crack of thunder. The lights blinked on and off. After several long seconds, Kopf leaned forward, placed his elbows on the table, chin in his palms and asked, "If I was there, as the photo contends, I still don't recall the gardener."

Maxwell paused, wanting Kopf to think hard, wanting him uncomfortable. "The frail little shit Francisco. He had a lot to get off his chest," he said, lying as he went. "He explained it all to me, Ewe, not in so many words but enough for me to draw conclusions. You knew Lillian almost as well as me. She would never have injected a concoction of moonflower to get a buzz."

"Wasn't that in the coroner's report?"

"Of course." Maxwell waited and watched Kopf's face flush with indecision. He continued. "The sheriff's report indicated the syringe in the greenhouse laying on a table with assorted parts of moonflower. A pitcher of iced tea and an empty glass were also found in the greenhouse. The syringe tested for remnants of atropine, as did Lillian. Atropine, Ewe, that's the main toxin in moonflower. Nobody tested the iced tea."

"For God's sake, Henry, what the hell are you driving at? I don't even recognize you anymore with all these bullshit facts. What's gotten into you?"

"I went and saw Roy yesterday. Thought he was involved. He did give me a piece of advice, talked about misdirection, like in the special effects of film. That got me to thinking harder, Ewe. I am convinced Lillian was poisoned from the insecticide found in a bag near the door. She never allowed insecticides in her garden. She would only have Francisco apply organic, natural products to control bugs. It never dawned on me until yesterday about the insecticide—diazinon, if I'm not mistaken." Maxwell's swollen eyes stared at Kopf. "Francisco laced the iced tea. It doesn't take much insecticide to cause severe reactions, even death. You know that, Ewe, being a doctor and all."

"Psychiatry, not medical."

"But you have a medical degree, all the same."

Kopf cleared his throat.

"And then we have the syringe filled with atropine, a drug any doctor could prescribe from any pharmacist, Ewe. My research indicated atropine could mask the insecticide poisoning. Convenient, don't you think? I just thought it would be only fair to let you in on all this before I talk to the police and have them reopen this case." He picked up his cell phone, umbrella and pushed up from the table. "Now if you'll excuse me, I have things to do." He reached for his cane.

"I think you'd best sit back down," Ewe said.

Maxwell looked at Kopf, a pistol pointed at him. He hesitated, letting a slim smile creep across his face. He sat back down. *The true Ewe shows himself.*

"Ewe, are you planning on shooting me?"

"Such a long time ago, Henry. Why would you consider resurrecting her death at your age? What were you thinking to gain?"

"The truth, before I leave this world. Interesting that you had the sense to bring a gun, Ewe. I think I deserve the truth. Why did you do it?"

"A simple calculation."

"Tell me more."

"What's to tell? My fault, but I don't apologize. I got her hooked on the barbs and benzos, totally intentional, of course. She was an easy target; the drugs kept her sanity. Genetically, she was easy prey. From my understanding her father had troubles with drugs and alcohol. After a while, two years, I suspect, she wanted out. Said she couldn't continue, and if I didn't agree, she would call the police. She was forceful in that respect,

Henry. I failed at diagnosing her strength. I give her credit for that. So, you see, I had to have her silenced. It would have been the end of a very lucrative business, and the end of me, I suspect. Psychiatry is a time-consuming profession that only fools would pursue." Kopf's eyes seemed to grow large, penetrating, like twin, flickering suns.

"I thought so, Ewe, but Francisco, why him?"

"A young kid, easily threatened, manipulated. I told him lies that Lillian didn't like his work. He began to believe me. Yes, he salted her tea with the insecticide. He kept hidden, waiting for the effects. It didn't take long. She stumbled out of the greenhouse toward the statues. She saw him, but it was too late. She collapsed. At that point it didn't matter. She was dead."

Maxwell felt his heart being shredded into a thousand pieces. He steadied his emotions and asked, voice creaking, "The syringe?"

"That's the beauty of it all, Henry. Prescription atropine in the syringe, to mimic the moonflower. I give the kid credit. He did his job admirably. She had crawled to the agora…and suffocated in her own vomit. Francisco waited, then checked for a pulse. None. I taught him well. He then injected Lillian. Now, this is the brilliance of it all—for the next two minutes he performed CPR…to insure the toxin would pump throughout her body. We practiced this beforehand so that he knew exactly what to do, how to compress the chest to get the blood flowing, even if the victim was already dead. Great idea I had, even had him work on a dummy to get the feel of what he had to do. A good student learns really fast. Genius, don't you think? The good news, it worked, and the atropine masked any residual toxicity of insecticide left in her body, just as you mentioned, Henry. *Voilà*, cause of death an overdose on moonflower."

Maxwell wanted to strangle Kopf with his bare hands. He felt crushed, having to hear about the pain Lillian had endured. His chest tightened, but he had to remain calm. Not now, not yet. This was his penance, his nailing to the cross. He had to suffer again…and again, aware the agonizing truth about Lillian would never fade away. He reached again for his belongings and stood up.

"And where do you think you're going, Henry?"

"Ewe, I'm going home, and I'm going to pour myself a stiff scotch. So, if you don't mind, I think I've heard enough."

"Now why do you think I would allow you to leave?" He raised the gun, keeping it pointed at Maxwell's chest.

"Because you have just admitted to Lillian's murder." He waved the cell phone high, so Kopf could get a good view of it. "Never had one of these contraptions, Ewe. Very inventive. You see, I recorded your confession, and thanks to Jessica for teaching me how. By the way, I just emailed the recording to a Detective Brown. Amazing how this thing works. I would suspect they'll find you in short order and arrest you. Jail's now in your future, although not the justice I would prescribe."

Maxwell placed the phone in his pocket and slowly walked away, leaving Kopf sitting at the table. Nothing was said. Kopf sat there, unmoving, a blank look on his face, sweat bubbling across his brow. He lowered the gun.

Another boom of thunder brought one more wave of

weather. Maxwell never looked back. He knew he would either receive a bullet in the back or Kopf would analyze his options. The lie about emailing Detective Brown was just that, a lie. Too many things to do right, too many steps. He did, however, get the confession recorded. It was a crapshoot, one he was willing to take. As he neared the front door, he opened it and saw the rain falling in sheets. His umbrella popped open, and as he stepped out, heard a gunshot echo from behind.

Chapter 40

You are my air
With somber heart, my breath set sail,
You are my air
To rocky shoals, my ship shall dare,
And weave our souls, beneath the veil
Of ancient shores, beyond the pale,
You are my air
—BB Barmore,
Lady Julia's Sarcophagus

After leaving the Terra Firma sound stage, Maxwell took his time returning home. He swung over to an area on the northside of downtown LA through the intermittent rain. He knew he had the right street and address, yet the apartment building he searched for was now a high-rise condominium. He pulled over and parked. What would make him think Lillian's old residence would still exist decades later? What a fool to think otherwise. Sadness crept over him.

He drove down another two blocks. At the intersection, he remembered the little Italian restaurant he and Lillian loved. The name escaped him, but to his astonishment, it stood on the far corner with a different name, as far as he could tell. The building hadn't changed a bit. He swore he could smell the strong garlic and tomato sauce he remembered. He sat for a moment, reminiscing about the many times they enjoyed dinner there, discussing their day. She was a student at California State University-Los Angeles. At that time, she snagged a part-time job working with one of the assistant directors on one of his earlier films. It was her spunk and beauty that caught his eye. He took a deep breath. A honk from behind broke his thoughts. Pulling across the intersection, he passed the little restaurant, leaving it and his memories in the past.

He took I-10 to Hwy 101 and arrived at Point Dume an hour and ten minutes later. Finding the spot where he and Jessica parked the other day, he exited the car. He walked along the bluff where he had a three-hundred-and-sixty-degree view. The rain ceased and the clouds were evaporating as they stretched lazily over the Pacific.

Steadying himself, he watched the setting sun sink into the horizon. It had only been a couple of days since he and Jessica were here. He took in a deep breath of the thick, salty air. The Channel Islands rose out of the cyan sea reaching for the sky, now a red-orange afterglow behind scattering cumulus clouds. For several minutes, he stood mesmerized. Like ancient seafarers who gazed out at the thin line separating sea and air, their ardent desire to see beyond the known world was written in the genetic code encrusted in their souls. Such a powerful elixir, this yearning to explore. Was the earth flat, riding on the back of a gigantic tortoise, or would unfortunate sailors sail off the edge into oblivion and into the dark abyss of hell?

Or did desire come in contrastive forms? Is desire love? Is love the catalyst that drives the human spirit, the spirit of discovery? Is it the strongest of emotions? But it took forty-some years for him to realize love does come in different shapes. And here he found himself, setting off on one last journey to prove love transcends all limits.

The orange glow dissipated, and the full moon reflected a silken repose off the water. He and Lillian last watched a sunset here together decades ago. He felt her presence. But the crash of waves below on the rocks and the squall of gulls soaring on the breeze washed out the sweet cadence of her voice. Now, he realized the importance of sharing the love of the sea with Jessica, who now filled his senses.

He'd best get home before it got too dark.

Chapter 41

Jessica gave David a goodnight kiss, walked up the entrance to the mansion and pushed the hefty door open. She waved one last time as he drove away, wishing she would have invited him in. He would have spent the night with her, but was she ready to commit to a relationship this soon, all with what had been happening concerning the grisly murders and Maxwell's arrest? At this point, she reasoned, some down time would be beneficial for all. Marsha called earlier and they discussed how much longer she would have to stay. Jessica fought the urge to move on. If she did, she'd be back in San Francisco and David would still be in LA. What would that have accomplished?

She stood for a moment, contemplating this monstrosity of a castle incarnate. After a few weeks, it didn't bother her like it did the first few days. How could she be so calm? Her former career in psychology brought her a plausible answer. Did she penetrate the realm of his troublesome background—or had Maxwell cast a spell upon her?

She entered, and paused, stopping in her tracks. The darkened foyer allowed feeble rays of moonshine to stream through the upper windows, casting oppressive shadows amongst the protrusions and niches. The tapestries appeared to ripple, preparing to slither down and wrap her in a suffocating mantle. The whole of the stone pulsated, like a bellows, nothing more dreadful than the wheeze of something alive and menacing. Why didn't she invite David in? For one, Maxwell clogged her mind, superseding David's presence. She realized she didn't have a flashlight, nor had she ever figured out where the light switches were, if they existed.

Taking a chance he'd be in the den, she rushed down the hallway, finding the door open. On entering, she saw a small desk lamp lit. Henry sat in his chair.

"A hunch you would stop by before you turned in."

Relieved she'd found him, she walked over and took a seat. "We enjoyed dinner."

Maxwell smiled. "You two seem to be spending more time together."

"We do."

"And?" His eyes twinkled.

"Friends, that's all. Too much going on to think about anything more than that."

"Keep all your friends. They will guide you through the rest of your life."

"And what about you, Henry? What about the rest of your life?"

He shook his head. "I'm not important. You are."

Both sat silent for a few moments.

She studied Maxwell's gruff exterior, his bifocals reflecting the desk lamp like a beacon at sea, flickering a steady "all is calm" as his head quaked back and forth.

"The other day, you took me to Point Dume. I want to thank you again for that."

"Happy to do it."

She stood, ready to leave, but sat back down. "Henry, I have a confession to make."

"And what would that be?"

"I want you to know, I never wanted this job.

He pursed his lips in, smiling. "Knowing you had to take on a cantankerous old fool like myself, I'm amazed you've stuck it out so long."

"To be honest, there were times…" She smiled.

"Uh, huh."

Her eyes fell on Maxwell. "To be honest, I failed in my first career."

"It might come as a shock to you, but I know. I'm aware of your previous profession."

"You are?"

"That worthless law firm of yours doesn't surprise me. Surely, Marsha suggested you for the job. She's not dumb. In any account, it's easy to get information—if you know whom to ask."

Her eyes dropped to the floor.

"So you've been psychoanalyzing me behind my back?"

"I don't know what to say."

"Say nothing. I know about the trauma you went through."

She felt the air escape her lungs.

"Hell, I'm not one to offer advice, not with my loony mental state the last few years. The deck was stacked against you. Everything is a coin toss in that profession. You did the best you could. Don't—ever—forget that."

She stared into space for a long time. Noah could never come back, but something in Henry's voice made the dreary and dark castle less frightening. "I kept all that a secret from you. I'm still a failure."

"Stuff it!" He leaned back and with a broad smile said, "Tomorrow you can continue to psychoanalyze me to your heart's content."

The Salvation of Henry Maxwell

She smiled, relieved.

"Listen, I need to show you something."

An ominous shiver shot through her when Maxwell pushed the button under the corner of his desk. The hidden door in the wainscot popped open, like it had several days ago. *What's this all about?* A chill rippled down from her shoulders to her toes. Surely, he remembered how frightened she was the last time the door had opened.

Maxwell's eyes fixed on her. "I wouldn't blame you at all for not wanting to follow, but I must show you something. Please, trust me, that's all I ask of you."

She was tempted to turn and run. But where? For what good? "That stunt you pulled the other day. Very callous."

He nodded. "It showed me a lot about your character."

Unconscionable. To descend again into the labyrinth beneath the castle? But she couldn't dwell on Henry's request. Hadn't he *not* harmed her since she stormed into his life, a house guest he never requested? She shivered in the warmth of the den. "You must have a reason for asking me to go down into your little playroom from hell again."

"I do."

"What you ask is not easy."

"Not much in life is."

She couldn't think straight.

"Please, this is important." He picked up his cane and disappeared into the opening.

She sucked in a wary breath and followed, her heart pummeling her chest. But, down the stairs she went. Once again, she viewed the dungeon-looking room with the two passageways side by side. The aged stone walls draped in cobwebs again closed in on her. Maxwell stood by a nearby table lighting a couple of candles.

For the briefest of moments, she wanted to scream at the top of her lungs.

****

Maxwell admonished himself for having the gall to force her down into the bowels of this bone-weary castle of terror again. Why would he torment this young woman to satisfy his own needs? —a woman who already had done so much for him. The wall torches illuminated her face. He had to tread softly or he would lose her.

He hobbled over, and, with a caring motion, put his hand under her chin, held it firm and studied her storm-green eyes. "I've had a long, abundant life—good, bad, loving, sometimes hateful. I want you to know who I am. Dragging you down here is not to bring you to the edge again. I understand the difficulty, Jessica." He paused before he spoke again. "I need you."

She kept eye contact. Nowhere did she recognize the evil blood-letting visage that roamed the screen years ago, now only a benevolent old man trying to deal with a life of rewards and tragedies, and deep secrets yearning to be free.

He pulled his hand away, sighing. "I bought this vast house from the estate of an industrialist named Nathaniel Ellis Pritchard. He immigrated to Southern California from England during the first oil strike and took advantage of the future booms in the Los Angeles basin." He swung his cane, pointing in all directions. "He rebuilt this in 1898, this mansion—whatever you want to call it."

"What do you mean?"

"All this hewn granite, brought over from the ruins of a castle in the Devon moors, each individual piece marked and catalogued."

Jessica gazed around. The last time here, anxiety clouded her thinking, nerves stretched tight. Now she focused on being a pupil taking in a lecture. She tried to relax, examining the walls, the pilasters, and barrel-vault roof in closer detail and the two passageways straight ahead as if taunting them to decide which way to go. The other terrified day with David flew across her mind.

"This place fit my desires at the time. It paralleled my passion."

"Movie acting?"

Maxwell shuffled over to the medieval trunk resting against one wall. He sat down, poking cobwebs with his cane. "An accident. I grew up in rural Ohio. Farming wasn't for me. Found my way to Hollywood. Started out as a truck driver, then an assistant gaffer. One day, I was offered a small role in a low-budget film. Did bits and pieces in more mainstream films. And then my break. I got a speaking part. The horror genre was beginning to snowball in the B-movie arena. Nobody knew if it would catch on. But did it ever. Wonderful escapism at the time. I played despicable characters, sadistic, deceitful, psychotic, sorry excuses for living creatures. But more than anything else, they were human, one way or the other."

"And you were successful."

His aged face smiled. "Things went my way. But happy? I didn't want to spend my whole life doing those kind of movies—not until I met Lillian."

"What happened after that?"

His smile now appeared genuine. "I found heaven. It didn't matter if I was back driving a truck or wasting away in front of a camera." He stood, walked over, handed her one of the lit candles and stepped into the left corridor.

She followed until he stopped in front of a door. "This is where David and I got separated. He went inside. The door slammed shut."

"Trick locks. After all these years, can't believe they still work. Fun in the day."

She stared at Henry, the light placing most of his face in shadow. Apologizing, he asked her to continue. Not having a choice, she trudged behind into the narrow confinement, passing a couple more crossing corridors. A few feet farther, an iron grille prevented them from continuing. He reached into his pocket and took out an old-fashioned skeleton key and inserted it into a lock. Hearing a click, he pushed it open with a protesting creak. Entering, they came upon descending steps. They both stopped for a moment. She saw the ends of rods protruding from the slots in the ceiling.

"That, my dear, is called a portcullis. It can be lowered as a barrier to keep others from entering this room below. Very medieval. Come, this is what I want to show you."

Taking his time, he ambled down. Her breath caught in her throat as she followed. Candlelight shadows danced over two stone coffins in front, raised above the floor on pedestals, decorated with what appeared to be a coat of arms and some other flowery designs.

"Most European castles and manors had a family tomb. That was the custom of aristocracy, and of course, of the massive cathedrals. Nathaniel Pritchard was no exception. He had this crypt built, one for him, and one for his wife Adelphia. As you can see, there's room to add more."

"More, what do you mean?"

"The Pritchards never had children."

Jessica examined the coffins. Macabre, yes, but something sacred about the way humans displayed their dead. "What's it like to have a burial chamber below your house?" she asked. "To me, it would be unnerving."

"Lillian thought the same thing even after learning the history."

"What history?"

"They're not here."

"Not here, why not?"

"It's a sad tale itself. They were coming back to the states in 1912…on the *Titanic*."

Jessica's eyes widened in the flickering candlelight. "Oh, my gosh!" So they're emp—" She stopped, gazing at Maxwell's played-out eyes across the way. At the front of the coffins, she noticed the name plates had been removed. It could only mean one thing. "Is Lillian here?"

He shook his head. "I realized she never would want to spend eternity in this oppressive space. We discussed a lot of issues back then. Our final resting spot was a big topic of conversation. Her place would have to be out of darkness, where the sun always shines, and within sight of the beautiful sea, like the Aegean she so adored.

"Is she buried in Greece?

Maxwell picked up his candle and gazed into Jessica's eyes. "No, she's not, but she has a grand view of the sea."

Chapter 42

"I'm sorry," the woman on the other end of the line said, "locating a book published before '65 would be problematic to find since ISBN or SBN numbers didn't exist prior to that year."

Talking with friend and colleague Miranda Faulkner, UCLA professor of English and Literature, David Grovene didn't like what he heard. "Are there no records of books published prior to 1965?"

"Back then, publishers used a different system of cataloging, but if you don't have the publisher's name for the book—what'd you call it, *Lady Julia's Sarcophagus*?—that's a huge task to undertake."

"I'm thinking the author may have been British, so the book could have been printed in Great Britain at the end of the nineteenth century."

"And is the publisher still around, or were they swallowed up by another publisher? It's a fickle business."

"Gee, Miranda, I'd thought you'd have all the answers."

"I wish I did. What about tracking down the author? Have you done a web search?"

"BB Barmore. Nothing came up."

"Another thought. Have you ever been to Odyssey Books downtown?"

"Isn't that the used bookstore on West 5th that must

256

have every book published under the sun?"

"That's the place, next to a tattoo parlor, if I remember. They might be able to help. You'll find it fascinating. It's a whole different world. It's like you've walked back in time, wall-to-wall hardcovers, and all I want to do is grab a volume and stick my nose in it and suck in a deep breath."

"Really?"

"Not unlike you sticking your snout in those old canisters of celluloid."

"Miranda, I know I have a fetish, but it seems like you do too."

"Call Eden Neel," she said. "He owns the store. A matter of fact, he's also British. Maybe he can shed some light on the novel, or the author."

"I appreciate your help."

"I'd like to hear what you come up with. Take a moment, and sniff the old books. It's the breakdown of volatile organic chemicals in the paper, ink and binding adhesives that give them that distinctive fragrance. Like your films, you'll find them irresistible."

"If I come across anything, I'll let you know, and how high I get." He chuckled. "Thanks, Miranda." After hanging up, he checked the Odyssey website, and made a phone call.

That afternoon, David walked into Odyssey Books. He remembered being here on a couple of other occasions, but now he took Miranda's suggestion and let his nose take control. The store, a long rectangle filled with bookshelves everywhere, housed a second-floor mezzanine at the rear. Stacks upon stacks of books greeted him. And the redolence, saturating. He moved along the cavernous shelving containing what appeared to be thousands of hardbacks. He stopped and pulled a book out, opened it and took a whiff. Mirada didn't lie, something unique about the aroma. Unlike the vinegar trace of nitrate films, old books had a vanilla, floral scent. Addicting, like celluloid.

"Looking for something?" a voice said, coming up from behind. David turned. A short man with round rimless glasses, a well-trimmed gray Van Dyke beard, attired in a blue polo shirt and beige chinos, smiled.

He noticed a slight English accent. "Are you Eden Neel?"

"I am," he said taking the book from David's hand. He opened it and read. "*Beau Geste* by P. C. Wren. Published in 1927 and priced at one hundred and seventy-five dollars." He pointed to a sticky-back price tag on the inside front jacket. "Not bad for a first edition, and it is signed." He gave him a smile and reinserted the book on the shelf. "You must be David Grovene?"

"Yes, good to meet you." They shook hands. "Thanks for seeing me. I explained what I was looking for, hoping you could help me out. You come highly recommended by Miranda Faulkner."

"Nice lady. She comes here quite often. I'm always willing to assist academia. Follow me, we can talk in my office."

He followed Eden Neel up a flight of stairs to the mezzanine and back through another forest of stacked books, appearing to be much older than the ones on the first floor. A sign at the top indicated the public not allowed without being escorted by an employee of Odyssey Books. They entered an office. Heaps of books littered a table at one end with Neel's desk at the far side. He sat down, pointing to a nearby chair. "Have a seat."

"Thanks."

"So, let me see if I have this correct," Neel said, his English accent now obvious. "On the phone you were inquiring about an author by the name of…" He picked up a loose-leaf notebook and read, "…by the name of BB Barmore."

"Either that, or the novel he wrote, *Lady Julia's Sarcophagus*."

He gave David a smile. "Comforting title, isn't it? It helps to have in possession a copy of the journal, *English Literature in Transition, 1880-1920*, focused on late-Victorian to early-twentieth-century British literature. I took a stab on your theory this author had written around the turn of the century, based upon the era of the film."

He felt his hopes rising. The scent of volatile organic compounds in old books again invaded his nostrils, mingling with his fond memory of vinegar in old nitrate films. Incompatible, dissimilar—two mediums that were the glue that bound past with present.

Neel continued. "BB Barmore was born in 1859 in the Cotswolds. Beautiful area. Died in 1927. He didn't have great success, as he wrote only three novels, *Lady Julia's Sarcophagus* being one, which was published in 1892. He penned several short stories for *The Strand Magazine* around the turn of the century."

David couldn't contain his excitement. "So, the author is real?"

"Indeed, and he had interesting friends, more well-known contemporaries like Irving and others."

"The reason I'm trying to find this novel is a film with the same name exists. Never finished. Details of the novel are unknown."

Neel stroked his goatee."

"So you have a copy?"

"No. I'll put a few feelers out to connections with other antiquarian dealers across the country. You never know if a copy is still in existence."

"Thanks, I'd appreciate that," David said, disappointed.

"Anything particular you're looking for in the book?"

"Just the ending."

Chapter 43

The next evening, Jessica finished pouring a cup of tea, went to the library, sat down, and booted up her laptop. While waiting, she phoned David. He answered on the first ring.

"Now I know I'm losing it," she said.

"Hard day?"

"I was exhausted last night. Fell asleep early. How's your day been?"

"Can't complain. I'm making progress on the film of my dreams. Found out today *Lady Julia's Sarcophagus* is based on a novel published in 1892. I still haven't been able to track down a copy, if one exists."

"Do you have time to come over later?"

"Sure, that might work. I'm driving back from Santa Barbara, attended a conference. Think I can be there in half an hour, assuming traffic isn't a bear. Headed to see Dart for dinner near Grauman's Theater. He's at a canned film fair, hoping he'll find some treasure to claim. By the way, you're welcome to join us. I'd like you to meet Dart. He's a character."

"Thanks for the invite. I think I better take it easy. You two boys will have a better dinner date without me."

"Okay, see you later."

A smile spread across her face. She enjoyed David's company. She lifted the cup of tea to her nose, the invigorating scent of jasmine, then a chill in the air invaded her spine, followed by cigarette stench as a rough hand pressed hard over her mouth. The cup went flying, her arms restrained. A wet rag clamped around her nose and mouth; a sweet, antiseptic-like smell overtook all the others as she drifted into oblivion.

****

Henry Maxwell massaged his eyes. For the last two hours, he lay in bed, staring into space. He hadn't slept a wink. Grunting, he stretched and rolled out. Fresh air out on the veranda might help him relax. Sliding on a pair of slippers and a robe, he put on his bifocals and grabbed his cane. A minute later, he took the elevator down. He crossed over to the center gallery, hesitated, gazing at the medieval weapons hanging from the walls. *Really, a battle axe and a spiked club.* Would the next owner of this monstrosity of a house want all this crap? Hell, the next owner may never materialize. This place was only for the macabre. His time in the Gothic arena was over, and the Munsters were off television a long, long time.

On the veranda, he eased into his favorite chair and stared out over the garden. Closing his eyes, his mind kept churning, reliving the last two days. When would this all end? He had to move beyond all distractions. His eternal future relied on it. For the time being, though, the recent vile murders took hold. *Dark Stairs*, the sickening corpse lure, for the sake of butchering the unsuspecting. The first of the string of movies he should have turned down. Followed by *The Sins of San Rafael*, an insidious journey into religion—and bloodletting. Curiosity and sadness. Why had he visited the mission all these years? Why? Why not? And the third, *The Chains*. Everything comes in threes, don't they? A sudden shudder penetrated his wrinkled frame. When would that hideous film be revisited in real life? What unnerved him the most, that someone would copy those bloody sequences in those films. One sick psychotic, and what was the point of mimicking the exact locale where the barbaric scenes were shot? What was the point?

He assumed Brown would investigate the connection after they released him from jail. *He damn well better.* Without knowing, he wondered if the killer had a grudge against him. Did he know this person, or was it a psychotic wanting nothing more than to imitate a fool?

What about that crazed Arlen Silvers? *Fan club bullshit!* An excuse. That should have ended years ago. Silvers, himself, was an unhinged lunatic from outer space. Last time Maxwell perused the website, *The Trilogy* movies took center stage, overshadowing his influential work. Mind made up. He'd call him and have him disband the club. No need for that crap floating around. The more he tried to figure things out, the faster his thinking fogged. He gazed out over the garden, lifeless, although Jessica had it weeded, watered, and manicured. What he needed was conversation. Rising from the chair, he entered the house and shuffled through the dreary darkness toward the library. That was where she spent her time. She used it as her office, which was fine with him. He was surprised she had done it there after her foray into the passageways under the house with the professor. He admired her courage.

Entering the library, he found himself disappointed, no Jessica. Maybe she'd gone to her room. He turned to leave when he spotted her cup overturned on the edge of the table. He looked closer. The contents were splashed in all directions. The stench of cigarettes and chloroform permeated the space. A disturbing thought flashed through his mind. He spun around, frantic. "It can't be, it just can't!" He stumbled out of the library, crossed the massive guts of the castle and went to the motor court. Jessica's Subaru was still there. "No, no, no!" he shrieked.

He remembered his revolver. This time he would make sure it was loaded. Ten minutes later, he slipped behind the wheel of the Bentley.

****

David pulled up the circular drive at 6:15 and spotted the Bentley coming out of the motor court. Knowing Maxwell was behind the wheel, he exited and dashed over before the old man could leave. "Jessica told me everything," he said, peering into the window. "I'd be glad to help you or her in any way."

A disturbed Maxwell rolled his eyes. "She's missing, you fool! Out of my way. No time to chit-chat."

He stepped back, surprised at the bellicose tone. "Henry, what the hell is going on?"

Maxwell's moisture-laden eyes tore into him. "*The Trilogy* has been set in motion, Professor. If you want to help, find out where that sick scene from *The Chains* was filmed. Somewhere downtown, in an old underground speakeasy in the tunnels. I can't remember. Too long ago. Then call worthless Detective Brown. For God's sake man, Jessica's gone! I'm convinced she's been kidnapped. I must get there before the scene is replayed, do you understand?" He stepped on the accelerator, coming close to knocking David down.

A few seconds later, Tom Caswell drove up. "What was that all about?" he asked, exiting his vehicle. "If that was Henry, he almost ran me off the road."

David's face flushed white. "We have a problem."

"What's going on?"

"Something happened to Jessica. She's missing!"

Caswell's jaw dropped. "Missing, what do you mean?"

"Henry mentioned the movie, *The Chains*, says that's where Jessica is."

"Oh, my God!"

David found it hard to breathe. He had to do something. "Where was the bloodiest scene filmed in *The Chains*?

"Why would I know? I don't remember that one."

David spun on his heel and ran to his car. He couldn't waste any more time.

"Where are you going?" Caswell yelled.

"How the hell do I know?" He slid into the seat, and sped off, watching Caswell in the rearview mirror, like one of Lillian's statues, a man turned to stone.

Chapter 44

Racing down the canyon, David's mind kept repeating over and over, *The Trilogy...The Trilogy...The Trilogy*. The other night, three films, two at the center of all this chaos. The third film, *The Chains*. He now feared its climax. *They come in threes, don't they*, Dart implied. He pushed harder on the accelerator. *The Trilogy has been set in motion*. Isn't that what Maxwell said in a panicked fit? David palmed his phone and made a one-handed dial.

After four rings, Dart answered. "Now what, gonna cancel our dinner date?"

"Dart, Jessica's missing! Maxwell said they're trying to complete *The Trilogy*."

"Who the hell is 'they'?"

"Don't know. Just describe the most depraved part in the film, goddammit."

"You want to know?"

"Yes, damn it, Dart!"

"Brace yourself. It's the bloodiest, shut-your-eyes scene I've ever seen in a movie. The victim bleeds to death from the sickest piece of knife graffiti one can imagine. It's too graphic to go into detail."

David's face prickled with sweat. He couldn't remember when he experienced such a hollowness. He should have dragged Maxwell from his car and forced him to tell where he was headed.

"Professor, you still there?"

"I'm here. There has to be a way to—" Arlen Silvers popped into his head, the so-called expert on *The Trilogy*. In his basement, the three films, the posters grouped together by themselves, glorified, the ones he held in immense fascination. Could that dumpy little shit be involved in Jessica's disappearance? Only one way to find out.

"Dart, I'm on my way to pick you up."

"I'll be waiting on the corner of Hollywood Boulevard and Highland Ave. I'll look for you. Can't miss that beat up Honda you drive."

Thirty minutes later, Dart flagged him down and jumped into the passenger seat. "So, where to?" he asked.

"That fan club president, Arlen Silvers. He's beginning to creep me out. He worships those blood-dripping movies as the best Maxwell films ever. The guy's a fruitcake—and maybe a killer, at that." David explained his visit and what he knew about the fan club president and his captivation with *The Trilogy*.

"Damn, you don't suppose—"

Fighting traffic and frustration, David pulled in front of Silvers' bungalow. If he was involved in some manner with Jessica's disappearance, the possibility of him being home would be close to zero. "If he's here, my theory's wrong. God, I hope I'm wrong."

"One way to find out. Let's go."

He sprinted up to the door, Dart on his heels. He knocked. He knocked again…then pounded…and pounded again."

"Easy, cowboy, you'll break the door down."

"Maybe that's what we need to do." He tried the

doorknob. Locked. Without thinking of consequences, he stepped back and kicked in the door, shearing the frame. The door swung open with a whimper.

"Now the cops will be on their way," Dart said, surprised at David's sudden turn toward breaking and entering.

"He doesn't have an alarm system—surprising, considering all the memorabilia below."

"What do you suppose we'll find here?"

"Not sure, but him not being here is evidence enough that he could be involved. Listen, this guy's got a screw loose. I have no doubt after I met him. He worships those three films. That's why I'm concerned." Finding a light switch, he turned it on. The stairs to the basement illuminated. "Down here is his poster museum. I'll show you what I mean." He stepped into the basement. Dart followed.

"Wow," Dart exclaimed. "I'd love to have a few of these vintage posters. What a collection."

David snooped around and found a light on in the office where Silvers conducted the fan club business. Nothing out of the ordinary. Exiting, he located *The Trilogy* posters. What he found stopped him in his tracks.

A shriek drew Dart's attention.

Taped over the first two posters was an assortment of several clippings about the murders from various newspaper articles. Only *The Chains* poster didn't have any newspaper articles. Distressed, he glared at Dart. "We have to find her! This guy's a fucking serial killer!"

In less than a minute, both were back in the Honda, fireballing it downtown.

Chapter 45

Night has fallen, and darkness smothers Miss Vanessa in a stupor of senseless motion. Pacing—back and forth—pacing, pacing, pacing! The madness of her prison is as wide as her outstretched arms. Only the ardent trill of a lone nightingale reaches her ears through the narrow opening high above in the tower. She shudders. The cold, stone floor draws away her strength, and between diligent struggles to replay in her mind the sinister ploy that brought her here, she surrenders to the very edge of saneness.
—BB Barmore,
Lady Julia's Sarcophagus

It was that region between narcosis and drowsiness, where blindness and silence were merging. Jessica struggled to make sense. A massive headache pounded her thoughts. The last she remembered, a strip of duct tape wrapped across her eyes and mouth, and an antiseptic, sweet-smelling rag shoved tight over her nose.

She pulled at her arms. They were locked in place, spread out like a vulture's wings. The jangle of chains ripped the silence. Her legs, the same, separated and restrained. She was upright flat against a wall. Her only sense that functioned was her hearing. She heard a slow hum somewhere nearby. And walking, the shuffling of feet scraping the floor, getting closer.

Someone grabbed at the tape and yanked it away from her eyes, ripping at her lashes and stinging her cheeks. An intolerable brilliance of light blinded her. She blinked as someone pulled one eyelid up, then the other, as if she were having an eye exam. Backing off, the glaring flashlight beam went dark. Shaking her head, she attempted to rid the orange spots from her vision, and her surroundings materialized: a low-ceiling space, thick brick walls, a string of incandescent bulbs angling down casting shadows on runners of pipes and wires.

She cocked her head and there, standing close by, a man grinned, a sickly grin, wearing a baseball cap and sweatshirt. Body odor saturated the room as did the stench of cigarette smoke.

Immobile. She couldn't move. She tried to scream, but only a garbled, muffled sound came out of her taped mouth.

****

Maxwell stood outside the door to Little Solomon's Tavern on the east side of downtown LA an hour before midnight with traffic beginning to thin out. A light breeze swept along the street bringing the urban odors of vehicle exhaust and a backed-up sewer. He couldn't remember the last time he'd driven down Wall Street. It had to have been in the daylight. In the evening, the neighborhood had a rougher look to it, unlike when they filmed the sinister part of *The Chains* in the old speakeasy. At that time, the area thrived. Now, on the edge of Skid Row, it was peppered with vacant buildings, crumbling warehouses and a few sleazy-looking businesses. Not a good place to be alone at night.

Little Solomon's looked its age, battered from the

outside, likely the same inside. Maxwell pondered his next move. He barely remembered access to the tunnels from the back stairs. And from there the old speakeasy, or so he thought. So how could he convince the bartender to allow him into the back room? Then an awful thought invaded. *What if the bartender was involved?*

Scared, his face shrouded with an undeniable pathos, he felt the urge to barge in, take the bartender at gunpoint and have him escort him to the tunnels. And what was he thinking? He was an old man, visually impaired, slow on reflexes, sluggish on brain power. He should have cued David on his plan. Hell, he should have contacted the sheriff, that Detective Brown. What a fool he'd been.

But here he was, not about to give up. He didn't have time to call the sheriff or the police, he reassured himself. Looking around, he saw a man pushing a grocery cart. He waited until in ear range. "Mister, you familiar with the tunnels below?"

The man, clad in a heavy jacket and black stocking cap, glanced up from his cart of treasures and held out his hand.

"Tunnels, below the city. How do you access them?"

The man didn't respond, still extending his hand. Maxwell shook his head, reached into his pocket, and handed him a ten-dollar bill. Thin and wrinkled, the man snatched it and continued pushing his cart down the street.

Disgusted, he spotted another man slinking from an alleyway, carrying a plastic trash bag over his shoulders. The man, in ragged trousers, cupped his hands around a short stub of cigarette he attempted to light. Checking the traffic, Maxwell stumbled across the street, cane in one hand and his other in the pocket of the windbreaker he had put on before he left his mansion.

"Hey you," he said, approaching.

The man peered up. He didn't speak.

"You live around here?"

The man flicked his eyes up and down over Maxwell. A slight grin eased upon his face, a grin of curiosity and not of happiness. "Well, you don't," he said. "Wrong part of town, Mr. Bigwig. You can get in trouble down here."

"Can you help me, beings you know the area? How do I find access to the tunnels?"

The man dropped the bag onto the sidewalk. It clinked. Aluminum cans. "What tunnels?" he said, keeping his attention on this stranger from the better side of the tracks.

"You know damn well what tunnels. They're not a mystery. In fact, I would wager you use them to flee bad weather. Hell, you probably sleep down there once and a while."

The man postured, coughed up a plug of something and spit it out. "I have a price."

"I have no problem with that. Show me access and I'll give you a hundred."

The man's eyes bulged. He put out his hand. "Might beat the hell out of scrounging for aluminum. Give it now and it's a deal."

He shook his head, growing impatient. "That's not how this is going to work. You produce, I pay. That's how commerce gets done. Now let's move, or I'll—" He shoved his hand in his coat pocket and thrust it forward.

The man caught the drift and backed away. "Hey, no

need, I'll take you. No problem."

"How far?"

He pointed up the street. "One block, maybe two."

Ten minutes later, Maxwell stared at what appeared to be a freight elevator for one of the dingy warehouses in an alley. Breathing heavily, the walk had sapped his strength. The security light from a nearby building lit their progress.

"This way to the basement," the man said.

"Then move it," he demanded, feeling his stamina return.

The man opened the steel gate and moved into the elevator. Maxwell followed, gingerly watching his every step, prodding with his cane. Once inside, the man pulled the cover off the control box, touched two wires together and the elevator sprang to life. "Don't have the key, but I can operate this thing," he said.

"I'll keep it a secret," Maxwell assured him, steadying himself against the downward movement.

The elevator came to a lurching stop. The man opened the opposite gate and stepped into a dark space, lighted a match. They were blocked from going farther by a security grille.

"Now what?"

The man leaned down and picked up something hidden in the bottom joint of the masonry wall. Maxwell thought it looked like a flat piece of steel. The man pushed it into the lock, working it back and forth. A motor hummed, and the grille rolled up.

He took out another match, struck it on the wall and shined the flame on a door to their left. "To the tunnels. Now, the money you promised."

"Not just yet. I must be sure."

Flustered, the man opened the rusted metal door.

Maxwell pulled out a small flashlight he had taken from the Bentley and beamed it inside.

"You could have used that earlier, save my matches."

He saw a sheet of plywood lying on the floor. "Now what?"

The man moved over, picked up a corner and leaned it against the wall. "Okay, there you go. The C-note, that's the deal."

"You first. I want a guarantee these are the tunnels."

"Hey, I fulfilled my end of the bargain."

"You first. Once I'm convinced, I'll pay."

"Never mind, I don't want the money." He turned to leave.

"Not so fast." Maxwell pulled out the revolver and pointed it at him. "Now, go down!" He shined the flashlight into his eyes.

The man began to shake, but stepped down a short flight of concrete stairs. Maxwell followed, one foot at a time, panning the flashlight around. Sure enough, they reached a long underground tube where the dripping of water into puddles reverberated. They were in the old subway tunnel that never came online because of WWII. Abandoned, flood-prone, the rat-infested tunnel was closed to the public—except to urban spelunkers like this man.

Maxwell stared at the man, knees banging together. "Don't worry, old boy. You did a good job." Reaching into his pocket, he pulled out the hundred-dollar bill, waded it into a ball and tossed it his way. The man grabbed it in midair.

"Now, get the hell out of here!"

The Salvation of Henry Maxwell

The man darted up the corridor as Maxwell shifted the light around, attempting to get his bearings. He was standing on one of the never-used subway loading platforms. Back in the day, the tracks had never been laid. His flashlight probed the tunnel, illuminating the semi-circular roof of concrete as it disappeared into the blackness. For a moment, the confinement reignited the memories, the odor of mold hung in the stagnant air as the production crews set up lights and cameras for the filming.

But memories weren't always a hundred percent; there would be missing bits and parts. He reasoned the tunnel fading into darkness to his left would be the direction of Little Solomon's Tavern. Knowing time was a factor, he hurried along the platform the best his old body allowed, eyes peeled for rats in the shadows and debris that would block his way.

Chapter 46

David followed Dart's directions, negotiating through the streets of downtown LA, hoping not to get pulled over for speeding.

"After you left the other night, had a premonition, that's what you call 'em, ain't it?" Dart offered. "My curiosity is killing me. I threaded that film onto the reel. I rolled the credits. Two caught my eye, the Los Angeles Historical Preservation District and a place called Little Solomon's Clothier. Did a little snooping. Now, it's a tavern. Somewhere below is an old speakeasy in the tunnels beneath the streets. Hundreds of these illegal drinking places existed during prohibition. The one in the film, don't have a clue, but I would guess it had entry from the clothier. Back in the day, many reputable businesses hid access to the tunnels below so those on the know could get a drink, cops included. Wild, don't you think?"

After parking, David stood in the shadows across the street from Little Solomon's, Dart at his side. Traffic thinned and the homeless population gone, surprisingly for this time of night. He checked his watch. Now 10:45. Not knowing when Little Solomon's Tavern would close, he had to figure out how to enter the basement that led to the tunnels, assuming access still existed. He had no plan, no gun, no training, nor was he equipped to tackle this situation. What the hell was he thinking? His feelings clouded his perspective, now more personal. Maybe he was already too late. His emotions centered on Jessica—overwhelming emotions.

His eyes roamed to Dart. "Make a distraction. I'm sure there's an entrance to the basement from the room behind the bar. I need to find it without being seen. Any ideas?"

"My chance at acting? I'll make a fuss, distract the bartender, that's your clue to duck into the back room. Hollywood, here I come."

David ignored Dart's humor. "Let me question the bartender first. You do your scene. After I disappear, you leave the bar and call the police. Tell them the story. Have them contact Detective Brown at the sheriff's office in Lost Hills."

Dart agreed.

They walked across the street. Stopping in front of the door, he gave Dart a onceover. *Doesn't look like a man of means to me. Fits the pattern here.* "Your outfit is perfect. Go for it."

Dart opened the door and vanished inside. David pulled his shirt tails out, ruffled his hair, waited a minute, then entered. Little Solomon's Tavern, one of those downtown beer joints that catered to a mistrusting and cynical clientele. Bored stool sitters at the rail stared at nothing. Around the perimeter of the stale-smelling space, the patrons nursed a variety of beverages. No one paid him any mind. At the other end of the bar, Dart ordered a beer from a fiftyish fellow with a Hercule Poirot black mustache accented by side chops.

David motioned for the bartender.

"What'ya have?"

"Bud Light on tap."

"Only bottles."

"Then a bottle." After receiving the beer, the bartender exited into the back room.

Damn, he swore to himself. He looked down at Dart and mouthed the word "wait." A moment later, the bartender returned, carrying a metal box which he stashed under the bar. David let out a sigh of relief.

"Curious," David said, "I understand this place might have been part of a movie back in the sixties. Any truth to that rumor?"

The bartender moseyed over. "I've been told such, a speakeasy below where filming occurred. The former owner mentioned it once. Tons of speakeasies back in the day. Can't recall what movie it was. Hey, that's a lot of years ago, you know?"

"They accessed the speakeasy from here when this was a clothing store."

"That's my understanding."

"Have you ever been down there?"

"Naw, too creepy for me. Stairs are tight, narrow, and dark below. Old lumber sort of blocks the way." He moved over to chat with another customer.

David nodded Dart's direction. It didn't take long. A sudden gag erupted. Dart fell from the stool onto the floor hard. All eyes fell on him, including the bartender, hurrying over to give aid. David didn't waste time, slipping through the back door and out of sight. The back room served as a storage room and office with a desk in a corner. For the briefest moment, he panicked, unable to find the stairs. He found the door to the alley, hurried over and opened it. Relief crept up his spine. Pulling the door closed, he cruised down a set of concrete steps. At the bottom, a hallway littered with cases of bottled beer, old bar stools and tables. Hidden behind a stack of upturned chairs, he saw a sheet of particle board against the concrete wall. He slid it to one side.

Another door, this one metal. He checked for a doorknob, noticing a padlock.

"Damn," he cursed. He shined the light again on the padlock. Unlocked. He pushed the door open and entered a narrow corridor, moved down another set of creaky, wooden stairs, dark and tight, sidestepping old framing lumber.

The stuffy, musty air greeted him in the complete darkness as he hit the bottom. Pulling out a small flashlight, he moved without fear into the blackness, although the thought of creepy Arlen Silvers made him nauseous.

****

Maxwell was surprised at how well he remembered being down under the streets, as if filming *The Chains* happened only a few days ago. The odors, the confinement, the realism. The abandoned subway tube never carried a train, disappearing into blackness each direction. And it didn't take long to find a small man-tunnel, the entrance hidden beneath a set of stairs, never used, leading to the street level. Traversing the tunnel, he moved toward Little Solomon's Tavern.

The passageways, built during the twenties, threaded beneath the city to a score of forbidden speakeasies and private clubs where alcohol flowed only for those with access. He stopped and listened. In the silence, there were far-off sounds, the rumble of a heavy truck above, the slow hum of air breezing through from ventilation ducts.

This had to be the tunnel that would lead him to his

destination. He remembered well the production crews hauling down the gear for the shoots. It took them hours, if not days. Cameras, lights, sound equipment, all hand-carried. Well worth it because the speakeasy was authentic, an existing set, decorated from the days of prohibition. Hand-painted murals on all the walls, genuine enough that recreating the scene on a sound stage didn't make sense.

His flashlight probed ahead, casting shadows along dips and curves in the brick walls. Every few steps, he paused, ears alert. His years may be many, but he was fortunate to still have excellent hearing. If his recollection served him, he couldn't be more than a block away from the streetside tavern.

He moved through the tunnel as it took a curious bend to the left. He stopped. Voices? A faint light at the end? His pulse accelerated, the pounding in his chest, so loud he worried it could be heard.

****

David moved down the last few feet, his flashlight cutting through the gloom, but it wasn't bright enough to dislodge the claustrophobia in the narrow corridor. He couldn't envision the horrors that repugnant Silvers had planned. Dart's description of *The Chains* twisted David's guts. The blackness and foul odor overwhelmed any rational thought he could muster.

Arlen Silvers, goddammit! Why hadn't he made the connection sooner? After visiting the depraved son of a bitch, he should have been suspicious. The posters were adored and worshipped. Casting aside his nervousness, he plowed ahead. The corridor jogged to the right and came out into a sizable room. He was now standing on a loading platform of the never-finished subway extension. The tunnel reeked of piss and feces, rotting garbage, and a sickening dampness that penetrated his skin. Even though the tunnels were closed to the public, those aware knew the way to access the world of LA's underground. Fanning the flashlight revealed concrete walls decorated with elaborate graffiti. The stench of sewer and other noxious odors grew.

Which way to go? He had no idea. Maybe it was to his right. He stepped down and walked along the old track bed as the tunnel made a sweep to his left.

A light brought him to a stop. Straight ahead, a couple hundred feet, through the gloom, another platform. His breathing increased.

Jessica, for God's sake, where is she?

He moved on. At the end, a rusting staircase rose to the second floor. An old control booth. Below the stair was a door with a broken window. A pinpoint glow flickered on and off. As he neared, he caught the acrid whiff of a cigarette.

A voice echoed from the dark. "Not a place to be lost, friend."

David shined his light on a man sitting on a wooden crate, tapping a cigarette between his fingers. "What about you?"

The man took a drag and exhaled. "No, not lost. I come here to escape the madness streetside. Down here, time doesn't move. Above, it's a goddamn social construct, something meant to screw civilization since the beginning of time." With the philosophical expression of a cynic, he took another puff. "Time is lost. Time is saved. No more time. Time heals all wounds." He grunted. "That one's questionable. Time flies, time is wasted—and worst of all—time is money. Need I say more? The clock is ticking."

David didn't care for the rambling. "Okay, I'm lost. I'm hunting for a historic speakeasy. It was entered from the basement below Little Solomon's Tavern. I thought it was this direction."

"The historical preservation folks stopped giving those tours years ago. Off limits now." The philosopher with unkempt hair looked up at him. "You could be arrested for being down here."

"And you?"

"They won't arrest me. I have nothing to offer."

"You talk about time. Time is getting short. Do you know where the speakeasy is?"

"Lots of them." He took another hit of the cigarette and tossed it onto the platform. "Yes, I know of the one you seek. Last time I checked, there was a lock on the door to keep undesirables like you out."

"Please, help me? A woman's life is at stake!"

The philosopher lit another cigarette. "Go back the way you came. On your left, a doorway hidden by a concrete support. You'll find a man tunnel."

"Thanks." David whirled around.

"Be careful, friend. Activity going on, I'm afraid. I'm quite convinced it's not on the up-and-up."

David took off at a jog, his chest thumping wildly.

****

Maxwell shuffled off into a nearby doorway, thinking this was where he should go. Raking his light around, he saw a large open space that was filled with what appeared to be cross stacks of old creosote railroad ties. He guessed they were a part of the subway construction never used. He paused to catch his breath, eyeing a rat scurrying across an expanse of dirt floor and puddles of water.

Chapter 47

Jessica feared she would suffer the fate of a torturous, painful death. Shackled with chains to the wall, every vulnerable cell in her body exposed, her thoughts turned to memories as a young girl, frolicking in the backyard of her parent's home in Santa Rosa. Playing with Cooper, she hadn't a worry in the world, until she fell over a sprinkler head as she tossed the ball to the five-year-old Golden Retriever. The crying came easily, as did her mother to the rescue, with love and a Band-Aid.

There would be no rescue this time, her mother more than four hundred miles away. In the tear-fogged light, she saw him. He drubbed the palm of his hand with the flashlight like playing the drums. As her eyes cleared from the tears, the man's image became clearer. He walked over to where two incandescent bulbs hung from the ceiling. He stepped around a bar, the kind one would find in a pub. Painted murals decorated the brick walls circling the perimeter of the space. Paintings of what, she couldn't tell.

****

Maxwell spun to leave when he dropped his cane. It rattled off the side of the stacked ties. Panicked, he fumbled to find it. With relief, he located it under an extended tie. Picking it up, he spotted a narrow space between the brick wall and a high stack of railroad ties.

He squeezed in, brushing them slightly. The stack, ten or twelve feet high, teetered outward on the brink of falling. He held his breath, watching the period of sway diminish. He looked closer, noticing the bottom ties were rotten and the dirt floor had settled from years of high humidity and a constant drip of water. He surmised it wouldn't take more than a strong push to topple the pile. He would stay hidden a moment until he felt it was clear and nobody had been alerted to the noise.

****

Jessica's captor reached down and produced a bottle and a glass. He poured a drink and tossed it down. "You should've watched the movie," he said. His voice was rough and scratchy, the kind of voice that foretold a smoker. Sure enough, he pulled a pack from his shirt pocket, shook out a smoke, struck a match and took a deep draw. "Or maybe not," he explained, then coughed harshly. "Probably not a good idea seeing the original movie—especially considering your—predicament." He poured another drink, downed it like the last. "You've got company coming, so I'll let you be. Now, don't go anywhere," he chuckled, then laughing out loud. A distant sound made him frown, ears perked. He slammed the glass hard on the bar, disappearing through a far doorway.

****

Maxwell heard a noise, a steady stomping of footsteps, someone coming his direction. Now his imagination played tricks. He turned his flashlight off. Frozen in place, he waited…and waited. Several seconds, a full minute. He couldn't stay here. Time in the dark would become the enemy. Jessica's life depended on him arriving soon, if it was not too late already.

A bouncing beam of light kicked off the walls, flickering down the tunnel and through the door opening, swallowing shadows. From his vantage point, the outline of a man stepped inside. Maxwell's emotions took a spike when he smelled the stench of cigarette smoke. The light came his way, the man shining it in every nook and cranny. He advanced his direction, then the beam flashed off his face.

"Out of there, now," he commanded.

He had to think fast. "I'm coming out the other end. Got more room." The man shuffled around in front of the ties. Now or never. With all the muscle he could muster, Maxwell pushed on the stack. Sure enough, the whole tower collapsed. With a scream of surprise, the man stepped back. Too late. The ties crashed down, reverberating throughout the room.

Maxwell raked his flashlight over the pile. An arm and one leg were exposed, the rest of his body buried under the massive weight of crisscrossed ties. He did not move, either severely injured or dead. Maxwell bent over and focused an ear on the man's breathing. Not a sound. Satisfied, he straightened up and exited through the opening.

****

David backtracked to the first platform where he spotted a support column and, behind it, a small doorway only four feet high. It looked as if it at one time was covered by a grille, as bolt holes were seen on both sides. He stooped down and pushed through the opening. Inside, he found himself in a passageway that had a higher ceiling. His light pierced past the brick walls, the tunnel twisting through a series of sharp bends. He came upon another opening, shined the light on a chaotic heap of railroad ties. He took a second glance, noticing something sticking out of one edge of the pile—a leg, an arm, a body. *Oh, please, not Jessica.* Something clamped around his throat, telling him to investigate. He had to know. He walked over. To his relief, a calloused hand and arm half protruded from under a mountain of ties.

Then Maxwell came to mind. But the man wore jeans. He'd never seen Maxwell in jeans. He bent down, listening. No breathing. He clasped the man's wrist, cold and clammy. No pulse. One of the ties levered off another where his head was hidden. Reaching down, he picked up the end of the tie and pushed it to the side. Another tie shifted, crashing to the ground. He jumped in time to prevent it from crushing his foot. Cursing his stupidity, he noticed a gun next to the victim's elbow.

****

The slam of a door shook Jessica to the bone. She looked up. In the shadowy background, a man approached. As he neared, the dim light illuminated the left side of his face. She paused. And in that moment, she knew she was on the edge of madness.

"Jessica, I am so sorry," Tom Caswell noted with little fanfare. "I was delayed, left your boyfriend, that David fellow. He is your boyfriend, right? Well, not important. We had a polite conversation. Said he needed to find you. That's nice of him to be concerned." He moved close, leaned in inches from her face. His hot breath sickened her. "I know this doesn't look good, but you had to involve yourself. So sad."

She pulled at her restraints, crying out, "Tom, I don't understand. What's going on?"

Caswell turned, walked back into shadow. He returned, carrying a wooden stool. Placing it down near her, he sat and stared in her eyes.

"Tom, what's this all about?"

"Oh, it's quite simple. You're the conclusion, and fittingly so since you stuck your nose in Henry's problems. The old man has grown rather fond of you. But Jessica, did you have to win his release from jail? Never thought you'd last that long. You stayed; you just wouldn't leave."

She fought paralyzing panic. Her head began to spin.

"The first two scenes, yes, they were magnificent. I do believe I had directed them to perfection. Oscar material? And of course, I performed them better than Henry ever did. Another award for set design. I accept."

The stark reality hit her. The first two scenes, the first murders copying Henry's movies. She blinked her tears away, realizing Tom was a killer, the vicious butcherer of innocent people. But why mirror old scenes from two of Henry's movies? She pulled at her restraints, the chains clanging, jarring her ears. "Let me go!"

"Oh, no. I think not. I can't have a woman ruining my plans. You are here, so now you have the opportunity to star in my final masterpiece. You called my hand. You gave me no choice but to complete *The Trilogy*. *The Chains*, superb cinema! Did you know Henry hated these films, wished he'd never starred in them? He loathed them all. Once you and I finish, he will regret making them even more. So let's not dally, get on with the shoot, since he's taken an interest in you." He walked back to the bar, picked up a tripod and video recorder.

Jessica struggled, thrashing with all she could manage. Steeped in sweat, out of breath—and for all intents and purposes—out of luck.

"Henry and I go back years," Caswell continued. "I was only a boy in the beginning. We loved, and we were loved or not loved, for varied reasons. And then it all…ended. The years racked up; the pain never ceased. Grief ebbed and flowed for both of us. For me, I knew I was left astray. Love is never easy to obtain. Unlike a mother's love, my time with women, how shall I say it…unproductive. In fact, some of the bitches never survived our encounters. Oh, well, water under the bridge." He slid off the stool. "Why am I telling you this? It's irrelevant now. The first two scenes weren't filmed. This one will be saved for posterity. I think Henry will have to watch it again…and again…and again."

Caswell retrieved a stanchion of production lights, the type used in film and television. Working with the stands, he adjusted their position, taking care to place them correctly.

"Notice the two-point setup. We would have done the standard three-point, but we can't since we have that wall that binds you. This is a kind of *noir* lighting, perfect for dark films such as this. Shadowy subjects, that's our goal here, the subject being you. I learned a lot in the old days from my dad when I would watch the shoots. Of course, he was a zero in my life otherwise. Never an ounce of love came from him."

Caswell placed the stool to the right of the camera, went behind the bar and retrieved something. When he returned the lights came on. Everything in front of Jessica became dull suns, her universe a mere ten-foot radius.

"Now, that's not too bad, is it? The lights aren't blinding, are they? That's what we want to achieve, a subject in fright, and from the terror on your face, I would say you're already in character. There is pure fear on your face. Fantastic! Maybe you'll win an Oscar."

She tried to think. What could she say to slow things down? Frantic, but with enough awareness, she asked, "Is this all about love? What was it that ended?"

"Love," Caswell responded. He rotated a six-inch knife, its keen edge shimmering and reflecting in the high intensity lights. "Lillian, she's the only one I ever really loved."

Jessica watched in horror as Caswell examined the glint on the knife's edge.

"And the more I think of it," he said, "I thank you from the bottom of my heart. You gave me the opportunity to complete *The Trilogy*. If not for you, Henry would be just another mass murderer serving life in prison. At his age, the suffering wouldn't amount to much—but because of you, the mental anguish will swirl around his mind like electrons circling a nucleus. You are the catalyst that will drive him to total insanity. It will pummel him to a pulp. He will suffer as I have. So yes, you made my task easier."

Jessica was stunned, rattling the chains as she pulled in futility.

Caswell approached, took the knife and, with the blade flat, stroked it across her cheek. "It's a shame. To Henry, you are the new Aphrodite, the Greek goddess of love and beauty. I see that now." He stepped back, probing her. "You are a beautiful woman, I can't disagree." He continued to caress her with the blade, flicking it side to side as if re-honing a razor on a strap of leather. She felt the heat of his breathing, becoming heavier, thirsting.

"He was beginning to treat you in a fatherly way. A

father's love so complete, how loving." He pulled the knife away, running his fingers through her hair, circling her lips—a tweaking of her breast—a conquering display of possession.

Jessica wrenched her head away and closed her eyes. Tears soaked her blouse as she anticipated the final moment. She would be dead, any second, the knife slicing from ear to ear. She waited…and waited, like minutes, hours, forever, but nothing. Except her chest now experienced coolness. She opened her eyes. She was alive, but her blouse had been cut away. She stared at Caswell, his eyes were on fire, his lips saturated with saliva. The knife floated to her throat, and in a steady fashion, he scribed down to her abdomen, splitting her bra. Blood trickled out in a thin line between her breasts, a river dribbling red.

She never sensed the pain, only the edge of fleeting consciousness.

Chapter 48

"Tom. It's time to end this."

Caswell turned suddenly, surprised to hear the voice. He pulled the knife away from the carving above Jessica's left breast. "Henry, what a surprise. I never expected you to join in the festivities."

Henry Maxwell stood at the door of the speakeasy, the revolver aimed at Caswell. He swallowed hard, seeing Jessica chained to the wall, her clothes shredded, her body covered with blood. Her head shifted, her eyes fell on Maxwell, but she remained silent. From a distance, he could see her lips tremble.

"Jessica, can you hear me?" his voice squeaked out.
She nodded.

"Oh, Henry, for hell's sake, she's still alive. I've said it time and time again, you need to relive your greatest moments in film. This is one of them. So happy you came, so don't let it go to waste. Would you like to do a little engraving yourself? Her face is a raw canvas awaiting your signature. Come on over. I'll share the knife."

Maxwell's head was thick with agony. His past, creepy, nightmarish films never prepared him for what he was experiencing now. This was no movie; this was sinister reality straight from the depths of hell. "Tom, drop it!" he cried feebly. The words trembled from his mouth. "I won't let you continue."

"Won't let me continue? That's a strong command coming from such a pitiful old man like you."

"Tom, why?"

Caswell's lips twisted unevenly. "Really, you don't know? Have you been that mentally impaired?"

A feverish memory overwhelmed Maxwell's vision, fiery circles of darkness in the speakeasy. The murals on the walls still portrayed smudged scenes, brimming mugs of beer on tables and joyful customers making merry in the background. Lovely paintings from a time long forgotten. Prohibition—days of happiness forced below the grimy streets of Los Angeles. Now, sadness engulfed both worlds, a finality that was not meant to be. The murals seemed to spin; the revolver felt heavy. His hand quivered. He had suspected for years Tom could be unhinged. He was a lone wolf, never had any longtime friends, never could keep a relationship. Maxwell didn't remember a girlfriend, or a guy, for that matter. Lillian had mothered Tom. She brought him under her wing, showering him with kindness, since his father never showed interest. The killings based upon *The Trilogy* films now made sense. Tom, the loner, a killer.

"Why kill? What have you gained by copying those films?"

"Satisfaction, pure and simple."

"Satisfaction?" Maxwell's voice was reduced to a low undertone, almost a whisper.

"Simple, Henry. To remember all the women that have ignored me—each uncaring—unworthy. They misread me. they teased me, they played me, made me feel inferior, sexless, a boy in a man's body, socially clumsy." A sneer crossed his face. "Most paid the ultimate price. Their loss, what can I say. Love is all one ever asks for in life."

"Why reinvent those hideous scenes?"

"Because of you! I only had one love, and you were responsible for her death. It starts—and ends—with you!" Caswell was close to frothing at the mouth, his face contorted.

In that very instant, Maxwell had confirmation of what he had suspected over the years. "When Lillian became aware of your thoughts, she told me."

"Now, you get it. You finally see!" Caswell shouted. "I loved her as much—more than you—and she loved me. Your world was your work. Lillian understood my loneliness. She took me in when my father didn't give a damn. Don't deny you didn't know who he really was. On the set, at your house, wherever she was, she gave me the affection I craved when my father was still trying to grapple with who he was. All the while, you were busy doing Hollywood, leaving my Lillian all alone. She treated me with love when no one else cared. I saw a future with her. Is it so wrong for a boy to be in love?"

Maxwell moved closer. He had to keep the upper hand. He was an old man, prone to mistakes, prone to letting his guard down. He didn't have the physical ability that Tom possessed, but he had tears. They were on the verge of filling his eyes, blinding him. Lillian was his greatest love. No one else came close. No one's love would match his. Tom was wrong. Maxwell spoke weakly, "If you have a grudge, it should have been against your father for his lack of caring. Lillian recognized that and accepted you for who you were. She understood your needs. What you're doing now would break her heart. Is that what you want?"

"Oh, no, no, no! If she were alive, she would be

praising what I'm doing. You, Henry, you killed her! You know it, don't deny it!"

For an instant, Maxwell felt the pain resurface—the emotional pain, the guilt, ten thousand nights of what-ifs. It wasn't his lack of love. "Lillian and I worked tirelessly to sustain the most glorious, loving relationship ever. Yes, she had depression problems. Prescribed drugs didn't help. They attacked her very soul, taking a piece of her mind. She was strong, she quit the drugs." His tired old eyes looked beyond Tom to Jessica and the connection he felt toward her. "How do you justify what you are doing to Jessica? She has nothing to do with your past, your pain."

"Henry, don't you see? It's because you have taken a liking to her. She has started to give you hope. I won't allow that. You don't deserve hope, only misery. What you see here is a fitting penance."

Maxwell lurched. A faint pain crept across his chest. *Not now*, he begged. *Not now, please.*

Caswell moved close to Jessica, knife raised. Maxwell shook off the discomfort and pointed the gun.

Caswell backed away, smiling. His opportunity had waned for the moment. "At your age, you're liable to blow a gasket."

"Not quite there yet," Maxwell said, rubbing his chest. But the pain kept coming. He dropped the cane, grasping at his chest. Caswell rushed him. Maxwell's arm fell as he pulled the trigger, the bullet ricocheted off the floor and cratered the brick wall beyond. As he lost his grip, the revolver fell from his hand just as he curled forward and fell onto his knees.

Caswell picked up the gun. He pointed it at Maxwell, who was struggling to get a breath.

"Henry, I really didn't want this to end this way. You deserve your remaining days to be spent in total agony."

Maxwell felt the pain subside. With willpower, he stood, wobbling, pushing his bifocals back up his nose. His cane remained on the floor, but he didn't have the energy to pick it up. "Let Jessica go, Tom," he pleaded. "Shoot me instead."

Caswell's faced brightened with excitement. "I have a better idea, Henry." He picked up the stool and placed it next to Maxwell. "Sit, Henry."

Maxwell leaned on the stool. "Let her go," he begged.

"Oh, I don't think so. I have you both. It was your decision to join the party. You still have an unobstructed view from where you stand." With the gun in one hand, and the knife in the other, he moved over to a bloody but still conscious Jessica. "This dear has just had a few minor scratches. Now the real work begins, you know, you did it once in *The Chains*. This time, it will be for real. You've always wanted to do it for real, haven't you, Henry? Watch closely, my friend."

Maxwell's unease had become a canyon of despair. "Tom, don't. I'll do anything you ask." He struggled for a full breath.

"I want you to watch, that's all. You like her, don't you? You recall this scene, Henry. You scratched symbols masterfully on the young woman, but not much blood was shown on the big screen. You know, the film rating had to include the younger matinee crowd. Even though you detested that movie, you couldn't allow a restricted rating. Money was at stake. Always about the money. No money here, just an R rating. Like the petroglyphs that the Native Americans left on rock walls all over the Southwest, we will do the same—but not with symbols of suns, snakes, and great warriors with shields. Our symbols could be of life and death, love, and hate. But I have a better idea. How about dates, you know, like the date of Lillian's death."

The dagger of words was too much to take. He hobbled toward Caswell without his cane, knowing he didn't have a chance to stop him.

Jessica blurted out, "Please don't, Henry, it's not worth it."

****

The sound of gunfire caught David off guard. Running down the tunnel, he saw light at the far end. A door slightly cracked. No time. He wrapped his fingers around the gun he had retrieved from the dead man, and kicked the door open. Rushing in, he couldn't believe what he saw. His eyes first fell on Jessica, lit by the lights. Chained to a wall, clothes shredded.

Blood.

Caswell dropped the knife and pointed the revolver at David. "More cavalry to the rescue. How nice." He cocked the hammer and pulled the trigger. Nothing.

Caught in a moment of unbelievable shock, David pointed the gun, pulled the trigger, missing his target. Caswell fled, slipping through the back door. David rushed to Jessica.

Maxwell stumbled over, pulled her blouse back over her breasts and offered David his handkerchief to stop some of the bleeding. With his other hand, David cradled her chin. She looked up, tears streaming, her breathing irregular. He pulled closer, cheek to cheek, and whispered in her ear. "It's over, sweetheart, all over.

We're going home."

Several gunshots echoed down the tunnels.

****

It was Brown's first visit to the legendary underworld beneath the streets of LA, the trash-strewn darkness, the intricate network of putrid, musty passageways and abandoned subways, a world within itself. He found it hard to breathe as he followed an LA police officer through the abandoned subway tunnel. He was panting when they approached another group of officers, but it was not from exertion, it was from uncertainty.

Light stanchions had been set up, providing an eerie glow that bounced off the confining walls. As he approached, several officers surrounded a man on the ground. He was lying on his side, blood seeping from several bullet holes that had riddled his body. Brown felt a gnawing chill in the air. Now, more than ever, he didn't want to know the circumstances.

One officer handed Brown a plastic bag containing a revolver. "He pointed this at our men. They returned fire."

Brown nodded, examined the revolver, and handed it back. He noticed there was only one empty shell, no other bullets.

"You ready for more?" the officer said.

His voice cracked. "If you must."

"Follow me." The police officer walked toward a cross-tunnel that intersected the subway at an oblique angle. "This one's an old freight tunnel that connected several basements along Wall Street. Crazy, don't you think?"

Brown didn't comment.

Another policeman came out of the tunnel and recognized Brown from the sheriff's department. "Detective, you've got to see this."

Once again, Brown got that dreadful, sinking feeling that Henry Maxwell and Jessica Barrow were involved. Could he handle another gruesome scene, now with people he knew? He felt the need to disappear into the blackness and never return.

The officer caught the distress on his face. "Everyone's going to be okay. We've called for medical assistance. It's nothing short of a miracle."

Brown took in a breath of stale air and let it out slowly. For the first time in days, he wanted to breathe in a sigh of relief, maybe inhale the soft scent of pine at Big Bear or the salty spray of a warm breeze off the Pacific.

Lovely dreams. If they'd only come true.

Chapter 49

It had been less than twelve hours since she'd been released from the hospital. The lacerations were only surface deep, although one required four stitches. The mental scars were yet to be fully determined. Searching through her minimal wardrobe, she found a navy button-down blouse hoping the collar would keep the dressings hidden. Her pale skin and anguished eyes were enough indications that she'd experienced a life-threatening event.

She zipped her suitcase tight after looking around to make sure she'd packed everything. It was inconsequential. Material items were, well, material items. They could be replaced, they could be forgotten—unlike things that mattered—flesh and bone, reality and awareness, relationships and trust. Marsha asked if she needed help packing, but Jessica declined, convincing her she had to do this alone. Even though her mind held chaos, she maintained a certain calm that overshadowed the courage it took to return to the castle.

The conservatorship was still in force, but rumors were it may be lifted. She realized she would not be continuing with Henry Maxwell after all she'd been through. Without the final ruling from the judge, it was an impossibility to continue. All well and good, she had her own reckoning to deal with, a terror-filled aspect of her life that she might never get beyond.

Exiting the guest room, she walked toward the stairs, thinking about the nightmarish first few nights she had spent here. Henry wasn't the monster she envisioned. Somehow, each night became a little more forgiving, the castle evolving into something acceptable. No dungeons, no torture chambers, no vats of acid, no rooms of horror, no creepy bedrooms with rotting corpses hiding under the blankets, only underground passageways which became more docile with every visit.

She took her time, following the spiral staircase as it wound down. She moved into the Grand Foyer and dropped her suitcase on the floor, the sound resonating off stone walls careening down from the high ceiling. She looked around for the last time, remembering when she first laid eyes on this threatening space, her heart then accelerating at a rapid pace, wrung with fear. Today, it beat calmly. The space no longer caused panic; the walls did not pulsate. She studied the octagonal room. The shadows held no perils, no slithering tapestries, and the perverse did not float in stale air. Glancing down the hall toward the library, she held her breath. Would she ever have the nerve to set foot in it again? *Hard to say*, escaped her mind. Shaking away the thought, she realized Henry's presence kept the castle masked in mystery. With his absence, this stacked stone behemoth had no stories to tell, or mysteries to untangle.

She took one last look around the foyer, picked her suitcase up and exited through the large door. Marsha sat at the wheel of the car, waiting. Jessica walked down the steps, stopped and whirled. The mansion stayed the same, the Gothic towers and battlements non-threatening. *The flying monkeys are nowhere to be seen.* Maybe they didn't exist in the first place.

In this moment of difficulty, she had hoped to see Henry. Marsha told her he was at the hospital for tests to determine the severity of his health. She may have seen him the last time in the speakeasy. She ached for him, the eighty-five-year-old, coming to the rescue with a revolver that had only one round. As much as she wanted to shred this terrifying experience from her mind, she knew the look of resolve that penetrated his wizened face would forever be a fixture of her soul.

For now, she and Marsha would spend the night in a hotel near LAX and take a flight back to San Francisco tomorrow morning. JWB had granted her an indefinite leave of absence. Whether she agreed or not, it was set in stone. The good news: David promised to come up in a few days and spend some time with her. If anything could be done to help her through this period, he might be the cure she most desperately needed.

Sliding into the passenger seat, she looked away from Marsha, not wanting her to see her emerging tears. The engine started and the vehicle turned down the drive past the twin gargoyles and disappeared into the canyon below.

Chapter 50

Early the next morning, David dropped both Jessica and Marsha off at LAX for their flight to San Francisco. He promised he'd come up after he wrapped up a few things at UCLA. He didn't share his schedule the rest of the day, knowing it was not the time to bring up anything to do with Maxwell.

After leaving the airport, he drove over to Silvers' bungalow. He called a day earlier and told him it was imperative they get together. Silvers agreed they should meet, since *The Trilogy* movies were all over the local and national news.

Walking up to the door, a carpenter fixing the door jamb turned. "If you're looking for Mr. Silvers," the man said, "he's downstairs."

"Thanks." David entered and headed to the basement, thinking this would be an interesting discussion. He would inquire about the posters with the news clippings attached, having no idea how Silvers would react. He found him in his office, sitting in front of his computer.

Silvers looked up with a rather contrite expression.

David stepped into the room, took a seat on a metal folding chair next to the desk. "You've read the papers."

After an apologetic sigh, Silvers spoke in his nasal voice. "I pulled all references to those three films from the website. I don't think I'll ever be able to talk about them again."

"They do have a history that's not pretty."

"These last few days have made me analyze Henry's career in detail. You were correct, Mr. Grovene, he should be remembered for his Gothic roles. Those—" He coughed. "Those *Trilogy* films, I thought they had all the merit in the world. I dreamt of a whole new field of horror, the slasher genre. Then his wife died unexpectedly, ending his illustrious career. No more dripping blood, so to speak. So, I will admit you were right in your assessment earlier about his legacy."

"How do you feel now?"

Silvers curled his neck. "I appreciate him more now. A true Gothic actor, as he should be remembered. The slasher genre was not meant for him. He belongs in the realm of actors who presented good entertainment, a positive examination of good versus evil."

From the office, David could see the wall where *The Trilogy* posters were hung. All three were missing. "Where did the posters go?"

"I put them in storage, maybe never to see the light of day again."

"Then tell me about the recent newspaper articles plastered on two of them detailing the killings?"

Silvers looked more suspicious than surprised. "How'd you know that?"

"Yeah, well, I'm the bastard who broke your door down. I apologize."

Silvers' eyes swept across David with disbelief. "You broke down my door?" His nasal voice disappeared.

"I did, and I will pay for the damage. The truth is, I pegged you wrong. I had every reason to think that way after hearing you immortalize those disgusting ribbons of celluloid. Your love of those films made me blame you without merit. I overreacted. I did knock a few times. After a while, I bashed in your door, and cringed when I saw the articles taped to the posters, convinced you were involved. At that moment, Jessica's life, or death, crowded my thinking."

Silvers took a deep breath. "I should call the cops and report you for vandalism."

"You have every right to press charges, but what about the newspaper articles?"

Silvers leaned back, smacking his lips. "After I realized the connections, I cut out the clippings. It got me to thinking about those films. Silly that I taped the stories to the posters. My way of comparison, I suppose." He shook his head. "I couldn't honor those movies after I read and reread the articles."

"I admit breaking and entering, but it takes guts to confess a change of heart."

The fan club president eyed him with admiration. "It takes integrity to admit you broke into my house."

"I'm still wondering about *Lady Julia's Sarcophagus*."

"You're persistent." His nasal voice returned.

"I'll cut to the chase. I know you have or had possession of the film."

He paused. "Why would you think that?"

"I have an email from a collector in New Jersey. Says you were fishing for a buyer."

The air appeared to be sucked out of Silvers' lungs. He stumbled to answer, but nothing came out. He stood and walked out the door. He moved past the remaining posters. David followed, seeing him admire them one at a time. Reaching the last one, *Once Upon a Nightmare*, he gazed at it for a long time. "I always thought this was one of Henry's greatest achievements, the way his magic with Tiffany Cobb lit the screen, the melding of a great love story with tragedy and horror. Nothing could be better for the human soul, until I—" He stopped and looked at David. "Until I saw *Lady Julia's Sarcophagus*. Henry had out done himself. That, in my opinion, was his best, even though he never finished it."

"Do you still have the film?"

Silvers nodded. "I guess I'm in a shit load of trouble?"

That afternoon, David sat in the film lab at UCLA after watching the digital recording of *Lady Julia's Sarcophagus*. He then examined the original reel of celluloid frame by frame in the Steenbeck 35 mm flatbed editor to check out the preservation qualities. Except for the last scene, which was missing, he would rate the film as excellent—a pure Gothic masterpiece of movie making, superlative in plot, directing and outstanding acting. He had seen most of Maxwell's films, and this performance in his humble opinion was by far the best. Maxwell outdid himself, and the absolute tragedy of it all—the film was shy of the final scene. If there ever was a moment when he needed to see the end of a movie, this was it.

He looked over at Arlen Silvers, sitting nearby, a face of sorrow and shame. He took his eyes off the fan club president and reread a few notes he had scribbled. After spending the last couple of weeks around Maxwell, he could see how he seemed to emulate the main character, Chatsworth—hallucinations, odd things, and all. The credits indicated the film was based upon the novel *Lady Julia's Sarcophagus* by BB Barmore.

Moorlands of Devon, England—Late nineteenth century Gothic tale—Sir Alston Chatsworth played by Maxwell—his wife Julia dies mysteriously—Chatsworth suffers perpetual grief, hallucinates, does strange doings—redemption, greed, and fits of terror. Lord Dedrick is his adversary and schemes to get Chatsworth off the land he desires to possess by masterminding horrible events for the purpose of intimidation and fright. He goes as far as kidnapping Chatsworth's daughter, Miss Vanessa. After a frantic time finding her, she is freed and Lord Dedrick commits suicide, knowing his life of misdeeds has caught up with him. The final resolution of the film is unknown—need to see if Maxwell will provide it.

He sat silent for a moment. Arlen Silvers had given him the reels, knowing his future depended on his explanation of why Yasuo Tashiro was killed. "Sad that there's no last scene."

Silvers added, "If Eddie and I had known, we wouldn't have tried to steal it, and—"

"And Tashiro would still be alive. I get it." David studied the fan president. He swore he detected remorse in the man's eyes. Silvers repeated it was an accident and no intent to kill the former editor. Involuntary manslaughter came to mind. Eddie must have put a dart in the barrel by mistake, intended for an elephant instead of a bobcat. The dosage was lethal enough for a small man like Tashiro. Their scheme, to render him unconscious, steal the film, replace it with another, and hope he would never notice. Unfortunately, Tashiro's heart stopped. A court of law would make the final determination as to guilt, whether homicide or manslaughter.

"Before you came over, and at your request, I called Detective Hardrick," David said. "He's flying down tomorrow to meet with you and take your statement. Whether he will arrest you or not, I don't know. I'll put in a good word for you. The Caswell incident has us all on edge. Hardrick did tell me the courts would take into consideration everything that occurred."

"I—I appreciate that." Silvers shook his head. "I should have known better."

"How did you find out Tashiro had the only copy of *Lady Julia's Sarcophagus*?"

"Just like you did. I knew he worked editing for Global. I talked to him on occasion. He sent me a list of his films but said none were for sale. He said I was welcome to check them out, which I did. That's when I verified the film was real. I didn't view it in its entirety, so I never realized it didn't have the final scene. Like you, I became intrigued. I had to have it, knowing it would be worth a lot of money on the market. There are collectors all over this country who would spend big on rarities like that. Henry had talked about it, but he never told me it was incomplete. He's a hard man from which to get information. But now, that doesn't matter."

"When Hardrick arrives tomorrow, I'm obligated to turn the film over to him. We must keep him in the loop."

Silvers nodded. "I understand."

"I made a digital copy just in case something happens to the original. A court will decide who has legal rights to it. Henry Maxwell might well have some ownership."

"The fan club will be grateful for that. Part of Maxwell's history, you know, even if I'm in jail."

David stood, and patted Silvers on the back. "Hang in there. I think you'll be fine."

Chapter 51

Maxwell sat in the library, staring at the chair Jessica had occupied when kidnapped. The stain from spilled tea still marked the table. He refused to have it cleaned. For a long time, he stared at it, his thoughts fractious, like a continuous reel of film never ending, never beginning. He looked up watching a blurred figure enter. As the form sharpened, he recognized the professor. His eyes followed as David sat down across from him. "I just got back from some tests at the hospital. Heart still ticking but on borrowed time, and after all this stuff with Caswell and—" He stumbled to mention Jessica.

"Relieved you and Jessica are doing better than expected," David commented. "She needs some down time. After a while, I'm convinced she'll want to see you again. She doesn't blame you for Tom Caswell."

With trembling lips, Maxwell untangled his threaded hands. "Professor, you've no doubt noticed I'm a stubborn old man, set in his ways, grumpy and indecisive."

David smiled. "I've noticed."

"I won't belabor the point. I'd like to thank you for being here for Jessica." Jessica, there he said her name.

"That's not necessary. I'm just grateful it's over and ended better than expected. That's what counts."

"At one time, Jessica told me you wanted to discuss

some of my other films."

"That's true."

"*The Trilogy*, off limits! Other Global pictures, it would be enjoyable to reminisce."

"Fine with me."

"So, what's on your mind?"

"Tell me about *Lady Julia's Sarcophagus*."

He stared hard at David. "Why am I not surprised you'd bring that one up?"

"When I first met you, I said I knew every one of your thirty-two films. You corrected me and said thirty-three. So *Lady Julia's Sarcophagus* was the last one?"

He grumbled. "Never finished. Nothing to talk about, discussion over."

"Oh, come now, Henry, you know that's not true. I've heard some say it would have been the best film ever released by Global."

"Who in the hell would say that?" Maxwell's throat tightened.

"Emma Sandstrom."

"What, that old bag? She still alive?"

"She was when we talked a while back."

His eyes squinted angrily. "What else did she say? Blamed it all on me, I presume."

"I'm not one to make judgments."

"She should have died years ago, the old bitch."

"*Lady Julia's Sarcophagus*. Great title. What's it about, and why wasn't it finished?"

A sadness flushed his face. "I had my reason. Leave it be."

"Let me give you a little of what I know about that film." David proceeded to explain Tashiro's death and how Arlen Silvers was in the thick of it.

His jaw fell. "Such a fiasco, that fan club. I should have shut it down. That Silvers is a loose cannon, had been since day one. How the hell he got control of the club is beyond me. My history doesn't need to be kept alive. My fans are older than the hills, long dead, or worthless losers who don't have anything better to do than go to Saturday matinees in their dreams and envision a sick overpaid bastard like me playing bullshit make-belief on the screen."

David leaned in. "I believe Silvers when he said Tashiro's death was an accident."

"I remember him back in the day. When Global folded, he must have taken possession of whatever wasn't claimed by the creditors. Easy then to clean out the vaults of a dying company. I was in such a miserable state at that time. I never thought much of it once I ended the filming. Unfinished, so be it, at that time. So it ended up in his possession. More power to him. Thanks for filling me in."

"Would you like to see it?"

"You've seen it?" Maxwell's eyes flared.

"Silvers and I had a little talk. He gave me the only reels of the film. I had no right, but I took the liberty of making a digital copy. The Sacramento Police now have the film, the legal rights up in the air. The digital copy, I have no right to keep it."

"Thanks, but no thanks. I don't have any desire to relive that awful time."

David studied Maxwell closely. His last sentence didn't register as truth on his face, a face that somehow had a continuing connection to the film. "But what about the finale? When I saw it, I was captivated. You can't leave me in limbo. As a fan, that's not fair. I need the ending."

He pushed himself up. "I'm a little tired. I think I'll go take a nap." He rose, and walked away, then stopped. "Oh, the ending." He turned and stared at David with a promising smile. "Yours, mine, Jessica's. We all have beginnings…we all have endings. You choose, but choose wisely." He hobbled out the door.

Chapter 52

The day was clear and warm, the type of day Bay Area residents had come to expect this time of year. Jessica walked by the high pagoda in Golden Gate Park, attempting to end the nightmare she endured beneath the streets of Los Angeles. No doubt the abundance of azaleas and Japanese maples, coupled with the incredible miniaturization and asymmetry that defined a Japanese garden, should have provided a sense of tranquility, yet the desired calmness couldn't erase her living hell in the speakeasy. Would she ever move on, or was the notion of a demonic death a lasting scar branded forever in her gray matter? Was her anguish really about surviving a near-death experience, or something else? She knew the answer before she even formulated the question.

Wandering along every path in the garden for close to an hour, she left and drove over to Lands End. She parked and took the trail toward Point Lobo, passing endless hikers and sightseers. After all, this was a popular spot within the confines of San Francisco and crowds would not be uncommon. For some odd reason, she felt a sense of peace as the urban trail wound its way through groves of cypress and eucalyptus. Wildflowers and chirping birds kept her mind focused away from Los Angeles. After fifteen minutes, she reached the cliffs above the bright blue Pacific and sandy beaches below, granting a spectacular view of Golden Gate Bridge in the distance. Finding a bench to take in the view, she sat and let her mind take a path of its own. The swirling seagulls drifting over the cliffs forced her thoughts back to Henry Maxwell and Point Dume.

Maybe this wasn't such a great idea. She needed a complete purge of the last few weeks. But Point Dume now took front and center, in fact, it became a mirror image. Both areas were similar—the cliffs, the sapphire Pacific stretching to infinity, the salt, the gulls—and Henry Maxwell. Her time spent with him at one of his favorite spots drew both together in an inescapable compact. Scanning south to north, she swore she saw a transparent Henry trudging up the trail, an aberration in his own right, cane testing each step of the way. He stopped, adjusted his fedora and then his ghostly presence looked her way. Her lips quivered as her mouth opened wide. Was she hallucinating, and was he smiling at her, or had she gone completely mad? She rubbed her eyes hard, then looked back at the trail. Only real flesh-and-blood visitors were visible. Henry no longer filled her vision.

Back to the Marina District, she sat on her condo balcony, gazing out at nothing in particular. It had been one full day since she and Marsha returned to San Francisco and she was forced to take an indefinite leave. Her whole world was now in slow-motion collapse. To do what, sit here and obsess? Marsha recommended taking a walk on the beach, visit the Japanese Tea Garden in Golden Gate Park, Fisherman's Wharf, on and on, do all the great things San Francisco had to offer. Relax, for goodness' sake! Neither the Tea Garden nor Point Lobo calmed her nerves. They exploded them. She'd thought about going back to work, but would they let her, and would she be effective? She knew the answer, shaking her head in despair. No, she'd be a wreck, wouldn't be able to get anything of value accomplished.

She stood and returned inside, her mind now awash in indecision. Although she rationalized she might return one day to Henry's castle, time became her enemy. What if it was too late? What if his heart gave out? What if he fell and broke his hip? Those possibilities began to tighten her in a regretful, never-ending vise.

A premonition. She would do better on her leave of absence if she went back. Crazy. And why question herself? Wasting no time, she opened her laptop and, as quickly as her fingers flew across the keyboard, booked a flight to LAX.

The following morning, Jessica arrived in Los Angeles, picked up her rental car and headed for the castle. She dialed David's number and explained her plan.

"What, you're back? Are you sure this is a good idea? I was coming up tomorrow, remember?"

"I couldn't stay away. I've had this foolhardy notion something is dragging me back. I can't ignore it. It's like an omen, like maybe a cardiac issue and he'll be gone. I would never forgive myself if something happened before I returned. Do you understand?"

"I do. Does he know this?"

"I didn't call, not wanting to frighten him. I'm being drawn back there. I can't explain it, that's all. I do sense he's aware I'm coming."

"Listen, I'll call later. I might have something to share from my end."

She paused. "David, it helps hearing your voice."

"Yours as well."

An hour later, Jessica turned into the circle drive and parked. Without thinking twice, she knew something inexplicable was drawing her. She walked to the door and pulled the latch. It opened with ease, never locked. Off to her right, a meager light emanated from the hallway beyond the pointed archway. Any light would be welcome until she could calm her train wreck of nerves. She moved under the arch toward the den, disregarding her last visit down this hallway. The door was open. She stopped in a self-induced panic—her frenzied thinking left her paralyzed, a condition that could only be cured by continuing. Fearful that her mind was playing tricks, she closed her eyes and exhaled. She entered, and like she thought, Henry sat at his desk. She felt relief that she had found him. She casually walked over and eased into a chair.

Motionless, he watched her with satisfaction. "I knew you'd return."

For the briefest of moments, she sensed a joyous lump in her throat, an emotional constriction that rippled down to her toes. "Marsha said you saw your doctor. What'd he tell you?"

"Had some tests taken. Old ticker. Maybe a stent, or some other wild medical procedure. At my age, I can assure you, it won't be rocket science."

"You'll do fine. I know it."

He shook his head. "I'm not important. You are. I have shown great stupidity for not recognizing the signs of Tom's instability. Will you forgive me?"

"No forgiveness necessary." Seeing Henry alive and not struggling for breath was all the forgiveness she needed.

"I knew Tom had serious mental problems. This dimwit of an old man never connected the dots. I kept trying to avoid him. On top of that, my guilt for having birthed those three movies will never go away."

She smiled. "It's over. There will be no more reenactments."

"Sorry to have brought it up. You must be exhausted. And to come back here, I can't imagine you haven't put this god-awful place out of your mind."

"I had to."

"At the hospital, they told me your cuts would heal."

"I'll be fine."

Both sat silent for a few moments; neither one of them knew what to say. Just as they were bound by court order, they were now inseparably connected emotionally. What had once been a forced association was now a forever pairing.

She studied Henry's gruff exterior, his bifocals reflecting the desk lamp like a beacon at sea, flickering a steady SOS as his head quaked back and forth. She spoke. "I was worried about you, your health."

"Is there another reason?"

"An inclination. Something told me to return."

He smiled, then rose out of his chair.

She stood, and for a moment, their eyes connected.

He limped over, embracing her in a meaningful hug. "You being here means all the world to me."

Chapter 53

That evening after the sun set, Jessica left the veranda. The night chill had convinced her to make a cup of soup. Her cell phone chimed. "Hello," she answered.

"I'm on my way up." David sounded alarmed.

"You sound out of sorts. What's going on?"

"I am a little spooked. I've stumbled across the most unnerving thing. I was hoping to be there within the hour, but traffic is crazy, bumper to bumper."

Then for some unknown reason, the line went dead.

A banging on the massive wooden door echoed throughout the high space. She gasped. She tensed, scared to death. Why wasn't David here already?

****

Stanley Brown pounded the dragon head a second time. D'Angelo looked on, more stupefied than amused at such a monstrous door knocker. His expression seemed to ask, *Where the hell in Transylvania are we?* The door opened.

Jessica stared at them across the threshold.

"Ms. Barrow," Brown said, his voice gritty. "Is Mr. Maxwell here?"

Puzzled, she said, "He's upstairs resting. What's the problem?"

"A couple of incidents have come to our attention. Both involve two men who are now in the morgue."

Her jaw dropped.

"Trust me, I hoped I'd never see you again, let alone Mr. Maxwell."

****

Jessica swore she was living a never-ending nightmare.

D'Angelo stepped forward. "If you don't mind, we have questions for Mr. Maxwell."

Brown gave D'Angelo a "down boy" glare.

"For me, I'd love to hear them," Maxwell's voice boomed from the other side of the darkened foyer.

All eyes turned to the dusk-cloaked recesses of the castle. Slowly, an image formed under an arch shrouded in shadow. Maxwell appeared from the shadows, plodding across the stone floor in a burgundy satin dress shirt, matching tie, black coat, slacks, and black wingtip brogues with a notable luster that glowed.

"Detective Brown, so nice of you to come. I see you have your trusty sidekick with you as well." He gave D'Angelo the eye.

D'Angelo took a step forward but held off responding.

"Our recent investigative work points to you as a person of interest," Brown said. "Very interesting, to say the least. A body was discovered yesterday in Culver City, been there a few days. But not until a few hours ago did we make the connection."

"Oh, yes, that would be Dr. Ewe Kopf, if you haven't already figured that out."

"What?" Jessica gulped.

"Sorry, dear, I didn't tell you. Ewe, I'm afraid, shot himself in the head." Maxwell turned back to Brown. "If you like, I did record the conversation I had with him prior to his demise. I think that might clear some things up. That was one thing I knew how to do with that new-fangled phone Jessica convinced me to acquire."

"And another man, a Francisco Cuervo. Finally your name came up after your Bentley was identified."

"Lillian's gardener eons ago. Yes, poor bastard in tremendous pain. What could I do? I hated to observe him in such agony."

Brown rolled his eyes. "It appears you have important details about both these cases. We are asking you to come down to the station for your statement."

"I'd be delighted. If you'd be so kind, I need my wallet, and the recording on the phone. They're in the den."

Brown nodded. "I don't see a problem. We'll wait."

"I'll come with you," D'Angelo said.

"Of course, Tony. I'd appreciate the escort," Maxwell said, giving D'Angelo a creepy smile.

Jessica shook her head as Maxwell and D'Angelo exited under the pointed arch and down the corridor.

Brown's sympathetic eyes fell on Jessica. "How are you doing?" he asked. "You've been through hell, no doubt."

"I'm in shock, to say the least."

"Welcome to the club," Brown added. "Has to be an end somewhere on the horizon, don't you think?"

"Right now, I don't know what to think."

****

Maxwell shuffled down the hallway, turning to look at D'Angelo, close on his heels. He smiled at the unease he saw on the detective's face.

"Never been in a castle before, Tony?" he asked, pausing in front of the door to the den. "You ought to find one. They really help the mind regress, so to speak."

He chuckled.

D'Angelo cleared his throat; the kind of gesture meant to portray *I'm not scared*. "I don't think so," he dribbled.

Maxwell stopped and leaned D'Angelo's direction, grinning. "A lot of fun goes on here, Tony. You're missing out." He entered the den. D'Angelo, looking a bit intimidated, followed.

"Don't you need a light to find the phone and wallet," D'Angelo asked, noticing the scant amount of light coming through the two elongated windows high above.

"Oh, no. When you live here, the darkness is your friend. It's better for the soul, assuming Satan doesn't have yours." He chuckled again, moving to the other side of the desk. He picked up the phone and handed it to D'Angelo. "Here's the recording. Now, where'd I put the wallet," he said, rummaging through drawers.

"We don't have all day," D'Angelo said, exasperated, glancing back and forth between Maxwell and the exit.

Maxwell reached under the desk and pushed the button.

The sound of creaking hinges spooked D'Angelo, who lurched backwards. "What the hell—"

The hidden door rotated out, exposing the wall cavity. Maxwell stepped inside. "I bid you good day, Tony." He disappeared and the door closed with a thud.

****

D'Angelo rushed to the door and couldn't open it. In a fit of panic, he ran back into the hallway and into the foyer out of breath. "That bastard disappeared behind a wall!" He wiped the sweat from his brow.

"Oh, no!" Jessica exclaimed.

"What are you talking about, Tony?" Brown asked.

"In the den, a door popped open," D'Angelo described, breathless. "He went through before I could stop him. The door closed. He's gone, goddammit!"

Brown shot Jessica a look of dismay.

"There's endless passageways underneath the castle," she said. "Why he's gone there, I don't know. A button beneath his desk. I never imagined he'd use it. It's no easy chore to find your way below. It's quite the maze."

"Then show us!" D'Angelo ordered.

She turned to Brown. "Henry's scared, that's all. Imagine all that he has been through. Please don't go rushing down there with guns drawn. He has a weak heart. Let me go first and talk to him. He'll listen to me, not a bunch of armed deputies."

Brown thought a moment. "Okay, we'll do it your way. If it doesn't work, we'll have to track him down ourselves. Any other access?"

Jessica figured she had to be honest. "The storage room in the motor court. Stair goes down, but it's a maze of corridors. Don't try it. You'll get lost."

A minute later, they were all in the den. Jessica pushed the button behind the desk. The door swung open.

"Tony, you stay here," Brown said. "I'll go to the motor court and keep an eye on that door in case Maxwell exits. I'll call headquarters and tell them our dilemma."

She took a flashlight out of the drawer, sucked in a deep breath and hurried out of sight, racing down the stairs. Stepping into the confines of the first room, she stared in a trauma-like state at the two passageways ahead.

"Henry," she spoke with authority. "Henry," she said a little louder. She waited, listened. Nothing.

She beamed the light right to left, just as they did yesterday, moving without thought or fear. This whole *macabre-dungeon-thing*, her mind rummaged, a part of Henry's past, composed of smoke and mirrors. Finding the intersecting passageway on her right, she found the iron-grille gate open. Moving through, she stopped at the top of the stairs that dipped deeper beneath the castle. A lone torch flickered, casting swaying shadows on the walls. She crept down like a cat, searching every crevice and cranny, and there, Henry sat on the edge of one of the stone caskets. He had unbuttoned his suit jacket. His satin dress shirt reflected the yellow glow emitted from the wall torches.

"I am beginning to understand you so much better, Jessica. I knew you'd follow."

She stepped into the massive space. "I had to, no choice. I'm not sure what the detectives would have done."

"Brown's okay. Tony needs some anger management skills."

She nodded, moving closer to him. "What's there to gain by running? I won't question what happened to Dr. Kopf and the other man."

"A valid reason for everything. After I'm gone, this whole affair will become clear."

"Henry, I don't like the tone of your voice, and I don't like the finality of 'after I'm gone.' She moved closer, sitting down next to him. "Please, Henry, what's this all about?"

He reached up and wiped the sweat off his brow. "Remember the first day you moved into my life?"

Jessica sighed. "How could I forget? I was scared to death. You, your house, the unknown."

"You had reason to feel that way. My attitude certainly would've made anyone have second thoughts. I wanted you to be miserable, thinking that would stop this conservatorship baloney. In any event, that night, I decided to take control of my destiny, in not so pretty a manner.

She didn't know what to think, but the question was unavoidable. "Was it because of me?"

Maxwell shook his head. "On the contrary, My mind had been made up before I laid eyes on you. Before I could carry out this *Mors Voluntaria*, a Latin phrase I had to memorize from *Ancient Eyes*, if I'm not mistaken, an image appeared, drawing me outside in the beating rain. I've been known to have these hallucinations, and this was just one more in a long list of crazy visions this crazy man has experienced. I got sidetracked. *Mors Voluntaria* never happened."

"If I understand the translation of the Latin phrases, I am happy it never happened. The apparition? The image—Lillian?"

He nodded.

"Was it real, or just another hallucination?"

He didn't respond.

"What else?"

"You, Jessica.

"Me, I don't understand."

"It all boils down to fate, Jessica. And sometimes fate can be irrational, abhorrent, painful, unwanted…but necessary."

"What do you mean?"

"Your fate, my fate. It took me awhile, but I realized, they're one of the same. For an old man short on years, my fate is intertwined with yours. Your entrance into my bleak existence was more than an inconvenience, it was the spark that transformed everything. It took me a while, and when I finally caught on, it made me the happiest man in the whole world."

She looked at him, confused and alarmed. "My psychological training, which I've tried to distance myself from, has reentered my life uninvited and is not helpful at the moment. I still don't understand. Where is this all going?"

"Before you interrupted my sorrowful, crappy life, I was headed down a road with a dead end. When you showed up, uninvited as you say, the road I was on came to a fork. Which way, the right or left, just like the two corridors in the anteroom of this appalling underground mess. Your arrival on the scene forced me to decide—which road to take. If I take the wrong one, I lose, the correct one, we all win. Enough soul searching, I chose the path that brought me to you, just as fate has devised."

He slid off the stone coffin. She followed. Within arm's length, he put a hand on her shoulder and drew her close. She acquiesced and didn't fight it. He gently hugged her and whispered in her ear. "In due time, it will all make sense. You're part of my life now, and the final glue to bind our fates. Don't ever forget that."

She pulled away. There were tears in her eyes. Now, he'd shown a loving gesture twice. So much progress had been made. From a depressed and miserable old man to one who finally opened his heart.

"Enough of the games," D'Angelo yelled, standing

on the lower part of the stairs, his gun drawn.

She flinched, holding her hand against her breast. "Why'd you follow me," she angrily cried out.

"Simple, I don't trust him—or you, for that matter." He stared at Maxwell. "Now let's move, back up those stairs."

"Tony, are you threatening us with that gun?" Maxwell asked, clasping the crown of his cane, stepping to the side of the casket. "Jessica, please remove yourself from the line of fire and step over there. It appears Tony might hurt someone the way that weapon is jumping in his hand." He motioned her to retreat, waving her farther back.

She didn't resist, backing away from D'Angelo.

"You are now under arrest," he raved. "Now, up the stairs, let's go, no more bullshit." He kept looking at the caskets, unnerved.

"Tony, you look a little spooked. Never been in a crypt? I mean, you've seen a crypt, haven't you, Tony? The final resting place…for the dead." Maxwell cackled.

D'Angelo waved the gun, the barrel bouncing back and forth, unsure of what to do next.

"What is it you fear so much, Tony?" Maxwell hobbled to the nearest casket bending down to read the inscription. "Oh, my, now I understand." He shot D'Angelo a biting glare. "Antonio Federico D'Angelo, born 1967, died—" He stopped. "Oh my!"

D'Angelo's eyes bugged out. "What're you talking about?" he screamed. "How'd you know my full name and date of birth?"

He shrugged his shoulders. "I read it right here, Tony. If you don't believe me, check it yourself."

D'Angelo's face went pale, sweat beginning to boil

on his forehead. "You—you're insane, a crazy old man," he shrieked, his eyes glancing at the coffin. He stepped closer, the gun trembling in his hand. "You and your fucking tricks. We should have kept you locked up."

"Oh, no, Tony. You wouldn't have wanted to do that. I would have infected the whole substation with the demonic plague, you included. Evil spreads, it perpetuates, you know? It was best you released me, lest you and your colleagues all go mad."

"You're spewing gibberish, you crazy old ass." D'Angelo took another couple of steps toward the coffin.

Maxwell glanced again at the name plate of the casket, D'Angelo not yet close enough to see. "Name's still here, hasn't changed, still yours—and the date of death. Oh my!"

D'Angelo rushed Maxwell. The sepulchral clanging of dragging chains echoed in the claustrophobic crypt. The detective froze in midstride, eyes bulging as the moving shadow of a dropping portcullis spun him a hundred and eighty degrees. He pulled back in time to escape being sliced by the barrier. He clutched at the cold bars of iron. Turning, he glared at Maxwell, who stood silent, grinning.

"Are you mad?" D'Angelo screamed. He saw Jessica on the opposite side of the portcullis. He pointed the gun at her. "Get me out, or else!"

"Tony, she can't help you," Maxwell said. "You're with me now, for eternity. I do apologize."

D'Angelo faced Maxwell, the gun shaking in his hand. "I'll use this, just try me. Now raise that fucking gate!"

"Jessica," Maxwell said, calmly. "Go upstairs and find Mr. Brown. Let him know the dilemma Tony and myself have found ourselves in."

She hesitated. "I can't leave you."

"Now, dear. I will be fine." He waved her up the stairs. "Now go quickly."

Sensing the urgency in his voice, she disappeared into the narrow confines of the mesh of corridors.

****

A lone tear dribbled from the corner of Maxwell's eye, as he saw the last vestige of Jessica disappear into shadows. He now drew a deep breath, knowing he may never be in her presence again.

He composed his thoughts. "I must warn you, Tony. She will be too late to save you. So here we are. You and me. Whether you shoot me or not, you'll spend your remaining days down here, your bones crumbling to dust. Is that what you want?"

D'Angelo kept his shaking gun pointed in the general direction of Maxwell. "You just sent her for help. I guess I'll wait it out with you."

"Tony, what makes you think they'll find you in time?"

"What the hell you talking about?"

"You found us by following voices. I commend your Boy Scout skills. You see, Tony, I am pure evil. Always have been. I can do things mere mortals cannot fathom. I can create confusion in these narrow, stone corridors solely by my thoughts, my vicious, despicable thoughts. The passageways are alive. They breathe, they smell. they move, they consume, they replicate. They have a way of shrinking, disappearing and being reborn, twisting and lashing into a wild inextricable network, like a bowl of oozing worms tying themselves into knots. When they do find you in a hundred years, there'll be nothing left. This crypt is your final resting place. Get used to it."

D'Angelo's face flushed with terror. He studied the portcullis, trying to lift it. He shook it, thinking it would budge. He stepped back and, with both hands, steadied his pistol and triggered off several rounds, shooting at nothing but stone and shadows, as if the portcullis were a living, breathing monster.

His face ravaged with sweat; his eyes turned blood-red. He spun around ready to fire again.

Henry Maxwell was nowhere to be seen.

Chapter 54

Maxwell smiled. *Damn, that was fun*. He opened the unobtrusive panel of stone, exposing the hidden passageway. He shook his head in delight, surprised it still worked after all these years. Escaping the crypt, he reveled in pulling off a Houdini-style type of showmanship. Getting away from that idiot Tony was fun and games. It was likely the mentally challenged detective was shitting his pants, wondering if he'd ever see the light of day again, his pale face displaying his tortured emotions. Looked like he was about to croak hearing his date of birth chiseled on the coffin. Easy to torment the pompous ass. Maxwell was giddy.

****

Breathless, Jessica made her way through the passages and outside the castle onto the motor court. Unaware that night had fallen, she found Brown waiting at the door to the storage room, watching her appear from the secondary access to Henry's subterranean world.

"I went to find Henry, hoping to calm him. D'Angelo followed me, blew things up. Now, both are locked in the crypt. He threatened Henry with his gun."

"Crypt, what? That dick, damn him!" Brown cursed.

Their conversation interrupted when David drove up. Seeing Jessica, he hurried out of his car, walking at a fast clip. "This doesn't look good," he said, eyeing Detective Brown. "What's going on? Where's Henry?"

Three more sheriff's vehicles rolled up the circle drive while Jessica tried to explain the craziness to David. Brown directed Crowley and the other two deputies to set up a perimeter. "Ms. Barrow, you and Mr. Grovene are ordered to stay away until we can extract D'Angelo and Mr. Maxwell from below. As of now, Maxwell's under arrest."

Alarmed, Jessica fought back. "No, he's an old man. If you'd all leave, he'll come out on his own."

Brown lost his patience. "I won't repeat myself. It's an order." He gave her a stern look. "Mr. Maxwell may not be as squeaky clean as you think."

"But—"

David curled an arm around her and herded her away. "Let's do what he says. Disobeying his orders won't help." Shaking her head in disbelief, she didn't fight, allowing him to guide her to his car.

Pulling her close, he tried to calm her. "It's for the best, considering the circumstances."

"But I—"

He opened the car door and nudged her inside. He slid into the driver's side and pulled out a book from the glove compartment. "We need to talk."

****

After his game with D'Angelo, Maxwell found himself having a hard time remembering which way to go to escape the jumble of passageways, all the electric torches still on. He pushed forward, eyes wide and anxious. Minutes passed. The space began to suffocate him. Strange shapes emerged from around the corners, rising out of the walls, bizarre, flittering, phantasmic images smirking, laughing at him, feeding his fears. How could this be? Had his terror turned on him?

The Salvation of Henry Maxwell

Soldier on! Keep the objective in focus. The west side of the castle, which way? So many years ago, so much memory of the underground maze lost in his foggy mind. The old parties, his friends and fellow moviemakers, all vying to outdo the others—discover their way out of the subterranean labyrinth—be the first to figure out the escape route back upstairs to the booze and other high jinks activities. He could only remember one person ever complaining, a young actress named Nancy Purnella, who had a fierce fear of dark spaces. It didn't help the situation that she slipped and twisted an ankle. Maxwell never invited her back. He hated whiners.

Shake the images, revive the memories. Keep moving!

****

Jessica couldn't believe her eyes when David showed her the book, *Lady Julia's Sarcophagus*. "You found it!"

"I visited Henry a day ago. After he left to take a nap, I thought I'd explore his library. Shame on me for snooping. Didn't think he would mind. I was curious to see what he might harbor there. He has an exceptional collection, some valuable, rare books. One caught my eye, an old hardback buried between reams of screenplays. I pulled it out, and low and behold, right under our noses, *Lady Julia's Sarcophagus*. Taking the liberty of borrowing it, I took it home, devouring it in one sitting. It's the original novel, over a hundred and twenty years old. Then I decided to put some pressure on Arlen Silvers. It worked. He came clean, admitting he possessed the only existing celluloid copies of *Lady Julia's Sarcophagus*. I watched it, sans ending, working late into the night comparing it with the novel." He sighed. "I hope you're not mad at me, keeping you in the dark."

"Considering everything that's happened," she said, slinking back into the seat. "Not at the moment, anyway."

Relieved, he pulled her close.

"How'd the book end?"

"There's a hell of a lot more to discuss before we get to that. Much to my dismay, Henry's been reliving this damn film in front of all of us."

"What?"

"Several things, parallel things," David said. "And now, with him having disappeared into his subterranean world, it's more frightening."

"What do you mean?"

"The book takes place in Victorian England before the turn of the century. The main character is a man named Sir Alston Chatsworth. Trust me when I say Henry has been inadvertently recreating key scenes. He's playing the part of Chatsworth in real time like he did in the movie. I'm not sure he's aware of the similarities he's living through. You're the psychologist. Could there be some psychosis that drives him to do these things without his knowledge? Coincidentally, the film doesn't deviate one iota from the novel."

Stunned, she didn't know what to think.

"Here's the strangeness. Henry's experienced hallucinations. You've mentioned them. Same thing with the fictional Chatsworth who later raises havoc at a country roadhouse. Think Olsen's tavern."

"A fluke?"

"Maybe. There's more. We have our foray into the

maze below the castle. Chatsworth manor had a network of catacombs and a crypt below, as well. In the novel, he had friends get lost down there while he stayed above, laughing. He wasn't all there, from what I gather from reading. It's like Henry subconsciously is replaying a modern-day twist of the novel."

She shook her head in confusion.

David raised a brow and continued. "And then there's the party, Henry going crazy, insulting old acquaintances and friends. Chatsworth lived a similar embarrassing episode at a gala at his castle."

"Don't remind me."

"Here's where I got spooked. There are other incidences that involve Henry that are similar to the book—things that he didn't have control over—yet something unearthly is occurring. In the book, Chatsworth had an acquaintance with a Lord Dedrick who is killed after kidnapping a family member. He's the antagonist in the novel." He reached over and gave her a reassuring hug. "The kidnapping is a coincidence, no question."

"Oh, my God," Jessica said trying to calm her runaway emotions. To keep her stomach from lurching, she asked her next question. "Who was kidnapped?"

"Chatsworth's daughter, Vanessa."

She swallowed hard. *Off the rails. Plain old coincidence. I'm not his daughter, off the rails.* Still, her heart fluttered unchecked.

"This whole reenactment is still taking place. When I drove up, I couldn't believe my eyes, you and Detective Brown together and now all these deputies. Henry's role playing is coming close to matching scene for scene."

She tried to form a sentence, but nothing came. The

uncanny similarities had her speechless.

"And Henry hiding from the sheriff, it's all déjà vu. Chatsworth did the same thing, only he hid from the constable at a village called Walton-On-Sea, England!"

Jessica sat silent, then whispered, "I—now understand."

David took her hand. "What's that?"

"Why I came back."

He looked at her, questioning.

"I came back because I was concerned for Henry's health, but—something else pulled me in—something unexplainable. Henry mentioned my fate and his being joined. I'm all goosebumps right now." She squeezed his hand for courage. "Henry has a plan. He's carrying it out now."

David's eyes met Jessica's. "Now it makes sense. Lady Julia, Chatsworth's wife, died under mysterious circumstances."

The confines of the Honda radiated like the inside of a blast furnace, and the old castle with ominous Gothic windows stared back at her, huffing, heaving with terror, turning fiction to reality. She felt numb, a senseless paralysis. Coincidences, frightening similarities?

"I know what you're thinking. I'm reading your mind, and I wish I had an explanation."

She found it hard to breathe, her thoughts dreamlike. "David, have I been summoned to help Henry enter Lillian's world?"

Chapter 55

Maxwell slogged along, regaining his composure. It wouldn't be long before they discovered the false wall revealing the hidden corridor. He stopped, listening. Voices from somewhere ahead. Footsteps. They were circling through the spaghetti network of passageways hoping to trap him. Closer than he wished. He thought hard, trying to coax his memory. To be caught in his own folly would be a fool's dilemma. Suddenly the bouncing beam of a flashlight moved toward him, skimming down the corridor. Two men, yacking back and forth. "Do you believe this shit?" one of them said. "This guy's one crazy sonofabitch."

Shadows danced along the wall. He quickly retreated to the crypt. Finding the false panel, he shoved it open, sneaking inside undetected. At the far end D'Angelo observed deputies on the other side using a blow torch on the portcullis. He stuck his ear against the panel. He could hear one of the men. "This is a dead end. Let's get the hell out of here."

Waiting a minute he pushed the panel, watching it swing open, then ducked back in the passageway. The voices that had been following were retreating. With relief, his memory gained life. Another false wall, if only he could find it.

****

"I can't sit here anymore," Jessica said, pushing the

door, and sliding out. The fresh air cooled her overheated mind. She gazed at the castle. Two deputies were stationed out front talking to one another.

David followed, moving to her side. The moon was now high, highlighting the stress written on her face. She was part of Henry's drama. *The book/movie has now come alive.* David waved the rare novel in the air. "Second to last chapter, police in England chasing after Sir Alston Chatsworth. Detective Brown here, hot on the heels of Henry."

She gazed at David. "My nerves are on fire. Henry's summoned me."

He looked at her, unsettled. The final scene. He had read it more than once. Only he and Henry knew of it. Would Jessica play along? "Sir Alston Chatsworth had one final wish—to spend eternity with Lady Julia."

"So you think Henry's determined to do the same with Lillian?"

"Lillian's grave, is that what you're thinking?"

"She's been gone a long time. Henry never told me where she's buried." Jessica paced, wracking her brain. She grabbed David. "I just remembered. He said she had to have a view of the sea, like the Aegean. The Pacific?" She pulled back, shaking.

"You okay?"

"Yeah, something else," she said, unease in her voice. "Tom Caswell mentioned a third terrace beyond the statuary garden, out on a point."

David's eyes reflected in the moonlight. "*Lady Julia's Sarcophagus*, Lillian's final resting place." His face turned dour. "Of course, if Brown and his men capture Henry—the ending, his ending."

"He must have closure. Why would he be dressed to

the max? He has a plan and he's ready for fulfillment. We can't let the deputies stop him. There's a small path, a deer trail, indiscernible, that hugs the face of the cliff on the west side. I couldn't see where it went, only south, but it has to start somewhere under the castle. Henry went below. At one time, he likely could navigate the maze of passageways. If he needs finality, that must be his escape avenue. He was dressed to a T for something big, like a formal affair. He's ready to meet up with Lillian. I can feel it!"

David eyed the deputies. "They're not watching. Quick, let's make a move." Slinking back into shadow, and still grasping the book, he disappeared behind a high hedge that ran along the east side of the castle.

"David, what about the ending, dammit?" she demanded, racing after him.

Chapter 56

Regaining his focus, it didn't take long for Maxwell to find his way out into the open. Extricating himself through the narrow confines of a split in the stone foundation, he came out on a small sandstone ledge below the west side of the castle high above the canyon floor. A wildlife trail nearby followed the face of the precipice, no guarantee it was still passable. Now, with the fall of night, the gamble he took to reach his destination became clear. The full moon exposed itself intermittently as clouds floated by, providing a semblance of light to guide him. Breathing in the welcoming cooler air, his old eyes were appreciative, and his worn body still retained some moves.

D'Angelo most likely had been freed from the crypt at the expense of destroying the portcullis. A small price to pay. Once the authorities determined he eluded them, they would search everywhere in the mansion. How hard could it be to find a crippled eighty-five-year-old man? They may have already converged on the garden terrace, going over every square inch with a fine-tooth comb. Now, he had to take extra precaution. The narrow, uneven trail had to be negotiated with care. It would be visible from the edge of the terrace above, depending upon the ever-changing moonlight, which crept toward the west.

With his cane probing each step, he gambled on. Not

more than three feet in width, the rocky path was full of dips and rises. He took his time navigating the treacherous route, estimating it would take forty-five minutes or so to reach the far end of the third terrace. A deep silence accompanied him, save for the noise of a few vehicles traversing the canyon, the swooshing of tires on asphalt, their headlights sweeping from side to side piercing the darkness, likely more sheriff deputies on their way.

Guided by the generosity of the patchy moon and a small flashlight he kept in his pocket, he hugged the overhang, testing each footstep before applying pressure, not wanting a loose rock to cause him to tumble over the edge. Below, the darkened ravines and chutes of tangled shrubs and trees loomed, no doubt habitat for the growing population of urban cougars and the ever-present rattlesnake. Those creatures would be immaterial, as a fall would likely kill him.

Voices from above stopped him. Clambering back and forth, getting closer. A shaft of light struck him in the face. He recoiled, pulling tight against the cliff.

"He's down there," a voice shouted. More flashlights raked the darkness.

The trail dipped back under the concaving sandstone face. He looked up. A couple of deputies attempted bushwhacking down the steep slope. *Bad choice*, he considered. *They'll never make it.* He took a raw breath and shuffled along, staying in shadow.

****

Jessica moved toward the statuary garden; David close behind. *Oh, God, please don't let him die.* Reaching the end, they found the path winding onto the second terrace. Sprinting into the trees until they thinned,

David stopped in awe, staring down the promenade of statues. The massive figure of Zeus reflected the luster from the moon. With any luck, they were a step ahead of Brown and his men.

****

Maxwell's heart raced like wildfire. Oh, how he prayed the reoccurring chest pains would cease as he struggled to catch a breath. He cast a glance over his shoulder; The deputy conversation and radio crackling had subsided. They were wandering about on the upper terraces unable to find access to the hidden trail, and the deputies who attempted to crawl down the steep slope likely gave up.

After a moment of rest, he resumed shuffling along the trail, circling down into a small ravine. At the bottom, he stopped, figuring he was about halfway along the length of the statuary garden far above. The moon didn't penetrate the shadowed dip in the trail he found himself in, making it difficult to see ahead. Taking a downward turn, it levelled off, the soil beneath saturated, spongelike. The air cooled; a sudden humid zone sheathed him. He paused, taking note of a slow gurgle of water trickling across his path and pouring off the edge of the jagged declivity. The seep, still flowing after all these years, began halfway up the ravine, near Lillian's overlook if his memory served him correctly. *Some things never change, the seep still seeps*. The indelible harmony of jubilation refreshed his desire, an indication of his destination within reach. Still, he had to cross the shallow flow without slipping and going over the edge.

A sudden anxiety challenged him to glance back the way he'd come. Swaying in the distance, the flicker of a flashlight came into focus. Panic settled in, knowing the fulfillment of his mission was now on the cusp of being stopped. The deputies had found the split in the castle wall. Examining the seep, he contemplated the danger of crossing. It was too wide to do in one step, and with his worn-out legs, impossible to do it in less than three or four strides. If he slipped, he'd plunge down a slippery chute and end up two hundred feet below in the chasm. But did he have any other choice? No other option existed. He took one cautious step into the trickle, not more than a half inch deep. Before he took another one, a voice rang out.

"Stop in your tracks, gramps," a man ordered.

He turned as a beam of light hit his face. He recognized the voice. "I see you've broken out of jail, Tony."

"Quite the horror chamber back there," D'Angelo said. "Your little crypt game didn't stop me, nor your maze of insanity, and your escape route deciphered. Brown demands I act respectfully, so I'm asking politely: come back this way slowly," he said, gun aimed at Maxwell.

"Come now, Tony. Do you think I'll oblige? I'm an old man, what do I have to lose?"

"I could care less what you have to lose. I've had it up to here with your tricks. You're either coming voluntarily or you'll force me to drag your old-man ass up this hill. Got it?"

Maxwell wiped the sweat building on his forehead, pondering his options. "Is this the end, Tony?"

"For you, yes. Don't force me to manhandle you," he said, lumbering down the incline.

Maxwell kept one eye on D'Angelo and the other on the seep. Taking another step in the water, the moss-covered rocks convinced him that friction between shoe and rock was fragile. Another step and his foot slipped. With the help of his cane, he regained his balance, sucked in a desperate gasp and quickly stepped again, reaching the other side. A deep exhale escaped his lips. He glanced back at D'Angelo. "Tony, I would suggest you go home. I have things to do." He swore the detective's face pulsated a bright red as the moon appeared from behind a cloud.

"If that's the way you want to handle this, then let's do it." D'Angelo whooshed down the remaining incline and moved into the seep.

"Tony, take care what you're doing. That's slick, moss-covered."

Too late. The detective skidded sideways, landing face down, his gun dislodging and bouncing down the chute over the ledge. Stunned, Maxwell watched in horror as D'Angelo continued to glide down the narrow chute and disappear into darkness. A rush of adrenalin forced Maxwell to tread closer. Shaking and gasping, he dropped his cane and beamed his flashlight into the void. He couldn't believe his eyes; half visible, feet dangling over the precipice, both hands clasping a spur of rock above the moss, D'Angelo was still alive.

"Tony, don't struggle, just hold onto that rock."

"Oh, my god—" the detective wailed.

He panned the flashlight around, not sure what he was looking for, thinking he could find something, anything to help. He gazed back at the detective. "Tony, you're a strong man. Can you pull yourself up?"

"I can't—" His eyes sucked back in their sockets as if trying to keep from peeking into the void. "I don't want to die!"

Maxwell thought, analyzing. What can an old man do in a situation like this? "Listen, Tony, I know you can hang on. It's in your makeup. You're one hell of a detective, you handle tough situations, I've seen you in action."

"My fingers are cramping, can't hold on too much longer!"

His first thought was to move on, the one night he had waited decades for, now in peril. Should he let D'Angelo suffer a deserved fate for not heeding his warning about the moss-covered rocks? The detective seemed to have had it in for him ever since the interrogation. But could he saunter up the hill and forget about him? Even the most despicable characters he played on film had both good and evil traits. Yes, they lacked compassion, but would they change if given the chance? Some could, others, not so much. He had to understand their background, their psychology before delving into portraying them. Human nature was fluid, he had discovered. Evil was evil, but he wasn't. No fiction here, just reality. He couldn't leave the poor man on his own.

His muscles pained, turning spasmic. Moving closer, he spotted a gnarly oak springing out of the sandstone on the edge of the chute. If he could reach it, he may be able to extend his cane over to D'Angelo. He could then clasp the end and pull himself up.

Maybe.

"Tony, hang on. Today's not the day you die." He bent down and placed his hands on the ground until he turned over on his backside. Every joint in his arthritic body was on fire; his bad knee spasmed and flamed. Sucking in the night air, he shimmied down on his butt, cane in one hand, until he felt the oak's woody trunk with his feet. "Tony, hang on. Keep the faith."

"What are you doing? How can I trust you?"

"Do you have a choice, Tony? I'm your only saving grace at this moment."

"At the crypt. You wanted me to die, I just know it. My name on the coffin and all."

"You should know me by now, Tony. I'm all make-believe. I lied about that inscription. You gave me your age when you first interrogated me. Remember? I still had my pj's on."

"But my name, all of it!"

"Oh that. Simple. Your photograph and full name were displayed along with every other Lost Hills station staff member on the hallway leading to the interrogation room. My mind can still recall things like that."

D'Angelo didn't respond.

"You still with me, Tony? If you are, that's how I made my living. Had to memorize scripts until blue in the face." He slid to his left, straddling the trunk of the oak. He sensed the eeriness of the ledge as his feet dropped over the edge, vertigo clouding his thoughts. Shaking it off, he only hoped it was strong enough and well rooted.

"What you going to do? Pound my hands with that cane, finish the job?"

"Oh, Tony, Tony. You do have an active mind." He took a deep, excruciating breath. "I give you credit for that. Must have seen some of my old work? Either that or you have the genius of a screenwriter. Great idea you have there." He now heard D'Angelo's harried panting.

"My fingers are wet, slippery, I can't—"

"Can it, Tony! You of all people complaining, being

a sissy. Now, I'm extending my cane over the edge. Look at me, dammit! You can grasp it if you so desire. I've hooked the handle around the trunk of this sad excuse for a tree. It's not going anywhere."

D'Angelo turned his head back toward Maxwell, who now beamed his flashlight on the end of the cane.

Maxwell recognized the indecision. "Trust, Tony, it only takes a little bit. But it's your decision, of course. Am I the evil you've always detested, or your savior? You decide."

Anguish and fear flittered across D'Angelo's face, and in one wild moment, he released one hand and lunged for the cane, grasping it, and with the other, hand over hand like a man possessed, pulled up, then clutched a lower branch. After a few seconds, his feet found stable ground. Breathing heavily, he turned back at Maxwell straddling the oak. In an act of contrition, he leaned down and helped him up. A minute later, both stood on the trail.

Maxwell brushed the dirt and mud off his suit coat and slacks. "Damn, Tony, you've caused a dry-cleaning problem." He looked D'Angelo over. "You okay?"

The detective, still breathing heavily, raised his head, eyes glazed. "Thanks…you…saved my life."

"I suppose I did. Now do me a favor, Tony. You're a good man, let me continue my hike. It will be the best for both of us." He ambled out of the ravine not looking back.

****

Detective Brown, followed by Deputy Crowley, worked their way along the trail. Coming over another short rise, they shined their flashlight down at someone sitting on the ground. After a few more yards, Brown exclaimed, "Tony, is that you?"

D'Angelo looked up, the flashlights blinding his eyes. He waved them off and said, "No sense to go any farther."

Brown looked confused. "What happened?" he said, taking in D'Angelo's wet and muddy clothes.

D'Angelo rose slowly, flicking a clump of moss off his shirt. "I saw him in the distance disappear over the hill. When I got here, he was no longer in my sights. Poor bastard must have slipped over the edge. I moved into the trickle of water, skidded myself, lucky to have caught a branch before it was too late. It's too dangerous to go any farther, no need."

Brown pointed his flashlight down the ravine, shook his head. "Not the way I wanted this to end. Let's go back. Morning will tell."

Chapter 57

Arriving at the statues, Jessica and David moved with speed along the agora, passing the mythological gods one by one. The far point of the promontory went down a steep wooded and rocky embankment. To Jessica's knowledge, no clear path led to where she thought would be Lillian's final resting place.

"Henry's aware the only access is a cliffside wildlife trail," Jessica said. "We'll have to pick our own route through this tangle of trees and shrubs. We need to go slow. There are gnarly trees on the rocky incline. Be careful on the scree."

"You lead the way," David said.

She stopped in stride. "Me? I haven't been any farther than the statue of Zeus at the head of the line."

"Ask Zeus for guidance. He's a god, for God's sake! Even if he doesn't help, the moon should give us direction when the clouds don't interfere."

She turned her ears to voices growing. "Brown's deputies are coming, we must hurry."

"Quick, mustn't let them see us."

Passing the large Zeus, they came up to the chaparral indicating the end of the terrace. She pointed to an opening. "Maybe a way to negotiate through the thicket."

Minutes later, shafts of light broke through at the opposite end. Several deputies appeared, hovering along the west side of the statuary garden, flashlights panning, searching, their chatter increasing to a feverish pitch.

"They're hoping to find access to the trail below," she said. "Pretty steep. I can't imagine them locating a way down."

Sinking farther into chaparral and small trees, they vanished from view, picking their way down the incline riddled with rocks and prickly pear cactus. She rubbed her bare arms. "It's chilly down here."

David looked up, the clouds solidifying, the humidity rising. It might rain. "If there's a cemetery on the third terrace, a tough spot for a burial. This is steep and wooded, no easy way down."

She stopped and took a breath of air, exhaling a foggy vapor. "What makes you think she's buried?"

David sidestepped a rock. "Well, I only assumed—Damn, she's not buried, she's in a crypt just like in the novel."

"I would think so. You're the Gothic expert. Victorian England, rich people, tombs, private mausoleums, all that stuff. There's a crypt under the castle. Henry made it quite clear she's somewhere else, somewhere where the sun always shines. I can only assume he had a mausoleum built out on the point."

David nodded. "But how did they build it? No access road that I'm aware of. Not a lot of room between both sides of the ridge."

"Helicopter?"

"That would mean heavy equipment to ferry up, and materials." He checked his watch. 4:58. He then looked to the west. "Rain coming."

She squinted, giving him a queasy look. "Dangerous enough without rain."

"The June Gloom, rain and coastal marine fogs."
"What about Henry? "she asked.
"If we make it to the point and don't find him, we'll backtrack up the trail toward the castle."

She gazed up at the faint moon, its luster dimmed by the clouds. If rain could affect their traversing the steepness, what would it do to Henry? She let out another long breath, stepped off a rock and screamed. "Ouch!"

"You okay?"

"Dammit!" She lifted her foot off a prickly pear.

Balancing on David's shoulder, he picked her foot up, searching for the multitude of spines that pierced the side of her sneaker. One by one, he plucked them out until he felt sure he'd removed them all. "Okay?"

She placed her foot on the ground, testing for more pokes. "I think you got them, thanks."

Jessica's knees ached from all the downhill maneuvering. The slope steepened, rocks, snags, cactus and chaparral all working against her. A slight drizzle began, adding to the challenge. The eastern light of a new dawn grew. They hadn't heard any more from Brown's deputies. That concerned her. It could only mean one of two things. They gave up—or they found Henry. Dead or alive? She ushered the negativity from her mind.

****

Maxwell stopped at a level spot, allowing his aged frame to rest. It did not trouble him that he hadn't been this far in decades. After Lillian's death, he feared entering her space, the realm of the unknown, but now, that had all changed. Soon, he wouldn't be burdened by her death, for her gentle touch that had been missing for over forty years would now be his.

As the trail moved higher, the air sweetened, and a

scarlet glow haloed the top of the ridge. It must be the reflection off of Zeus, the highest statue along the terrace catching the last vestiges of the moon's rays. *Or could it be High Haven?* The soils beneath his feet changed from a spongy, softer layer to rocklike crust. At that moment, he knew he was coming home.

...and ere morning, his journey would be complete, the sea of peat and bogs would forever be in his mortal past.

The slope flattened and shrubs of buckwheat and coastal sagebrush gave way to brighter, showier shrubs, predominately Mexican manzanita. A smile unfolded across his face. Lillian had worked to revegetate the slopes of the third terrace and the native manzanita was her plant of choice. His destination now close, he sensed a deep joy ready to take control. But then an unexpected rain began to fall.

****

Determined to be optimistic, Jessica pushed on. Their trek became unmanageable as a slight drizzle turned to a full-fledged downpour. Brush and trees thinned out. They found themselves on a flat sandstone bench devoid of vegetation except along cracks where tufts of grass could be seen.

"The rain is chilling. This isn't helpful. Is that a path over there?" she asked, pointing to her right through the relentless rain.

"Could be the deer trail Maxwell may have taken," David said, placing the copy of *Lady Julia's Sarcophagus* beneath his shirt to keep it dry.

Without discussion, they moved toward the now-visible trail. The sound of shuffling and clicking on hard sandstone broke the patter of falling rain. And in that moment, a stooped-over man with a cane came into view.

"Henry!" she exclaimed, all but forgetting her shivering.

Maxwell stopped, hearing his name, bewilderment on his face, his suit coat soaked. "Jessica, what are you doing here?" he said trying to catch his breath.

She didn't know how to answer. "Henry, are you okay?"

A smile spread across his face. "Back at the crypt, I thought I'd never see you again."

As fast as the rain started, it slacked and a fog drifted upon the point, as if machine-generated, flowing across a stage. For a moment, they stood riveted. Not more than forty yards ahead, a heavenly temple rose above the sandstone bench, above the vapor, a splendid marble building towering above the Pacific.

...and the neoclassical mausoleum in all its grandeur rises from the barren peat below the pinnacle of High Haven.

Jessica turned and glanced at David. He smiled, stepped back and pulled the book out from under his shirt so Maxwell would recognize it. Time was short. She rushed over and wrapped her arms around Henry.

Maxwell wiped the rain from her face, noticing the book. "I give you and the professor credit for deciphering my destination. He's a keeper, hang onto him." He nodded David's direction.

Tears welled in her eyes. Still grasping Maxwell, she paused long enough to let the moment blend into her soul, knowing this was the last time she would ever see him. "Go, this is your longing," she choked out.

Maxwell's tired face seemed to glow with

contentment. "To see you again has renewed my faith in kindness, compassion, most of all love—discovered again." He wiped the wetness from his eyes. "I will carry you in my heart for the rest of eternity."

"Go," she repeated, trying to contain her tears. "The rain may have delayed Brown and his men."

He hugged her tight one last time, gave a thumbs-up to David and moved as quickly as his old bones allowed, disappearing into the rolling fog. The rising sun torched the eastern flank of the Santa Monica Mountains, and beyond, the waters of the Pacific began to turn from sluggish black to a rejuvenated blue-green.

Chapter 58

There appears, through the lattice of a soft spirit night, a whispering mist of incandescent imagination and swirling dreams, summoning all his presence to the silent gate. There, below the sentinel of High Haven, the ivy-laced beauty of entombed dust takes shape and wraps her emerging arms around his laden soul. And Lady Julia's ethereal voice beckons, "Come, my love, for the ache in your turbulent heart has been banished."
—BB Barmore,
Lady Julia's Sarcophagus

Henry Maxwell had come home.

Rooted in a dream-like daze, he gazed at a replica of the Greek Temple of Poseidon, mesmerized by the copper rays on the gleaming colonnades. The mausoleum drifted in and out with every wave of fog. Only a matter of time now, like all the other nights in the statuary garden, only the essence of time…

But Lillian did not appear. Could he have been so wrong in expectations? Patience by the wayside, he hobbled forward, creeping up the steps to the front portico. He moved between two Doric columns supporting the entablature, reached into his pocket securing a key. Closing in on the high patina-coated door, he fumbled in the dim light for the lock. Before he could shove the key home, he realized the door was ajar.

A strong emotion gripped his throat, his anticipation flew out of control. *After all these years, years of loneliness, years of lost love.* His weakened heart spiraled wildly. Keeping his balance with the aid of his cane, he pushed, with the last of his strength, the heavy door open.

The squeal and squeak of hinges broke the early morning reverie. Inside, the darkened space played upon his mind in a series of melodious acts, bringing to life visions of past cinematic efforts. How many scenes such as this had he acted in throughout the early years? Dreary settings, creepy cemeteries, burial crypts at night, he'd done them all. There was but one scene that had his attention. He felt the drama closing in on him. *Sir Alston Chatsworth will fulfill his fate.*

He stepped inside, turning his head as the door unexpectedly closed. Sensing the tension of the moment, the nebulous space he remembered encapsulated him with decades-old air from the past. Taking a much-needed breath, he convinced himself he sensed Lillian's fragrance floating through his lungs.

In the dim room, he allowed his vision to adjust. The blackness of the small room lifted, the pronaos if he wasn't mistaken. In the earthly silence, he recalled the parts of a Greek temple as Lillian taught him. She insisted that authenticity was paramount throughout the design of the mausoleum, using the pronaos, naos, and opisthodomos, all temple components. She decided the naos, or sanctuary, be the final resting place for the twin sarcophagus where she and Henry would spend the rest of eternity. *If one must tolerate eternity in a mausoleum,* she said, *it had to be the realm of joy and serenity.*

After she was interred, he never returned, the pain too vast to bear. Forty-plus years and nobody had ever stepped foot inside until now. He tried to remember the layout of the pronaos, a room with an opening at the far wall, like a small foyer. Each side contained intricate black marble tables supporting ceramic amphoras, contrasting with the creme-colored walls.

It took the better part of thirty seconds for him to enter the naos. The interior finishes were of the finest white and pink marble, now thick with decades of dust, intricately detailed with classical corbels and ceiling medallions. He blinked, in disbelief. A series of candles circled the long rectangular room, all lit, peacefully flickering. His heartbeat quickened without pain, the edge of eternal bliss now within his grasp. *She is guiding me with her light, she is waiting.* He took off his mud-caked coat, pulled away the collar of his satin dress shirt, and rubbed sweat off his neck. He took another step, the soft flames from the candles rippling shadows over the twin sarcophagus no more than ten feet ahead. Statuary reliefs covered the sides, Grecian angels and otherworldly deities etched from the finest white marble. As he neared, he stopped with a gasp, noticing the stone lid halfway off Lillian's sarcophagus. He shuffled over and stared inside.

Empty!

He clasped his chest, attempting to chase away the pain that shot through his body. Eyes strayed from the sarcophagus and glided around the naos, from the floor to the stained-glass windows high above on either side.

"Lillian, my Lillian, where are you?" he asked. Frantic, he hobbled into another room, the opisthodomos, the back room of a temple. On one wall, a glass case displayed physical reminders of her life—birth certificate, college degree, a few written poems that she penned to him, an assortment of other memorabilia, and in the middle her wedding and engagement rings.

A tear rolled down his cheek as he gazed inside, his face flush, his breath fogging the glass. In the dimness, he could see the mesmerizing glow from the diamond, a brilliant-cut solitaire emitting light on its own. He pulled back and rubbed his eyes. Before turning to leave, he looked at the other wall where his history would be displayed. But who would carry out his last will and testament? Jessica, of course.

In a hurry, he spun around and returned through the pronaos, opened the door and stepped outside. Sweat bubbled on his forehead. To the east, the sun rose above the horizon and the fading fog. The lights of Los Angeles began to recede. Unable to think straight, he trundled along the colonnade, tapping his way with his cane. "Oh, my Lillian, where are you? Answer please. I am here, waiting." Nearing the south end of the mausoleum, there on the edge of the point...*Lillian appears in a white flowing gown. Her long hair glows like brilliant gold, the color of wheat fields on a cloudless day, her face a smooth pearl, and her soft lips radiating a sweet scent of plumeria. She moves toward him as if floating on air. Her hand extends in a welcoming gesture.*

And then the transformation...aches and pains fade; his clothes again too small. His imagination takes flight, knowing his dream will live. He stumbles toward her. She holds his hand, as he drops his cane near the edge of the cliff, and guides him back to the mausoleum.

Chapter 59

They waited a half hour for Henry to come back. Jessica knew he wouldn't return, realizing this was the end. She understood her role. Her throat constricted, her lips quivered, and a lone tear escaped. On sacred ground, they approached the mausoleum. Neither of them spoke. Above the entrance, Maxwell's family name, carved in hand-tooled Grecian letters engraved on the entablature, stared back at them with a sense of mystery. She walked under the portico and reached for the handle on the massive door and pulled. Locked. Another tear rolled down her cheek.

Something near the edge of the cliff caught her attention, out of place, unnatural. She took a closer look. A surge of grief overwhelmed her senses. Henry's cane. Below, only steep slopes and jagged sandstone crevasses. Trembling, she moved out from under the portico, bent down, and picked it up. The answer to where Henry was now shredded all her hopes.

David came over, placing a steadying arm around her. "Henry's at peace," he assured her.

She cradled her pounding head. "I can't process all of this."

He gave her a smile she would never forget. "You're the reason he's now with Lillian. Your arrival in the castle set things in motion the first day. He despised you, he loathed you, and then, he began to see you were on his side, his friend. It took time and perseverance, but you brought sunshine to his life after all those lonely years. More than that, you listened, you consoled him. You did things for him he never imagined possible. You got him out of jail, not once, but twice. He started to appreciate you, respect you, share with you his deepest feelings. During the Caswell affair, he realized the worth of your companionship. He found his *salvation* because of you."

The first rays of sun crystallized the cascade of tears rolling down her cheeks. After several minutes and without a second thought, she rubbed her eyes dry, moved back under the portico and, for some strange reason, tried the handle again. Still locked. Why would she expect anything different? She glanced at David, his face an expression of finality that she knew she had to accept.

Convinced she'd been summoned to witness Henry's final wish; she looked over her shoulder toward the cliff. Somehow, if believing in reverence and spirituality were possible, Henry and Lillian were together in peace and eternal love.

David opened the worn cover from the hundred-and-twenty-year-old novel, *Lady Julia's Sarcophagus*, and read the last paragraph. Clasping his arm, she listened.

And as the empyrean rays of the rising sun wash over the mausoleum, a halcyon breeze disperses the mist, and the deep-seated fervor of his grief and suffering has ended. In the most passionate and tranquil manner, Sir Alston Chatsworth and Lady Julia, now together until the end of time.

Chapter 60

The library, antiquarian in every respect, stale…musty…reflective. Jessica sat in her chair, musing about the past month or so. How did she have the will to set foot in the library again? Only a fool would have the courage to do such a thing. God only knows, good and bad, traumatic and comforting. Memories of Henry Maxwell flooded her thoughts. She would always believe that Henry and Lillian were together again. The police report did not give a cause of death, only assumed he died from the fall off the promontory. Heavily wooded, steep slopes marred with sandstone crevasses made it impossible to retrieve the body. The possibility of a mountain lion dragging the carcass off was likely. Closure.

After all, it started as an unwelcome assignment, an old man, stubborn and caustic as they came. She made much progress, only now to think that her time with him had been wasted. *No, not wasted*, she reprimanded herself. He had a caring side, and she was richer for it. He showed her things she didn't know about herself. She lived the adventure of a lifetime, a stirring and perilous journey she would do all over again. She tried to bury her memory of being carved into a thousand images, but like magic, a free flow of friendship and love she'd never experienced before came into her life.

Her phone pinged, scattering her thoughts.

"I'll be the first to say you've had one hell of a ride," Marsha said.

"I wish it had turned out differently," she said, letting her eyes rest upon the hundreds of books surrounding her.

"With the reality of the situation, the conservatorship has come to an end."

Jessica blinked, still staring at all the hardbacks and bound screenplays with a sense of emptiness sticking her like dull harpoons. "What happens to all this since Henry's body hasn't been found? Maybe he escaped somehow."

"Jessica, you must move on. Don't hold out hope. His Will explains a lot. And he revised it recently."

"He had no family. Doesn't California law require five years before the estate can be distributed, if he's presumed dead and the body hasn't been found?"

"He took care to ensure the estate can be parceled to avoid probate. I'll send you a copy. After you read it, you'll understand. By the way, he left a letter for you."

"A letter?"

"Dated three days ago, the day he went missing. No one in the office has read it since it's addressed to you. But we are curious, if you're inclined to share it."

"I'm a bit in shock."

"I'm emailing it. After you've soaked it all in, give me a call when you get a chance. No hurry. We'll talk more later."

The conversation ended. She felt the tension rise, wondering why he sent her a letter before his accident.

Clicking the e-mail icon on her laptop, she found an attached copy of Henry's Will and the letter addressed to her.

The Salvation of Henry Maxwell

Jessica,

I assume you are reading this after I have left this planet, and that is how it should be. First things first. You were sent to me because of the legal fiat that had been authorized by the state of California. I was furious that you invaded my world. At that time, my life had been hell. I had no desire to continue. I fought you at first, I deplored you, I tested you, I tried my best to break you and make your life as miserable as possible for interfering in my dismal existence. That said, you performed your duties admirably, following the directives laid out by the courts exceedingly well. You brought my estate back to respectability. You ushered an awakening into my dreary soul that vanished long ago. Yes, a cantankerous old fool I was, and you never gave in to my irascible moods and schemes.

Soon after, I began to have future expectations, thanks to my many visits to the garden at midnight. Then Tom Caswell. I spent all my time grieving with my own miserable life that I forgot how dangerous a man he had become. His loner personality, his early history (that I overlooked), and other signs were brushed aside. Yet I did nothing. I ignored him. I should have paid more attention when he was a child and Lillian was still alive.

And then there were the two men found dead just a few days ago, former gardener Francisco Cuervo (you never knew him) and Dr. Ewe Kopf (whom you knew). I take responsibility for both men's demise. I sent a full accounting to Detective Brown on the situations leading up to their deaths. There is no need to describe what happened between them and me. I believe Detective Brown will be more than happy to share what he knows. As an aside, Lillian did not perish from a drug overdose.

She was murdered. Both men were responsible. Although a court of law would have a hard time proving those facts, at least I have comfort in bringing closure to myself, having avenged her death.

As time marched on this last month, even before Tom Caswell killed innocent victims and had his sights on you, I had a genuine sense of why you were sent to me. It did not come easily. It came in spurts.

And this is where my inner self woke up. Jessica, my fondness for you grew even before you brilliantly sprung me from jail. When you agreed to take me to Point Dume afterwards, you let me pour out a part of my soul. You listened with genuine concern. I recognized real sympathy in your eyes. I then realized you were someone extraordinary. I could tell that you grasped my devotion and love for Lillian and how her death impacted my life all these years. You had been sent to me for a purpose other than conservator, please believe this. Later, I wanted to tell you everything, but it had to wait. I will tell you now.

You see, Lillian was ten weeks pregnant when she was murdered. Whether it would have been a boy or girl, does not matter. My wife and child, taken from me. This burden has now been lifted. To me, you are the daughter I never had. I do not say this lightly. I say this with pure joy and love in my heart. You have compassion, you have honesty, above all you have empathy, and you are all and more anyone could hope for in a daughter.

Please do not grieve my passing. The spirit of Lillian never died. Since you arrived, she called for me and I had to follow. Your presence brought her to me and reignited our love that was abruptly taken from us. She was waiting for that moment, and as you are my witness, she asked me to join her in eternity. I entrust that you will carry on. In that regard, do not take this burden as an unwelcome task. My last Will and Testament have been revised to leave fifty percent of my liquid assets to my favorite charities. The other fifty percent and property (including this estate) is to be left in your name.

I wish the best for you and yours in the years to come.

With eternal love,
Henry Maxwell

Jessica stared at Henry's name on the laptop screen in total disbelief. For a moment, she felt the library come alive with tales and stories from yesteryear, all wanting to escape the dusty shelves of books and screenplays to entertain a new generation of believers. She stood, gave the library a tearful smile, and walked through the door, moving across the slate floor and the creepy confines of stone and wood. Reaching the back door of the Great Hall, she stepped out onto the veranda and took the deepest breath of fresh air under a bright sun, cheerful as any she had ever seen. She looked beyond the manicured gardens, the woodland hiding the secretive mythological gods of centuries past, and farther out, the Temple of Poseidon, silent and majestic on the point in full view of the blue Pacific.

Epilogue

Thirty-Six Years Later

Los Angeles (AP)—A powerful earthquake hit Southern California on August 17, damaging buildings, knocking out power and causing several house and business fires. The 6.9 magnitude quake struck about 68 miles (110 km) northeast of Los Angeles at around 5:30 PM PDT (1230 GMT), according to the U.S. Geological Survey (USGS). The epicenter hit remarkably close to Lancaster, a city with a population of more than 242,000 in the Western Mojave Desert. The area has suffered earthquake swarms in the past, but not of this magnitude. Prior to this event, the largest ever recorded in Lancaster was a 6.5 magnitude in 1971.

The USGS said the quake was shallow—only 4.0 miles (6.5 km) below the surface—amplifying the effect. The temblor was felt throughout the Los Angeles basin, as far north as Fresno, and as far east as Las Vegas, Nevada. It was even felt as far south as Ensenada, Mexico.

One week after the quake, Lilly stood next to the west tower of Maxwell's Castle watching the trio of masons repointing the joints in several cut stones that shifted with the recent earthquake. A stickler for perfection, she wanted the new mortar to match the existing color, a difficult task since the castle approached a hundred and fifty years old. Once completed, the estate would reopen to the throngs of tourists who would descend again, drawn by the allure and mystery of Henry Maxwell, and his incredible legacy. The magnificent, terraced gardens were always a popular draw, along with the statuary garden of mythological gods on the agora. She served as executive director of the Henry Maxwell Foundation, a philanthropic organization started a couple of years after Maxwell disappeared. Lilly's mother inherited the estate and decided to open it to the public.

Yes, Henry Maxwell, one of the most famous Gothic horror actors from the mid twentieth century. Along with the esteemed Vincent Price, Christopher Lee, and a host of others, they brought a Gothic genre to the screen that entertained so many in the past. Only Henry Maxwell had a monument to his life and death— Maxwell Castle. Not yet on the registry of National Historical Landmarks like Hearst Castle a little farther north, it operated as a non-profit museum highlighting his career and life. Lilly's parents created the museum and set aside the estate as a living monument to the man that played an important part in their lives, even though they had only known him a few short weeks before he died. And she was part of that history, named for Maxwell's wife, Lillian, an honor that now more than ever tugged at her with a sense of pride.

After approving the new mortar color, she went to check out the mausoleum, as the extent of damage hadn't been ascertained. A rockslide blocked the serpentine path and it took a week with heavy equipment to clear it.

She walked through the statuary garden, following the path built twenty years ago, offering access down the steep slope to the mausoleum on the point and the incredible view toward Malibu and the Pacific. The former wildlife trail along the cliff face had been abandoned because of safety concerns. Henry Maxwell himself was the last to have used it.

She let her thoughts drift to the story her parents told a thousand times, how they bushwhacked to get to the mausoleum in hopes of finding Henry. His final hours were highlighted in the historical guide the museum gave to all visitors who took the tour.

Taking the switchbacks down the slope, Lilly reached the point, stopped, and stared. Like all visitors, she never tired of viewing the amazing replica of the Temple of Poseidon and the azure Pacific beyond. Soaking in the emotion, as she always did, she took time, walking around the mausoleum, jotting notes. Several cracks were seen in the marble entablature and one of the Doric column bases had a split corner. She took the key, unlocked the decorative door, pushed hard. It wouldn't open. Again, it didn't budge. The door jambs were skewed. Raising her shoulder, she leaned against the massive door and aggressively pressed as hard as she could. It stubbornly sprang free. Shaking her head with frustration, she entered. No need for lights, as the array of windows near the ceiling sunlit the space and appeared to be unbroken.

Entering the naos, she froze. Lillian's sarcophagus inclined at an angle; the marble lid had slid to one side exposing the red velvet lining. At that moment, an image etched in her mind that would live on for the rest of her life. It was *there*, where the remarkable mysteries surrounding Henry and his Lillian were exposed. It was *there*, where the themes of Gothic films jumped from the screen into the imaginative minds of moviegoers around the world. It was *there*, for those who yearned to be transported into the realm of melodramatic imagination; *there*, where a hidden singularity rose, an apparition of romanticism taking place high above the gloom of a stormy world. She swore she heard voices sing a sanguine melody, a forever song of the rising sun shining a light of beauty and serenity upon a distant sea.

Lilly stood transfixed, caught in a Gothic era that no longer existed. And *there* in Lillian's sarcophagus, two bodies rested side by side, dressed in the finest satin and silk ...*and in that movie moment, they fade to crumbling bones, lovingly embracing one another until the end of time.*

Author's Note

Henry Maxwell is a fictional character molded after a long list of Gothic horror actors of the '60s (think Vincent Price) that dominated the Saturday matinee. Oh, yes, those wonderful double features, complete with fountain drinks, popcorn, candy bars, and who could forget—Roger Corman, master of the B-movie, producer and director of the Edgar Allan Poe films for American International Pictures—most notably *The Fall of the House of Usher* and *The Pit and the Pendulum*. B-movies, for those who have never heard the term, refer to the second half of the matinee double feature, similar to the B-side of 45 rpm records in the music industry.

For the younger generation who don't have a recollection or knowledge of that era, I hope by reading this novel, it will evoke an appreciation for the artistry of this genre of Gothic horror movies that birthed Henry Maxwell. I would recommend searching out those magnificent celluloid masterpieces and immerse yourself in a world of psychological complexities and macabre settings, a timeless power of the past, frame by frame. By all means, *The Salvation of Henry Maxwell* is not a work of horror. It is an attempt to transport the reader into the realm of melodramatic imagination and romanticism by calling attention to those masterful literary themes envisioned since the time of Poe.

A word about the author...

Award winning author and Colorado native, Lee Lindauer has a BS in Architectural Engineering and a MS in Civil Engineering and was a principal of a consulting structural engineering firm he founded in Western Colorado. He is a member of the International Thriller Writers, has appeared on author panels at ThrillerFest and has served as co-editor on the Big Thrill magazine. He and his wife Teri divide their time between Colorado and Nevada.

www.leelindauer.com

Thank you for purchasing
this publication of The Wild Rose Press, Inc.

For questions or more information
contact us at
info@thewildrosepress.com.

The Wild Rose Press, Inc.
www.thewildrosepress.com

Printed in the USA
CPSIA information can be obtained
at www.ICGtesting.com
JSHW021333170824
68167JS00003B/21